Pitching the Petticoat

by

Maryanne Ross

Victorians Unlaced, Book 3

Pitching the Petticoat

Cover Art by *The Wild Rose Press, Inc.*

The Wild Rose Press, Inc.
PO Box 708
Adams Basin, NY 14410-0708
Visit us at www.thewildrosepress.com

Publishing History
First Edition, 2023
Trade Paperback ISBN 978-1-5092-4886-5
Digital ISBN 978-1-5092-4887-2

Victorians Unlaced, Book 3
Published in the United States of America

Her heart kicked into a hard tattoo. Was he going to *kiss* her?

Curiosity spiked in her blood. So. In the interests of Science…

His lips hovered. Closer. His breath tickled her lips. Every cell in her body hummed with awareness of him, with eager anticipation. Her hands unaccountably itched to stroke and grip his brawny shoulders. Her breath tangled in her throat.

Two large, warm, knurled palms cupped her cheeks. And then he gently bit her bottom lip, followed by a tender kiss, light as a butterfly's wing. Her blood sang like a Scottish bagpipe band in her veins. Shock and delight rippled and raced through her body.

"Raider!" She wrested herself from his grasp. "I'll have you know I'm the pirate here. Named for the infamous Ruairidh the Turbulent. Nobody takes what is mine, whether my Picti artifacts, or…or…" She coughed and stepped three paces back, out of the danger zone of his magnetic physical pull.

She fisted sharp-knuckled hands into her hipbones. "What do you here, marauder? My brother Roderick will have your guts for guitar strings. That is, if I don't slice you from neck to knee first."

He laughed, and the sound rolled through her like a charm.

Praise for Maryanne Ross

Praise for Crushing the Corset

"…awesome romance. Page-turner, romantic, unpredictable, witty, wonderful characters."

~ 5 stars, Brenda, BookBub

"A feisty, beautiful heroine in need for rescue - check, an outlaw hero helping her - check, a wicked villain plotting against our heroine - check. The book is intriguing, interesting and will keep your attention focused on the plot from the first sentence you read. It is definitely worth your time."

~ 5 stars, Netgalley reviewer

Praise for Bouncing the Bustle

"I love the way Lilwen Jones takes charge of her life and the way she upends Sawyer Thane's life. Oh my!"

~ 5 stars, Dee, BookBub

"…an immense pleasure to read…storytelling, characters and vivid descriptions are captivating."

~ Neeha, Reedsy

"…definitely recommend this to my friends."

~ 5 stars, Hani, Netgalley

Dedication

To my mother, Elizabeth Ross, who bequeathed genes from Ruary "The Turbulent" MacNeil of Barra, Outer Hebrides, and gifted her booklover DNA to us all. With love and thanks for all those walks to the library!

To my brilliant editor, Eilidh MacKenzie, whose supersonic editing powers, laced with laugh-out-loud humor, has guided me through five books.
Thanks to you I hold my dream in my hands.

Chapter One

Outer Hebrides, Scotland, 1839

Ruari MacDonald hefted the Highland bagpipes in her arms, balancing her body on the crumbling castle battlements. She filled her lungs with salty evening air, blew hard into the blowpipe, squeezed the bag under her arm, played a tuneful blast from the chanter—and paused.

Her ancient maid grumbled from within the tower bedroom, "What ails you, lass? My heart longs for a MacNeil tune while I tidy your mess."

"Sìneag! A foreign ship rides in the bay." Ruari scanned the countryside, lit lilac-gold in the long gloaming. "There! A stranger stalks among my ancient Picti-carved stones." She rested the heavy pipes against her hip and frowned, seeking clues. The intruder's hair gleamed copper-bright. His coat flapped like a predatory hawk's wings. "He is pacing and bending, stretching out his arms—"

Measuring distances? Her mind fizzed in a rush of mad hope. A scientist, with whom she could discuss her precious research and theories? Her pipes emitted a faint moan, as though in sympathy.

Nonsense! Fury surged in a prickling tide. "No doubt he seeks artifacts to sell in Glasgow and Edinburgh. How dare he plunder our beloved heritage?

1

I'll give that brigand a MacDonald welcome."

"Ye'll bide here, Ruari the Turbulent. The spit of your wild mother, God rest her wayward soul..." The maid's scolding subsided into mutters.

Ruari grinned and ducked into the tower room. She wrapped her grandmother's bagpipes tenderly in their MacNeil plaid. She kissed Sineag on her brow, evading a shaky grab and Gaelic curse, and clattered down the inner stone staircase and out into the night.

The enormous standing stone circles on the hill lurked like frozen giants. Small pointy-winged bats flitted from their sea caves. The restless ocean on her left sang its hypnotic song.

Blast! In her hurry, she'd missed the shallow peat hole, a darker purple in the twilight. She wrenched herself upright, rubbing bruised shins. Scraped, stinging hands fueled her ire. Tripping on her own land! All the interloper's fault.

She wiped clinging mud from her skirts. What *was* he doing? In the magical half glow, when the wee folk and fabled heroes walk, his height and blazing hair lent him the ghostly glamor of a Viking warrior returned. A superstitious shiver trickled down her spine.

MacDonald, get a haud o' yersel'!

She sprinted to the ruined blackhouse and flattened herself against its one remaining wall. Ignoring her drumming heartbeat, she peered around.

The tall figure examined the standing stone semicircle rising from the sea cliff, and the three Picti carved stones wedged in the landscape. He radiated frowning concentration and—annoyance!

She inhaled a fortifying breath and stepped around the blackhouse wall. "What on earth do *you* have to be annoyed about, trespassing on someone else's land?"

His face snapped up and scanned the landscape. His focus arrowed to the blackhouse. She slammed back against the wall, the blood pulsing in her muscles, panic spinning in her brain.

She clenched her fists. *Victory or Death!*

The scree clattered with rapid bootsteps as he approached the ruin and stood, looming over her. He reached out a large hand and gripped a fold of her MacDonald tartan between thumb and forefinger.

A squeak, quickly swallowed, escaped her throat. She raised a foot, preparatory to stomping on his instep. Or kneeing his privates.

Gold-peat eyes like the best island whisky, blazing with intelligent curiosity, burned her. His intent gaze traversed her face, lingered on the exposed skin at her neck and throat, and tracked the slide of peat mud adhering to the curve of her hip.

She lowered her foot, still wary.

His hollow-cheeked, harsh-boned face was strangely beautiful. His height and athletic balance seemed conjured from the landscape. So close, his body warmth leached into her skin. An exotic, delicious, spicy scent teased her nostrils.

Attack! urged her pirate ancestors. "Thief!" she spat. "What are you doing on my land, without permission?"

His glower softened. His lips curved. "Thief? Well, then. I'll suit the action to the accusation." His voice rumbled through her, deep and rich, igniting tingles in her veins. He pulled gently on the tartan until her body curved toward him, her chest high and her hips pushing forward. His head bent to her.

Her heart kicked into a hard tattoo. Was he going to

kiss her?

Curiosity spiked in her blood. So. In the interests of Science…

His lips hovered. Closer. His breath tickled her lips. Every cell in her body hummed with awareness of him, with eager anticipation. Her hands unaccountably itched to stroke and grip his brawny shoulders. Her breath tangled in her throat.

Two large, warm, knurled palms cupped her cheeks. And then he gently bit her bottom lip, followed by a tender kiss, light as a butterfly's wing. Her blood sang like a Scottish bagpipe band in her veins. Shock and delight rippled and raced through her body.

"*Raider!*" She wrested herself from his grasp. "I'll have you know I'm the pirate here. Named for the infamous Ruairidh the Turbulent. *Nobody* takes what is mine, whether my Picti artifacts, or…or…" She coughed and stepped three paces back, out of the danger zone of his magnetic physical pull.

She fisted sharp-knuckled hands into her hipbones. "What do you here, marauder? My brother, Roderick, will have your guts for guitar strings. That is, if I don't slice you from neck to knee first."

He laughed, and the sound rolled through her like a charm. "Men warned me about these islands on the edge of nowhere, filled with savages and heathens." He closed the space between them in one long stride. Her pulses beat in staccato tempo. His voice lowered to a rasp, scoring her senses. "They neglected to warn me of their beauty, however."

"*Beauty.*" Ruari rolled the word around on her tongue, savoring it like a dram of Laphroaig, piquant and wickedly alluring.

She snapped her lips into a firm line and shook her head. "I well ken the difference between fools' glitter and true gold," she retorted with as much whiplash scorn as she could muster. "You are addressing Miss Ruari MacNeil MacDonald, of Castle Callanish over yonder. Named for my ancestors Black Ruairidh the Pirate and Ruairidh the Tartar. You will address me with the courtesy due to me, aye, to any woman, and you will explain why you stalk around my lands without warrant."

He snorted, the infuriating man. "Your lands?" he repeated, his tone silky and dangerous now, sliding over her senses. "Curious. I was given to understand they belong to a Lord Balgair MacDonald. Who is currently auctioning his authority—"

"That weak excuse for manhood!" she spat. Fear curdled in her guts now. "What has that *fèineil, droch-dhuine*—"

"Selfish villain?" A flash of a crooked grin.

Alert! her ancestors whispered. *The interloper kens the Gaelic too.* A Highlander accent abraded his words: a different music to the tongue of the islands.

"My cousin, may the old gods rot his evil, greedy, shallow heart," she muttered. A cold fist squeezed her entrails into knots. The night lost its magic. Weariness crept like a malaise through her bones. Her feet throbbed.

She summoned one last barrage of vitriol. "Touch those Picti artifacts or any of the standing stone circles and my wicked cousin will wonder what happened to his friend." She thrust her chin at him defiantly. "I'm here. He's far away wasting the last dregs of family money in frivolous London, like the fribble he is. He won't come to your aid when you find yourself on the point of a sword."

The man laughed.

Ruari said, "You laugh one more time when I threaten you, and you'll never see dawn. I'm the daughter of Vikings and pirates, many of them bold, brave women. Despite what the misguided English law believes, *this is my land.* Go back to your ship, sail away, and never, never return. Plenty of bodies buried in this peat." She hissed the *s*'s and spat the *p*'s.

He bent close to her, those tawny eyes alight with wicked glee.

Her heart flipflopped, with terror and fascination both. How would he respond?

He surprised her. Again. "And who then will wake you from your slumber, Sleeping Beauty? Those sweet curves, those tempting wide, red lips are not meant to wither away in salt-scoured islands filled with bird shit and little else."

Ruari hunched her shoulders as though to ward off a blow. Most shockingly, her eyes suddenly filled with tears. Her beloved islands. Her precious, mysterious Picti artifacts, their strange and beautiful carvings a puzzle that nobody could solve.

She knew the world saw her islands thus. But it hurt, to have it told with such bare truth.

She turned and ran, before he saw that he had struck a wounding blow.

****

Lochaber Gordon stood like a man poleaxed. He stared after the fleeing minx, utterly be-spelled, realized his mouth was agape, and snapped it shut. The urge to chase her almost overmastered him. He fought the impulse with rigid self-control.

But he *felt* his hardened, bitter heart crack a little. *Tears* had shone in her brilliant amethyst eyes and sparkled on her rosy cheek before she fled.

He'd been in some dangerous situations—and every cell in his body buzzed with the knowledge that this one promised unforeseen hazards of the worst kind.

He took a step to resume pacing out the potential site for the main factory building. Hesitated. Better to return to the ship for the night? In case of sudden attack by a horde of Miss Ruari MacNeil MacDonald's male relatives? Despite himself, a foolish grin slid over his face. She might attack the ship too, commanding her own pirate band.

The image lured: her eyes as violet-blue and storm-filled as the ocean before him. That lush, wide mouth promising riches, spouting invective as she thrust forward her sword—and her breasts...

Did the woman not know her own appearance? Far from a pirate wench indeed. Curves and apple cheeks, thick shining dark hair dancing in the breeze. More like a sweet, juicy peach, with a satisfying tartness...

He'd *bitten* that irresistibly plump bottom lip. *What had possessed him?*

He knew. Too long dwelling on revenge until it lodged in his belly, an everlasting fire simmering low. A fire that flared into a sword of vengeance baying for blood, the closer he came to the place of his birth. Too long denying ordinary human needs.

Lochaber shook himself. Back to the ship. He'd swallow some Islay whisky instead of planning his mentor's damnable distillery.

He'd had enough of standing in the Highlands—the first time for so many years—even if it was just the desolate, remote Outer Hebrides, so many miles from his boyhood home.

There. That thought cooled his lust like a drench of freezing hail. His urge for revenge consumed him once more and accompanied him like an old, evil shadow down the cliff path, across the small beach, and back onto his vessel.

****

Ruari stood on the battlements outside her high octagonal tower room in the crumbling MacDonald Castle, breathing hard. Twisting emotions battered her as she gazed over the landscape.

A half circle of standing stones stood sentinel on the curve of the bay, as it had for untold millennia. To the northeast, a huge double ring linked earth and sky. More circles, hidden from view, loomed south of the castle.

The artifacts' steadfast strength soothed her—empowered her!—despite her pricking anxiety about her slippery cousin and his latest folderols.

The pale moon cast a cold golden trail over the heaving sea to small wave-gouged islands, hunched in the inky swell like phantasms. Dolphins leapt in the waves, the silver light catching on arched fins. Stars glittered in a lavender sky.

Restlessness jangled in Ruari's muscles and itched under her skin. The castle wouldn't thank her for a stirring bagpipe blast this late, so she pulled her tin whistle from her pocket. The whistle's sweet tone would blend with the call of seabirds and the sigh of the wind.

As she raised the instrument to her lips, she halted mid-action.

She wasn't the only one restless this night.

Down there by Callanish Bay, believing himself

hidden from castle eyes by purple twilight and the cliff overhang, the stranger stood stripped to the waist in the cool night air. Fascinated, Ruari leaned farther over the low stone battlement.

Holding two queer curved swords aloft until they flashed silver in the starlight, his whole body stretched high. Then utterly balanced, with the fluid physical grace she had already noted, he began to whirl and jump in a complicated sword dance. Faster and faster he moved, until sweat shone on his naked torso and the twinkling swords borrowed streaks of silver glitter from moon and stars.

Excitement rushed through Ruari. She raised her whistle to her lips and softly blew a fierce, wild victory tune, guaranteed to stir the blood of every mortal who heard its plaintive tones.

As though he danced to her music, the intruder sprang, rolled, and cartwheeled with astonishing athleticism.

She could not tear her eyes away. Her blood hurtled in her veins, her brain sang, every cell sparked as she blew her song and feasted her eyes on the man's magnificent strength and grace.

His flaming hair spoke the passionate truth of him. The rest was concealed under a steel-hard, mocking intelligence.

But what did he want? What harm did he and her horrid cousin intend to her beloved islands—her Picti artifacts, and her precious research?

****

"A letter for you, my lady."

Ruari waited, sipping her breakfast tea, as her maid Sìneag limped arthritically across the huge main hall.

Neither flinched as a chill wind whistled through a gap in the cracking stone wall; they were both well inured to the privations of residing in this decaying castle.

"My cousin, rot his degenerate soul." Ruari flung the letter on the table and stabbed it viciously with her knife. How she wished it were the fool's vitals.

Sìneag lowered herself onto a hard chair and poured a cup of tea with a shaky hand. "Ye best open it and see what the wicked wee man wants now."

An image flashed in Ruari's mind: flaming hair, height and strength, a powerful, mesmerizing attention that melted all the bones in her body. Something to do with her cousin.

She hadn't told Roddy about the stranger. A part of her yearned to banter words with the mysterious fellow again. But too late. Everyone on the island would already be aware of the visiting ship and would arrive soon to report the stranger's doings.

She inhaled and tore open the letter, unfortunately still readable despite the stab holes.

"My dearest cousin, blah de blah rubbish." She held the missive in the air, preparatory to ripping it in two.

Her maid snatched the letter away. "Stop your foolishness and read it out now."

Ruari scanned the contents in a single fast gulp, like taking unpleasant medicine. Choked. Sìneag bashed her on the back with her sinewy strength.

"That devil!" Ruari gasped. "I will not!" She gulped tea.

"...*As you have proven not up to dick with acquiring English graces, nor husbands, as head of this family, I must nab the racket. I have arranged a plummy match for you. Your future leg-shackle will arrive close on this letter. None of your mouth-pie! Do* not *give him a disgust of you—I order you to behave as a docile woman for once in your rambunctious life.*

"*He is an English swell, well-breeched.*"

Ruari gripped Sìneag's thin hand. She spat an oath.

The intruder's whisky eyes swam in her mind. *Him!* Excitement stirred in her belly. And somehow, she wasn't as cross as she should be.

But then—the next section. She ground the words out through the claw squeezing her throat.

"*...You have no choice in this matter. The horrid alternative must be that you come to live with moi. As I am assured it would be nothing but collie-shangles for us, you must marry. I am in barter with three flash lords for a hundred-year lease for the MacDonald lands. It is high time those barbarous islands yield me the needful as befits my station in life.*

"*It follows that there will be no home for you, as I will lease the whole.*"

"He breaks the agreement between our fathers." Ruari wanted to break her cousin's skull.

"You knew when your beloved father died that it might come to this," Sìneag said. "That villain always wanted whatever he could clutch and snatch with his greedy, grasping fingers. This castle is rightfully his. You knew he would not allow us to bide here if there is gold to be bled from it."

Ruari fumed, plans and schemes flipping and swirling in her desperate brain. "The Lord Balgair MacDonald lacks honor—and literacy. How I would have loved the education he despises! I'll go to stinking London and slaughter the *nàmhaid* myself."

So much at stake: their antique family servants,

MacNeils and MacDonalds, who all needed a roof over their heads and food in their bellies; her brother, Roderick, with his croft and his anger and temperament best suited to lonely, wild places.

Worst of all—Balgair risked her fantastical, mysterious Picti stones and standing stone circles scattered over the Outer Hebrides. Her obsession and passion. Her marvelous research.

All uprooted. Deported. Smashed into oblivion.

"I can't be married." Ruari heaved back her chair and paced the draughty hall. She wrenched a bloodstained, ancient sword from the wall and swung it in an expert swishing arc.

She pointed it at poor Sineag. "If I were a man, I'd be a scientist: a recognized authority in Neolithic and Picti artifacts. Standing stone circles. Carved steles. Ancient defensive brochs. *Hell and damnation*, shred my skirts, I *am* a scientist!"

"Language, lass," Sineag said, wholly unruffled.

Ruari swung the sword with satisfying energy. "That's for my new husband's head! I've no time to pander to some troublesome male. *Nobody will develop these lands.*"

A shadow darkened the doorway. Ruari swung the sword to point at her long-limbed elder brother, as he ducked his head to enter the hall. He uttered one of his charming laughs that lit his whole face from its usual dark glower.

"Who are you killing now, Ruari the Turbulent?" He pulled out a heavy chair. "And whose is that ship by the bay?"

Ruari and Sìneag gazed at each other in consternation.

How to tell Roderick this fell news?

Chapter Two

"Your mission here is doomed. You will never succeed." The words drilled his back like a barrage of bullets.

Lochaber straightened from his perusal of the eerily engrossing, intricately carved marker stone, as high as his hip and as broad as his shoulders.

The flushed cheeks and angrily heaving bosom of last night's pirate maid filled his vision. So. Not a fantasy conjured from the bitter pangs wrought by standing on Scottish soil. And she glowed more glorious, if that were possible, in this pink-streaked, fresh dawn. *Control.*

He curled his lip. "Believe me, I have more urgent matters at hand than this tedious side affair."

"Oh! *Tedious side affair.*" Ire sparkled in those magnificent lavender eyes.

He stepped closer to her. "But once I have made up my mind to embark on a project, I inevitably succeed."

She clenched a dainty fist. "Well, in this matter, you will taste defeat. You need my sanction, whatever my bloated cousin tells you."

A spear of warning stabbed Lochaber. She was right—her cousin was a foolish fribble consumed by thing-lust and crawling ambition. "If that bootlicking gigglemug is attempting to defraud my mentor, I will return to London and see him ruined. And I can and will do it, never doubt."

"Ha! At last, we are in agreement, sir." A wicked grin lit the wench's face. "Though you restrain yourself with the insults. I prefer fawning lickspittle."

Lochaber snorted a laugh.

Miss MacDonald emitted a musical peal like the song of seabirds, wild and free, that rippled through him like a charm. He swallowed, rendered temporarily speechless.

Her chin rose. "For I have no need of a husband at present. *Or ever.*"

Kamadeva, these island women were forward. Surprise curled through him like soft fingers teasing— *part of him would not object*. His jaw tightened as he sought control. He snarled, "One stolen kiss does not make a handfasting."

Her slashing dark brows snapped together. "I do not refer—" Her wide red mouth creased. Uncertainty shadowed her face. "Your Scots accent is very strong."

"I fear being in the Highlands has called it forth."

"The Scots accent and an English title seldom march alongside." She mashed her lips together. "Unless your ancestors were turncoat traitors during the dread Culloden years…Well! In that case, even if there were a thread of temptation, I am decided. You can get back on that ship and sail away—because I will *not* marry you!"

Thread of temptation. A strangled noise burst from his throat. Wrongfooted again by an island minx! Lucky his business rivals were not present. He sought a calmly sardonic tone and gritted, "I'm glad to hear it! I'm busy this week."

The woman stared. "My cousin sent a horrid letter, commanding me to ma—"

Oh ho. Light glimmered. Lochaber waited. "Yes?

Ma—?"

Temper flashed across her adorable apple cheeks. "Did not my cousin send you here, with an express command?"

Lochaber wrestled two temptations. The urge to tease the spirited and delicious Miss MacDonald almost overmastered him. But the idea that sniveling worm Balgair MacDonald could order him! Pride won.

Pride *always* won. It drove him.

He snapped, "Your puling cousin has no power over me. I am here as a favor to my mentor, a man more like a father to me."

"Then who…?" she muttered. "Balgair says my new husband comes."

A whirling dervish of emotions smote him. Fury. Envy. Desire… He spoke to squash the unwelcome stabs of feeling. "My mentor has a vision for these islands, the birthplace of his grandfather. I owe the man everything. I intend to see his dream realized, before I attend to my own concerns."

My cold-planned revenge in Aberdeen-Shire. He itched to sail away, just as the minx wished, and implement his final, bitter coup.

She transformed before his gaze into a serious pillar of woman, all cold fury and lethal threat. He blinked. A tiny inner part of him quailed. Some lost childhood part of him stirred. Highland women were not to be messed with.

Her freezing glare could have turned him to stone. "What vision? *What has my cousin done?*"

An accountable urge to calm her fear consumed him. He paced around the site, waving his arms for emphasis. "A boon for the islands, I assure you, that will bring much-needed prosperity. Jobs for the crofters currently eking out a poverty-scarred existence. Fame for Callanish and the islands. Your cousin and my mentor are discussing a hundred-year lease for use of the MacDonald lands."

Her cheeks paled. "What? No!" She uttered a mere whisper of sound. "So soon?" Her lithe form swayed.

He stepped closer; Miss MacDonald appeared on the point of collapse. Clearly, she had misunderstood. He clarified, his arms poised to assist her, "We shall construct the largest whisky distillery and factory ever imagined over this desolate landscape. The distillery will conjure the most seductive, glorious, complex Scots single-malt in the world."

The fierce pirate maid went white. Her legs appeared to give way, and she flung out her arms as she half fell onto the hill behind her. Lochaber stepped forward and scooped her against his chest.

For one long moment, his arms wrapped a delicious bundle of melting curves and pliant women. Twin heartbeats met and fused.

One all-too-brief instant. Her shaking calmed. Her inner fire ignited.

She glared up at him, eyes blazing violet-sapphire fire, temper riding in crimson cheeks, palms pressed flat against his chest. She spat, "Over my bleeding corpse! And even then, my shade will haunt and curse you."

All the bones in his face turned to lead. He leaned in and growled, "I am cursed already. Bitter shadows haunt me night and day."

She struggled, and he released her. Loss pinged through him like an ache in his blood. She stood one pace away, white-knuckled fists clenched, radiating fury.

The skin on his cheekbones stung too tight. "A burning mission drives me to Aberdeen-Shire. Yet I owe my mentor the making of me—*and I always pay my debts*. Whether debts of gratitude, or of ruin and obliteration." He matched her furious glare. "The distillery will be built."

Her slender throat bobbed as she swallowed.

An unwelcome wash of pity melted his bones. To disguise it, he snapped in his harshest tone, "Don't be foolish. These islands will sink over the edge of history without new industry and enterprise. A whisky manufactory! What could be more perfect? Birthed from pristine waters, heather honey, and peat smoke. The world will pay any price, I assure you."

"Some things are worth more than money. Irreplaceable, once gone."

"These islands need to be introduced to the glorious nineteenth century before they rot away entirely."

Color mounted once more in her cheeks. Red flags of warning. "I will permit no man to steal my heritage." She crowded his space. "These peat bogs are deep, and our farmers a silent lot."

This close, the urge to embrace her again lit a fire under his skin. *Blast it all to hell. No.*

She squared her shoulders and put up her chin. "I am a daughter of valiant warriors and pirate raiders. Nobody will take what is mine."

She walked over to the stone he had been examining, his gaze tracking her, utterly magnetized. She rested an elegant hand on its lichen-spotted, gray-flecked surface. Turned a serious face to him. "What of my Picti stones and their impenetrable carved symbols?" She gestured to the eastern hill. "Our eerie, beautiful, yet forever cryptic, standing stone circles?"

What indeed. "That's why museums exist. So everyone can gawk and wonder at our lost Scots heritage."

"Museums. Ha!" She spat on the ground. "In Edinburgh or Glasgow, I assume? Who would travel all the way there?"

Interesting perspective. Lochaber stifled a laugh. "Far better than losing the artifacts completely. The Picti carved stones are certainly beautiful, a unique art form. Many more people will enjoy them in a museum."

"You totally miss the point. These ancient stones are anchored in this landscape, this place, have meaning *here*. In some faraway museum, they are merely curios, a moment's entertainment for bored city-dwellers." She stroked the stone. "I will protect them with my considerable brains, my body, and my life!"

Considerable brains. An imp of mischief possessed him. The best way to inflame an intelligent woman? He said, "You are hysterical. Irrational."

Miss Ruari MacNeil MacDonald paced forward and slapped the air by his cheek. Then she gripped her hands on her hips and let him have it. A torrent of furious words lashed him. *"...heritage...unsolved mysteries...must remain in situ...I am a scientist..."*

A deep voice split the air like a thunderclap. "What goes on here? Ruari, what are you doing to this man?" A tall, lean, black-haired man appeared on the brow of the hill and stalked toward them, radiating temper.

"Who are you?" he asked Lochaber in a gravel voice and, without waiting for a response, turned to Miss MacDonald. "Where are your wits? A ship floats on the horizon and will be here anon. Our cousin's *package*

19

arrives, no doubt."

He snapped a suspicious chocolate glare at Lochaber and raised a heavy black brow. "What are you, the welcome party? You clearly don't know my sister, or you wouldn't be upsetting her. You'd be running for your life."

Lochaber emitted a surprised burst of mirth. He recovered himself and grated, "I grow weary of being lumped with your spineless cousin's schemes. And I have no wish to marry your terrifying sister, Mr. MacDonald."

Both siblings rounded on him. "You insult her!" the gloomy-visaged brother growled.

His sister laughed, then prodded Lochaber's chest hard with an outstretched finger. She hissed, in threatening tones which tingled over his skin, "Peat bog!"

She hooked her arm in her brother's. "Come, Roddy, we will give our new visitors the welcome they deserve."

Roddy paused. He glanced back at Lochaber and looked him up and down, taking his measure. "Your name?"

"Gordon. Lochaber Gordon. Delighted to meet you and your—charming—sister." He bowed.

Roddy ignored the bow. "Perhaps you will honor us at Castle Callanish with your company, Gordon, in an hour. You look as though you'd be handy in a fight. Able to incite chaos and confusion."

Lochaber scratched his head. "Handy in a fight. Well, yes. There is one thing, at least, I am good for."

He was rewarded by a bright periwinkle stare, avid with curiosity.

****

She had a little time yet. She needed to slough off some of her restlessness, fueled by her interchanges with the stranger. She bid Roderick return to the castle without her. "I will not dally long."

Checking over her shoulder to ensure the handsome stranger was not in pursuit of her—no tall figure stalked fast and intent in her direction—Ruari hurried to the Picti stone which marked the cliff path down to sea.

She paused to trace the familiar, cryptic carvings: a stylized flower, V-rod, and lunar crescent, with a later Christian cross superimposed on the top.

"Guard them, Ruari." Her poor dead mother's voice rang in her mind. "They are our treasure. Marker stones of the star folk."

Girlish Ruari had hoped her mother alluded to ancient treasure maps. She had imagined cracking the stones' secrets and unearthing riches that would save her family from grinding poverty and sickening dependence on her uncle, the laird.

And then, she got all tangled up in their mysteries. Studying the Neolithic standing stones and Picti carvings, documenting their mystic etchings, became her life's passion. How she adored those lightning bolts of insight, that thrill of discovery!

No room for husbands. Ergh! She needed to expend some fizz.

Ruari hurried down the hidden cliff path to her secret sea cave. She stepped into the cool dimness, the sand chill and damp under her feet. The air tasted of cold rock and seaweed. She lifted her selkie costume from its hiding place, fingering its plush, rubbery quality.

Shivering in the cold air, she removed every stitch of clothing until she was stripped to quivering cold-pink flesh. With care, she pulled the shaped sealskin over her legs, then wrenched the tight skin up and over her hips, torso, and breasts, contorting herself to thrust in each arm. She tightened the drawstring on the waterproof hood, which fit snugly over her hair and around her face.

The selkie-woman emerged from the cave, arms stretched high to salute the bright day. White seabirds wheeled and screamed around her. She strode into the freezing ocean, inhaled sharply, girded her will, and dove hard into the delicious salty embrace of the heaving sea. One fierce shock of cold smacked into her and then her seal-suit warmed.

The waves rushed against her body, sending thrills over singing skin. Ruari swam over to her sisters and brothers, her ancestor spirits, the seals honking and surfing in the foaming blue breakers on the edge of the cove. She dived and swam with the creatures, their sleek pelts rushing over her body and bumping her up over the breakers.

Ruari caught wave after curling wave, swimming with hard strokes until the sea flung her high, her torso suspended in air as the wave rushed her into the shore with the exhilarating speed of a runaway horse.

At last, enlivened by her swim, she strode happy and heavy-legged out of the sea. Back in the dim cave, she shivered as she stripped, rubbed herself dry and dressed. She washed the salt from her selkie-suit in a barrel of fresh water and hung it on the rock to dry.

Her brain pinged with ideas and new courage. What power did an impoverished, lone female have? *None*.

She needed higher powers. She needed *Science!*

Fabric stuck on her damp skin as she tugged her garments straight and braided her hair with numb fingers. Transformed back into Miss Ruari MacNeil MacDonald, she skipped back to Callanish castle, thrilled with a brilliant idea.

Months ago, she'd rescued and hoarded an Edinburgh newspaper discarded by her incurably bored cousin on his last brief visit. The article swam in her vision: a group of distinguished, bearded men with intelligent eyes. The Royal Society! She'd spent hours in the castle library laboriously looking up their areas of research: Astronomy—the stars. Natural history—animals, birds, insects, and plants. Paleontology—fossils. Archaeology—human prehistory and artifacts.

Elation pulsed through her again. Her own areas of passion and study! These men were her true soul's clan. How they would marvel when they heard her findings.

She would enlist the aid of the powerful Royal Society. Sponsored by the queen herself, no pompous laird of the MacDonalds could gainsay Science. As she strode, the letter formed itself in her active brain.

Curse it all! *Already* a sleek vessel bobbed close at the Callanish dock. A skua bird screeched above it like a discordant warning horn. A grand mothership rode the waves a league out beyond the breakers.

Her supposed husband had arrived.

Ruari hurried in through the garden door and took the steps two at a time to her tower room.

A thought flitted across her mind like a welcome breeze. Perhaps the man had brought his sister or female relative. The female crofters and aging castle retainers were warm-hearted, brave women, but how she yearned to converse with other women who had seen a little of the greater world.

More for the imaginary sister than the man waiting

below, Ruari donned a fresh dress and replaited her hair.

Energy like a foaming breaker surged through her. She must begin her plan immediately! She took a precious page of notepaper and rapidly drafted her letter.

Her research. A hint of her own theories about Picts and Vikings—and the stone star maps—saving the detail to enthrall the scientists later. Ha! She would foil her cousin and his dread plans yet!

She would be no wife. She would enlist the Distinguished Fellows and preserve her heritage with their interest. They would embrace her into their world, marveling at her bright brains. She would smile from a future newspaper image, surrounded by men of science.

Dear Sirs...

****

Raised male voices echoed from the hall as Ruari strode toward it, chin high and shoulders back. Her bones whispered that these were enemies, come to wrest away her freedom and everything she held dear, even their corroding castle.

Be alert, she cautioned herself. *Watch and listen.*

The deep-toned babble ceased as she entered the hall, as regal and gracious as a Scottish queen, despite her modest stature. Two men, clad in the finest Victorian fashion, leapt to their feet.

Two husbands? What now?

Chapter Three

An excess of unwanted grooms.

Roderick wore his cynical, wary face. He rose to his full, towering height. "Ruari, we have Lord Rupert Stavelet, Earl of Kilmore, come to visit us and grace us with his presence. And you know Alasdair MacLeod of Dunwary Castle, Skye. My sister, Miss Ruari MacDonald."

She stepped forward, and each gentleman bowed over her hand. The Kilmore resembled a storybook wicked earl. A small man who held himself very erect, Rupert Stavelet looked her over with cold, pale, unblinking eyes. His thin lips curved downward in disdain as he flicked a glance at her feet. "Barefoot!" he muttered.

The Earl of Kilmore's vicious reputation preceded him. The man had ruthlessly cleared many Highland clans from their generational lands. For sheep. A shiver coursed through her. "*Danger!*" the ancestors whispered in her ear. He barely touched her fingers, as though Catholicism and poverty were contagious.

What could such a man want with her?

The MacLeod she had met several times before, in her childhood and young womanhood. The MacLeods were ancient enemies and allies both. The main MacLeod clan of Skye had fought with the English at Culloden and then ravaged their Stuart-supporting

Catholic relatives on Raasay for decades. Alasdair MacLeod took her hand in his warm grip.

If Alasdair bid her to wife, she would be rich indeed. If she consented.

He gestured forward a woman, a tall, scornful-faced redhead. "My sister, Flora MacLeod, who has been away with my aunt in Inverness."

Despite the woman's sneer, Ruari grasped both her hands. "You are most welcome to Callanish Castle, my dear," she said. "Though I am well content here, I do lack for female company." The sneer softened a fraction. Ruari looked around and caught her brother, Roderick's, gaze. He stared at Flora MacLeod as if he had been blindsided by a bolt of lightning.

Into the middle of the cold and tense atmosphere, a sudden awareness prickled her skin. She whirled. Lochaber Gordon stood in the entrance to the great hall, standing very straight and bearing a politely blank expression. Ruari discerned a rising temper lurking under that pleasantly bland visage. Did visitors unravel his schemes? Or was he already acquainted with the earl or the MacLeod and disliked them?

A strange excitement lit her veins. He had come.

Three husbands.

Ha! She would have none of this folly. She had things to do.

The Kilmore broke the tense silence with a hissing speech praising Ruari's beauty. He surveyed her through his lizard eyes, as though he would soon dart out his reptile tongue and swallow her up as if she were a plump juicy fly.

The man made her bones feel hollow. Trepidation clawed at her belly.

Fight! shouted her pirate ancestors. Ruari smiled brightly. "My goodness! What hold can my cousin Lord Balgair MacDonald possibly hold over you, Lord Rupert, to compel you to travel to our desolate, primitive outpost? As for my 'famed beauty,' as you can see, he has dealt you false coin."

The elderly housekeeper, Gormshuil, tottering in with a tray of warm, scented pastries, muttered, "Now, Miss Ruari. Mind your manners."

The earl flashed the woman a death stare. "You are addressing your mistress! I would quash uppity, revolutionary—"

Gormshuil gave a particularly strong wobble, and a hot pastry slid from the shaking tray onto the earl's pristine boot. The nobleman shouted and cursed. Ruari grinned. A snort of amusement emanated from the doorway.

While the earl viciously abused the housekeeper, Lochaber Gordon sauntered in, put a strong arm around the old woman's shoulder, lifted the tray, and placed it securely on the long wooden table. Ruari's heart gave a strange flip-flop. Oh! A true gentleman. She smiled her approval.

The faintest pink tinged his carved cheekbones. Did the man *blush*? He bowed to Ruari and to the assembled company, then stalked over to a tall chair, arranging his long lean limbs in an elegant posture.

The Kilmore glowered at Lochaber. Ha! The slithery earl was disconcerted by Lochaber Gordon's clever, worldly presence.

As was customary, the guests had brought supplies and gifts: great wheels of cheese, potted meats and pastries, sides of venison, and whisky from the Skye distilleries.

The castle servants staggered in, grumbling about the weight of great platters of food suitable to welcome guests to a magnificent breakfast: haggis, roasted lamb and fresh potatoes, neeps and greens, oatcake bannocks, fresh soft cheese, cockles, and delicious smoked fish. Bowls of oatmeal dotted the table for people to roll their potatoes in.

"What news of the greater world?" asked Ruari, as the meal progressed. The company talked stiffly of the young queen, the old prince regent and the mad king, the Canadian rebellion, and the war with the Qing dynasty.

Finally, the enormous table was cleared, leaving only platters of rich fruitcake, shortbreads, and fruits.

"These islands will make excellent grazing lands," began Kilmore. Everybody around the table stiffened. The players had been assessed for weakness, and the game had begun.

Roderick waited, regarding the earl with repressed fury, a dangerous glint lurking in his dark gaze. She made no attempt to calm her brother. Give her the fight. Give her the truth. She was no peacemaker.

Lochaber Gordon suddenly grinned at her. *Did he just wink?*

The Earl of Kilmore continued in stuffy tones, "In these times, small crofts merely beggar large estates. One is always propping up the tenants until the whole family and all their dependents are ruined. Better to act now. These islands could support fat lambs and fine rich wool. The demand in the new nation of America increases daily, not to mention across the entire British Empire."

"Do you have an interest in the MacDonald castle and lands, or did you sail all this way to give Roderick the benefit of your no doubt practiced advice?" asked Lochaber pleasantly.

"Don't be a fool, Gordon. Balgair MacDonald needs funds. Currently he expends it on supporting his poor relatives." The earl traded narrow-eyed stares with the Gordon. Alasdair MacLeod tried to conceal his bright-eyed interest.

A cold hand gripped Ruari's throat. Was their poverty so widely known then? The earl clearly thought he could come here and the negotiations would be all but completed. The Kilmore did not miss Ruari's shock.

He pounced. "Your sister deserves a dowry, if she is to attract a high suitor. Balgair will give her one, when he secures the leases." He took a swallow of wine. "Or agrees to my offer." He sneered.

Ruari choked a little. "What is your offer, my lord?"

"What does business have to do with women's brains?" Then triumph lit his narrow features. "I don't lease. I buy. I have made him a handsome offer, while the land is still in good heart, which he would be foolish to refuse."

"We have generational dependents!" Ruari gasped. *Dowry* clanged like a bell in her ears.

The earl looked at Roderick. "MacDonald, I believe it is best to remove your sister. Perhaps she would accompany Miss MacLeod for a stroll around the castle or a lady's ride across the farmlands."

Ruari was surprised Roderick's glower did not fell the earl on the spot. He said in measured tones, redolent with lurking danger, "My sister has the right to sit in the hall of her ancestors. Miss Flora MacLeod may wish to retire to her room to rest and refresh, if she so pleases."

The tall redhead with the scornful smile flashed fire

back at Roderick. "Women of the MacLeods of Skye are no less doughty than Leòdhas women, I assure you."

"I doubt that," Roderick replied and wrinkled his lip. She jerked as though she had been shot. The expression on her face as she opened her mouth to respond augured a blistering retort. Ruari laughed.

The earl banged the table. "This is exactly why women are banned from rational discussion at the best tables. The conversation veers off track. Business is unable to be canvassed effectively."

"Your business, perhaps," retorted Ruari. "Not ours." The redhead Flora MacLeod gave her a chilly but approving half smile.

Lochaber Gordon twirled his glass. "Am I to understand, Kilmore, that you come to Callanish to inspect the MacDonald estate? With a view to purchase?"

"What of it? I do not have time to waste making polite conversation with such as the MacDonalds. The supporters of Charles Stuart lost all at Culloden. They have all been hanging by a thinning Catholic rosary ever since."

Alasdair MacLeod cleared his throat.

No! *Dowry*. Now we come to it. She could not stay and hear herself haggled over, like a prime piece of castle property.

Ruari leapt up, her heavy chair screeching across the floor. "Nothing is for sale," she declared, in the ringing tones of a practiced piper. "You must fight us for every inch of soil. Every crumbling stone."

Shaking, she fled the room. The Earl of Kilmore and the MacLeod laird had hatched a plan between them. Ruari's stomach churned. She must thwart them in their tracks.

Could she count on Lochaber for aid?

Or like a shark in the great sea, did he circle in ever-decreasing spirals as he waited for their weakening, in order to move in for the kill?

Four days. Perhaps five, for her letter to reach Burlington House, by messenger, sail, mail coach, and the fast steam train from Edinburgh to London. And then, the Royal Society would come to her aid. She just had to delay these interlopers for five little days.

So many ways.

Make Roddy take them game fishing among the shattered islands floating in the great ocean and pretend they were stuck out on St. Kilda. Ask Angus to hole their boat. Give them the herb woman's receipt to ensure a two-day sickness.

Her namesake Black Ruairidh the Pirate would simply cut their thieving heads from their grasping bodies and bury them forever in the peat.

****

Lochaber wrapped himself in his frustration and strode away from Callanish Castle, heading alone across the flower-studded fields and through tiny, ancient crofts adorned with traditional island dwellings, the blackhouses. Several redolent, moss-covered buildings appeared half collapsed.

This place! Calm and wonder unfurled in his brain, wrought from the ageless feel of the dwellings, the sour-sweet smell of the soil, birds silhouetted black and wheeling high in the sky, and the ever-present sound of the slapping sea.

"*A new clean, healthy village,*" Billy Bentinck had roared back in his London office, clinking his Laphroaig-filled glass with Lochaber's. "Not those smoke-filled blackhouses where only the strongest children cough their way into their ninth year. *A grand new industry*—a top-notch whisky distillery—will bring prosperity to the starving islanders. Capable management, to wrest a living from those forgotten islands."

"The future. If anyone can conjure it," Billy had said, his hand squeezing Lochaber's shoulder with his familiar affection, "it's you, Lochaber Gordon."

Fresh resolution steeling his veins, Lochaber crested the hill.

His jaw dropped. His brain jangled.

He took five paces and reached out a hand to reverently touch an ancient lichen-encrusted stone, as tall as himself and broader, somehow wedged upright in the ground, many eons ago. In fact, five standing stones, each six to ten feet high, another two fallen, arranged in a stone circle. A long stone slab in front of the western standing stone pointed to the center of the circle—and to a massive cairn, almost thirty feet wide.

He stepped within the ring. The tiny hairs on the back of his neck prickled. His skin shivered.

This circle was as strange and eerie as any of the marvels he'd seen in India.

The ground hummed with power, as though a current connected him to the earth. The stones seemed to vibrate with invisible force.

And there, barely three hundred yards away—a double standing stone circle, one within the other, perhaps fourteen yards across, with at least thirteen stones.

And on the far summit! Back toward Callanish Castle…

Lochaber's whole body stilled in wonder.

An enormous circle complex crested the rise to the northeast of the castle. Long arms comprised tall stone avenues in a massive cross, all leading inward to a magnificent stone circle, rearing high into the sky. The air shimmered all around it, as though it formed a veil into another world.

A huge stone circle complex on this lost island on the edge of the world.

Unbelievable.

He shook his head.

Hundreds of acres of good arable land—and fields perfect to situate a new village—were abandoned to the circles. And if Billy Bentinck did not beat the Earl of Kilmore to an offer on this land, he had no doubt the earl would clear the lot for his sheep.

Under Billy's scheme, the islanders would get new housing and hope for future prosperity. He had seen—created—progress and prosperity in India, with the formidable East India Company. Billy Bentinck would do the same here. The circles could be recreated in an outdoor museum in Edinburgh perhaps. Or London.

He strode away from the huge circle dominating the skyline, mentally measuring distances, erecting villages, laying roads.

Ignoring the sour taste of guilt and shame on his tongue.

****

He was stunned. Filled with a kind of religious awe. He had chanced upon a shoulder-high carved stone positioned at the edge of a hidden path down to Callanish Bay. The carvings spoke a language as mysterious and alien as something from another planet. Their magnetic power called like a lodestone, their strange meaning lost in time.

Carved stones. Visions of his lost boyhood crowded his brain. Pain sharp as an Indian *khanda* sword lanced his guts.

A light touch on his shoulder pulled him from a quicksand of bitterness. The scent of sea, wildflowers, and peat soothed him. He whirled.

"What are you doing *here*, Lochaber Gordon?" Ruari the Tartar hissed the words. A furious rosy flush crept over her cheeks, and her eyes blazed. Small fists clenched at each hip. "Why do I find you at our Neolithic and Picti sites?"

He couldn't lie to her. She didn't wish for soft words, palatable untruths to calm her. She would crush them underfoot.

He countered, "What use are these sites? Spread over so much of the landscape?"

"What use? What *use*? Can you be serious? These sites are many thousands of years old, containing mysteries and secrets as yet undiscovered. They belong to the Hebrides. They *are* us." Her nostrils flared. Temper sizzled from her, blending with the carved stone and the harsh backdrop, lending her dignity, power, and authority. Her figure crackled in the ancient landscape.

Lochaber was not a man to quail. He leaned in. "The future is coming. The past only holds us back. The past tries to anchor us, to define us—when we should be free to define ourselves, to fly up and create ourselves into people we want to be."

An agile brain ticked beneath that lovely face and form. Temptation rippled in a wave over her features.

He had her.

And then he ruined it. He snarled, "Do you truly want these remarkable objects left to rot—or for them to be recognized in the eyes of the world? With *you* as the acknowledged expert? Admit it!"

Her nostrils flared. An angry flush mounted her cheeks.

He kept at her. "What do these old stones give you? Nothing. They hold you back from the woman you could be."

Her cheeks hollowed. Desperation and despair washed over her face, chased by a determination so strong her cheekbones blanched white. "Fine words, Lochy Gordon. There speaks a man, and like all men, accustomed to easily getting his way. What do *you* know of the woman I could be? What do *you* care about my passions?"

He reached a hand. Touched a round shoulder. Stroked a curving upper arm. She didn't flinch. He made his voice soft. "What do you crave, Ruari MacDonald?"

She tossed her brown braids. Her moment of weakness had passed. "What do you propose for 'these old stones'? Tell me."

He deflected. "I met a lad, Kenny, on my walk here. He longed for new experience so much he hoped I had come to clear the tenants from the land, so he could escape this dreary life. That clever child is wasted as a crofter. Has he been to school?"

"He attended the village school for a few years, like all the island children. They don't like it, because the school makes them speak English."

"A useful attribute, surely?"

The mockery returned. "What for? To count the cows in two languages? Gaelic is the language of song

35

and story, of beauty and history and love. Why should they speak that hard hissing language of the oppressors?"

"That lad should be sent to school and university."

Ruari the Pirate was back, glaring at him. "What is the matter with you, Lochaber Gordon? Cannot you understand the prime importance of land and heritage? The *absolute necessity* to the soul of standing on the land of your forebears, that deep link to the past and the future, the rhythms of life as they have always been? Where are you from, yourself?"

Clàrsach Castle at Cluny. Aberdeen. The word itself tolling like a doom. *Aberdeen. Vengeance.*

He wrenched his mind back. "There is a wide world out there, which would welcome that lad and his quick brain."

"Are we talking about Kenny of Lewis or you, Lochaber Gordon?"

Ho! She hit true. "His talents could be used to greater effect in the world—to benefit that very family."

She glared, amethyst eyes flashing fire.

He wrestled with himself—and lost. "So. You would not wish your own bright sons to make their way in the wider world? You would tie them to duty and land?"

Why did he hold his breath for her answer?

"Why would you care?" she snapped, echoing his thought. The full rosy color mounted higher in her cheeks. "And what of my bright daughters?" Her voice rang out over the screaming of sea birds and the rhythmic swell of the sea. "Why should my imaginary sons have all the adventure, all the learning?" Alarm passed over her vivid features. She clamped her lips shut and turned her beautiful face away from him.

He stared at her elegant profile, awakening suffusing his agile brain. Could it be possible? Had he found a key to the mystery that was Ruari MacDonald? By the angry blush on her cheeks, he suspected that he had. *She burned with a rampant desire for escape, adventure, and learning.*

She stared out over the machair, her face taut. "The world would gobble up poor Kenny."

"Nonsense. He would excel at a profession." Testing her. Yes, there it was. *The tell.* Lips pressed back hard against her lovely white teeth. Frustration, Desire. Determination. A strange expression softened her features. Vulnerability. And suddenly he was all male, desperate to protect her. "What is it?"

"I believe...I believe these Picti stones are star maps...recording moon, season, direction—" She shook her head, scrunched up her face. Slapped her own forehead so hard he winced in sympathy. She gasped, tone cracking in despair, "Oh, why did I tell you? These are my secrets!"

"I've seen carved stones like these! Many times. With different symbols."

"What?" A full violet-lightning gaze sent every hair on his body on alert.

He desperately did not wish to speak of his childhood, did not want to release those writhing, bitter snakes of old hurt, but to save her pain..."There are many such around—" He coughed.

"Yes?" Urgency laced her tone. "Where?"

"—Aberdeen. Cluny. The land of my boyhood." There. He'd said those place names, for her, and the earth did not open, nor the heavens explode.

"But I must see these marvels! How do you mean,

37

different? In what way? Unique symbols, or the same, but rendered stylistically—" Ruari stopped just short of gripping his biceps.

"Mercy!" He emitted a laugh like a sheep's bleat. *Pull yourself together, man.*

She pinned him with a gaze so burning bright any resistance was consumed in her fire. "I have written to the Royal Society. To tell them of my marvelous artifacts. The carved stones—called steles, you know." She puffed out her chest delightfully.

His cock twitched.

Her lush lips parted. "The standing stone circles. My hard-won scientific research. My *scintillating* theories!"

He had to do something. Never had he been so bespelled by a female. The island atmosphere—being back on Scottish soil after all these years weakened him, perhaps. He gritted, "Don't count on their support."

"What? Why ever not?" She narrowed her eyes. "Are you going to destroy all my hopes?" A playful half smile danced on her curving red mouth.

Yes. Must break this spell. "You are a woman, are you not?" *Too much so.*

"What of it?"

He hesitated. Instead he said, "Live in the real world. You will get further, faster."

"Nonsense. One must dream first, before we can act. All right, say it. Why will the Royal Society not aid me?"

"They will dismiss your letter, because they believe women are weak-brained and illogical."

Her lips compressed. "They are men of science. Their motto: *Nullius in verba*. Take nobody's word for it. Gender is irrelevant." She shot him a venomous look. "You propose a blighted future which threatens my island, my artifacts."

Desperation to impress her, to woo her, pressed in his chest. "We will build a new healthy village. Construct an industry that puts Lewis and the Outer Hebrides on the world stage. Picture it! Prosperity for the crofters and villagers. Education for the children—like that wee lad Kenny." He waited, heart in his mouth.

Why did he hope, even for a second, that she would see things his way?

The torrent broke over his head in a hail of Gaelic. Fury, insults, threats. She pummeled his chest with hard fists. Huge storm-filled purple eyes, swimming in angry tears, glared at him, wet-lashed. Her body quivered.

And then she whirled and sprinted back to Callanish Castle.

Later, the men spent supper covertly eyeing each other and making stilted conversation, spiky with concealed barbs. Neither lady made an appearance.

Chapter Four

Burraidh! She hardly knew if she called herself or
the Gordon a fool. Why had she revealed her carefully
guarded theories about the star maps? What strange
power did he exert over her?

Ruari shifted her grandmother MacNeil's bagpipes
against her chest. She inhaled and gazed out at the
magical green and purple sky. The northern lights
danced and flickered, echoing her sparking mood.

Ruari balanced on the high battlements and gave a
fierce blow on the MacNeil Highland pipes. She
welcomed the ache in her arms, back, and thighs as she
supported the great instrument. The buzz in her muscles
helped to counter her tumbling emotions.

The soaring music spun free, its discordant jangling
notes a harmony and counterpoint with the roar of fierce
seas, the scream of gannets, and the excited leaping of
dolphins through foaming green breakers.

To the northeast, the silhouette of the great standing
stone circle pierced the vivid sky. She played a song to
their beauty and mystery, to her own Norse and Pict
heritage, to her forgotten ancestors who ventured far
over strange seas to come here.

Finally, she finished and rested the pipes on a
buttress. She cast a glance down over the castle
grounds—and stiffened and bent forward.

Lamp light emanating from the castle bathed two

figures below, lingering in the castle garden walk. She would recognize the height and curling black hair, the leonine stalking walk of her brother, Roderick, anywhere. The person accompanying him—regal, disdainful even from this distance, masses of gleaming red hair piled on top of her head and curling around her ears. Flora MacLeod, walking with her brother, by Neptune and all the gods of the sea!

Secreting herself behind one of the thick battlements, she bent farther over the wall of the castle walk.

"Be careful, Miss Ruari!" called Ceitidh from within her tower bedroom.

Ruari ignored the young chambermaid. She'd been leaning over these battlements her whole life. During her childhood, she had climbed the castle walls and towers too, beating her heavier brother to the highest spars.

Raised voices floated up. The Lady Flora gesticulated angrily, her magnificently styled hair releasing curls and shedding feathers in her unwonted animation. Roderick loomed over Flora with a forbidding expression. Ruari knew that scowl well: he must be vexed. And now he shouted at Flora! Roderick at his most tempestuous—worlds collided! Thunder roared.

Oh dear. Flora gathered her skirts around her and hastened off down the walk back toward the castle. Roderick glowered after her, his expression furious, then stalked off in the direction of his farm.

Oh. This visit got ever more complex. Filled with zest and lively curiosity, Ruari endured Ceitidh's help in putting herself to rights, and then she hurried down through the secret inner stone staircases to the garden exit.

****

Roderick's tall silhouette paced black against a sky heavy with stars. Ruari ran across the farmlands, assuming he padded to his favorite croft blackhouse. Though she ran as swiftly and silently as she could, Roddy's excellent hearing betrayed her. He turned and waited for her.

She hastened to the cottage doorway. He bent under the low lintel and scrabbled around, lighting a lantern and setting a small fire blazing. He put the old black kettle on the hob and pulled the Lagavulin from a hidden cupboard. Roddy's books lining three walls glimmered in the half-light of the single lantern.

"Ruari." He pushed his long dark curling hair from his forehead. Made her a cup of tea with a dram added. They gazed at each other for a while, relaxing into their mutual warm, safe regard.

Roddy's deep, slow voice held a turbulent undercurrent. "We must expel these invaders. Fix my cousin for good."

"Yes! I am weary of that scoundrel foiling my plans. What do you suggest?"

Her brother's black eyes flashed. His throat bobbed. "Ruari, I cannot lose these farmlands." He scraped his chair back, unfolded to his full height, and kicked at the fire with the toe of his worn boot. "I would go mad living in those cities." Desperation curdled his tone.

A shout of laughter escaped her. "Yes, I can see you now, felling those prancing fops with one single, well-aimed glower! Stomping around in your farm boots and your gloomy moods…you'd probably set a fashion and within a month every fribble would be paying *riches* for well-worn farm boots, practicing their fiercest frown…"

Roddy snorted a laugh. His brows descended once more. "Equally, I cannot stay here, to be commanded and overseen by some fool who barely knows his peat from his peter—"

"Ha! Roddy. But yes. Impossible."

"That infernal earl will outwit our vapid cousin in a heartbeat. We will lose all." He leaned his forehead on the mantel. Muffled voice. "Could you marry him?"

"Ma—?" Ruari's world stopped. No sound, except for a roaring in her ears. "You want me to marry that sinister snake? Roddy, look at the man's eyes! He is cold and nasty, through and through."

"You might save us. Save the Picti stones. Preserve the standing stones."

"That creeping white worm would never listen to a wife. He'd marry me and then threaten everything we value to exert control over me. No and no!"

He rested his head in his long-fingered hands and tugged at his inky curls. "The ledgers don't balance. The cursed English aristocracy hold the reins of trade too tight. Our small yields cannot compete."

"The earl will not save our farms."

"Yes. Merely an illusion of hope."

She rose and patted his shoulder. "I have a plan, Roddy! Science will aid us. I have written to the Royal Society, and they will rush in to protect the artifacts." As she uttered the words, sudden doubt assailed her. If the Gordon was correct—that plentiful Picti stones scattered Aberdeen and Cluny—would the professors even care about remote Hebridean archaeology?

Cold fingers of fear gripped her bones. Invisible walls pressed her mind. Maybe she *would* have to marry the reptilian earl.

Roddy's gravel voice penetrated her worry. "You have another option."

"*Yes?*"

"Lochaber Gordon will offer for you." Roddy's intelligent gaze sharpened as he noted her reaction. The quick flush.

"Don't be absurd!"

"His eyes follow you as though you are his one hope. He had intended to wrest our lands from us. But I watch his mind spin and his face follow you with his heart in his eyes, longing after you. He is making his mind up to an offer—a deal which involves the possession of you."

Repulsion filled her. "I will be no man's possession."

"I will not give my permission. He is not the man for you."

"You will not give your permission because you don't have the ordering of me, Roderick Ranald MacDonald." She tossed a stick on the fire and waited until it was engulfed in bright flames. "No man will determine my actions, not my craven cousin nor an English earl nor a well-set stranger from Cluny. No Scottish lord from Skye, *nor you*. Do you hear me?"

She glared at her brother. "What would you all do to curb my womanly disobedience, Roddy? *Imprison me in a sea-locked castle tower?*" She widened her eyes and gestured in the direction of the castle.

He barked a harsh laugh. Approval beamed from his dark eyes. "There's my Ruari the Turbulent."

Despite her words, she did hang on Roderick's approval. She did listen to him. Perhaps the only man she attended to. His words about Lochaber disturbed her. "Why isn't Lochy Gordon the man for me?"

"He is bitter inside. He must best and master everyone and everything in his path. He will douse your fire and turn you by degrees into a simulacrum of a biddable wife. He will attempt to control your actions and the way you live and, in so doing, make you both miserable."

He towered over her, not touching. "You will try your valiant heart out because that is you, that is how you commit to anything and anyone you love, with a strong and willing heart. But in attempting to be something other than you are, your own affection and loyalty will destroy you."

"Nonsense!" she retorted. But she could never fool Roddy for long.

As she strolled from the croft back to the castle, the soft night air kissing her cheeks, a gadfly of unease fluttered in her stomach. As usual, Roderick had seen more than she had where her welfare was concerned.

Would Lochaber Gordon really offer for her? A flash of his intent peat-honey eyes and strong muscular body assailed her senses. Her body leapt in a thrill as she pictured him. She felt again that kiss, which had sent fizzing sensation racing through her blood. Her heart skittered.

When would he kiss her again?

She should kiss *him*. Show him she was no passive maid…Her mind lingered, imagining her lips brushing his, her fingers tangling in that sunburst hair…

But currently he threatened everything she cared for.

And he hailed from way across the great Scottish mainland, far from her home and family, born in a mountainous eastern land which spoke no stories to her western isle-bred heart—but new *Picti stones!* Exactly what her research lacked.

And…admit it.

How she yearned for excitement and adventure, to explore other lands and places. *How she secretly craved love.*

The ground shook with hoofbeats. Her musings shattered into splinters.

A long shadow fell over her, darkening her vision. She whirled. A thin, upright figure on a great black horse clattered toward her from the direction of the village.

The horseman drew alongside. The greeting died on her lips when she spied the wicked earl's white, leering face. A low-toned hiss slid into her ears. "No innocent maid is abroad at this time of night. Creeping to an assignation, my sweet?" A hand stretched out and wrapped a braid, snapping her head and body back toward his mount.

What? Shock slammed into her like a punch to the lungs. "Release me!"

"Good peasant maids are all tucked in their beds. Which means you are the other sort. Forget your lumbering swain. I will show you more *interesting* sport."

Cold chills coursed down Ruari's spine. Fear spiked in her jumping muscles. Mad options for escape rioted in her brain.

A strong hand hooked under her arm and lifted her in the air several inches. He was dragging her onto his horse! She grabbed the thumb clenching her upper arm and wrenched it back until he released her with an oath. In the starlight, his thin face twisted. He raised his whip.

Snapped it back in the air.

Ruari stood her ground. "Lord Kilmore! How dare you molest any woman on this island. Keep your filthy habits to the degenerate cities."

He lowered his whip but stroked it lovingly over and over in his black-gloved hands. "Why, Miss MacDonald. Skulking around like a randy farm girl. Hmm. Damaged goods. That will lower the asking price for you."

The horse shifted. The earl flicked the whip at the beast's ear.

"You won't get me at any price." She turned and began to walk as rapidly as dignity permitted, back to Callanish Castle. Feverish plans ran in her mind. The Evil Earl must be ejected from Lewis. Somehow. What had he been doing in the village? She would check tomorrow that everyone was unmolested. Warn the women to keep everyone safe until Kilmore was expelled.

Hoofbeats sounded behind her. "Ah, a chase! I do love a hunt." The earl's sinister tones slithered over her like unwelcome fingers.

Ruari broke into a run. Mounted or not, he could not best her in a race over her own ground. She dodged and ducked as the whip whistled and cracked about her ears, and the earl's laughter rang out.

A sting on her shoulder gave her fresh impetus. The man must be mad!

She headed straight into peatlands too thick and sticky for a large horse. Sprinted to where the men had been cutting peat sods yesterday. The horse. It would break a fetlock. She halted, her gasping breath slicing her lungs.

The earl bent over his steed, coming fast. She cried

out, "Peat holes wrapped in darkness here. You will lame your beast."

The Kilmore pulled on the reins, and the horse reared and danced to the side. "A race to the castle, then. You will not escape me."

His poisonous shadow remained staring after her, dwindling as she ran through a standing stone circle, ducked low along the shadow of a hill and finally reached the seaward side of the castle. She cast a final terrified, furious glance around her and entered by the small, secret garden door, wedging it shut behind her.

That demon. May all the saints protect her!

By my ancestors! *May your Viking blood in my veins lend me courage and cold ruthlessness.*

Now, she had to save her precious artifacts, Roddy's farm, the village women—and herself. She prayed her letter from the Royal Society would come soon. How many days until it arrived?

She clattered into her room. Stripped to her undergarments, washed her face and all the places the Evil Earl had grasped.

Oh! The professors might be so intrigued, they came themselves. A delightful vision of those men of Science expelling the hateful earl swam in her mind. Even the Kilmore must give way to the mighty Royal Society.

Partly comforted, she went to bed.

Chapter Five

"You'll keep a MacDonald man with you at all times."

"Roddy, no!" She stopped, frustration squeezing her throat. Her brother wasn't responding at all as she had envisioned. Furious, broody, gloomy, yes. Active in vengeance against the earl? No.

Predawn ruby light washed the castle estate room, a delicious round room on the ground floor of the north turret, filled with worn and comfortable leather seats and bristling with racks of guns, swords, bayonets, axes, fighting bows, and spiky hammers. Papers, ledgers, account books, and other castle detritus crammed cabinets and shelves. Ancient glassware gleamed with red and gold lights from the reflected firelight and old ornate lamps.

Roderick threw a document down on his great desk. He stood, his great height rendering shifting black shadows around the walls.

She picked up an axe. Pricked her finger with its sharp blade. "What about the village women? They're not safe! The man was riding from there when he assaulted me—"

"Tell them to stay within or bide near their menfolk, until the pestilent man is gone."

She replaced the axe. Hefted a small sword. "I'm not sure he is going! He wants the MacDonald lands, for some fell purpose. He can acquire them more cheaply if he takes me too."

"That fool Balgair invited him. There's nothing we can do."

Why so passive? Fight, Roddy! "I'll write a letter to our cousin, acquainting him with what manner of man he has foisted on us. Balgair is stupid and greedy, but not evil. I hope." She grabbed a pen and a sheaf of paper, ready to begin at once. Slammed them back down on the table. "No doubt a useless appeal. He'll blame me instead for willfulness."

"He'll claim it's your fault and insist on a hasty marriage."

"Our ancestors rid themselves of our enemies without a pang. A million ways! The Earl of Kilmore's head in a deep bog. Abandoned on one of our tiny islands surrounded by savage seas. Run through with a sword. Shot, stabbed, beheaded—"

"Enough, my bloodthirsty sister." Roddy quirked a grin and drank his cooling tea. "Keep a MacDonald man by your side. The earl means you harm."

"No and no! This is *my* home, *my* lands, and I refuse to be afraid on the ground walked by my ancestors!"

Roddy frowned. Shrugged. "As you will." He opened a thick farm manual, palpably dismissing all women's concerns.

Keep a MacDonald man with you. She snorted. Her brother did not look up.

Blast him then. She would find her own solutions. As always.

She strode back around the outside of the castle, dodging through the gardens to avoid encountering a guest, and in by the secret stair. She hoisted the MacNeil pipes from their table.

Ruari balanced on the high battlements. She inhaled a full breath and blasted out the famous MacNeil military tunes, the ancient songs calling the Barra clans and bondmen to fight.

Below, Murdo and Donald MacDonald marched up and down the castle bailey while Ceitidh MacNeil linked arms with Malcolm the weapons master and whirled in a dance.

The music calmed her most murderous impulses. Still, she needed help.

There were only her ancestors to lend her courage, the Neolithic ones, the early Norse who populated these islands on the edge of the world. The Shining Ones who dwelt within the largest, most magnificent standing stone circle on Lewis, the Callanish Stones.

****

In her tower room, she covered her head and upper body in a MacNeil tartan *earasaid*, securing the fabric with an ornate Picti brooch carved with sea animals and strange beasts. She hesitated, then selected a gold brooch treasured for generations by the MacDonalds and hooked it through a section.

Pulling the wide tartan wrap farther over her hair to shadow her face, she ran lightly down her inner stairway and out through the secret garden door of the castle.

Ruari cast a furtive glance around from under the wrap, then walked swiftly across sweet green farmlands toward her place of sanctuary: the largest circle of Callanish standing stones, positioned high on the northeastern hill.

The machair this glorious morning glowed with yellow celandine and pink ragged robin, studded through the grass like tossed gemstones. The sea-scented breeze shivered the blue loch and lifted and teased the curls of her hair like soft hands of long-departed spirits.

On the hilltop, the enormous ring of standing stones stood tall against the pale blue sky. Ruari arrived at the great cross of standing stones, the arms forming entrance avenues to the grand inner circle. The stones vibrated with recognition, their eerie and ancient majesty offering welcome and dwarfing her own concerns.

She inhaled a steadying breath, then strode along the tall avenue, her pulses hammering a vigorous rhythm in her veins.

Halfway along, she paused and placed her hand on a gray granite lichen-encrusted pillar of stone, twice her height and much wider than her girth. "Help me!" she urged the *sithche* spirit inside it. "Enemies come. Strangers threaten my peace. Your mighty works face damage and extinction by uncaring hands. And I know not whom to trust."

She stroked the weathered rock, feeling the fissured surface with her fingertips, worn smooth in places where many fingers over countless years had stroked the stones before her. The massive size of the monument awed her but lent her comfort with their immensity and antiquity. Breathing deeply, she walked more slowly until she arrived in the center formation, the loci of the powerful magic of the standing stone circle.

Hands flat on two of the tallest standing stones, she stood proud and spoke aloud. "*Ancestors, I call you!* I fear your ancient lands will be ripped from us by a greedy landlord supported by unjust English laws. I am in terror that our people—*your people*—will starve in body and spirit; aye, will lose themselves laboring mindlessly in dark factories or be tossed onto great ships to sail far away to strange foreign lands, too distant for Scots *sithchean* to find. You and all your mighty, ages-old art and architecture will be broken up for industry. The magical Picti star maps will be lost forever."

Comfort snaked over Ruari's skin and infused her mind like a benevolent mist. She was strong. She would endure as the Circles had, for millennia. She could fight with all her weapons.

The image of Lochaber Gordon shimmered in her mind. He had traveled and lived far away, fighting for recognition and worldly rewards—*and he had won.*

Confusion bubbled in her mind. She pulled her hands from the pillars. Did the standing stones send her this message? *Trust the Gordon?* He was astute, intelligent, worldly—but patently plagued with his own inner demons.

She curled a lip. Or did her wishful heart speak? She shook her head. The *sithchean* were often tricksy. One did not always like the things they sent. Their messages were notoriously difficult to interpret.

"If your descendants are forced to yield their liberty, cede their lands, who will honor you and preserve your ancient monuments, my ancestors? The English and English-loving Scots will tear you down for their blasted factories and sheep. We will become Little England and you—" She swallowed. "You will be fading memories and dust."

The stones vibrated power and hummed with the slow measured heartbeat of the earth turning, but no more visions sprang to her mind. Ruari had asked for their help and now she must pay. Even if she did not understand the message.

She hurried down to the edge of the sea loch. For a moment she clutched the MacDonald gold brooch in her hand. Her science-brain whispered, "Superstitious nonsense!" But Ruari knew all the old tales about people who had sought advice from the *sithchean* and then reneged on paying the price. She held the brooch tight in her fist for a moment longer, repressing a bitter surge of grief and loss. And then, with a quick gesture, she threw it into the loch.

Back to the stone circle, she walked slowly up the avenue once more, this time drinking in their strength and resilience, easing her heart in their ancient embrace.

When she stood once more in the central circle, a sudden stab of awareness between her shoulder blades bade her spin around and stare back down the main avenue.

Lochaber Gordon himself stood smirking at the entrance!

A shiver ran down her spine—had the standing stones and her ancestors in fact sent her a warning, when she had seen the shimmering image of him earlier?

The Gordon grinned, his white teeth flashing in the sun, curse his English-tainted heart. He sauntered toward her, his bright brown eyes sparking with mischief.

"Quite the performance, Miss Ruari the Tartar!" he said, his voice as teasing as the breeze that tickled her flaming cheeks.

She opened her mouth, but he had her on the defensive. She could summon no fiery retort here in her deep place.

The Gordon kept walking, approaching steadily, mercilessly, like a nightmare, like fate itself. Her hand stuck to the stone she leaned against, unable to speak, unable to move.

He arrived at the standing stone next to hers and leaned to her. "A flaw in the clever, quick-witted Miss MacDonald!" he mocked, his voice rumbling as deep as the pillars were rooted in the earth. "Superstition. Throwing perfectly good gold into nearby water as offering to the old gods of land and sea! You know that never works, my love. There is only you; only your strong will and quicksilver mind and the strength of your determination. The *sithchean* are so very old. Now they sleep. They cannot hear you any longer. Their time is long past, Ruari the Pirate."

She stared back at him. Had the *sithchean* sent him? Or not?

With one step, he closed the distance and placed a hand on one side of the pillar, his dark honey-toffee eyes intent on her face. "I want to kiss you again, Ruari the Glorious."

Kiss you again. His bass voice vibrated through her. Sensation tingled over her skin. A bell in her brain rang with caution—and curiosity. A hot wave of desire turned her blood to fire.

Ruari reached her palms to his wide shoulders, gripping their breadth and strength. She studied his heated copper gaze and the flush bronzing his hollow cheeks. A faint scent of cinnamon and an unknown exotic spice, caught in the folds of his clothes, enveloped her. He stood motionless except for the rise and fall of his chest, his eyes narrowed to gleaming slits.

Ruari jutted her chin. "In this sacred place, my place, *I* will kiss *you*."

The man hissed in a breath through his teeth.

She stood on tiptoe and brushed her lips on his, her

heart pounding so hard in her chest, he must be able to feel it. His lips pressed firm and lush under her own. She froze, panic prickling in her belly. Could he tell she had little experience?

He uttered a low growl and wrapped her in burly arms. His mouth touched hers in a gentle greeting, then withdrew. She gasped in air, and then he met her lips once more, his kiss fervent.

Desire raced across her skin in fiery trails. For a moment, she pressed her body into his, his hard muscles and body heat mingling with her own flexible strength and soft places. She pulled back, her heart thundering.

He tangled his fingers in her hair, pushing back the *earasaid*, and held her cheeks in gentle palms. Her back rested against the tall, hard stone.

His deep voice sent spicy sizzles right to her curling toes. "Ruari MacNeil MacDonald. Your beauty enslaves me. Your fierce spirit enthralls me."

Their gazes locked. His whisky eyes lit with passion, a strange fury. "I am famous for my iron will and self-control. But with you…" He bent his head and ran the tip of his tongue around her mouth, tracing its shape.

Her lips sprang apart, and then his velvet tongue slid into her mouth, dancing against her own. How lush and smooth, slippery and intimate. *Intense*. She jerked back.

He studied her with hot eyes. "Do you wish me to continue?"

She met his gaze. Nodded.

His thighs pressed against hers. His sturdy arms, the breadth of his shoulders, the brawny width of his chest, all surrounded and possessed her, as though the stones themselves had come alive, with all their demands, their warm comfort, and their ancient strength.

This time when he bent his mouth to hers, their lips met, frenzied, devouring and tasting.

He pulled the wrap from her shoulders and cast it on a nearby rock. His fingers traced her delicate throat, the shape of the bones across her chest, touching soft white flesh.

Now Lochaber's face was taut with desire, aching with hunger and need. "You are extraordinarily lovely," he grated. "Your body is a music I yearn to dance with."

A flash in her vision: Loch and the sword dance, his whirling athleticism. Her blood rushed in her veins and pulsed in her lower belly.

His breath warmed her ear; his gravel voice shivered through her skin. "Your amethyst eyes and wide red mouth charm me—yet it's the heart of you, Ruari the Magnificent, that calls to me. Your passion for your artifacts warms my cold, black core." He smoothed a hand down her hair. His voice husked. "You are a strange and rare bloom growing at the edge of the known world."

She stared back. Such words! Such poetic images, here in this ancient, magic place. A well-bred lass would pull away and rush home. An English debutante would pretend shock, mimic outrage, a faint, pale hand quivering against her brow.

Ruari curled her lip.

Right now, in this instant, in this suspended bubble of time, she and the *sithchean* chose this man, whose bright hair flamed like an ancient crown in the sun.

Holding his hot-coffee gaze, she raised her right hand and deliberately drew down the fabric shielding her bosom until the cool air caressed her white skin, until only the corset propping and half covering her breasts lay between his devouring gaze and her flesh.

"You may plunder a pirate maid. If you dare." Her voice came throaty and inviting. Her pulses raced as she awaited his reaction.

He seized her upper arms. Immediately gentled his grip. "Ruari, blast it all, you are an innocent—"

"—An intelligent woman who decides her own path. In this moment, I choose you, Lochaber Gordon. I want the man who dances with swords on the beach in the moonlight."

"Ha! So you saw that…Then you shall have me. I can resist you no longer, pirate queen."

His lips slid against hers. He kissed her languorously, luxuriously, his silky tongue sweeping against hers. He ran long fingers lightly up and down her arms, waking her skin with delicious tingling ripples of sensation. His large, warm palms slid over her hair, cheeks, and shoulders.

She curved her form toward him, a slave to the sensations swelling her feminine parts and racing in her blood. She jutted her breasts at him.

His jaw clenched, then relaxed as he gave in. His fingers stroked the secret skin bared to his touch. His touch circled the tops of her breasts, dipping under the edge of the corset to probe the swell of each fat globe. She gasped as his finger touched her left nipple, the nub immediately hardening under his delving fingers.

She half slid down the standing stone at her back; he scooped his left hand under her buttock to hold her while he pleasured her with his right palm and fingers.

His voice gritted in her ear, sending spikes of pleasure through her with each rumble of sound. "So beautiful. Such lush, sweet skin. Such passion!"

She sucked in air, pressing back against the stone, tracking his fingers with her gaze as he unlaced the ribbons tying her corset. Her breasts sprang free, the cold air briefly clasping them before his warm hands began to stroke and tease her there, clever fingers urging her nipples into passionate peaks.

A low moan escaped her throat, and her body writhed under his caress. Her hands sought him. His muscular shoulders. His chest, waist, lean muscled thighs. She freed the buttons on his waistcoat, slid a hand between the fastenings on his shirt, pressed his warm skin. His heart beat strong and fast under her palm. She grazed wiry hair under her searching fingertips.

His hand slid down her waist, hips, legs. The air kissed the skin on her legs, bared now as he lifted her skirts with a long arm. He hauled her skirts above her knees.

"I would give you pleasure, pirate queen," he murmured against her neck.

"*Do it!*" She pressed back against the stone as her legs turned rubbery. Her heart rampaged under her ribs, and her breath strangled in her throat. Every cell in her body called for his touch, his kiss.

His hand lifted one of her legs and nestled her thigh against his hip. Dancing fingertips trailed up her ankle, her calf, tickled behind her knee—she hitched a breath.

"Like that, do you?" He repeated the action and smiled as she curved forward. His fingers traced the shape of her thigh, the outside, the tender skin on her inner thigh, and stopped, just before the junction of her thigh and her hidden folds of feminine flesh, now throbbing with delicious, searing want. She gripped the solidity of his upper arms, an anchor to the earth and the moment.

"This is the way to honor the old gods," Lochaber rumbled in her ear, the bass tones sending a responsive wave right through her. He dragged a gentle fingertip across her sensitive seam.

"Oh!" She jerked in surprise. And delight. And wanted him back there.

"No?" he asked.

"Yes, blast you!"

He laughed, a low, savage sound. His lips trailed sweetly down her neck, lingered in the hollow in her collarbone. He bit her earlobe. Sensation arrowed through her again.

She whispered, "Do it. While I still belong only to myself."

His body stilled. A fingertip teased the lobes of her secret parts. Then he stroked her there, spreading slickness, circling and pressing. Her breath wrenched in urgent gasps. She pulled him closer. He plunged a long, hard finger deep within. She bucked against his touch, seeking his firm heat. Then he withdrew.

His lips pressed on hers, as she ached and sizzled all over.

He obeyed her frantic wriggling and stroked and circled her tiny bud with a fingertip, until she throbbed in an agony of pleasure. Her body crushed against him, wanting, needing more of him. A finger slid inside her softness, and she clamped around him. He set up a rhythm with his fingers, pushing in and out, firm and hard, and she rubbed and rocked against him, with him, all her attention on his touch and her rising pleasure.

Ruari writhed, small involuntary moans escaping her, but she was beyond caring. Lochaber himself, his hot male presence overwhelming her, insistent, demanding…a bagpipe blast built within her as a delicious tension wracked her body, centered on that universe of friction and sensation he created deep inside her. Waves of sensation flooded her mind, and rippling sparks collected at the edges of her vison.

The universe exploded. A shout tore from her throat and sang down the avenue of the Old Ones. Stars sprayed in her vision, and a great wave threw her high up into a sunburst sky.

Ruari returned to earth. Lochaber held her tight against him. His firm heartbeat under her cheek pulsed as hard and strong as did hers. His muscles shook against her body. He put his mouth on hers and kissed her slowly, lingeringly. Lovingly.

Ruari couldn't speak. She pulled away from him and stared at him with wide eyes. She hardly knew if she was shocked, or languorously pleasured, or alarmed, or utterly in love with Lochaber Gordon. Or all of them at once.

"I believe you are the pirate, Lochaber Gordon," she finally managed with a shaky laugh. "Plunder and theft. Charming your way to the treasure you seek like all the best pirates."

"I did not steal what was freely given!" he replied, but his voice caressed and his eyes shone deep honey with wicked need. A smile flirted at the edge of his mouth, a dimple flashing in his right cheek. "Be careful I do not ask you to walk my plank, my lady," he added. "At this present moment, my wood is very long indeed."

Ruari's eyes fluttered wider as she caught his meaning. "Well, you certainly plundered my chest," she retorted in kind.

They looked at each other and laughed, foolishly and longer than necessary for such small jokes.

Lochaber's brilliant mind, the sharp brain that had got him halfway around the globe and rising high in a complex, dangerous business world of shifting alliances, bright opportunities and harsh setbacks, sudden allies and deadly enemies, was completely and utterly…tangled. As though Ruari the Pirate Queen had turned his clever brain as soft and knotted as the MacDonald cable pattern in a family sweater. With merely a lift of a delicate, curving brow and the touch of a finger. *And* that sparkling mockery, which had him in thrall and frustration from the instant of their meeting.

His body, though! A strident clarion call to possess this seductive witch shouted within him. He needed every ounce of his considerable will to resist tearing every stitch of the MacNeil tartans from her shapely form. He wanted to know those lush curves. He wanted to stroke that ivory skin all over. He wanted to meld her kiss with his. He wanted to know her entirely.

Not just her body. He wanted to stay with her, walk with her, talk with her, breathe the same air, learn the complicated mystery that was Ruari MacDonald.

What a fool. His triumph in the Highlands teased within his grasp…and all he could see, think about, *desire*—was this forthright, charming, fascinating woman.

"Are you well, Ruari MacDonald?" His fingers reassembled her clothing for her, taking every opportunity to stroke her silky skin. She smiled so enticingly he could not resist kissing her again.

She said, "I am well. It is a pleasure to meet a man so surprisingly knowledgeable of a woman's body."

Danger! He heard the unstated question. *Had he enjoyed many women thus in his past? Did he have someone now?*

Let her wonder. For now. He preferred to speak of her interests. "These eerie sites—they are most intriguing, are they not?" He coughed a little. His voice rattled harsh in his throat as though he had forgotten how to speak.

He and Ruari leaned together against the strong stones, a little apart. He feasted his eyes greedily on the beauty of her face: her feminine, defined jaw and cheekbones, her lustrous eyes sparkling now with liveliness, the rosy flush mantling her cheeks, as sweetly rounded as her breasts. He managed—just—to keep his eyes—and his hands—from her person.

So Lochaber saw the change in her expression wrought by his words. Her eyes brightened with interest. Her body snapped to attention. She leaned toward him. "Yes indeed," she answered him, no longer embarrassed at his excess of civilities.

She did not think of him at all.

Her eyes lit and her voice sparkled. "There are several great standing circles scattered over this island, and many single, carved stones, Neolithic and Picti monuments." Her wide red mouth curved in a lush smile. "Some folk insist they are giants turned to stone. Others believe ancient peoples built the rings to track the movement of the sun and seasons—and to predict good and evil for humankind. Others say the circles were used for ritual human sacrifice upon bloodied altars."

Her face glowed in a sweet expression of wonder. Lochaber drank it in like a man with a thirst. She said, "The old Callanish folk say that early on midsummer morning, the Shining One walks the length of the avenue of this, the largest standing stone circle. His coming is heralded by the call of the cuckoo."

She reached out a hand and stroked the line of his jaw with absentminded sensuality. Lochaber stood stock still, unwilling to make a sound or movement which would cause her to snatch her hand away. She murmured, "Everyone who encounters the great stone circles feels their power, radiating from the great gray stones themselves so deeply planted in the Callanish earth and emanating like an invisible beacon from the core of the central ring."

She took her hand back. A pang of loss smote him. She said, "I study these ancient circles and carved steles and the people who made them. Their magic possesses me…" The color mounted along her fine cheekbones. "…and seduces me."

He craved to know more of the secret passions which drove her. He desperately sought the vital key to this brave-hearted woman.

He smoothed a dark chocolate strand from her heated cheek. "When I was a lad, I explored many Picti sites and standing stones carved with their unknowable, but very beautiful, symbols and designs. Stylized horse's heads. Sea creatures. Zagged lightning flashes. Circles and dots and lines."

She stared at him, transfixed, wanting more. Her swollen mouth parted in delight. He swallowed against the need, deep in his throat, to kiss her again. A flash of insight blasted through him—this woman demanded that he intrigue and tantalize her clever mind, if he was to gain further access to her delectable body.

Her whisper shivered along his skin. "So you will

not recommend this land be cleared for a village. You understand."

And yet, we must create the future.

He could not utter the words aloud. He could not break the spell. He basked in her attention. Greedily desired to keep her focus wholly on him. "In Aberdeen-Shire, between the great Cairngorm mountains and Aberdeen city, near where I spent my boyhood, significant Picti sites abound. The Maiden Stone near Inverurie is carved with fabulous creatures, including a centaur, a man with his arms outstretched between two fish monsters, known as Picti beasts, and a mirror and comb."

"Oh! How I would dearly love to see those!"

He could stare at her vivid, entranced features all day. "Four Picti stones are built into the kirk wall at Inverurie. They are carved with serpents, horseshoes, lightning flashes, a mirror case, and double discs."

Her eyes shone bright as periwinkle stars, intelligence and curiosity searing into him, no longer masked with polite fictions of feminine dullness. As he had suspected. Here was a formidable intellect—fated to rust away in this godforsaken backwater.

She paled with excitement. "What do they mean, these unique, eerie engravings? What do folk say, in Aberdeen-Shire?"

How he hated to disappoint her! "No one knows. Not even the archaeologists from the universities. The Picti stones offer an impenetrable mystery, thus far."

Her brows rose. "These Aberdeen carvings—they sound...yes! They could contain the answers, the evidence I seek. I am compelled. How I wish I could study our ancient artifacts—as a profession."

He swallowed and took her hands in his. "Easily done," he gritted. "If you are brilliant, wealthy, *and male*."

"Ha to that!"

The beginnings of a plan began to flower in his mind. When he described the Picti remains, he had set a lure. He watched her quick brain turning over options.

She said, in a halting tone, "Do...do you have a sister, Lochaber Gordon?"

What? He dropped her hands as though stung. He could not mask his expression; the blood drained from his face. *Had she discovered his secret?*

His lips tightened. He clamped his jaw against unwitting words tumbling out while under her spell.

What had he been thinking?

He had been toying with an impossible dream. A sharp stab of reality punctured his golden fantasy. Excellent. He hated to waste time in the realm of dreams and wishes. "It is past time I returned to Callanish Castle," he said in his most formal tones. He stood straight and tall, assuming a distant, mildly disgusted expression.

She jerked as though stabbed. Her dark eyelashes fluttered rapidly, and then a wave of temper flushed her cheeks.

He said, "Please allow me to escort you back to the castle, Miss MacDonald."

She showed her teeth in a ferocious grimace. "So that is how it is, is it, Lochaber Gordon? No doubt you are accustomed to—" She heaved several gasping breaths, making her breasts jog up and down in a most attractive manner. Lochy tore his gaze from her chest and back to her face.

She found her words, and they tumbled out laced with fire and lightning. "No doubt you are accustomed to *plundering* exotic maidens in far lands, whenever and as you will. *Plunging* your fingers into their most secret..."

Tears refracting into mini rainbows spangled her eyelashes. She dashed an angry hand across her face, leaving a sparkling trail of moisture across her red blazing cheek.

"I meant no disrespect—"

"No *disrespect*!" Ruari shouted the words, grimacing as though they tore her throat as they emerged.

"I could not resist your charms."

"My *charms*!" She gulped in air. "You call us barbarians! Oh yes, I know. The servants told me. You hold us in such low esteem that you think to take what you want: our lands, our history and heritage, and even the secrets of my body!" Her lovely mobile lips thinned over her teeth. She hissed, "*Secrets I barely know myself.*"

With a last chagrined glare, she tore herself away. Holding her tartans close about her, she ran down the standing stone avenue and took off across the field.

Lochaber stared after her. Should he follow?

Too late, he realized the purpose of her question about his sister. She had wondered about coming to visit his home. To explore the Picti sites. For that to be acceptable, he would need a sister, mother, or female relative present in the house.

That was all.

He began to run.

He inhaled the sweet fresh air as he ran after the flying figure some yards ahead. It felt good to stretch his long limbs and stride over good Scottish farmland. His blood sang with the hunt. The realization slammed into him like running full tilt into a stone wall—he craved this woman with every cell of his body.

"Ruari!" he bellowed. "Miss MacDonald, wait!"

He heaved in more of the good sweet-salty air and put on a burst of speed. "I am the greatest fool. Wait for me, minx!" His words floated off over the grassy fields. Hairy island sheep stared at him in surprise, their expressions so comical a bubble of laughter burst from him.

She stopped and turned.

Yes! Victory was at hand. "I apologize!" he called in a stentorian voice. "No need to call your men."

Even from yards away, he read her scorn.

"For what?" Her voice, redolent with mockery, floated back. "I run for my sharpest sword, Lochaber Gordon!" She bunched her hands on her hips. "And believe you me, I know how to wield it." She raised her right fist high in the air.

Once more she became a figure of flying tartan, running fleet and swift away across the grassy fields, away from him.

He bellowed, "I've been threatened with far worse than a sword and won!"

An urge to pursue her and tumble her down to the fields came over him, stronger than any he had had since he was a stripling boy struggling with passionate urges. A vision of him pressing her into soil and kissing her into passion fired his brain. His arms and hands reached out toward her of their own volition.

But no! He would fight to his strengths: his strategic, cunning brain and indomitable will. Right now, he flexed that will to the utmost to allow her to flee—this time. Give her an illusion of victory.

He had two keys—two cracks in that fierce façade— to the heart and mind of the delicious Ruari MacDonald: her capacity for enormous passion and her fascination with Picti artifacts. Her bright brain could be tantalized with new data, to overrule her iron will and addiction to clan.

Smiling bitterly, Lochaber adjusted his clothing and smoothed his wild red hair. He bowed theatrically to the astonished sheep and strolled nonchalantly back to Castle Callanish.

Parama padam.

Snakes and ladders.

Chapter Six

Ruari rushed headlong into Callanish Castle, seeking the comfort and safety of her private tower aerie. Her cheeks stung salty with furious tears. Her stomach roiled with a storm of conflicting emotions she dared not examine until she was alone.

She hastened into the low back door and began to mount a small back staircase.

"Miss Ruari! There ye are!" Sìneag, the MacNeil maid who had come with Ruari's mother to Callanish, stood above her in the dimness of the servants' stair.

"Sìneag. I go to my tower. I do not wish to be disturbed."

The elderly maid stepped closer and peered into her face. "Whatever is the matter, young Ruari, my heart?" the woman asked softly. She enfolded Ruari into her work-strong arms.

Ruari took a deep breath in. She would not cry in the maid's arms, despite their blood connection, despite the maid's ready sympathy, despite her terrible need to bawl out her confusion…She managed to tear herself away.

"Excuse me, dear Sìneag." She pushed past her and had not stepped more than two steps toward her escape, when the maid said, her voice urgent, "But my little love, you are wanted. In the castle library. We have been searching all Callanish for you. Your brother and his guests grow impatient." Her gnarled hand stroked

Ruari's hair. "It does not do to send Roderick into one of his tempers."

Ruari tossed her hair. "As if I am afraid of my brother! Nonsense!" She met the maid's concerned gaze. "What do they want, do you know?"

"We were unable to ascertain."

Sìneag's face was so grave, Ruari found—at last— a small laugh bubbling inside her. "What? The Callanish Castle retainers unable to find out what occurs! Unheard of!" A smile flashed, and her expression grew somber again. "It cannot augur anything good. That wicked Earl of Kilmore bides with him within."

They stared at each in mutual consternation.

"Ask Donald or Murdo to inform my brother that I am tidying myself in my room after a wee sojourn outside. I will join them in a short time." She grasped the maid's hands. "Please. If one of Callanish's people learns anything, bring it to me in my tower."

"We will, my lady." Sìneag nocked a finger under Ruari's jaw, tilting her chin up. "Remember! You are the valiant daughter of braw-hearted MacNeils. Call on your stalwart mother's blood to succor you. Call on the Clan MacNeil fighting spirit to sustain you. I heard your battle songs the morn."

The words made Ruari's blood leap strong and proud in her veins. "*Victory or Death!*" she replied, and the maid hit Ruari's shoulder with so much force she staggered on the stair. She laughed and kissed her fierce gray-haired kinswoman.

She ran quickly up the stairway to her tower, praying nobody else would catch her.

****

The atmosphere in the castle library could have

burnt all the paper within to flinders, Ruari thought. Sìneag MacNeil's words had stirred her blood, and she had long learned to take the fight to her stormy brother, so she decided to open proceedings in a suitably warlike manner.

"Men are dreadful at waiting, are they not, whereas they expect women to wait for everything," she began, smiling prettily in her best hostess manner.

The five men in the room reacted according to their temperament, before they could hide their responses.

The Earl of Kilmore, Rupert Stavelet, jerked as though shot. His sallow cheeks colored with a tinge of savage temper. His thin lips thinned even more, and a nasty gleam shone in his cold eyes.

Ruari curled her lip and glared. It was the first time she had set eyes on him since their encounter in the darkness. The Earl of Kilmore was not kind to women, and female Scots in particular, he wanted to grind under his heel.

Well, he would not grind her.

The laird of Clan MacLeod, Alasdair, stood tall, lean, and arrogant. He had the bright blue eyes common to the Hebrides, proclaiming the Norse blood flowing strong in his veins. At this moment, those azure eyes shone chill with disapproval. He was accustomed to commanding men, as laird and as an army captain for the English. His most attractive feature, in her view, was the jagged scar across his left eyebrow, which lent a jaunty, buccaneering flavor to his military stance.

Her brother, Roderick MacDonald, gave her a secret approving grin, his black eyes glinting with mischief. One hoary MacDonald man, Murdo, grimaced at her in gentle rebuke, and Donald MacDonald smothered a laugh.

Roddy waved her to a seat, and the company sat in chairs ranged around the room. The two MacDonald retainers stood to attention—more or less—either side of the door. Roderick smoldered behind his large desk. "Clan MacDonald has received an offer," he said.

"Oh?" Ruari raised an enquiring brow at Murdo, who merely stared back at her steadily, not indicating by nod or shake of his head that he had an opinion on the matter.

She was out of charity with all men, at present, and in quite a temper. "You have all been discussing matters that concern the MacDonalds of Callanish without including the daughter of this castle?"

The earl snorted and practically pawed the ground like an angry bull. Ruari repressed a smile and began to enjoy herself. The MacLeod blinked. At least he was accustomed to fiery island women, despite spending many years with the milk-and-water misses of English high society.

Roderick continued in his dark chocolate voice, keeping his expression schooled and closed. "The offer concerns you, Ruari MacNeil MacDonald, only daughter of Callanish Castle."

She widened her eyes and waited, a chill fist of foreboding squeezing her heart.

Alasdair MacLeod stepped forward. "I have asked your brother for your hand in marriage." He made her a formal bow. "I would unite our lands and our families, in these uncertain times."

Shock speared Ruari. She had not really believed…

The offer had come with no preliminaries: the man shot straight. She opened her mouth, but the mad shapes rocketing in her brain could not resolve into coherent words.

Before anyone could speak, Roderick added, "Should this arrangement not be to your liking, my sister, the Earl of Kilmore has made a counter offer to purchase Callanish Castle and most of our lands—for a respectable sum."

The room spun around her. She could not get breath into her body.

Roderick rose. "And now, we will leave you, with the exception of Laird Alasdair MacLeod of Dunwary, who has asked leave to plead his case with you." Roderick's frowning, satirical grin danced for an instant on his dark-browed face. "I explained to him that the decision would be yours, and yours alone."

The MacDonalds all bowed. Roderick led the way from the room. On the threshold, the Kilmore paused and gave her a lingering adder stare.

"Roderick!" Ruari said, but it was too late. He was gone.

For a long moment, Ruari remained seated in her chair, her hands gripping the carved armrests in a palsied white-knuckled grip. She could not look at Alasdair MacLeod. Her brain was paralyzed with a kind of seizure.

Vivid flashes of what she had just done with Lochy Gordon heated her cheeks and sent her blood spiraling madly in her veins.

She swallowed against a grainy throat. "Before you speak, I must talk further with my brother," she began. She rose from the chair and at last met the MacLeod's vivid gaze. As blue as the wide sky she looked upon every day. As blue as the seas in the Little Minch, that stretch of water between Leòdhas and Skye, which linked their two lands, as their families were linked throughout history.

"Miss Ruari," the MacLeod said. "This declaration was not perhaps in the manner you may have imagined. But please allow me to add the elements of a proper proposal of marriage, which were necessarily omitted by your brother."

Ruari made a stifled sound, then found some words. "I have known you and yours since childhood. Our families have been kindred as both ally and enemy for centuries. I will always give you the courtesy of my attention, Alasdair MacLeod."

He strode forward and took both of her hands in his. "I have long admired your beauty, your elegance, and your clever wit, my lady. I know our families fought hard on opposite sides in the last century, but I offer you now the chance to unite once more."

"Your family committed shocking atrocities on your own relatives, especially during the tragic Jacobite campaign. You have blood on your hands, and your blood is tainted with those crimes. Besides, I am Catholic."

"Yes, there have been many terrible MacLeod wars, with winners and losers as the wheel of fortune turns, but that was generations past. And you are as Catholic as I am Protestant. It is the islands that is our true religion, for both of us, is it not?"

"Heresy!" She could not repress a small smile.

"Nonsense. We will marry in the Church of England, but you will be permitted to practice your faith as you will."

Ruari struggled with multiple retorts stinging her

tongue. "*Permitted?*" She glared her outrage. "Marry into a church which practices divorce? So you can shed me when you will it?"

The MacLeod frowned and drew back. He said, his tones wounded, "This is a respectable and heartfelt offer. Your brother knows it is a greater offer than you have a right to expect. Your future—and that of your family and dependents—will be secured. You will not have to leave the islands that you love so dearly. You will have a great increase in status as my lady of Dunwary." He bowed. "My castle is beautiful and very comfortably appointed. My grounds are extensive and laid out in sumptuous gardens."

He must have read the sudden desire on Ruari's face, for his voice softened and his hard cobalt eyes at last revealed his want of her. "I understand you are an independent spirit who needs the wild landscapes of your islands. In my castle—in my arms—I offer you those unspoiled landscapes, my protection, and peace."

Ruari studied him. "Alasdair, why me? You could have your pick of charming English maidens who will support your rise in society, who are trained to be perfect hostesses and mistresses of large estates. Surely your marriage is a vitally important thing, to earn you favors and preferment, or confer new titles and nobilities on your clan? I will admit to you—I am a veritable hoyden!"

The MacLeod regarded her gravely. "Many English misses would not even conceive of such strategy and forethought; and those that did would be so horribly ambitious as to be unbearable. You immediately grasp the situation and discuss it dispassionately. Your intelligence and guidance, Ruari MacDonald, will be most welcome in my life."

He saw her hesitate and struggle for words. He added, very low and soft, "The islands are my great love. These harsh landscapes call to me wherever I have fought in wars or lived elsewhere for a time. My blood sings with the call of the sea. My eyes crave the blue horizons, which melt into misty landscapes. My ears find their best comfort and joy in the wild cries of sea birds. I would have a wife who understands and shares this greatest part of me."

"You could not have said anything more romantic to me, Alasdair MacLeod. You are right: the islands are my heartbeat and my blood and my joy. Truly I am honored by your offer."

The MacLeod stood more upright, and his face shone with victory.

Ruari forestalled him with a hand raised, palm out before her. "You will allow me time to consider this matter and to discuss it with my brother before I give you my answer."

His eyes flashed, and his jaw set hard. He looked once more the arrogant and commanding man who had stepped into Callanish Castle the day before. "What is there to consider?" he demanded in silky, dangerous tones. "You will not receive a more advantageous offer. And a possible—likely—future, includes you and your family evicted from the MacDonald lands, thrown onto a clearance ship with a ragged bundle of poor belongings and sent to the colonies, there to starve or...sell your body for bread!" he ended on a savage, triumphant note.

Ruari smirked at him. "I like you better in a temper, Alasdair MacLeod."

He banged the table. "My temper is determined. Should you deny me, Ruari MacDonald, I will wreak vengeance on you and your family."

"With your bonny new friend, the Earl of Kilmore, I have no doubt? What happened to love and esteem me?"

The laird regarded her steadily. "If you continue to provoke me in such a manner when we are married, I will have you whipped."

Ruari laughed. "You will have to catch me first. And fight off numerous MacNeils and MacDonalds. You would create a new clan war. But perhaps you would enjoy that, burning and pillaging the homes of the people you profess to love."

"Your brother intimated you were impossible."

"He is correct in all things."

Finally, reluctantly, as though it hurt him, the MacLeod laughed. He was a different man when he laughed, Ruari thought, his eyes dancing like sun on waves, that tall lean body at last relaxing into humor. She could do it. She could help this man find his softer side. She could live as his wife, on the glorious Isle of Skye, a short boat trip back to her beloved ancestral homes on Leòdhas and Barra. He was handsome, and rich, and could save them all.

She could save them all.

"Your offer is magnificent," she said at last. "And you yourself are a large part of the attraction. It would be an honor to be your wife. But! I must have time to consider."

"The request is an insult. However, I will indulge you this thinking time as a token of my esteem. You have twenty-four hours."

He bowed in crisp military fashion, wheeled, and quit the room.

****

When—at last—there was no one left to see her, Ruari's entire body weakened and folded, her legs giving way beneath her like the exhausted jelly-limbs of a newborn lamb. She collapsed onto an upholstered sofa, her mind in shreds and tatters.

For months—years!—nothing had happened to disturb the calm, boring tenor of her days, and now...!

Two men. One taking her, thrilling her, offering delightful promises of—she hardly knew. Adventure. Travel. The call of Science.

But his country was distant Aberdeen-Shire, far from the wide turquoise ocean and misty horizons which moved and sparkled within her like her very blood. Aberdeen and Cluny, filled with ancient curiosities. Her mind burned with eager fascination, leaped with urgent compulsion to see those marvels for herself, to embrace delicious new evidence.

And yes. She craved more addictive, intimate touches from the man himself.

But he carried some bitter secret within. How he had reacted when she asked of his family!

The laird, Alasdair MacLeod of Dunwary: a great lord, a fabulous castle, wealth and influence untold. A magnificent offer, there was no denying it. Her family, her dependents, the children of her body would be safe— and not just secure. They would thrive, be able to grab with both hands all the dizzying opportunities waiting in the wide world, with such wealth, such acceptance in the great English empire to propel them forward.

If she said yes to the laird, she could stay on her beloved islands. Her future and her life as the Lady MacLeod would roll out before her like a story already told a thousand times, worn smooth into the parchment of history. She could save her precious artifacts.

The man himself: she liked him. Fierce, bold, valiant, with a love of the islands in his deepest heart. *His English-loving heart.* Could all men make her feel as the Gordon did?

No. The earl. Her flesh shuddered.

How she longed for the friendship and counsel of another woman, at this moment! Flora MacLeod, haughty and frosty, might thaw toward her.

The urge to flee, to take time to understand her heart and mind, utterly possessed her. She craved the peace of her artifacts—perhaps the cool shadowy interior of the ancient broch to the south of the castle—with the advantage that the earl could not creep up on her in there.

No! He would not alter her ways. She would not live in fear on her own ground. Better to strike his head from his body and bury him in a bog.

Besides, the ancient library clock showed the hour nudged noon. She'd better attend luncheon, attend to her duty as hostess, for Flora MacLeod's sake. No matter the turmoil of her emotions, and despite the awkwardness of both Lochaber Gordon and Alasdair MacLeod present at the meal! Oh dear.

Fight on, Ruari the Turbulent!

She rose and stretched the aches and problems from her limbs. She took two steps outside the library, but a mad impulse overcame her. She turned and lightly skipped up a hidden staircase to her tower room. She burst through the door, startling a maid, flung open the shutters on her balcony, and stepped out onto the castle battlements, huffing and gasping in gulps of brisk fresh air as though in the midst of an apoplexy.

She surveyed her domain, seeking to calm her swooping emotions and her churning belly. The sea loch shone brilliant glassy green today, dotted with fishermen's skiffs bobbing far out on the horizon. She cast a glance down over the castle grounds—and stiffened and bent forward.

Roddy and Flora—again! Locked in passionate embrace. Flora pulled herself away, flush-faced, disheveled. Spat a few words at poor Roddy like poisoned darts and flounced away.

Roderick stared after her like a man bereft.

Oooh. Nuncheon promised sparks and fireworks. Ruari tore down to the hall, eager to fan the flames of this tantalizing romance.

Chapter Seven

Ruari arrived in the dining hall to discover everything in turmoil. Servants limped around, packing picnics and serving snacks and drinks to the men, who stood in attitudes of expectant waiting, clad in sturdy outdoor clothes.

"I am taking the men for a sail around the sea loch," Roderick informed her in a low gritty voice.

"Thank you!" Ruari breathed.

At that moment, a freshly groomed Flora MacLeod arrived at the entrance to the hall and stepped forward, emanating a thick cloud of icy disdain. The titian beauty held her dainty nose high in the air.

Ruari watched with interest as Flora's chilly gaze met Roderick's thunderous one. Flora's nostrils flared, and her cheekbones flushed a pretty rose-pink. Roderick's eyes darkened to almost black, and they remained fixed on Flora as she glided around the room and took a seat under the window embrasure.

The men departed in flurry of shouted orders, trailing a retinue of castle servants.

Ruari took a deep breath. She walked over to Flora and sank into a curly-legged chair nearby, its handworked cross-stitch cover a medley of jewel-colored flowers. "We are two women alone in this gaggle of men," she began, searching her guest's pale, pinched expression for any kindle of warmth. Flora slanted her a chilly look, lips pursed.

"I wish to make overtures of friendship to you!" Ruari tried to press down the surge of temper. She held her right hand firmly in her lap with her left, rather than slap the frostiness from the woman's face.

Around them, castle servants prepared luncheon for the two ladies, their domestic rustling and soft Gaelic murmurs a counterpoint to the stiff formal atmosphere of this encounter.

In desperation, Ruari cut to the heart of the matter. "Your brother has asked me for my hand in marriage."

Flora answered, her cool tone barely masking her fury, "And you have accepted him."

Ruari stood, anxiety and temper propelling her limbs into movement. "I have asked him for a boon of time to consider."

Now she had Lady Flora MacLeod's full attention. "*What?* I do not believe you. Why would a—" Flora sniffed. Nose wrinkled in a haughty sneer, she raked her gaze up and down Ruari's person in a manner calculated to offend. "Why would an impoverished, feckless woman such as you, from a decaying family, decline one of the most advantageous offers you could ever hope to receive?"

Ruari's nostrils flared and her chin flew up. "Why, Miss Flora," she retorted in sick-sweet tones, "I do believe you are against the match." Satisfaction welled as the redhead visibly wrestled with her own temper.

Flora leapt to her feet too, and glowering, attempted to loom over Ruari with her greater height. She hissed, "I advised the laird against the proposal. In fact, I *begged* him not to offer for you. To be allied with the sad, tattered remains of a once-great family is no match for the laird of Clan MacLeod."

"No match for the laird of Clan MacLeod? The family who tore riches from their own relatives, who betrayed their birthright and fought with the English at Culloden, who have stamped all over the people of these islands instead of caring for them as is their ancestral duty!"

Ruari's hands itched for the sword on the wall. One quick strike, and the woman's bloodied head would be tumbling from the MacDonald castle battlements. Dimly, Ruari became aware of the steady gaze of the castle housekeeper, Gormshuil MacDonald, silently warning her to calm herself.

Flora glared. "The clan is all. One can only help one's dependents if one is successful, if one builds wealth to share, builds social capital to sponsor other MacLeods. What use is your regal duty if you are losing all—so you can all starve together?" Contempt dripped from her like water from an icicle.

Ruari had a flash of her brother, Roderick, and Flora arguing behind the castle. A laugh bubbled into her nose. "There is perhaps another way our family could be allied," she said slyly, the smile dancing on her lips.

Flora stared, uncomprehending, narrowing her eyes. When she realized the import of Ruari's words, her mouth dropped open and her glare brightened to an incendiary flare.

Flora released her rage in a torrent of wild Gaelic, cursing the MacDonalds, their ancestors, their castle and lands and all the children of an uncertain MacDonald future. Pushing the disordered garnet curls back into a rough topknot, drawing her skirts around her, she pranced away across the great hall.

Gormshuil stepped forward from her place by the long table and smoothed her hands on her apron. She said to Ruari in island Gaelic, "Your bràthair and that red-haired baggage will have fierce, feisty children then."

Flora turned and spat, "I curse the lot of you."

Ruari laughed. "Flora, wait," she urged, all temper gone now. "Please. Stay and eat some luncheon. I see now you have the mercurial island blood quickening in your veins and a bright mind. I would value your conversation."

Her visitor halted in the doorway. Her mouth had flattened into a slash of ire and her cheeks blazed. Ruari raised her brows at her and jerked her head in friendly invitation to the laden table.

Flora said, voice low and venomous, "I have no need of a friend such as you. *Nor a husband like your brother*." She whirled and quit the room.

Ruari heaved a sigh and said, "Gormshuil, my dear, would you please have a tray of food sent to Flora MacLeod's room? We prefer to slash the heads from our enemies than starve them." She smirked and added, "Poverty-stricken as we supposedly are."

Gormshuil stared after Flora MacLeod, a look of luscious satisfaction on her plump cheeks. "The lady will make a fine strong wife for Roderick," she said. "Not such a chilly one, after all."

Ruari took a bite of a bannock smeared with game pâté and topped with wild greens. "Mmm. Delicious." She finished her mouthful. "Has my brother chosen a bride then? How astonishing. The lady does not seem overwilling?"

Gormshuil snorted. "That's as may be," she responded and stalked away to her myriad duties.

****

Foiled in her attempts to bask in another woman's friendship and counsel, Ruari longed for peace and privacy, so she could examine all the yammering in her mind. She made a hasty luncheon and then, checking no one saw her, pulled her tartan about her and fled south over the fields, the wind streaming in her hair and teasing her plaid cloak out behind her. The sour-sweet odor of peat soothed her lacerated spirit. Squawking clouds of black gannets and white gulls exploded around her as she strode.

Her boots crunched over the rough gravel around the ancient ruined broch. She crept into the dim entrance, made her way up the curving inner staircase, narrow and cool between the two stonework walls, and emerged onto the high platform, roofless now for many centuries. She made a cushioned seat with her plaid and stared out over the crofts to the restless, endless sea.

Marriage and men. How to make a decision? What parameters should she set? Logic or sensation?

She tingled as she relived the touch of Lochaber's clever fingers on her flesh, stroking her secret places and calling forth that shattering, exhilarating response. Would she feel such a thing with the MacLeod too?

How did one tell, without trying them out, each one? She gasped aloud at the notion of such breath-stealing wickedness. In any case, she must not allow Lochaber any more liberties while she considered the MacLeod's offer—despite her willful, sensuous body craving more. That would be the height of dishonor.

She clenched a fist. Above the fields, a hovering hawk screamed a harsh cry and dived. Diamonds of light sparkled on the ocean as it called to her with its song of travel.

Aberdeen-Shire. The notion of visiting there fired her with both a belly-tearing, grieving sensation and rippling excitement. Leaving her beloved island...yet strange new Picti markings and artifacts to study.

Lochy himself. She loved his long lean frame. She loved his magnificent red hair and fierce brown eyes. She adored his kiss and clever fingers. She loved his acute brain. The unusual life he'd lived in far-flung countries drew her like a snare.

But did he love her? Why did he not offer for her, if he wanted her?

A *very* good question.

How to choose? And what if she chose the wrong path?

A sudden chorus of childish yelling brought her to her feet and scanning the fields. There! A trail of village children ran toward the castle, shouting in alarm. She called and waved until she caught the attention of the lead boy. She gathered her tartan and clattered down the broch inner stairs and out into the light.

"Miss Ruari! *Miss!*" The lad Kenny bolted over the peatlands toward her. "The fell men came!"

Ruari caught the boy as he slammed his body into her. A trail of younger girls and boys, the sun glinting on golden and fiery heads, milled around them in a babel of high-pitched Gaelic, many red-faced and sobbing.

"What now, Kenny Matheson?"

Tears glistened on his thin cheeks. "They galloped in on tall horses. They stomped all over our wee cottage and sneered at Mam's things. They broke her best vase from Grandma and laughed when she shrieked fit to wake the dead."

"What men?" Ruari went cold all over. She kept hold of Kenny but held him away, until he met her eyes.

"The small silent one with eyes as chill as the hoarfrost—" Kenny sniffed and wiped his nose on his bare arm. "Some great lord, for his men wore crimson and black kit."

Black and murrey—a dark crimson-red—the livery colors of the Earl of Kilmore.

Fury lit a fuse under her skin. She said, tight-lipped, "Did he have the grace to mention what he did in your home?"

"He said we'll all be cleared, lady. He said not to hide any valuables, as they'll all be found. If he finds any crofters trying to run for the hills, they'll be hunted by dogs and dragged to the ship in chains."

Ruari pulled the boy to her body, releasing her embrace to pull more crofter children to her as they told more dread tales in a chorus of piping Gaelic. "Are the men still there?"

"I dinna know, Lady Ruari. They smashed in the Macaskills' door and frightened the wee lass and shot a Beaton sheep for sport, but then they rode awa' to Stornoway."

Her mind groped to make sense of this news. Had something changed during her brief escape?

She released the children. "Go back to your farms— carefully now! If the men are still there, watch from a distance and run to the castle and ask for me if they try to inflict any further damage. You are MacDonald tenant crofters, and nobody has the right to clear you from this land." *Unless our cousin has sold it or lost it this hour.*

If the earl behaved thus to villagers, what would he do to her precious artifacts? Smash them to dust, for the pleasure of seeing her distress. She must do something.

The crofter children, many holding hands, crept back over the low hills.

Where was her letter from the Royal Society—still not arrived!

The MacLeod. His fine offer of wedlock. She could beg him to buy the MacDonald holdings from her dishonorable cousin as a wedding gift. And expel the wicked earl from the new MacLeod lands with immediate effect.

A fine man, Laird Alasdair MacLeod, she instructed her heart. Yet that reluctant instrument squeezed itself into a tight fist in her chest as she walked back to the castle.

If she hadn't met Lochy Gordon...

One couldn't leave a group of men alone for a moment. What had they done now, her brother, her cousin, Lochaber Gordon, Alasdair MacLeod, and the Evil Earl? Surely Roderick could not countenance such savagery.

She picked up her skirts and rushed headlong to the castle, slowing to a walk once she was within sight of its battlements. Stepping up the shadowy internal stairway, she ran the fingers of her left hand along the cold, hard stone wall to anchor herself both emotionally and physically. The desires, the schemes, the desperate hopes of hundreds of MacDonalds before her had breathed into its centuries-old stone, their resilience and fighting strength becoming part of the fabric of Callanish Castle itself.

She stopped on the stair and placed the flat of both hands on the wall. Suddenly, those hard walls whispered a message which penetrated into her bones. Certainty overcame her.

She must accept the MacLeod forthwith. There was no other way Kenny and all the children and families of Lewis would be safe, else. No other way to save the Picti steles and standing stone circles, her ancestral birthright and her passion. She was the daughter of Callanish and it was her duty.

Unless she summoned the men of MacDonald and MacNeil to war. For a tiny instant, her heart sang. Then crashed in flat despair.

Those times were long past.

She entered the great hall, into an atmosphere twanging with tension. The earl was present, smirking. Lochaber's admiring gaze brought a pang of guilt and longing, which she ruthlessly quashed.

Once every eye was upon her and the room had gone silent and expectant, she spoke in ringing, formal tones. "Laird Alasdair MacLeod, you have done me the honor of offering your hand in marriage, to unite Clan MacLeod and Clan MacDonald." A loud sniff echoed in the ringing silence—Flora. From the corner of her eye, she saw a man move—Lochaber Gordon, his hand resting on a wall sword.

She spoke swiftly. "I accept this offer. I will marry you and be your wife. For the good of these islands. For the safety of the folk whose welfare is in my care. And for your honorable self."

Into the cacophony of English and Gaelic, one voice rang out above the others. Lochaber Gordon strode forward, a column of blazing fury, his angular jaw determined, and his brown eyes bright and wild. "*You will not.*"

Noise swelled all around her.

Lochaber Gordon turned and faced the assembled company, the sword held aloft in his right hand. "The Lady Ruari MacDonald will not marry Laird Alasdair MacLeod."

"No, Lochy—"

He spoke over her. "This woman is mine. *I claim her.*"

Roderick drew to his full height. His black gaze flashed over the Gordon like a Viking choosing the most vulnerable site in which to sink his axe. "My sister has spoken. The decision is hers."

The MacLeod had stepped forward, eyes glowing, but now he frowned.

Lochaber glared at the company. He fixed a fulminating stare at Ruari. Her heart picked up and thumped painfully in her ribs.

Lochaber Gordon said, his voice strong, clear and unrelenting as summer sun, "Ruari MacDonald is mine. Her fierce heart is mine, her quick clever brain is mine. *For I have already taken intimate liberties with this woman.*"

The room spun around Ruari's vision, and sound roared in her ears.

Chapter Eight

Burly arms caught her. Clean-skin scent of fit male. Faint exotic spice in his garments. *Lochaber.*

The hall echoed with deep-voiced shouts and curses. Roddy. Alasdair. A female exclaimed in high-pitched horror. Flora.

Gritting her teeth, Ruari forced herself to her feet. She slapped Lochy hard on his cheek, the sound snapping through the hall like a gunshot. "How *dare* you?" Rage consumed her. Fear. Dread. "How *dare* you attempt to constrain my choices?"

"Because they are also my choices."

A musty smell penetrated her nostrils. The earl's face swam close in her vision, stepping in on her left flank. His gaze flickered over Ruari like a snake choosing the most tender site in which to sink his fangs.

The earl's voice slithered through the noise. "Damaged goods? You'll retract your offer, Laird MacLeod. I'll take her, and the lands off the MacDonald's hands, for a song. I know how to break willful women." He pushed a long-nailed finger under Ruari's chin, dug its sharp, grimy edge into her delicate skin. "I'll enjoy it," he added silkily.

A fist like a hammer blurred through Ruari's vision. *Crack.* The earl's nose exploded in a fine spray of blood; some of it spattered on her cheek. The man swirled and staggered, then fell like a log to the hall floor, red blood leaking into the polished boards.

Lochaber. Again.

She stuttered into the sudden silence, "I'm shocked that villain has red blood like everyone else." Angry tears pricked the back of her eyes. "Men! How you do muck everything up." With her last reserves of courage, she whirled and made for the door. Her legs wobbled like rubber. Her pulses clanged in her temples. A vise squeezed her throat tight so she could not get breath.

"Let her go." Her brother's deep voice drifted behind her.

****

Early morning. Weariness dragged in her skin after a night full of dark dreams, tormented by the earl's dreadful vengeance visited on the Gordon, on her and Roddy, and on the MacDonald tenants.

Still no letter from the Royal Society. Soon, a missive would arrive too late.

She replaced her bagpipes, unblown. The minutes stretched and stalled.

A boat bobbed toward Callanish Castle, rowed by Angus McPhail. What had her man found this time? He spied her on the battlements and waved a greeting. Almost a smile! The find must be a great one. Excellent. She was tired of worry.

She skipped down the stone stairway to the tack room and assembled her research equipment. The kitchen packed her a nuncheon, and she ran to the castle boat landing, as Angus pulled up his boat.

"Another find, Miss Ruari."

Ruari grasped his hoary arm. "Same bog or another?"

"Not a bog. An ancient fairy dwelling—" Angus

McPhail crossed himself with his gnarly weathered hand and blinked terror from his bright blue eyes. "—around the bay."

"Dwelling?" Excitement and disbelief exploded in her mind like a storm. Ruari restrained herself from shaking more information from the poor man.

"The great storm last month reshaped the beach near Tolstachaolais. And then last night's high tide…"

Ruari nodded, keeping tight rein on her impatience. Someone could come at any moment.

" 'Twas the hand of the old gods. They stripped the dunes and now there is a building, may the gods have mercy. And bones in a grave."

Ruari jumped as though pricked with a fork. "An ancient house? *At Tolstachaolais?*" She felt her expression mirroring Angus's, a comedy of raised brows and wide startled eyes. And a grave. Her blood thrummed with the promise of gold and treasure. *Her ancestors, come to rescue them.*

Angus crossed himself again. "My lad Donald guards it. But come quick. Neither Catherine nor myself like him to linger so close for long. He will be bespelled or, worse, be drawn into those other realms, and we will never set eyes on his bonny face again—" Angus interrupted himself and gave a manly cough. "So my Catherine says, Miss Ruari," he added hastily.

"I'll come now." She clutched both of Angus's hands in hers. "And I thank you. Keep this secret as long as you can, aye?" She lowered her voice. "*Especially* do not talk to the guests we have in this castle at present. They are not friends to the MacDonalds."

"I'll not talk," Angus replied.

"Get you yon the kitchen and have a hot drink. Not

a word now!"

"I don't need a drink, Miss Ruari. 'Tis but two miles. I'll fetch yer pack."

In moments, Ruari was ensconced in the boat, sharing the space with woven bags, shovels, buckets, and her pack. The little boat bobbed and danced on the waves as the boatman pulled strongly through the sea loch.

She cricked her neck around and scanned the castle battlements, terrified she would be seen by the Evil Earl and that, curious, he would pursue her. She strained her ears against the plethora of familiar sea sounds: the slap of waves, the happy scream of sea birds, the whistle of the wind in her ears. No human shout emanated from the castle. She sank lower in the boat and draped a McPhail tartan over her head, disguising her brown locks and upright posture in case enemy eyes should look out.

The sun glowed brilliant gold in a bright pale sky. White sands stretched away in a great curve along the coast. Seabirds cried their harsh mournful cries, and the far horizon misted and mingled sea into sky. She found comfort in the glorious scene.

Sizzling with impatience, Ruari tried to relax as the craft skipped along the coast. The secrets and mysteries of the ancient peoples who once lived in these islands gripped her mind.

The Iron Age peoples—the Picti. Were they the wee folk for whom the villagers left out bowls of milk and grew red-berried rowan trees by their doors? Were they the elves of folklore, or a race entirely different? The Picts had left beautiful carved direction stones and the most intricate gold and silver jewelry. The meaning of their symbols, the stylized engravings and curlicues, enticed every imagination.

Before the Picts existed were the Neolithic ones, those ancient, terrifying people who had erected the three gigantic standing stone circles near Callanish Castle and all around Leòdhas.

Angus steered the craft into the tiny landing beach at Tolsta and shouldered the shovel and heavy tools, while she pulled on her pack filled with rope, flints, sketchpad, pens, and charcoal sticks. Fierce fingers of wind patted their faces and pulled their hair in streamers as they strode over the dune.

Ruari's heart hammered within her bodice, and her lips tingled with anticipation. The past was a mystery whose grip tightened on her with every boggy and coastal find.

Angus's son Donald waited, as sturdy and taciturn in the desolate landscape as a Pictish standing stone himself. Two ponies nibbled the rich machair grasses. "*Madainn mhath, mo bhoireannach,*" he said in the deep musical accent of the islands. *Good morning, my lady.*

"*Halò, ciamar a tha thu* to you, Donald McPhail. Thank you for guarding the site."

"A grave too is uncovered, beyond the dune." Donald and his father reflexively crossed themselves. "Twa Old Ones rest there."

"Please, show me these wonderful finds at all speed!"

"Will ye tell the universities in Edinburgh or Glasgow, lass?"

Ruari snorted. "Those city dwellers! They look down their long, clever noses and wrinkle them at the healthful smell of peat in our hair and clothes. They mock our customs and our Gaelic. They call us insular and superstitious and make us the butt of cruel jokes. So, no, I will not—until they are ready to hear us."

The Royal Society would be different. They were motivated by scientific principle. Sudden, clinging dread gnawed at her bones. She shook it away.

Angus and his son flashed approving grins in their weather-gnarled faces. They led her across the face of the dune, which faced into the great expanse of ocean all the way to Iceland and Canada.

That tug to adventure in her cells—that strong yearning for excitement and hazard on foreign shores. Surely her Norse Viking blood beat strong in her veins, their bold seafaring spirit infused her. She tore her sight from the beckoning horizon.

Early wildflowers carpeted the machair in a mosaic kissed with purple orchids and tiny yellow marigolds. The ever-present scent of seaweed stung her nostrils. Ruari's heart sang. The short summer had arrived. The sun's warmth caressed her cheeks.

And there! By all the old gods and saints of the sea and land!

Her heart skipped, and her stomach swooped in a great circle. Never had she seen such a thing.

An ancient dwelling had been revealed by storm and tide on the very edge of the old dune. Her mind clanged with trepidation as she stepped toward the structure, still partly covered by shifting dunes.

The dwelling appeared conical in shape, a central spike rising up from ancient thatch. A carved, weathered stone marker stood vigil nearby. Ruari halted at the shadowed entrance.

Whoever slept here, they would not like their rest disturbed.

"I am you," Ruari whispered, the superstitious part

of her eager to placate angry spirits. "I am bone of your bone, blood of your blood, and keep your stories safe. I would know more of you."

She cast a quick look back at the brawny McPhails cowering against the far dune, well away from the structure. The islanders had many old stories and beliefs about the ancient remains found in the deep peats and on the lonely coasts of the islands.

She was Ruari the Pirate, Ruari the Tartar, and made of sterner stuff. "Angus! Donald. I thank you. Leave me the boat, and I'll be fine alone." The men nodded, mounted the ponies, and vanished over the hill.

She was alone with her ancestors. Her whole body tingled with excited anticipation. She ducked under the low threshold and peered into the dimness.

The structure was shaped in a figure of eight, with a large round main chamber containing a rectangular hearth right in the middle of the floor, and a smaller chamber extending from the main room. The dwelling resembled their own blackhouses, with its smoky, shady interior and central fireplace.

Ruari took a deep a breath, then stood quite still. She imagined herself as an ancient princess or priestess of this lost culture. She saw herself reading the curling symbols of the Picts. She saw herself clad in blue-inked markings and animal skins, her long brown hair woven with colorful threads and trophy teeth from creatures of the sea and land. Engraved gold and silver arm-rings gleamed on her biceps and amulets hung from twisted cords swung lightly between her breasts. Power rippled in her veins.

Wait! Was that a hoofbeat? She stood, all her senses prickling.

The Gordon. Her body swayed as she relived his fingers on her flesh, his deep tones whispering of her beauty…Perhaps he had arrived and would kiss her again in this secret place…

Nothing. She stepped through the space, entranced, touched ceramic pots by the hearth, held in wonder a carved bone comb fastened with delicate iron rivets.

And now to—*the grave*.

Bright sun stabbed her eyes. The sands along the dunes felt warm underfoot, shifting and sinking as she walked to the burial site. There! Recently uncovered bones gleamed white in the sun. Something metallic flashed. Her heart jerked.

Two skeletons nestled in the oval grave, male and female by their size, laid out like Norse warriors, unlike the dark, curled-over bog bodies unearthed in the peat. Each skeleton's bony fist curled around the hilt of a fine sword. The sword in the larger skeleton's hand was broken.

Ruari sat on the sand and gazed out over the flashing sea to mythical lands. "Old Ones, if it please you. Aid me. Guide me." She patted the arm bone of the female warrior. "I have great need of your sword and your courage, my mother. Change comes. Your monuments and relicts are threatened. I vow on your bones that I will save them, protect them, to awaken the world to the marvels you left for us. I will fight for you. *Victory or Death*."

An albatross soared white-winged across the blue sky.

Ruari collected a leather pouch from within the grave and weighed it in her hands. She carefully undid the withered leather thong and peered inside at a tiny trove of hack-silver and gold fragments and coins. She would distribute this quietly to the islanders. Give some to Roddy to save Callanish Castle. Keep them all going for another season.

Ruari placed the bag down and plucked the ornate brooch from the female warrior. Terror and pleasure boiled in her veins. The ornament was large and very decorative, with swirling circular designs and bizarre animal shapes carved into it. "A Picti token," she breathed. "On a female warrior laid out like a Norse. Far from home? Or a local Pict?"

She pinned the brooch to her plaid. She stroked the ornament with a shaking hand and swallowed. Ruari braced herself and pulled out the long slender sword from the smaller skeleton's bony fingers. A lightning crack of pride smote her. "The women were dauntless fighters," she said aloud, leaping to her feet, whipping and whirling the sword, imagining slicing her enemies and defying her foes.

The sword in her hand warmed. Her shoulder blades pricked. A thin shadow fell over her.

The earl, mounted, clad all in black and crimson except for wicked silver spurs flashing in the sun.

Fury roared in her blood. "I'm glad your swollen nose matches your livery now, sir." A pulse of warning throbbed in her belly. She ignored it. Lifted the sword. Pointed it.

The earl's thin, pale face twisted. Two spots of color rode high on his cheeks. His lips curled in a sneer. "You will give yourself to me. If you pander to my will in a sufficiently pleasing manner, we will be married."

"Ha! Dreaming!" She swished the sword, deliberately just missing his black-booted leg.

He rocked back in the saddle, then slid from the horse. Despite herself, she took a frightened step backward, wishing for the burly McPhails to return—and then unwishing it. A man such as the earl could visit terrible revenge on poor fisherfolk.

No. There was only her.

Get to the boat. She would be safe from this man on the ocean. Her element, not his.

"And what do you here, hmm?" He cast his gaze around. She had been slowly edging away from the grave with tiny steps, toward the dune and the boat behind it.

But his vision locked on the grave. "Grave robbing? I should frisk you for pilfered treasure. That belongs to the Crown, and currently, I am the closest to the authority of the Crown here."

By all the saints. *Ancestors! Help!*

Time froze. Her muscles locked in helpless horror as the evil, slimy, repulsive creature strolled to her ancestors, who had slept so undisturbed for so long.

A flash in her brain. A Picti and a Norse together—this would advance her theories. It was evidence, if it remained preserved for Science to examine—

Why, *why* had she come here, knowing well that the earl would be bent on wickedness in payment for Lochaber's punch? *Why* hadn't she raced the gold and silver back to the castle? She forced her gaze away from the small leather bag still nestling near the bones.

With a poisonous deliberation, the earl stalked to the grave. With the handle of his long, black whip, he hefted one body in the air and tossed it.

"No!" The sound burst from her. Too late. And futile.

He whipped around to face her. "Oh? This causes

you pain?" Still watching her, his eyes avid, he kicked the other body, the male Viking, high into the air. Fragments of bone broke off in a gritty cloud and flew into the ocean from whence he once came.

"May my ancestors curse you and all your descendants!" She howled the bane at him.

"Why, my dear," he responded in his silkiest, most lethal tone, "you curse your own children."

And with his whip, clearly too fastidious to touch, he pulled and scattered the bones and the scraps of garments adhering to them around the dune and into the sea.

"And what is this?" He bent, then hefted the small, fraying bag in one hand. He unlaced the tie and peered inside. "Delicious. These gold and silver fragments I will take in compensation for the grievous assault on my person yesterday." He enjoyed her enraged expression for long seconds, then held up a thin white hand. "Be grateful. For I had intended to suborn several maidens and fire the village. This will do, however, instead. For today."

He tucked the bag in his clothes and mounted his horse. He spoke over his shoulder. "Should I get bored, my dear—for example if I find myself lacking your ready company—I may indulge myself with a little rape and pillage in any case."

He still did not leave but studied her with flat black eyes. "I begin to see…perhaps not the village. Perhaps I'll smash these historic sites, one standing stone at a time." His voice sharpened. "You have twenty-four hours, after which I expect your full and dutiful submission."

"Why me?" she whispered.

A grin crawled over his face. "Best I don't inform you, don't you think? Understanding what I want from you would give you the tiniest power over me—and that, I certainly cannot permit. Good day, madam."

The Earl of Kilmore finally rode away, but his black shadow stayed clinging to her, leaching her of strength, hope, every good thing.

Despair ran in her veins like slow poison. Twenty-four hours? What on earth could she do in that time?

The wife of the Earl of Kilmore.

Nausea collected in her guts. She slid down next to the destroyed grave and wept bitter, ugly, gulping, recriminatory tears.

A little later, she pulled herself together. Set about sketching the grave and its inhabitants as closely as she could recollect. Reassembled the grave from the bones left unshattered, the scraps of fabric adhering to the dune. A vital key to her theories, destroyed.

More tears moistened their white bones.

Her skin shivered. A presence…She whirled.

There! A tall, commanding warrior, his head wreathed in a flaming crown of fire. Fit, flexible limbs poised for action, silhouetted dark against the sky…

Chapter Nine

Before dawn, the delicious scent of baking had lured Lochaber down to the ancient kitchens in the bowels of the castle, built off to one side to prevent fire.

An enormous black range occupied most of one side of the kitchen. Massive gleaming steel pots and pans hung above the range and on one wall. White painted dressers groaned with clan-sized platters and serving ware. A long wooden table filled the center of the room.

Three cooks were plucking golden-crusted pies from giant oven trays. The smell was glorious. On his entry, the entire room went still. If glares could kill, he would have been dead in seconds.

"Worse than the bluidy English," hissed a voice in Gaelic. Lochaber shot a look around the room. Impossible to tell who had spoken.

"A traitor Scot, may he burn in hell." Also Gaelic.

Lochaber said, in English, and in as pleasant a voice as he could manage, "It appears my hopes of gaining one of those magnificent pies is diminishing by the second." If he had hoped for laughs, he had failed dismally.

"Bluidy English accent too," said someone else.

Lochaber blinked. He was famous in the East India Company for his thick Scots accent, which he had only managed to moderate so he could better facilitate business, after years of practice.

The Highlander in him could resist no longer. "Very

well," he replied in Gaelic, "I will just be myself—a Highlander like yourselves—and *steal* two of these pies." As he stepped forward and nimbly lifted two of the delicious-smelling pastries from the tray, a deep laugh curled around his ears. He spun. Roderick MacDonald leaned in the doorway.

Lochaber's cheeks heated. Caught—*losing*—the Battle of the Kitchen! He stiffened, waiting for Ruari's brother to make a mocking remark.

"I think those pies are the poisoned ones meant for you anyhow," Roderick said, also in Gaelic. The whole kitchen laughed, blast them all.

He repressed a snort of mirth himself. These MacDonalds were a damnably charming family. Lochaber juggled the stolen pies and tossed one to Roderick, who caught it neatly on a floral plate he had removed from the dresser.

He handed its twin to Lochy. "Gormshuil will have your guts if you spill crumbs."

Lochaber grabbed it gratefully, relieving his burnt fingers. He took a bite and coughed as the contents seared his tongue.

"At least may they choke the man," a Gaelic voice said.

"I suggest you take yourself away to breakfast." Roderick took a huge bite and grinned around his mouthful at Lochaber. "This place is riddled with murderous weapons—cleavers, heavy skillets, fire hooks. Best I don't leave you here with the kitchen staff. They are MacDonalds and MacNeils, or very loyal."

"Oh? You have concerns for my welfare? You needn't." He took his own massive bite and chewed determinedly.

"No," said Roderick. "When an enemy of the MacDonalds threatens, Ruari the Pirate prefers to do the killing herself."

Lochaber stood his ground, holding the pie plate, the malicious guffaws of the entire kitchen ringing in his crimsoned ears. "I am not your enemy. I merely hoped for sustenance before a morning walk."

"Good. In that case, would you be so kind as to hunt down my sister—" Loch had been planning that very activity. "—and tell her that two letters have come. One missive is addressed in my cousin's flamboyant style. The other bears an official stamp. Neither should be neglected, I fear." Roderick nodded his thanks and stalked out of the kitchen.

Lochaber surveyed the hostile glares, burly cleaver-wielding forearms, shining knife racks, and bared-teeth smiles. "I'd best deliver this message, then. I thank you."

He fled.

****

Traces of tears shone silver on her sweet rosy cheeks, flushing pinker as she spied him. Sitting by what appeared to be a partly covered grave.

With a sword.

"Did I startle you?" He strode toward her, unwilling to raise her anger—but unable to master a surge of protective feeling which consumed him, faced with such evidence of her distress.

"Recent enemies, I take it?" He raised his brows at the skeletons and the sword held loosely beside her.

A laugh bloomed in her face. Her eyes lit, then darkened. "My ancestors."

He hesitated, then lowered himself beside her on the dune. What ailed the woman?

She impaled him with a glittering amethyst stare. "*Why* does the Earl of Kilmore want me?"

He jumped. A spear of jealousy lanced him. "Do you not know, Ruari MacNeil MacDonald, descendant of pirates and Vikings?"

"I do not, except he enjoys tormenting and threatening me with impossible choices."

"Shall I tell you?"

They locked gazes.

He lifted a hand. Touched a fingertip to her tear-stained cheek. "Has he bothered you, my lady?" That unwelcome protective urge swelled and clamored for action.

Her nostrils flared. "Of course he bothers me!" She rose with fluid grace. Bent and covered the grave with carefully laid planks followed by a flurry of sand and peaty hunks of grass. Lochaber leaped to his feet and assisted her.

She twisted her lips. "What can one do against a rich, evil-minded nobleman, with the weight of English law behind his whip hand?"

His mouth, apparently sundered from his brain, said, "The earl wants you—as do we all. For your unique wild beauty, your splintering intelligence, and your fire. Men want to burn in that fire, want to flame and combust…"

Her eyes popped wide open. Her mobile mouth made an astonished pink *O*. Color rushed from her neck to her hairline. "Such words, Lochaber Gordon!" She blinked several times. Wiped her hands down the front of her skirts.

Perhaps to cover confusion, she launched into rapid speech. She paced the small site, words tumbling, waving her arms for emphasis and to indicate direction.

"My artifacts. The earliest are the Neolithic age, the standing stone circles. Constructed in a range of sizes over this island Leòdhas. The Picti carved stones and defensive brochs were created thousands of years later, and it's my belief the Picts and the invading Norse, the first wave, co-existed, that their civilizations overlapped.

"I need more information—more papers, more books. I can only buy books when I find gold and silver in graves or the bogs or we have a good harvest—ha to that last! Once, I sold my hair.

"The Picti symbols. I am developing a proposal, a theory, that the steles are *star maps*. Carvings which plot and record the return journey to their ancient homelands. Denoting constellation, moon phase, solstice and season, depicting which creatures feature at certain times, a key to when it is safe to sail. Also that some Picts befriended the invading Norse and made star maps for them too. Some steles mark clan boundaries, of course. We are strong on clans, are we not? Family ties are all."

She'd robbed him of breath. Such brilliance and unique ideas, igniting in his brain! He listened while his mind sifted and sorted his limited knowledge against her theories. "And the great standing stone circles?"

Her cheeks pinked, perhaps at the memory of what they had done there. She faced him, eyes alight. "No one knows. Star maps also? A stone calendar tracking the days? The site of significant religious ceremonies to which people came from all around Scotland?"

She suddenly ran out of words and collapsed down beside him. "All this, all this is at risk. You, with your distillery. The dreadful earl, with his disdain for all beauty, all science. And the MacLeod? He is angry with me now, and I doubt his offer of marriage still stands."

Lochaber's cool brain succumbed to an unreasoning tumult of contradictory emotions. He battled for composure. He ground out the gravel words. "Will you accept him?"

Ruari speared him with a gaze dripping with contempt. "Men! Out of everything I just said, words and ideas I have spoken *to no person alive*, you fasten on my *marriage*?"

Lochaber clenched his jaw. Damn it! Where was his famous, hard-won control, the self-mastery he strived for over so many hard years? This woman undid him.

His planned vengeance rested on his capacity for cold control. He inhaled, nostrils flaring. He calmed his heartbeat. Sought cool detachment.

Not very successfully. *Words and ideas I have spoken to no person alive...*A victory trumpet sounded in his ears, for Ruari the Turbulent trusted him.

"Tell me your dreams." Lochaber's voice sounded rusted in his own ears. He cleared his throat. No. Best to show her.

He picked up the ancient sword—small, but finely wrought, with intricate silver designs etched on the hilt. Perfectly balanced. A mighty weapon, honed to deadly precision—perfectly created for a female warrior.

And for Ruari's eyes alone, he performed one of the ancient sword dances, learned in India. The dance sang of love and respect for ancient objects and rituals, of power and self-mastery, of the triumph of the human spirit.

Her eyes glowed like stars. When he finished, with a somersault and bow, handing her the sword, he said, "I respect the mystery and power of ancient things."

And then, to his own astonishment, instead of

profiting by her capitulation, he repaid her frankness with a deluge of words.

His own bitter anger, his sharp longing for the place of his birth, his thirst for retribution swirled and burst from him. "I have a purpose in returning to Scotland after many decades away working as an executive in the East India Company. I yielded to a moment of affection for my mentor—*unforgiveable weakness*—which means time out from my schedule of financial takeovers, executed with military precision."

"You curse yourself for a moment of affection?"

"I stand on Scottish soil once more, as I have all the pieces assembled for a long-planned act of vengeance for an old wound in my boyhood."

"Vengeance on *whom*?"

No. He could not speak that vile truth. Could not bear to watch her withdrawal from him.

He dissembled. "At Cluny and Aberdeen. Yet right on the threshold of storming into my triumph, I hesitated, by agreeing to this ridiculous detour. Not in character. I owe so much to my governor—my friend and mentor, Billy Bentinck—that I agreed to survey and report on a new large whisky distillery on your island."

"Now, you will not proceed with that plan."

Could he deflect her with a jest? "You should be pleased. It was originally a small herring factory, to be *scaled up* from there. Requiring some *fin*-esse—"

Her lips twitched, and she smothered a giggle. "My artifacts are at risk and you make fish jokes?"

"I am a man of honor. I made a promise. And I will deliver it."

She leaped to her feet. Anger sparked from her, as sudden and furious as a summer storm. She lashed him with fury. "What, then is the point of that sword dance, those fine words? You will wipe thousands of years of history from the face of the earth. You will destroy my passion and dreams—and that is a grievous sin, because you do so in full knowledge! And all for your *pride*, your misplaced *affection*!"

"I am a bastard, Ruari." The words burst out, so long denied and now embraced, an eradicable part of him. The vile truth.

"A *horrid, contemptible* bastard."

He did not disabuse her of her misunderstanding.

As she collected her research tools together—carefully, he noted, despite her exploding rage—and prepared to storm off toward the boat wedged on the sand, he said, "I almost forgot. Your brother said two letters have come for you."

"Two—" Her face paled. "And you wasted time with your fancy dancing and lying speeches? Why did you not say *immediately*?" Satchel slung over her shoulder, she broke into a run.

****

The devil take all men!

Blight and blast male pride. Through great gobs of angry tears, Ruari reread the cursed letter.

Dear Madam,

We refer to your correspondence concerning the Neolithic and Picti artifacts on Lewis, Outer Hebrides.

Naturally the Society is pleased that an amateur takes such interest in England's pre-history. We understand that it is natural to become excited by their Mysteries and to fabricate imaginative Tales regarding their provenance and purpose.

We suggest however, that the more usual female

pursuits of sketching the landscape and recording carvings would profit you more. We urge you to leave Speculation and the weighing of Evidence to Men of Science, whose natural capacity for Logic and Science as per the male Brain, has been further trained for the purpose by many years of diligent study. Such passionate concern as is evident in your letter may damage the smaller female brain with unwonted pressure.

We thank you for drawing our attention to the Lewis artifacts, but tactfully suggest that your "marvels" are rather pedestrian compared with the rich archaeology of the English and Scottish mainland. In addition, we wish to regretfully inform you that our Archaeological and Philosophical Fellows are currently fully occupied with study of these.

We will Mention the Lewis archeological sites to the Fellows at the next Symposium. Perhaps next year or in subsequent years, the Fellows may wish to visit your island and add an interesting footnote to their Researches.

We wish you well with your sketching and contemplation of activities more suited to the emotive female mind,

Yours, etc.,
William Morrow
Secretary
The Royal Society.

She crumpled the letter and threw it at the heavy door. Ruari hefted her bagpipes from their cupboard, stepped through her long window, and balancing on the battlements, blew her despair and fury to the wild winds in a torrent of marching music.

What on earth could she do now? She must save her

artifacts. The Royal Society wouldn't even bother to come! *Pedestrian. Footnote.*

As always, there was only her. Her agile wits, her intelligence, and courage.

Ranged against a stupid, greedy cousin; a stranger suffering pride and driven by vengeance; an offended lord of the Isles; and a rich, evil earl, bent on her ruin.

"Victory or Death," she muttered. *Victory or Death.* The MacNeil motto.

Comforted by her fierce music and the weight of the pipes in her arms, she returned to her room. She retrieved the crumpled letter from the corner, smoothed it out, and laid it in a heavy envelope to create a file of correspondence on the subject.

This is not an end to the matter!

She must get to the Scottish mainland to inspect the other artifacts around Cluny and Aberdeen for herself. Whatever the fatal pressure on her poor, weak, female brain, she would apply the scientific method. Check and recheck every fact. Test her hypotheses. Seek new information, new data, new evidence to either support her ideas or transform them.

She would venture to the Scottish Highlands—and Lochaber Gordon would escort her there.

He could implement his mysterious vengeance, and he—the expert in cold revenge—would enable her to take her own retaliation on the fat-headed fools who called themselves Men of Science in the Royal Society.

Ruari MacNeil MacDonald had pirate blood racing in her veins and Norse strategy in her brain.

She would save her artifacts, develop her star map theories, and prove those fools at the Royal Society mere narrow-minded bigots.

And in the process, evade the earl, save Roddy's farmlands, avoid unwanted husbands, and open her heart to adventure and travel.

Oh! The second letter. By the stars! In all her anger and crushing disappointment, she had forgotten to peruse the no doubt hectoring missive from her cousin Balgair. She ripped it open.

Words flashed in her vision. *...bid you to obedience...advantageous marriage...and so, my dearest relative, I expect to arrive on the very heels of my note...*

May the man hole his ship!

She reread the letter more carefully, pondering the flavor of his displeasure and seeking a loophole for escape.

Shouts and bustle echoed from down below. She rushed to the long window and leaned out, gazing at the hive of activity at the castle dock.

Too late.

Her cousin Balgair, laird of the mighty MacDonald clan, had already arrived at Castle Callanish.

Chapter Ten

Music spilled through the air as Lochaber hastened back to Callanish Castle after a long uphill detour, which had not wrought the desired calm on his roaring emotions.

MacDonald plaids and coats of arms hung from the castle ramparts, snapping in the brisk cool breeze. Tenant farmers and crofters streamed over the hills and fields from all directions, rushing to the edifice, laden with baskets of food and clutching bottles of whisky of all shapes and colors.

He halted a hobbling villager, nodding to the castle. The man creaked, "The laird's returned, may his guts wither inside him." Lochaber stared at the crenellated towers, assessing this new surprise and deciding how he could work it into his plans.

The MacDonald. He'd not met the man. Billy had corresponded with the fellow, proposing the hundred-year lease for a distillery. By repute, an utter fribble. And yet, the fellow was also negotiating with MacLeod and Kilmore, creating a bidding war which scooped in the beautiful Miss Ruari MacDonald as part of the goods for sale.

Lochaber strode fast, picturing a Londonized version of Roderick. He grunted in annoyance. He had dawdled and dangled, enjoying a tryst with the delicious Ruari, and now he may have lost all advantage.

Worse, he'd yelled to the world that he had trifled with her. Lochaber missed his footing and almost fell flat into the murky peat. He wiped a muddy hand on the grass and brushed at his trousers.

Would the MacDonald harry Lochaber from Callanish Castle like an enemy of old? He had never failed his mentor Billy Bentinck yet—and he didn't plan to start.

The enticing Ruari had unbalanced him, thrown him off his game. And now he would pay. Well, no more. He summoned the sharp-dealing, persuasive, diamond-bright Lochaber Gordon who progressed so fast in the East India Company among the scornful English upper class.

He hiked his collar straight, attempted to smooth his uncontrollable flaming hair, put up his chin, and marched toward the entrance to the great hall.

Lochaber halted in the doorway, one foot raised, mouth open, taking in the scene.

The hall throbbed with music and vibrated with laughter. Servants drank with crofters, all talking island Gaelic at the tops of their voices; Flora MacLeod clinked whisky glasses with Roderick MacDonald; men clad in the MacDonald tartans linked arms and swung around to the music blasting from a group of pipers, fiddlers, and whistle players set up on the stage at the head of the room.

And surely that wasn't the Earl of Kilmore *smiling*?

He'd plunged into Bedlam Hospital.

An enormous cluster of laughing people gathered tight around a magnetic center at the head of the grand dining table. The crowd parted. The man at the center of the mayhem boasted, "…the famous Count D'Orsay, friend of mine, honoring *moi* with one of his likenesses…"

Middling height, red hair oiled into curls. Pinch-waisted coat, cutaway waistcoat, yellow *striped* pantaloons, heeled boots. Pointed nose. Pale skinned, smiling, affable. Spouting London slang: "…Feeling quite *afternoonified* in this backwater, though adoring this *enthusimuzzy*…"

The MacDonald.

Roaring for more whisky as crofters and tenants of all ages and styles of dress streamed into the hall, bumping Lochaber aside in their haste.

Roderick sat to the right of his frivolous cousin, glowering. A young farmer hung on Balgair's left, laughing and singing with his laird.

The laird spied Lochaber hesitating in the doorway, asked a question of Roderick. The MacDonald bellowed over the noise, frantically gesturing him forward. "The podsnappery 'Lucky' Lochaber Gordon! Come, drink with me. We shall speak of business and skilamalink dealings later."

Clever. His own advance cut from beneath him. And the man knew his nickname. It would not do to underrate the MacDonald.

Ruari brushed past, his skin leaping at her slightest touch. "My cousin," she whispered.

"Most unlike you and Roderick."

She laughed. "Roddy takes after our mother and the MacNeils: a dark-haired, flammable lot. My cousin lives for company and fun." She tossed him a wicked smile. "I'm from the stars."

Head high, she walked to her cousin, and he embraced her. The laird roared for music, waving his hand at the band, then he and Ruari danced a sprightly reel together while their clan folk clapped along.

Lochaber could not tear his gaze from her unrestrained, yet graceful form. How she danced! Lust jabbed through him.

He forced himself to calmly reassess, to recalculate all the economic currents swishing in this great hall.

The MacLeod sauntered over and handed him a glass, amber whisky sparking rainbows in the mellow light. "There is an elegant solution." The man raised his brows as he spoke, inviting Lochaber to share a comradeship. "You can withdraw from the fray with some well-chosen phrases. A fine gesture and one that retains your dignity."

Lochaber shot the laird a sharp look. He did not speak of business. "So you intend to press your suit for Miss MacDonald?" Curse it all, the thought left him entirely bereft.

Alasdair gave him a direct blue stare. "To inveigle yourself into the MacDonald's graces, you will be expected to game through the night, until you own nothing but a tattered Gordon plaid to drape over your sorry form. Nobody will want that, except to wave from a flagpole of victory."

A welcome surge of anger shook him alert. "Are you threatening me, Alasdair MacLeod?"

"You know verra well I am aiding you. Neither the MacDonald lands, nor the woman, is for you."

They locked stares.

Lochaber pressed his lips together. Weight collected on his brow into a glower worthy of Roderick.

The MacLeod jerked his chin high. "Balgair has created a bidding war. For the lands, and his lovely cousin. He has made promises to us all, damn the weasel. I am inclined to return to Dunwary Castle at Skye and be done with this slippery business. However, you are correct. I want the woman." His lips thinned. "Despite your claims of intimate knowledge. I trust you limited yourself to stealing a gentlemanly kiss."

Gentlemanly kiss? Did the man not understand the pirate maid's passionate nature?

A tall presence loomed at Lochaber's back. Roderick stepped between them. "There is only one way to win my sister. You must exert your own heart, your own brains and talents. Your only leverage over her is if she loves you in return."

He put a hand on each man's shoulder. "And if either of you hurt her, I will use all my wits and temper to hunt you down and make you suffer all the hells."

Lochaber growled, "A formidable threat."

At the grand table, Balgair regained his seat, mopping his face with his plaid and downing another gulp of firewater. His pale lilac stare, a faint echo of Ruari's, drilled Lochaber. The laird held a hand up and the band shut down, the clan folk quietened, and the room suddenly pulsed with silence.

Loch's heart beat steady in his chest. All his muscles calmed, preparatory to action.

Ruari's brilliant amethyst gaze met his across the room—and his stolen heart leaped and kicked like an enclosed stallion.

Time for the reckoning.

Had someone curried favor with the laird by whispering of Lochaber's declaration of intimate knowledge of Ruari? One of her cousin's bargaining chips.

His legs lost their strength at the doorway. His chest squeezed. He could lose all—*Straighten your spine, man!* Billy Bentinck's voice, from long ago.

He clenched his jaw, stood tall, and strode to the laird. The cluster of people parted to let him through, barely making room. Their body heat hammered at him. The scent of heated woolen garments enclosed him in a suffocating fog.

The MacDonald's lips twisted. Close up, those cunning violet eyes gleamed as they assessed him—arrowing through to his bones.

That piercing glare was not friendly, despite the fixed smile.

Lochaber wrenched himself from the laird's grip and pushed his way to the top of the hall.

He took one long last look at Ruari. He could not lose her. His heart cracked in his chest. *Forgive me, Billy.*

He was a Scot, despite all those years in the East India Company. In the deep core of him, he held the grandeur and harsh majesty of the mountains. He let those misty glens and soaring peaks possess his mind as he spoke, hoping that the longing for a home, for his own place, could invest his words with enough emotion to appease this drunken MacDonald rabble.

He drowned in her jewel eyes. He relived his fingers on her skin.

He held aloft two squares of paper.

"I am surveying the Callanish Castle and MacDonald lands—to build a brand-new village and industry."

The hall erupted in outraged shouting.

The laird held up a hand for silence. Cold warning glowed in those chilly eyes.

Lochaber spoke quickly. "I have led a nomadic existence. Since my father's house was burned in the Jacobite wars"—angry muttering—"I have not had a home, to call it as such. My adult years were spent wandering the Far East." He surveyed the company. "Besting the English at their own game." Cheers and toasts to his health.

"In the few days I have been a guest at Callanish Castle, I have enjoyed unparalleled hospitality. I have seen care of lands, tenants, and history. I have seen grace. And my own flinty heart has opened."

He choked. The words pressing behind his teeth were too raw. He cleared his throat, and declared instead, "I...*I love the daughter of this castle*. I yield to her desire that I do not build on her precious lands. I withdraw from this absurd auction, in order to win her regard."

He met Ruari's astonished gaze.

He pressed a hand to his forehead, covering his eyes, and banged his way to the hall entrance, cries and cheers ringing in his ears, hands slapping his back and head.

His long legs increased the pace as he made the passageway, and then once out in the crisp windy air, he bolted across the fields heading for an inland hill—the closest thing to his harsh childhood mountains within reach.

He could not recognize himself. He had failed his mentor. With deliberate intent. How he dreaded the letter he must write to Billy, and the man's bitter disappointment.

"Lochaber Gordon!"

His name carried on the breeze, shouted by many voices. He turned. A stream of MacDonald-tartan wearing folk streamed after him, calling and jesting.

Couldn't this pestilential clan leave him be?
"You are wanted by himself, the MacDonald!"
****

In the great hall of the MacDonalds, the laird smiled hugely all around, his glittering diamond-hard gaze landing on Lochaber like a warning blow.

Despite himself, his heart smashed in a mad fledgling hope. Had the laird heard of his foolish, anger-fueled pronouncement of *intimate knowledge* of his cousin? Was he about to enforce Ruari's handfasting—to him? He swallowed. Desire flamed rampant in his blood and muscles.

"And now all the company is present," the laird announced with a grand flourish, "I will hearten you all with glad tidings. Our future is secured! The MacDonalds reign victorious!"

Lochaber's blood thundered. Along with the entire hall, he waited.

"Great news!" roared the MacDonald. "Everyone wet your glasses! *Gabh deoch*! The great Clan MacDonald is uniting with...the House of Kilmore!"

By the window, the earl shuttered his hungry eyes and his thin mouth twisted in victory.

The laird glared in wicked jubilation at Lochaber. "My cousin Ruari will marry Rupert Stavelet, the Earl of Kilmore."

The ancient hall of the MacDonalds rang with silence. The castle staff froze, eyes wide as startled hares, toast glasses paused halfway to their lips.

Gormshuil was the first to react. She stared at the earl, looked wild-eyed at Ruari and then Roderick, and tossed the drink down her throat in one swallow.

The hall erupted in weak cheers, alarmed island

Gaelic rippling around the walls like a swelling full-moon tide. The laird showed all his teeth as he grinned at Lochaber in triumphant malice.

Lochaber was completely, utterly undone.

No! *This was all wrong.*

He'd opened his heart, admitted he loved Ruari, and instead of everything falling into his lap—what a blasted, silly fool he'd been to expect it!—the laird had pounced on his weakness.

Never again!

He'd learned young to hold in his feelings. He should not have had to learn the lesson again, in so sharp a manner. He'd confessed emotion, and had lost the long game, all in one fell swoop.

Hurt stuttered in his brain. *Had Roderick engineered this, in partnership with his cousin? And Ruari too*?

Of course. The neat coup had all the hallmarks of her clever brain and elegant finesse.

That black-hearted wench. *He could have given her riches, if that was what she desired...*

She'd played him.

Pain swamped him.

Blinded by emotion, he found the doorway by instinct. This time when he bolted into the cleansing air, he was finally alone.

Alone. That was how he worked best.

Never, never again would he open his foolish, flinty, scarred heart.

****

A conflagration of fury burned in every cell of Ruari's body. She stalked to her cousin's side. "You have *sold* me, Laird? I will not have it. I refuse."

Balgair called, "Pipes!" As Ruari jumped, he added,

"Dish this morbish mood. No pipes for you, my dear. More feminine pursuits are in order, what? Donald MacDonald will blast a victory song."

"Even the dread English, and certainly not you, can stop the MacNeil pipers!"

The first blast sounded through the hall. Donald MacDonald instead chose a lament, the keening music the sound of Ruari's heart shattering. For her laird's betrayal. For selling her to that cold, *terrifying* worm, who stared at her with a malignant expression, his mouth twisting in a slithery smile.

Ruari swallowed three excoriating retorts and stared wildly around the company. Her clamoring brain sought and discarded questions and responses that would not enrage her cousin and would keep her from this fell fate looming like a miasma of doom.

Her cousin—entirely uncaring—waved his arms, shouting, "This will be a good—nay a great!—marriage of two powerful houses. Never say the MacDonalds are stuck in the auld ways, not up to dick in the new Victorian world. Hurrah, we're bang up to the elephant!"

Ruari's eyes narrowed. That concept—in better English—had no doubt been fed to the laird by the arctic earl.

Temper and hurt erupted in a torrent of words. "This is an alliance with no power in it for MacDonalds! If your great earl lacks love or respect for his bride, how shall I protect the MacDonald lands and tenants? If the earl despises his wife, where is my power to perform our *ancestral duty*?"

The laird fake-laughed to the company and hugged his fuming cousin. She stood like an ancient bastion, fury sparking from every cell.

"Ruari, my sweet," he whispered. "Hold your head high. We will come about. Show an appearance of complaisance."

"What?" Cold certainty washed over her body, as chill as dead herrings in the icehouse. "Have you *gambled me away*, cousin?"

He had no need to answer. His cheeks reddened. As she stared at him, his eyes hardened to chips of ice, cold as a sea-floe. "This is for the best, cousin. The House of Kilmore is flush with swag and influence. You will be safe."

"Balgair! When have I ever craved *safety*, of all things?"

"But I crave it for you. You are a baggage and a burden to a sane man. This is best." He ran his be-ringed, white hand over her hair. "You are clever and bonny. You shall be able to vamp the earl as you will it, soon enough."

She shuddered. "The man is not human," she hissed. "The dice were no doubt loaded."

She put her chin high and plastered a smile on her face as the earl slithered over to her and put a slimy, cold hand under her chin.

Ruari blazed at him with undisguised hatred, slapped his hand away, snarled at her laird, and barged from the room.

The earl's chilly laugh resounded in her ears behind her. Like the scrape of nails on slate. Like the shriek of a hawk swooping on its prey.

She needed to swim, to wash this day from her body and brain.

Chapter Eleven

Lochaber strode away to the distant hillock. He climbed up its stony slope and headed around the peak until the castle ramparts were completely obscured from his vision.

He stared over the fields toward mainland Scotland, the unfamiliar blue sea and sky and gray sea-mists filling his vision. Somewhere through that pearly fog lay the Scottish Highlands. The place of his birth. A land of tall, harsh peaks, clad in green and brown, untamed burns running with intrigue, and drizzling mists redolent with poetry. Where the cold air seared his lungs and slapped his cheeks and made his blood dance in his veins.

But he would be as welcome there as in this hostile castle behind him.

The scene of his mistakes and missteps. This entire Hebridean journey was a broken rung in his stellar career.

And Lochaber Gordon didn't make mistakes.

Certainly not twice.

He plunged his heavy head into his cold hands, gripping his skull tight, gritting his teeth.

A flying figure crossed his vision. He dropped his hands and straightened. Ruari MacDonald! Fleeing the castle, running along the cliffs to the bay as though pursued by the hounds of hell.

Poisonous jealousy roiled in his stomach.

Leave the minx. Let her suffer the consequences of her traitorous family's machinations.

He groaned aloud. It was not in his nature, or his power, to leave that fiery woman without help, even though she would probably bite the hand he offered in friendship. It appeared that where Ruari was concerned, he would happily make mistake after mistake, endure any indignity, for a morsel of her attention.

Of their own accord, his heavy limbs rose, reassembled into a man of vigor and purpose, and stepped out to pursue the flying figure.

****

A jolt of pure fear smashed through Lochaber. His eyes stood out almost on stalks. Mythology come alive! Strange things lived on and around these islands…

His tongue cleaved to the roof of his dry mouth. His muscles clenched.

The selkie rose from the sea, water flowing from its smooth gray pelt in translucent lacy waves, and walked with athletic motion toward him.

The thing bore the face of Ruari MacDonald!

His heart almost gave out right there on the path. He looked around—he could escape into that small cove leading back into the coastal cliff—or maybe that was the thing's lair.

He stepped back a pace. The creature hadn't seen him yet. He melted into the sea cave, his blood hammering in his veins, sharp spikes loading his bloodstream, readying him for action.

The selkie dripped into the cave, bringing a wave of sea- and salt-scented air with it. Its form: so lithe, so female. Cheekbones, tip-tilted amethyst eyes, so like Pirate Ruari's.

He pressed himself back into the darkness, trying to regulate his breathing.

In front of his astonished gaze, the creature began to peel its skin off, facing the sea. Old myths and stories slammed into his brain—selkie women, stripping off their pelts; fishermen hiding their skins and taking them for wives.

The creature peeled back the skin on its head, revealing a surprising shock of wet, thick brown locks, just like a human woman's. One ivory shoulder shone in the muted light, then another. The back of a white-skinned neck gleamed through that thick dark hair.

A sharp blast of lust stabbed him.

Turn around, he begged silently, desperate to see her mermaid breasts.

He smothered a gasp. The creature stilled. Had it heard him?

Wearing the face of Ruari MacDonald, emerging from thick rubbery skin, it peered into the back of the cave. Lochaber stood frozen in the darkness. Every part of him waited, longing to see…

He stifled a moan of agonized desire.

The selkie peeled her gray skin from her torso, freeing bouncing snowy breasts, their sweet pink-tipped peaks hardening quickly in the cold.

Lochaber put his hand on his aching cock. He might burst from his trousers.

Slowly, the skin peeled down a slender waist which flared into rounded hips, firm with muscle. And then…the shadowed V at the apex of shapely thighs…

His throat dried. He smothered a groan.

The selkie washed herself in a tub of rain water left for the purpose, her skin pinkening as she slathered her breasts, her underarms, her thighs, until her body glistened and shone in the half-light.

How did one take a selkie? Like a sea creature might, chase and dance and finally subdue? He took a step forward, desire hammering like an unrelenting force in his groin, his blood, his head.

He would take her and watch her moan and sing under his fingers, that face of lovely Ruari bright with desire and satiation.

She reached for a towel.

What? *A towel?*

"You can come out now, Lochaber Gordon." The amused tones of the selkie whipped his desire further. She sounded *exactly* like his Ruari. A thought flitted in his red lust. How did the magic creature know his name…? Did she speak aloud, or in his mind?

The craving exploded, to possess her *now*, this instant, to roll her screaming with ecstasy on the floor of the sea cave, to pound out all his hurt and lust for her double. He stepped forward, fingers seeking the buttons of his flies. He held his large erection ready in his fist.

The selkie covered herself with the towel, wide-eyed.

He grabbed her rubbery gray skin and threw it to the back of the cave. That's what the myths said. Hide their skins and you could possess them, keep them…

He advanced on the pearly-skinned object of his desire. He placed his hands on her cool arms and pulled her to him. He halted, giving her time to pull away, to escape…or to choose him.

She nestled closer.

He sank greedy lips over hers. So warm and soft! Her cold, clammy skin on arms, neck, shoulders, warmed rapidly as he caressed, its silky texture like to drive him mad. He bounced a soft breast and groaned into her mouth.

"Ruari." Surely the selkie would not mind what he called her?

He squeezed the creature's warm, round buttocks in urgent hands.

He became aware the selkie was speaking, in Ruari's voice. He ignored her words, listening to the familiar beloved tones. "Say 'my darling,' " he whispered harshly into her ear. "Call me your stallion, your mate."

He cupped a rounded hip in his palm. Curious, he flicked a desperate searching finger across the hot wetness between her thighs. Oh. Exactly like a human woman. He moaned, "Come to me. Lie with me." The creature wantonly rubbed her skin against his body as he whispered, "That's the way, my selkie, my sweet sea-gift."

He lowered the alluring creature to the sandy floor of the cave and covered her body with his own. Really, it could be Ruari MacDonald he was about to deflower. His cock gave an almighty pulse, seeking the firm silky heat of her, rubbing along her sliding warmth.

He hesitated.

She pushed him off, rolled away from him, and stood. She grabbed the fallen towel and wrapped her luscious body in it.

And then she said, "Lochaber Gordon, I am promised to another. If you wanted me, you had time and plenty to request my hand. And you did not. And now, in some stupid male display of one-upmanship, you seek to rob another man."

A terrible snake of suspicion uncurled in his brain, hissing and stretching.

No. Could this be Ruari herself? In the flesh? In some strange swimming costume?

He was in terrible trouble.

He either was about to passionately make love to Ruari with few preliminaries, or he believed her a selkie and he was about to deflower a magical sea-creature.

What sort of man would she think him?

He had no defense at all.

So he leapt to his feet, gave in to his overmastering impulse. He pulled her tight and pressed his mouth to her warm, soft, sweet lips. He dropped tiny tickling kisses along their lush curve until she huffed a tiny gasp and opened for him. He darted his tongue into her silky depths, demanding, seeking, exploring.

She whispered approval, and he pressed her against the cave wall.

He filled his hands with her glorious brown hair, then slid them down to her splendid square shoulders. He bent his head to her breasts and licked and tugged at her rosy nipples until she bleated.

And then he tore himself away. He stood shaking and throbbing with thwarted desire.

"By all the gods, Ruari—if it is you…how I want you."

Her round cheeks were stained bright cherry with their lovemaking. Her plush crimson mouth twisted mockingly. With quick, practiced movements, she pulled on lacy white underclothes and a warm woolen dress. Damn. Now he would continually imagine her in those translucent lacy garments…He dared not touch her to help her with the fastenings. Her clothes would be as quickly shed once more.

"You thought I was a selkie."

Oh no. Here it came.

"You would force yourself on an innocent sea creature? You planned to hide my skin, did you not, so you could take your pleasures as you would?"

His mouth opened and shut, and a stuttering sound emanated from him. He coughed. "She had your face."

Worse. He was a condemned man. Hung by his own actions and words. Now, he had nothing to lose. "Ruari MacDonald...I adore you. I saw a selkie with your face, and lust completely overran me." His voice cracked. "I want you." He paced to the front of the cave and stared out at the sparkling, heaving sea. He swallowed. "Tell me—what must I do to win you?" A black certainty took possession of his mind. "You are not made for that cold devil, the earl." He turned to her and said, his tone stiff and cold, "Unless, of course, you wish to marry him."

She studied him. "Will you tell me why you have not offered for me then? When you had only Roderick to please? Or did this—*affection*—come on you suddenly when you saw the creature naked?"

Ooh. A blow to the guts. Direct and hard.

Her purple eyes glittered like the deep sea beyond, just as beautiful, and just as deadly.

A flash of her in the frothy undergarments stole his breath. *Concentrate, man.* This conversation mattered to her.

His nimble brain canvassed and rejected explanations. He could tell her the truth about himself—and watch the warm regard dissolve into scorn and disgust. No. he could not bear to have her treat him thus.

Scorn and disgust were already writ on her lovely

face. She tossed her head. "Just a quick tumble with an exotic creature, is that it? Shall I don my seal skin once more and slowly peel it away again for your titillation?"

Yes, shouted his whole body. His cock pulsed and reared. He put a hand on his trouser front to press it down. A futile hope, with Ruari standing there like a blazing goddess.

"If you wish." The words escaped him before he could bite them back. A faint hope possessed him—who knew what this tempting, ravishing, glorious woman would do next?

She laughed.

Thank all the gods. Not great for his male dignity, but at least she didn't batter him with a sharp cave rock. "My body knew the selkie was you, my Ruari."

In the glimmering half darkness of the cave, bright shadows leapt and danced with every pulse of the sea, as loud and insistent as the beat of blood in Lochaber's muscles. His mind replayed the vision of those creamy breasts, springing free from the tight skin suit as she peeled it down her body. Her eyes were huge deep pools as they locked gazes.

Her cheeks flushed. "Salty seaweed, Lochaber Gordon, where's a man when you need him? Just like all the rest of your cowardly species. Running and hiding when I need you most! If you wanted me, *why did you not fight for me?*"

Lochaber jerked. Despair froze his bones hard in his body. His face stiffened, cold as marble. Self-hatred and fury welled up, a fuel to keep his heart beating in his chest. "You betrayed me." *Keep silent, man!*

"What are you blathering now, Lochaber?" She fisted her hands on her hips.

"You and your brother. Engineering that coup, so I relinquished the land bid—" He recited in a mincing voice, " '*I love this daughter of this castle*'—and in so doing, I broke my promise to my mentor." He gritted his teeth. *Lock it down. Say no more.*

"Oh my ancestors, aid me! Help me drum sense into that thick male skull, awash with wounded pride."

"It's not wounded pride. It's a broken hea—"

"Yes? And? A broken?"

"Forget it. Do you deny it?"

"Of course I deny it, you sap-skulled foolish whelp of a Highland loon! As if I would be party to any arrangement which sold my freedom to that shark."

Could he believe her? A bright flare of hope speared his chest. He was all emotion, his cool business-smart brain entirely on leave.

She studied him, a smile animating her fierce, lovely face. "So. You did not fight for me because you believed I was part of a plot to make you lose your bid?"

He nodded. He longed to reach for her, to kiss her again, to feel those warm, pillowy lips under his.

"Well, I expect a man to fight for me despite the obstacles. But I will not despise you yet, *Lucky* Lochaber Gordon."

He strove to reestablish control. "I wonder what new humiliation you and your family will lay on me next?'

"Ooh, nobody can grow and nurture a grudge quite like a Highland Scot, can they, Lochaber Gordon?" She poked him hard in the gullet. "A bonny temper grows there now, does it not? Not accustomed to losing then? Enjoying wallowing in misery? Making harsh vows which punish you more than anyone else? It's all about your damaged pride, is it not?"

She took his breath away. How did she know these things about him? It made her more dangerous. To his tranquility, to his plans, to his conquering, imperial nature. She found cracks in his deepest self, which could widen into the fault line that tumbled his personal empire.

"Go away." He pushed at her hand. Even that slight touch sent tremors of desire rocketing through him. "Return to the Earl of Kilmore."

"Don't say it!" she held up an admonitory finger. "I've no idea where my so-called betrothed lurks. Nor do I care."

He turned to her fully, took in her lovely face, her bright eyes, her soft lips, her siren form. "I wish you well, Ruari MacDonald. Truly. If ever you find yourself in need, you may call on me." He clenched his fists in the effort not to pull her to him.

She studied him. "Do you mean that?"

"I do. As you saw in the hall earlier. To my loss."

Her eyes widened into violet pools fringed with dark curling lashes. "Help me now then." Her musical voice twanged with need.

His right hand went to her upper arm of its own volition. He must touch her. "You belong to another man. *Ask him.*" His voice in his own ears grated, harsh and uncomfortable as the spiky shale on which they sat.

"Lochaber," she crooned. His name in her mouth. He wanted to hear her scream it, sigh it, whisper it.

"Lochaber. Take me—early tomorrow—to those Scottish Highlands you told me about. I want to see those Pictish stones and monuments. I want to savor their stories, meld with their ancient song lines. I want to walk in your majestic mountains and cool valleys."

"I don't understand you."

"I must flee from here, you great *burraidh*. I cannot wed that slithery, cold, creeping adder of a man."

He tore himself from her magnetic gaze and paced around the cave. "And have the entire MacDonald clan and Kilmore armies chasing after us? And the fighting MacLeods for good measure? No, my love, this is a tangle you must solve. You must speak to your cousin."

"He wants rid of me. He believes he does not need my opinion, nor my consent. He is the laird, and that is an end to it."

"I cannot quite understand. Surely you are of age? He cannot force your marriage."

"The laird owns all our castle and lands, Roddy's farms, and all our income. We remain here only because his father promised our father. But that promise wears thin as Balgair's gambling debts grow."

"Don't MacNeil pirate queens stand and fight? *Victory or Death*? You called me coward recently." He taunted her now. His evil disappointment and frustrated love for her twisted his desire into petty vengefulness. "Tell your brother, Roderick, to speak for you."

"The only reason I can escape now is because the laird and Roderick are roaring at each other in the study. As always. Roderick hates his gambling, spendthrift ways."

She smacked his cheek gently, then squeezed his cold face in her supple hands.

His whole body tensed. Would she—?

She did.

Ruari raised her sweet lips onto his, so warm and soft and beguiling. He tasted her. Salt and wild air and Ruari. He groaned against her mouth. She nibbled his lip.

Pulled away.

Her clear voice rang around the cave. "Take me to your Highlands fastness. Far from the reach of my cousin and his evil transactions." She held his jaw in both soft palms demanding his focus. "But primarily because I *must* see your Picti marvels, for my research."

Her research. He nodded and plastered his lips back to hers.

The biggest mistake of his life, no doubt.

So why did his blood hurtle with delight and shout with the savage rush of victory?

Chapter Twelve

The fresh predawn breeze lifted her hair in a dance as she raised the blowpipe of the great Highland bagpipes to her lips.

She blew her crippling pain at leaving. She blew her intense love for her lonely island and its majestic seas. She blew her fierce desire and longing for the ancient Picti stones which called to her from the misty mainland.

And she blew her fascination and attraction for that red-haired *claidheamh dùbailte*—that double-edged sword—who had turned her life upside down, Lochaber Gordon.

When she had welcomed the dawn and played her grief, loss, and love into the free wind, she stood quietly for a moment. She filled her lungs with salt-sweet sea air, complex and redolent with seaweed and shells, fish and dolphins and seals, seabirds and salt spray.

Then whipped around as she sensed a hovering presence behind her.

Sìneag.

The tall gray-haired woman said, "I cared for your bonny mother, and now I look out for you, daughter of the MacNeils. Why would you abandon me here in this castle bursting with our enemies?"

Ruari grimaced as pain lanced her. "Sìneag. Are they our enemies, then? I am half MacDonald, you know."

"Aye, the bad half."

Ruari laughed. "Oh, Sìneag. You've been here nigh thirty years. Is this place not home?"

"It's too hilly and too big. Barra and the MacNeil castle is my home. Or wherever a daughter of the MacNeils dwells."

Ruari's tears did flow then as she embraced the fierce old maid. "If I land somewhere else, I shall send for you. But you cannot come on this journey. Your joints pain you in the cold. Rough travel will jolt and unsettle you. Please, stay here and care for Roderick and our MacNeil clan folk. They need you."

Sìneag departed, grumbling and cursing in Gaelic.

Another arrow of guilt lanced her troubled heart. Did she really know what she was doing? All she could hear was the siren song of the Picti stones, calling, calling to her.

And the Gordon's magnetic presence, warmth, and intelligence drawing her in.

She must go. She must try. She must follow this path and see where it led her.

****

Breakfast was a tense but riotous affair.

Disapproval and anxiety radiated from those two old retainers, Sìneag and Gormshuil. Sìneag slammed down Ruari's breakfast bowl of porridge and clattered her teacup in its saucer. Gormshuil tugged a loose curl of Ruari's hair as she glided behind her, so hard that tears sprang to Ruari's eyes. Her head jerked, and she covered the movement with an abrupt cough.

She smothered a smile in her plaid.

Lochaber Gordon acted for all the world as if this was an ordinary morning. He was so good she began to

139

doubt he was actually coming!

"Miss MacDonald. A fine morning." Alasdair MacLeod's blue eyes melted as he regarded her. "Please. Allow me to collect eggs and bacon for you. Or do you prefer toast and honey?"

Oh dear. Excruciating. His unwanted attentions made her guilty heart ping in her chest.

The earl said in an oily voice, "I believe it is my honor to collect breakfast for my affianced wife."

Even his cold voice sent shivers of repulsion down her spine. Hurry on, this day! She did not care about the shame that would visit him, but how she feared his vengeance! She dared not even meet his gaze.

She lowered her eyes and shook her head, afraid to lie to him, unable even to summon a false smile.

Sìneag saved her. "Sit ye down, Your Grace, and Laird MacLeod, and I'll get your breakfasts, so. This *mi-mhodhail* lass can save her breath and et her parritch."

She patted the MacLeod on the shoulder, guided him to a seat, and gestured for the earl to sit, while glaring at the "unmannerly" Ruari over his shoulder.

When the maid brushed past Ruari next, under guise of serving her, Sìneag leaned forward and whispered, "You are young, *m'eudail*. Look forward, not back."

Ruari squeezed her eyelids shut so she didn't bawl into her oats.

Her darling.

Sìneag's heart must be grieving sore.

****

The laird was not happy when Lochaber refused the tour of the tenancies.

Balgair's pale eyes flashed with incipient temper as he made a show of listening to Lochaber's reasons.

Suspicion sat on his brow.

"Your cousin has shown me some of the tenancies." Lochaber's pleasant tone grew steely. "I have viewed your lands. In any case, I have withdrawn my offer, on behalf of my principal, as you heard yesterday."

The laird's plucked auburn brows snapped together.

Lochaber made a sickly smile. His bitterness could have soured the cream. "I am unused to being bested in so complete a manner."

Ruari held her breath. Brilliant! A masterstroke. But would her cousin take the bait?

She exhaled. Balgair could not hide his delight. He laughed and slapped the Gordon on the shoulder. "No need to behave as enemies." He glanced at Ruari and arched his brows. "The reason for withdrawal no longer applies. You may reinstate your bid. Come and enjoy the day."

Oh no. Lochaber must know about the rules of Scottish hospitality. He could not be so rude as to refuse.

Roderick growled from his end of the room, "Leave the man be, cousin. I wish to ask him about the East India Company."

Thus, her brother drew her cousin's fire, protecting Ruari. The men spent a flammable few minutes shouting across the hall about the relevance of India to Hebridean concerns.

Balgair sneered. "You will require a new profession, 'tis true. I had thought the earl would make you factor or overseer—but he will wish to grease his own men."

The MacDonald men heard the racket and arrived to cajole the laird away with Alasdair MacLeod and the Earl of Kilmore to their planned excursion.

Ruari rolled wide eyes at Lochaber and bustled

away to wash and collect her things. Her skin fizzed with fear and excitement. Her heart skipped in her chest. She was traveling into the unknown with that compelling, fascinating man, Lochaber Gordon.

And her rock, her brother, Roderick, had kept her safe, as he always did. Her heart gave a lurch. Sharp pain lanced across her chest. How she would miss him!

Maybe she should tell him…?

No. He might think it his duty to inform the laird.

****

Her bedroom door opened behind her in a swirl of wind. She pivoted, heart jumping in her ribs. "Roddy!"

He surveyed the three dresses laid out on the bed, next to her underclothes, a flexible corset, lace scarf, tippets, gloves, and a pelisse arranged in a pitifully small pile. His lip curled and his eyes darkened.

"It's not what you think."

"It's exactly what I think." Roddy sauntered over, the air around him crackling with angry sparks. "Lochaber Gordon last night asked me to accompany him on a visit to the Highlands. *A very hasty visit*. He wished to depart at dawn. I asked him to delay until after breakfast."

"Oh!" All the air escaped her lungs, and she sat heavily on her bed. "He had no right—"

Roderick leaned in, eyes flashing, softening to deep pools as he regarded her. "Little sister. Is the rich Earl of Kilmore so dreadful an alliance?"

She shook her head. She plucked up a lace scarf that had been her mother's and drew it through her fingers again and again. "The offer is an excellent one."

"Ruari. You could save us all."

The room clanged with silence.

Roddy. Her best friend in childhood, running wild together, escaping the strictures of nurses. She felt flinty scree under her fingers again as children once more, they climbed the tallest peak on the island. Breathless excitement hammered in her chest as she and Roddy explored forbidden sea caves which crisscrossed under the limestone cliffs. He'd taught her to shoot guns and arrows and all manner of unfeminine things. He'd encouraged her to learn the bagpipes from auld Donald MacNeil. And in return, she understood him as no other did.

How could she leave him? Now when he needed her? Now, when she could *save them all*?

Roderick waited. Though his temper could ignite with the merest spark, he was also one of the most patient men she had ever chanced to meet. Maybe he relived their childhood adventures too, for his voice came out all soft and gravelly. "Ruari, what are you about?"

"I hardly know. The world calls to me, Roddy."

"Has the Gordon offered for you?"

"He has not." The confession wrung from her. Perhaps she was being the verist fool. Giving up everything for a man's light flirtation.

But it didn't feel like that.

Roderick's glower made even the hefty furniture cower back into the shadows. "And yet you propose to go with him? Ruin yourself, dash your passion and your bright light against the world's small-minded frowns? Ruari, you cannot win that battle. You must be handfasted at least."

She pressed her lips together to stop them trembling. Blinked, to chase away the two angry, humiliated tears. Roddy always had a direct line to her emotions.

She scrunched her shoulders high. "He will have his reasons. He has secrets. I do not quite understand them. Yet." A surge of excitement suddenly flickered through her veins. She smiled, chin up, her conviction restored. "Roddy, I do not believe he means me ill. He offers me the world! Ancient stones and strange Picti carvings. Experiences and knowledge I cannot get here on my adored island home. The Pictish Trail!" She beamed stars at her brother and laughed. "What do I care about this world? The ancient one calls me!"

His lips pressed against his teeth. "You are set on this course?"

"I'm sorry, Roddy. His stories pluck at my curiosity. He has ensnared my mind."

Roderick stood and gazed out into the starry night. "He is clever then. And smart in his arrangements. He will make your flight into an honorable holiday if he can. That's why he asks me to accompany him. You come as my sister."

He turned, and a wry smile spilt his grim countenance. "It seems I have no choice. Besides, I need to escape the laird for the moment, so I don't murder the profligate fool for gambling and wasting away the MacDonald's last small store of gold. Perhaps I should dispatch him before we go." He raised his brow and grinned.

"Roderick! You can't mean it!" She clutched his hands, joy spilling through her. "Not the murder bit, the coming with!" She studied him. "It would kill you to leave this island. No. You must not try to ease my path. I simply *don't care* what people may say."

He laughed. "This is the only way. I am decided. Don't worry, little sister. I am curious also to travel to the legendary Highlands. I'll send Sìneag to pack your bag and get Gormshuil to help with mine."

He turned at the door. "We will leave in half an hour. Our cousin takes the MacLeod and the earl—your betrothed—to visit our farmlands and tenant crofters. We won't tell them. It will cause too much fuss. I'll leave a note for the laird."

"He'll tear the castle apart in his fury! He'll send the men after us."

"It will be too late. And he will hate any scandal to attach to our name. He will promote our fiction."

"Roddy, I wish had your confidence. A female sees more of his ruthless vindictiveness than a male. You don't know what he is capable of."

Roderick merely laughed, shook his head, and raised his brows at her, before disappearing into the passageway.

Ruari sat on the bed, her mind whirling, planning, picking up ideas and casting them away again as though they were stockings. Her emotions shouted and clashed like a bagpipe band in disagreement.

Roderick lending countenance to their journey— how like him to protect her still.

A part of her was sorry it would not be just she and the Gordon. She shivered. Alone, just the two of them, she doubted they would have traveled far before she willingly lost her maidenhood to his clever fingers and urgent love.

****

Ruari stood on the mounting block and swung her leg over her horse. Lochaber held her horse, old Róisín, steady. Sìneag fussed around, patting the saddle packs and smoothing the riding plaid. Her grim expression belied the suspicious brightness in her eyes. Ruari smothered a laugh as the tall old maid glared icy daggers at Lochaber, still blaming him for stealing the daughter of her heart away.

Gormshuil stood in the shadows of the stables, arms crossed, snapping glances around. She stared with a graven face at Roderick, her eyes wretched with grief.

Lochaber kicked his heels, and his mount began to move. Ruari gave Sìneag and Gormshuil a wave. They must make speed as they could be easily seen from the castle. Ruari would not feel safe until they had disappeared over the hillock and out of sight half a mile away over the fields.

A wild Highland band played music in her ears. Her body danced a reel inside. Travel! Adventure! She laughed aloud and raised an arm in salute to her exciting future.

"Farewell, my ancestors," she whispered into the wind. "I go to unravel more of your mysteries. I will ensure your safety and protection."

"Wait!" A woman's high-pitched cry rang out behind them.

Ruari stiffened. Were they discovered already? She held her heels ready to kick her horse into flight. She would bolt rather than go back now.

Roderick reined his horse and turned back to the hurrying figure.

Of all the strange occurrences! "Flora MacLeod!" Ruari said, amazed. Flora staggered with the heavy pack she hauled in her arms. For once, the icy, proud woman was rosy-cheeked with exertion, her brilliant red hair flying out of its pins in the sun. Her bonnet hung from ribbons tied around her neck. Her plaid had been donned in haste, coming untucked over the plain blouse and dark split skirt.

She looked magnificent. Ruari's gaze flashed to Roderick's face.

Oh. He thought so too.

"Wait." Flora's chest heaved. She dropped her pack to the ground and bent over, gasping. "Take me with you. Don't leave me with those savage, brawling hellions!"

Fury flared in Ruari's veins. "That's my cousin and kinfolk you are calling hellions."

"Ruari." Roderick shushed her with a calming motion of his hand and focused on Flora.

Flora snapped back, "I'm including my brother too."

Ruari and Lochaber laughed. Roddy frowned. The MacLeod daughter stood tall and tucked a blazing curl behind her ear. Roderick watched as though mesmerized.

By the Old Ones! They'd get no sense from Roderick if the woman accompanied them.

Flora squared her shoulders and said primly, "I wish to rejoin my aunt in Inverness to observe the new fashions."

Suddenly her face collapsed, wreathed with desperation. "Please! I am kept in these islands like some marble statue of a saint for all the tenants to venerate. Soon, the laird will sell my hand in marriage. I want to live! I want new experiences." Her lips trembled. She fixed Ruari with a blazing, pleading blue stare. "*You* know."

She did know. "But Flora—the scandal!"

"I accompany the daughter of Callanish Castle, our long-time allies and friends. The betrothed of the Earl of Kilmore. What could be more proper?"

Ruari leaned down from her horse. "Flora, you nit, I

am running from that marriage. I will be ruined. The earl will not wish to marry me once he reads the note Roderick left for the laird." She grinned triumphantly and raised her arms in the air. "I go to find my future, Flora MacLeod, and that future is not likely to be a conventional one."

Gormshuil appeared with a horse newly saddled. "No time for chatting and lazing in the sun. Get you gone this instant." Her musical island Gaelic rang harshly. "And you mun take that baggage with you now." She jerked her head at Flora.

Gormshuil came to Roddy and gripped his ankle as he sat astride his steed. "She has left a letter for her brother, the laird of Clan MacLeod. I will deliver it when you are all well away on the ship to the mainland. Domhnall will collect the horses this evening."

Roderick and Gormshuil held a long, silent communion. Roddy nodded. He dismounted and assisted Flora to mount, helping Gormshuil to strap Flora's pack to the horse.

Ruari's lips tightened. "They will definitely come after us now! Not only a laird's cousin but a laird's sister too. We do not have their permission. We are valuable goods, for bartering, selling, or sealing a bargain. You had better not foil my escape, Flora MacLeod."

"They don't have you yet," Roderick grated. "At present, you are free and unencumbered."

Lochaber curled a lip. "And not entirely without protection." He put a hand on his short sword sheathed on his belt. "Come then," the Gordon said. "Make haste."

They all kicked their heels and sprang into movement, trotting quickly down the length of the long back entrance.

Ruari took one last long look back at her childhood home, her beloved island-dotted seas, and the harsh, jagged coast that was as much a part of her as her hands.

Farewell once more, my ancestors, she called in her mind. *Keep my kin safe from harm until I return.*

And then as Sìneag had bade her, like a true daughter of the fierce MacNeil and MacDonald lineages, she turned her face to her own chosen, dangerous, as yet unknown future.

****

The harsh, salty Hebridean breeze slapped Ruari's cheeks and teased escaping locks of hair into curls streaming out behind her. Gentle sun warmed her shoulders. Her body sparked alive with the movement of the horse.

Lochaber rode next to her, with Roddy and Flora trotting behind, deep in conversation.

She wondered if she had ever been happier.

"Are the mountains very misty?" she asked Lochaber. "What kinds of birds and flowers shall I see there? What are your folk like? Do they sing the same songs?"

He laughed, and his whisky eyes teased her. "Mountain folk are uncommonly tall and fierce, like the giants and trolls of tales. Even the women are seven feet in height, with arms like tree trunks and warts on their noses as large as mushrooms. You don't ever want to hear them sing—their screeching is so horrific that the hills shudder and crack. Their dancing is worse: the fearsome stamping with their platter-like feet creates sharp chasms into which lost travelers fall—prey for their dinners."

Ruari laughed in delight. This was a new Lochaber,

a playful, charming one. Would he continue to change as he drew closer to the home of his childhood?

"And you, Lochaber? Do you have this giant heritage?"

He glinted at her. "In one part of my anatomy."

Ruari blushed. Then she rallied, asking sweetly, "Does this part bear a wart too?"

Shock leapt over his cheekbones. He drilled her with a scorching glare, then threw back his fiery red head and gave a great belly laugh. His gaze melted into a caressing, heavy-lidded regard which drew rapid heartbeats kicking in her ribs.

She tossed her head.

Laughing, he glanced backward, idly checking behind them.

He jerked bolt upright in the saddle, all ease and teasing wiped from his expression. He shouted an oath. Her peace and joy splintered as she turned to check what had alarmed the imperturbable Gordon.

He stood in his stirrups, pointing into the distance. "Hellfire! *MacDonald*. Look behind ye. *We are pursued.*"

Ruari noticed through the growing alarm swamping her brain that his Scots accent thickened in his worry. She stared past Roderick, also standing in his stirrups and craning backward, and an increasingly flustered Flora.

Six tartan-clad horsemen hove into view. Sun sparked from weapons strapped to their backs. Dust rose as they galloped furiously toward the fleeing foursome.

One of them raised a weapon in the air.

The sound of a bullet cracked in the misty air.

Chapter Thirteen

Roderick's face darkened as though thunder crackled within. A stream of Scottish curses rose into the sky. Roddy and Flora caught up to Lochaber and Ruari.

"Everyone—keep riding forward!" Lochaber shouted. "We are yet twenty minutes from the inn at Stornoway. The women must escape."

Another bullet blazed, pinging off a nearby rocky hillock. Ruari twitched and jumped.

"How dare they…?" screamed Flora. Her eyes looked quite wild.

Ruari sneered. "Too much soft living with the English. Go back to them, why don't you?"

"Ruari," Roderick said in a warning voice. He hissed at Lochaber, "They are MacDonalds. They are merely firing warning shots at us. Keep riding."

"It won't do." Lochaber's face had strained into angles and shadows. He jerked his chin at Roddy. "You and I will go back and deal with your men."

He inhaled and stared at Ruari. His skin stretched over his cheekbones. His lips pressed together in a white slash. "You'll take Miss MacLeod to the Lord of the Isles Inn at Stornoway. Wait there for us."

"They'll find us there!" shrieked Flora. "It's where everyone stays who is leaving."

"Stop your maudlin whining," hissed Ruari. "Where's your fight? Call yourself an island woman."

"Ruari." Roderick snapped it this time. He cut her a vivid dark glare. "It's no use. They are gaining on us. We must take the fight to them. Look after Miss MacLeod. *For my sake.*"

Ruari felt her lips twist. "And who will look after me?"

Lochaber's brows shot together in concern for an instant, but her devoted brother snorted. "You'll wither them where they stand, if they are so unfortunate as to catch you."

Ruari bared her teeth. Flora whimpered.

Lochaber gave her another fulminating stare and said, "They will not catch you. Your brother and I will stop them in their tracks. We will meet you at the inn by sunset. Go now."

Suddenly Ruari couldn't bear it. "My love," she whispered. "Those MacDonalds have *guns.* Someone has armed them with *pistols.*" She raised her voice. "The two most beloved people in all the world to me, rushing back to certain death. *No*, I say! Come now. Ride like the wind. We will evade them."

Hot tears sprang forth, stinging her eyes and cheeks. Her whole body felt rubbery and trembly.

Lochaber rode closer. He stretched out an arm and pulled her closer. "Never worry, *mo chridhe.* I will bring your brother back to you."

My heart. For a long moment, she savored his warmth, his exotic-spice Lochaber smell, and the hard strength of his body. She nodded.

The two men wheeled their mounts and kicked their heels. The hardy beasts leapt forward.

Ruari pulled her horse to a stop and watched their dear forms recede, her throat thick, her stomach clenching.

"We have to go!" Flora quavered. "Now. The men are coming."

"A fine match for my brave brother, you are, you sniveling mess." Ruari wanted to tear the stupid woman's hair from her head and scream her fear and rage into the horizon.

Wait! A vision rose in her mind. The sword! She had packed her ancestor's fine weapon, from the grave by the sea. "Thank you, my ancestor," Ruari whispered.

"What are you doing now?" Flora's eyes had white all around the edges, like a terrified dog.

Ruari dismounted and rummaged in her pack. "Ride on," Ruari answered her, then drew the gleaming weapon from its wrappings.

"You don't know how to wield that thing."

"Don't I?" She made several large sweeping moves, enjoying the crack and swish of the blade slicing through the air. "I'm going back to the fight. You can wait or ride to the inn, as you prefer."

Flora surprised her. "Where's my sword then?"

Ruari studied her. The woman had her chin up, and her eyes shone flinty. A proud, brave effect, even with the betraying mouth tremble.

"That's the spirit!" Ruari considered. "I suppose you could throw rocks at the MacDonalds, from a distance? After all," she added sourly, "it's not as though your family is unaccustomed to making war on us."

"Oh, very funny, Amazon woman." Flora swallowed. "I'm useless in a battle. I shall wait here."

Ruari nodded. She mounted her horse with some difficulty, holding the sword out from her body. With a last grin at Flora, she galloped toward the fray.

Dust. Shouting. Gaelic curses. Flying plaid, rearing horses, a tangle of male bodies, smashing together with heavy slapping thuds which shook the ground. Brawny arms. Sun glinting on steel. The metallic gunpowder smell of fired ammunition.

As Ruari slowed her mount, the storm cloud of dust and bodies resolved itself into individual men.

Six MacDonald clansmen fought against Lochaber and Roderick. *Six against two*. She thrust her sword in the air with a murderous scream.

Six against three now.

Ruari kicked her heels into her mount and rode fast into the melee, screeching like a demon queen from hell, swishing her sword in crazed patterns in the air.

All the men saw, stopped in midmotion, hands clenched into fists or holding weapons, mouths open.

Her gaze snapped to Lochaber. His eyes sparked, and his whole face opened in astonished wonder, as though he had been hit by a thunderbolt. Only for a second. His eyes narrowed. His lips crushed together in a flat line. He shook his head in slow motion from side to side.

The fighting MacDonalds had the advantage of a lone Gordon. They were accustomed to Ruari's exploits. They recovered their wits faster. Three of them jumped forward to wrest Lochaber from his mount—and now it was Ruari's turn to be confounded.

Lochaber Gordon somehow rose with athletic grace and stood balanced on his saddle for a moment, then leapt the clutching hands. He somersaulted onto the ground—landing softly on his feet—and made a quick crouching kind of balance. A whirlwind of hands, arms, and feet met the unsuspecting MacDonalds, chopping and cleaving, knocking and smashing.

Ruari tacked her horse away from the fighting, her sword balanced across her pommel. She wanted to watch, to absorb every blazing moment. Her horse whickered, and she stroked its neck absently.

He was *magnificent. Never* had she seen such strange, effective fighting.

Her clansmen kept charging him, but he leapt agilely out of the way, cleaving heads together, or kicking them in the temple, his whole body airborne.

He was a whirlwind, a storm, a dance of death and destruction.

One MacDonald still held Roderick's arm in a loose grip, but both men merely watched the battle, mouths agape. The two other MacDonalds leapt for Lochaber. A strange curved sword appeared from inside the Gordon's clothing; at the same time, he bent and collected a long sturdy stick. The glinting sword and the stick swiftly became deadly, spinning dynamos, knocking legs out from under the aggressors, slashing plaids and belts, chopping a gun held in a shaking fist, and in one fast jab, slicing the red plait from a MacDonald's head. The clansman clapped a hand to his newly shorn head and emitted a shriek of agony. *Domhnall.*

She cupped her palms to her mouth and sang out, "That will teach you to attack the niece and nephew of the old laird!" She gave her newly shorn kinsman a fierce grin.

That lithe form, twirling the sun-kissed sword into slashes of fire. A snake of desperate lust uncoiled, deep in her belly. She couldn't rip her gaze from his muscles and skin, gauzed with shining sweat. She ached to tear him from the battle, to pull him over her, to have that

155

power focused on *her*, handling her with hands rough with desire. Greed throbbed in her core.

She'd heard whispers from the maids and tenants about men returned from a brawl: blood firing in their veins, seeking a woman to tumble, desperate to spend all that pent-up bravado and fight.

She shivered, desire licking her skin like tongues of flame.

And then, it was all over. With a few smoothing motions over his hair, tucks and jerks to set his disordered garments to rights, Lochaber Gordon once more became the steady businessman of the world, only his warm peat-gold eyes and blazing hair denoting the wild savage that lurked within.

Ruari could only stutter.

Lochaber gathered up Roderick, who bore only a grazed cheek and amused grin. The Gordon rode to Ruari and treated her to a rigid jerk of his chin. Fire still burned deep in his eyes, feverish and hot. She licked her lips. That flame fastened on her mouth.

A smile flirted at the edges of lips and eyes, bunching his cheeks. "Sword maiden."

She laughed. "I expected you would shout and storm at me!"

The lids of his eyes lowered until only a steely gleam drilled her. "You are not safe yet." His voice rasped like sand dragging under her knees.

"From them? Or from you?" Her heart picked up in a frantic rhythm. Slippery heat spiked and pooled where she sat in the saddle.

His nostrils flared.

Roderick's voice severed the spell they wove about each other. "Come then. That lot will wake soon enough."

She finally found her voice. "As they are MacDonalds, not only will they wake, but they will come after us like hounds of hell, burning for vengeance."

"Followed by the earl's men. Those vipers will not hesitate to strike down a MacDonald."

She swallowed and smiled at her brother. "Flora waits just ahead. She would not flee." She chose to relate the better truth. The woman had found her courage. In the end.

A savage grin lightened Roderick's dark face. "Miss MacLeod is a woman of the islands. Harshness and softness both ride in her veins."

Ruari rolled her eyes.

****

"The sword curved in a wicked crescent. He wielded it like the sword of an archangel, all power and vengeance. And then he grabbed a stick and fought with that too."

Flora swallowed ale and frowned. "He fought six MacDonalds. And the last one just gave up?" She snorted, most unladylike for Flora.

There was hope for her yet.

Flora was still talking. "Lochaber Gordon did this. The cold businessman from the East India Company, all ruthless focus. The man who calls *us* heathens? And then he fights like a savage barbarian?"

Ruari pulled her bread apart and crumbled it. She took another hefty gulp of her lovely refreshing ale. The food stuck in her throat, but the ale soothed her swooping excitement. "He fights like a warrior. All concentrated movement and balance and precision—oh Flora, I've never seen the like!"

The redhead shifted impatiently. "Yes, yes, sounds dazzling. If you enjoy that sort of thing." Her gaze raked the room. "Where is your brother?" Her voice rose an octave. "Our pursuers have arrived…Roderick is being attacked as we speak…"

Ruari ate a segment of steaming pie and a spoonful or two of mashed turnip. "Calm down, Flora. I tell you, the Gordon fixed my clansmen so they will be lucky to wake before moonrise. And their headaches will be monstrous!" She laughed. "We are safe here in this comfortable inn."

Flora sniffed. "The Lord of the Isles Inn. Named for my family."

"Or mine."

They stared daggers at each other. Ruari cracked first, laughing and then waving for more ale. She wouldn't waste this night trying to out-chill Miss Frosty Glare herself.

On the ride to the inn, Ruari had been tortured with imaginings and wonderings about this night at the hotel. Would the aftermath of the fight still blaze in Lochaber's veins? Would he look at her so, eyes glinting and promising…something? Would he make her body burn and sing for him? Would he kiss her and claim her with that athletic savagery he displayed in the fight?

Or perhaps he would frustrate her by transforming back into that cool executive that teased and fascinated, yet closed everyone out.

A door crashed open. Flora gazed over Ruari's shoulder and brightened. Ruari swiveled to see Lochaber and Roderick lope into the hotel dining room where she and Flora had claimed a cozy table in a protected corner near the fire, away from the window and curious eyes.

Lochaber had made some attempt to clean and tidy himself, with his bright hair darkened and smoothed almost flat with water. He barely bore a streak of dust and certainly no visible injury.

As they approached the table, Ruari's heart picked up and hammered a staccato beat. Her mind replayed the sight of him fighting in that powerful, mobile, ferocious manner.

"Miss MacDonald. Miss MacLeod. I am overjoyed to see you unharmed and rested." His words shocked, like a dowsing in cold water. He had pulled on his civilized veneer like a favorite tartan. Or a seal skin.

How could she find him again? How could she crack that cultivated shell to find that savage beneath? Savage was the wrong word. Highly trained, exotic, controlled *warrior*.

Flora gave Roderick one wide blue stare, then turned frosty as the machair in winter. "I take it you are unharmed and our pursuers have not caught up with us, as yet?"

Roddy summoned a heavy glower and matched her chill with dark thunder. "As you see. Don't expect pretty words. I have a thirst like a drought, and hunger claws at my belly like sharks in herring season."

The serving maid, eyes bugging out in admiration, was already hurrying over. Her hot gaze slid up and down Roderick like a dram of Lagavulin on a cold night. Ruari smiled. The maid had the wrong man.

Ruari allowed Lochaber to drink three jars of ale in quick succession and demolish half a large pie, a plate of chicken and potatoes and almost a loaf of bread. He ate it all with well-bred courtesy, putting down his fork to speak and listen, as though he had just come from a meeting with bankers and not just vanquished the MacDonalds' most feared fighters.

When he announced he would check on their mounts, she followed.

****

The stable smelt sweetly of hay and less sweetly of horse, leather, and oils. In the half darkness, lit only by a lantern hanging from a hook by the door, with his conventional clothes shadowed, he was not disguised by his apparel. She could see he moved like a fighter, with that balance, that poised promise of explosive action that she had missed before, fooled by his calm manner and tidy jackets.

"I know nothing about you, Lochaber Gordon."

He whirled and half crouched, slowly straightening. He stood very still for a long moment, his face sculpted and shaded in the dim, golden light. She couldn't read him at all.

"You know more than you did this morning." His deep voice curled around her like mellow honey.

"Not true. I know less." She inhaled and took a step closer. *Courage.* Her voice hitched. "But I would know more."

Long fingers clasped her jaw lightly. Stroked. "Ruari MacDonald. The woman who can call the selkies and blue men from the waves with her music. Who sings to her mysterious ancestors and bravely ventures forth to seek knowledge." He ran a hand down over the back of her head, the warmth cupping her hair sending tremors down her spine. His fingers played with the tiny curls at her hairline, tracing tingles over her sensitive skin. "I am as you see. A businessman who lost a bidding war. Nothing else."

Frustration exploded in her veins. "Nonsense! What did I witness today?" Impatience hummed within her. Disappointment. He was not going to kiss her, to hold her with desperate hands and tear the plaid from her body. She said, "Curse all gentlemen!"

A smile tugged at his lips, turning into a full grin. "What do you want of me, Ruari the Turbulent?" He came closer and his voice hissed. "Surely you know it is dangerous to closet yourself here with me?"

"I want the man I saw today. I want—" She swallowed. "—your hands on my body. Your mouth on mine."

His words came silky as bog cotton. "You saw the fire, and now you want to release it?" He shook his head. "You are right. You know nothing about me."

Ruari grabbed a nearby fork and pitched a wad of hay into an empty stall. "I have pledged my uncertain future with you, Lochaber Gordon, for better or worse, without any vow to keep me safe. My body trusts you. I...like your smell. I feel alive when I am near you."

"Very well. Here is my promise. As we make a tour of various Pictish sites, at each stone, you may ask one question of me."

"And you will answer true?"

"I will. One question. One true answer."

"And by the end?"

He only smiled and turned away. His voice muffled. "Go now. Before I forget I am a civilized man and you are a daughter of a mighty house."

Ruari was in her room and washed before she realized—he had called her the daughter of a mighty house, but had said nothing about his own. Only that he was civilized.

Mysteries and Picts and promises. How her future shone!

She lay in bed, words and ideas flitting and flying through her brain. It was like one of the old tales. Success hinged on getting her questions just right.

She must.

Chapter Fourteen

Breakfast. Ruari drank her coffee in grateful enjoyment of the enlivening liquid. "Come away from the window and eat, Flora. It's barely dawn. Too dark to spy anything out there."

She cracked her egg and slid a sideways appraising glance at Lochaber, who resembled nothing more than a Scottish gentleman consuming toast and marmalade. Except for that amused glint in his brown eyes. "No, stay as you are. Your expression will frighten any MacDonalds for leagues." She stopped her teasing as Flora's spine stiffened in alarm. Again. "For the old ones' sakes, woman, what ails you now? You are as nervy as an anchovy in fishing season."

"So much for your champion's fatal skills."

Lochaber stilled. Ruari put down her cup. "What can you—"

"*MacDonalds.*"

Lochaber and Roderick both rose from the table, faces wary. Ruari crowded Flora at the small window, peering into the misty gray light. "She's right! No, wait…it's our kinsman Malcolm…and my Sìneag!" Joy warred with worry in Ruari's mind.

Flora spoke Ruari's thoughts aloud. "What ill tidings do they bring?"

Roderick put a hand on Flora's shoulder, and she calmed, her body tilting toward him like a metal filing to a magnet.

"Wait—" Lochaber's command rang in her ears, but Ruari was away out of the room and running from the inn toward her faithful maid.

Ruari treated her liege-woman to a tearing scold while she assisted her from her mount. The woman was too elderly now to subject herself to the rigors of travel, even a day's fast ride to Stornoway would tire her. "Come into the inn then, and rest your bones. Shush, now. The news can wait until you are seated with a hot drink to warm you." She nodded to Malcolm, the aging weapons master who had spent many hours of their childhood teaching Roderick—and Ruari when she could wheedle him—all he knew about archery, swords, cabers, and weapons. He would need a reviving tipple too.

Ruari ordered tea and whisky and gave the maid a good helping of both. Malcolm sat with them, clasping his age-knotted hands around the steaming heat of his large mug.

"How is my cousin?" Roderick asked, the thunder already gathering under his lowered brows.

The old man grinned. "Furious."

Sìneag interrupted. "We care naught for that!" Her scorn at these mere male concerns could have curdled the cream.

She put down her cup with a plunk. Her gimlet gaze seared Ruari. "Gormshuil said that Roddy and the lass were leaving you at Inverness." She raked Ruari with a stern stare. "That you would be traveling alone with that blaze-haired son of the mountains there." She jerked a chin at Lochaber. "I forbid it. Your mother would tear my eyeballs out were I to allow such folly and *reubaltaich.*"

Lochaber said, clearly trying to lighten the atmosphere, "That sounds rather extreme."

Ruari snapped back, "You didn't know my mother."

Lochaber asked for the maid's name and said, "Miss MacNeil. Sìneag. Have you come to return Miss Ruari to her cousin, or to accompany her on our perilous journey?"

The whole table held their breath.

Now she had everyone's undivided attention, like a true MacNeil storyteller, Sìneag chose to answer a different question. "Your cousin the laird gave me a mighty telling off. He spat anger like a fury unleashed."

"Oh, Sìneag…"

"He asked me where you were bound and why. I told him you and your brother were on the track of the lost Jacobite gold. That silenced him."

Shock pulsed for a moment, and then the stunned company burst into laughter. Even Flora smiled.

Ruari said, "Inspired!" and hugged her maid. "So he called off the search for us?"

"Aye, for the bye. I harked on the need for utmost secrecy. That even the earl—especially the earl—must know naught of this."

"What did my cousin do?"

"I'm afraid the laird immediately began to hint of future riches."

"Of course he did." Ruari and Roderick laughed. Lochaber's face was blank with astonishment, carefully controlled. Flora merely sighed and tossed her head, impatient.

And then Sìneag deigned to answer Lochaber's question. "I am coming with you, Ruari MacDonald,

165

daughter of the MacNeils, warrior child."

"Sìneag. We go far away to the mainland. If my cousin is angry beyond bearing, why not go home to Barra? You know you long to."

"Aye, *mo chridhe*, I will return to my home on Barra isle. Before I die." Her gaze went abstracted. "I come to protect you…and to hold the bairn I saw. The next fierce daughter of the MacNeils. *Your bairn*. Cradled in your arms."

Ruari's eyes widened in her head. Sìneag had had a seeing? *A baby*? She swallowed against a suddenly thick throat. *Yes.* A pulse of greed slammed in her stomach. How she would love a child one day…Of all the mad reasons for the maid to come!

The room dimmed. Voices rose and fell around her. Ruari clutched the table edge as though to prevent herself falling into a dizzy chasm. A cup of tea appeared in front of her. Lochaber.

"Is the prospect so dreadful then?" Did hurt ping in those deep tones?

She speared a glance at him. "Never mind Sìneag. We are superstitious folk on these islands. All our mists and skies and oceans blend into watery horizons, from whence strangers bloom like apparitions. Tales spin from our long ghostly twilights. Anyone would see sprites and visions."

"You sound homesick, and we have not left this island! Don't break your heart, my Ruari. The Scots mainland has a harsh beauty of its own. Jagged cliffs and blue seas. Misty mountains to steal to your heart. Starry skies like heralds of the future. I have been away for far too long." He smiled at her, melting her resolve, washing away that brief pang of regret. "And now, we are safe from the sticky noses of the world, accompanied as you are by a proper dragon of a maid, to keep the proprieties."

Ruari grimaced. Nodded. She hardly knew if that would be a blessing or a curse.

****

The passenger boat set sail without further MacDonald trespasses or angry mobs come to drag the daughter of the castle home to that fell marriage.

She leaned on the side of the vessel as the ship hove away into the strait between Lewis and Ullapool in Ross-Shire on the Scots mainland.

Her heart divided: a sharp pang for the loss of her beloved islands, her friends among the tenants; a surge of untrammeled excitement for an unknown future.

How much she had to discover! Picts. New places. Mountains. Strange harsh coasts. A frustrating, mysterious, wounded, lovely man.

And—as intoxicating as the rest—her own guiding star.

The misty, pastel-hued horizons melted. Her homelands faded and disappeared as though made from legends and memory. Seabirds soared in the pale blue sky. Dolphins and seals dived and swam alongside the ship. Salt and sea air scoured her lungs and needled her cheeks with icy fingers.

Happiness bloomed in her heart and flowed like heady wine bubbling in her blood.

****

As day darkened into evening, the party arrived in pretty Ullapool and went to the inn for food and rest for the night. On the morrow, the party would head to Inverness, where Roddy and Flora would stay, and Ruari and Lochaber would begin to explore the trail of the

Picts.

And she would ask a question of Lochy with each stone.

As she lay in bed in the delightful inn, she turned her strategy over in her mind. Begin with the hardest question, before he changed the rules? Or start slowly, carefully, penetrating each layer with subtle skill so he barely felt himself being filleted? Perhaps that would serve her best, layer by layer, until she reached that deep, damaged part of him, the wounded lad who burned for vengeance.

Then she could help him deliver it! *And* help him knit himself back together, healthy and whole. For alone in all the world, he saw the true Ruari, respected her intelligence and passion. He lifted her closer to the glitter and lure of her particular star.

A snore emanated from the other side of the large bed. Sìneag.

Bairn cradled in her arms.

She squashed the bonny image away.

She had things to do.

****

Ruari hugged Roderick again, tears in her eyes. "Take care, you great *burraidh*." She turned to Flora. "As the Old Ones witness, look after this fine man, or my very ghost will haunt you to the end of your days. *Oh, Roddy*."

Over his shoulder, the view of bonny Inverness town stretched out below them, the glorious River Ness reflecting the dawn. The foursome stood on the brow of Castle Hill, looking over the town. A group of tartan-clad pipers were setting up near the newly restored castle walls. The castle, like so many others in the Highlands, had been fired and ruined after the Jacobite rebellion, decades ago. The band leader took a hearty gulp of air and nodded to the men.

As though to play the lament singing in her heart, the skirl of the pipes floated out over the air in the dawn, searing and mournful and catching at her emotions. The drums pounded the rhythm of her hopes and fears.

She ran to the band and gestured to a spare set. Without losing a note, the leader quirked his brows up, then nodded. Ruari hefted the bagpipes, blew into the blowpipe, filling the instrument with air, and her music soared out into the dawn's embrace. Grief. Heartache. Yearning for home and family. Hot tears tracked down her cheeks, leaving stinging trails which pricked with salt as the wind whipped them dry.

Goodbye my brother, sang her bagpipes. I love you. I'll never forget you. One day, God willing, we will all meet again, on the soil of our ancestors.

****

The first Picti stone.

The pretty village of Knocknagael nestled in the borders of grand Inverness, like a lace edging on a stalwart mahogany sideboard. The carved stone stood sentinel in a green field, still hazy with dew.

She and Lochaber had walked the two miles from Inverness, leaving Sìneag at the Caledonian Hotel to fuss with their clothing after their two days' journeying by sea and land. He consulted the map given them by an ancient scholar in Inverness the night before.

In the hotel last night, Lochaber had bought drinks and chatted amiably with suited Inverness professionals: accountants, mercantile owners, shippers, exporters; with farmers, come to trade their produce for sovereigns and guineas, dirt-encrusted hands raised with the glasses of whisky Lochaber bought them; with idlers and gossipers. Another Lochaber. This time, she glimpsed the man of the world, accustomed to making acquaintances and gleaning information with an open purse and an easy, relaxed charm.

A thrill of excitement had bubbled within her when, after dinner, he had taken her for a walk. The river sparkled rose and silver in the gloaming, and she could fancy sprites and piskies danced with the graceful-necked herons perched on fishing stones lining the rushing river.

They crossed a small arched bridge into Inverness township and strolled into a maze of narrow streets and gray stone shops and cottages, clustered under the towering Castle Hill and the castle ramparts overshadowing all in the magical twilight.

He knocked on a low door in a narrow brick alleyway, edged on two sides by towering walls. The door opened. From inside his coat, Lochaber produced a bottle of aged Dalwhinnie single malt. The old man's eyes lit, and they were admitted into a smoky, cozy room flickering with two lanterns and warmed by a leaping fire crackling in the hearth.

Cradling his whisky glass, the old scholar, Alexander Ross, asked questions and told stories and chuckled. He gulped his drink and poured another, forgetting to offer to more to his unexpected guests. When he downed a third dram, Lochaber rose and poured a measure into his own glass and a small amount into Ruari's. The old man didn't seem to mind, merely twinkling at them under his gray and black hoary brows.

"The Picts? The Picts, aye, a strange mystery.

Perhaps we'll never know the truth of them. They left beautiful works of art and intricate standing stones engraved with curious symbols: mirrors, boars, eagles, fish, zigzags, lightning bolts…" He took a hefty slug of his drink. "A fine wee drop, laddie. I thank you."

What to ask first, of the thousand questions brimming in her brain…"Did they have a language?"

"Aye, lass, we believe so. Something like our own Scots Gaelic or the Welsh down to the south. They intermarried with the Scotti and the Norse. You know why they are called Picti?"

She shook her head, pretending ignorance to please the old man.

"It's Roman for 'decorated ones' or 'painted people.' "

"Ooh. What a lovely description. It makes my imagination fizz."

Lochaber grinned, the lantern light gleaming on his teeth. "No rushing out to get tattooed, my Ruari. Although it would match the pirate blood beating inside and give the world fair warning of what you are!"

The old man switched bright eyes from Lochaber to Ruari. He might be old and adore a whisky or five, but Ruari would bet her Pictish brooch he rarely missed a thing.

"You have an interest in the Picts, miss?"

"I am completely obsessed with them." Such a relief to say it out loud! To be able to just admit it and have Alexander Ross nod, as though that was only to be expected, faced with such delectable, fascinating mysteries. She blessed Lochaber in her heart, to have brought her here, to this meeting.

She opened her mouth to share her ideas about the

star maps—what fortune! To have another intelligent mind grapple with the puzzle—and choked before the words could form. The Royal Society's mockery smashed into her enthusiasm. Shame corroded her belly. Anxiety sliced cold in her veins.

The fire to reveal her theories fizzled to ash. She faltered at this first challenge.

The old scholar clinked his glass with hers and took a long swallow. With some difficulty, he pushed himself up from his chair on arthritic legs and tottered over to his huge bookcases lining every wall. He pushed an ancient pair of spectacles on his nose and fumbled in a drawer, muttering to himself.

She pushed down her despair. Exchanged a bright smile with Lochy. "I'm in love!" she whispered mischievously.

Lochaber's gaze narrowed mock dangerously, then his face opened in a smile.

"Here we are." Alexander Ross held out a large crumpled paper, yellowing at the edges and soft with much folding. Some of the folds had been reinforced with stitching to keep the paper from splitting. "Here. Feast yer eyes on that while I find you a braw wee Picti-stone reference book, ideal for field research…" His voice faded to mutters once more as he talked himself through where the book might be. He fortified himself with another dram, then rummaged in a low bookcase.

"Ha!" He waved a tiny green leather-covered volume. "The Picti field guide. You'll find it most informative." His old eyes softened. "You may keep this book with my blessing. But…I'd give much to have you visit one day and tell me of your experiences and thoughts about the fascinating Picts."

"Oh! But how fabulous. Are you sure? We could return it when we return to Inverness."

"No, my dear. I'm so old that soon I will dwell more in dreams and memory than in life. Books must be read and appreciated, not hoarded like an old, smelly dragon with his gold. But I'd give my last dram of Dalwhinnie to hear your travelers' tales." He regarded his glass, frowning. "Perhaps my second last."

Lochaber and Ruari laughed. "No need to deprive you so cruelly, sir! We would adore to visit you again."

****

Now, they stood in the field, gaping at the Boar Stone. Lochaber's hands rested warm and heavy on her shoulders, his bulk protecting her back from the brisk wind scoring her cheeks. She pulled her plaid closer about her head.

She had no words. The magic and mystery of the lost tribes, her forgotten ancestors, sent thrills shivering down her spine and sparkling along her skin, as though she sat in a small waterfall.

The stone was a large, rough slab, carved with a stylized, incised figure of a boar. An ancient artist's hand had created a flowing outline, with three strange curling symbols inside the beast, like backward question marks. Above the beast, two concentric circles topped a small square.

Salty tears stung her cheeks. She scrubbed them with her plaid before Lochaber saw her crying. "Leave me a moment," she whispered.

He nodded and faded back across the field.

Ruari bent down and touched reverent fingertips to the stone. She traced the carving with the lightest of touches. "My ancestors!" she murmured. "I hail you.

You have bred brave daughters and strong sons. I come to hear your stories, to trace your lost histories." She swallowed. "To find my heart and its home."

So absorbed was she in communing with the carved stone, she jumped when she sensed his presence close behind her.

"Did you have a question?"

Oh no! The man sounded peeved. Ignored. She tried not to laugh. All that build-up about unpeeling his secrets, and then at the first sight of a Picti stone, she had clean forgotten her other mission: to unwrap the tightly held layers of Lochaber Gordon.

Invigorated, inspired, and renewed by the stunning carving, she whipped around to face him. "Yes, I have a question. We will start slowly, Lochaber Gordon—I don't wish to frighten you."

"*Frighten* me." Disgust laced his words.

"We will begin with an easy puzzle, needing a factual answer, not an emotional truth."

The man jerked. As she thought. He was afraid of emotions, keeping them locked tight in a black iron box of his will.

She met his brown gaze, the smile flirting and dancing on her lips. Deep in his eyes: a flash of fear. She snorted. "A Picti stone depicting a fighting boar—so a battle question. *Where on earth* did you learn to fight like that?" Facing him, she gripped his upper arms hard. His biceps rounded and bunched under her palms.

The strength of the man. A sizzle burnt through her, leaving a hot trail of simmering desire.

She still did not know if he would answer with truth. She waited.

"As you know, I spent many years with the East

India Company, in the deserts, mountains, and lush cool forests in the north of India. Also a little time in magical, mysterious China. I made many friends in India—not just among the English, Irish, and Scots. I am honored to call many Indians friend too, fine men, proud people, with deeply fascinating and diverse cultures, even within India. Princes and princesses. Hindus. Sikhs. Mughals."

Oh. Fascinating. But he was luring her with stories, away from his truth. She raised an inquiring brow. His lips curved, then he sobered and stared out across the field at the hairy Highland cattle grazing in the misty morning.

His voice deepened, gained a faraway quality. "I trained with the notorious *paika akhada*. Swords and sticks become fearsome weapons in their hands. They specialize in acrobatic maneuvers and use of the *khanda*—a straight sword—and *patta*—a gauntlet-sword—sticks, and other weapons."

The skin tightened on his face, his slanting cheekbones sharp above a jutting jaw. His throat bobbed as he swallowed. "I learned a type of martial art called *yuddha kalā* and *śastra kalā* and an athletic discipline called yoga, the regular practice of which keeps one's body strong and supple, even into old age."

She took a moment to absorb all this and to chase the expressions dancing over his features. Pain. Determination. An ache of love, or regret.

She dredged through her brain, desperately seeking snippets of secondhand information about the East India Company. She made a guess as to the reason for the ache in his soul. "And did you fight…with the English against your friends? Or with your friends against the English?"

His face slammed closed. A breath, then the mask of

charm was back, though she could see emotion simmering behind it. "That, my dear," he riposted in a light, amused tone, "is a second question. One per stone. That's the deal."

She could have sworn his body quivered as he turned away. In grief? Despair?

He had answered her question.

But a million more rose like an ocean wave. Had he faced a tragedy? Had he left friends behind—or betrayed them? *Did he have a lost love?*

Now her own mind shut down with a snap. That was enough of Lochaber's murky past for one day.

According to their guide book, the next Picti stone was located at Dingwall Churchyard, less than twelve miles and two hours travel away.

Ruari took Lochaber's arm, stiff under her hand, and walked with him silently toward the little bridge over the River Ness and to the Caledonian Inn, where a grand cooked breakfast awaited them. She smiled to herself. If he suffered now, wait until she slammed him with her next question at Dingwall. A blast of sun struck them through a break in the clouds.

Ruari released Lochaber's arm and gave three happy skips like a new lamb frolicking in the spring sun.

Chapter Fifteen

What had he let himself in for? He should have restricted the questions to certain topics. Unlike his usual cautious, precise methodology, he had omitted to set boundaries, to mark the deal with rigid borders, but had foolishly left the field wide open. The minx would not hesitate to take advantage.

What had he been thinking, to allow a pirate wench unalloyed access to his deepest self? He grimaced. Because it wasn't his brain that had been doing the thinking. As if in confirmation, his cock twitched and gave a thick pulse.

Their proximity in this small hired carriage helped not one whit. Thank all the gods for the irascible, elderly maid, Sìneag.

Now *that* was an unexpected thought.

He smothered a laugh, which brought Ruari's bright amethyst eyes to fix on his face. She was wedged next to her maid, who glowered at him the whole journey like a dragon guarding its favorite diamond.

"Tell me more of the *paika*…whatever. It sounds so fascinating."

"You have had your question."

"Oh, but now, there is conversation. Cannot we beguile the journey with a most remarkable topic, rather than commenting on the scenery, which we can all see, or those contented cows in fields and meadows, munching grass and herbs?"

"You are cheating."

"Lochaber, you malign me! Never besmirch the honor of a MacNeil, isn't that right, Sìneag?"

The maid intensified her glower and grunted an affirmation which sounded like a Gaelic malediction.

His blood stirred. This is why gently bred women kept their maids close. Else he would treat her liveliness with the physical response it merited. A kiss for those wide red lips, now taunting him, parted in a half smile, a glimpse of pearly teeth peeking through…and a wet tip of pink tongue.

Blood rushed straight to his groin. He shifted in his seat. This could get uncomfortable, fast.

Her voice rippled with laughter. "Very well, as you refuse to answer further questions on any subject, I shall read some Picti facts from the lovely professor's guide book. Pay attention now."

As if he could do otherwise. She compelled him. She plunked her feet on top of his, sending a sharp thrill spearing around his veins. Not the kind of contact he yearned for, but even this brief inch of stocking on cotton sock felt like the world.

"The Picts were a warlike tribe from the north, fond of tattoos and body art. They were artistic and cultivated—they left mysterious carved standing stones, artifacts, intricate jewelry, and echoes of fables within traditional Celtic stories."

Her sprightly tones skipped and danced over his senses. Her fascination with her topic lent a rosy blush to her cheeks and bright animation to her expression. She caught him staring and widened her magnificent eyes at him in silent reprimand.

"The ancient Picts fought with, married, and interbred with Scotti kings in ancient Alba, now Scotland. The Romans *never* conquered them. How about *that*?" She kicked him lightly. He grabbed her toes, got sizzled in Sineag's glare, and released the dainty foot, wishing he could peel away the stocking and suck each sweet toe.

"…And along with other Scottish nations, they stood brave and firm against all the marauding Goths, Huns, Vandals, Franks, Angles, and Saxons who subsumed Europe and England under their war hammers."

"Are you making this up?"

"I'm summarizing. For the benefit of your limited male powers of concentration. I'm focusing on the war, not the art, for you."

He grinned. "Please, do continue."

Never defeated. Pride. His chest swelled with it. His muscles hardened, and a happy song streamed through his brain like a triumphant war band. Every day, she reminded him of his Scots heritage; every day, his blood powered up, gaining strength from his Gaelic language, his culture, his roots. He stood taller in her company.

The broken, fragmented parts of him, hidden deep: they weren't knitting together—yet—but they were saying *good morning*.

Part of him cheered and rioted like a Hogmanay celebration. Most of him hurt. It had taken years upon careful years to build his cold, brilliant business persona.

Now, Ruari the Pirate had found her swords to merrily slash that social carapace to shreds. She cracked his hard shell, exposing quivering parts of him to the light.

Emotion. That tamped down fire. He had been cold so long, he was completely at the mercy of the blazing inferno of desire Ruari summoned in his brain and heart. He snapped his attention back to her.

"…the carved images include double discs, lightning rods, stylized creatures with organs, muscles, and feathers. The Pictish beast—is it a water kelpie of mythology? A sea creature? A horse…"

Mischief possessed him. "The greater claim for Picti blood is mine, as I am a product of Aberdeen-Shire: a Pict stronghold. Unlike two Hebridean interlopers." He ducked both the maid's outraged glare and one fancy shoe thrown with the precision of a woman with a brother.

****

Ruari stared in fascination at the Churchyard Stone at Dingwall. Her chest squeezed tight. Here before her eyes were the strange double discs and Z-rods, and crescent and V-rod. Their elusive mysteries gripped her tighter. Yes! These mainland steles could well be star maps.

Lochaber vibrated with tension beside her, shifting from foot to foot. The man dreaded her next question. So fearless in a fight! And yet, terrified of anything approaching emotion. *Men.*

Perhaps she had better put him out of his misery.

"Sìneag. Please fetch my drawing satchel from the carriage. I must sketch these."

The maid tore her amazed gaze from the stone, nodded, and set off back to the carriage. Ruari called after her, "And rest yourself there a bye."

She smiled at Lochaber. "I believe my Sìneag becomes as drawn to these ancient mysteries as myself."

Lochaber swallowed, then grunted through clenched teeth. "Indeed."

Ruari whirled to face him, fists on hips. "And now, my *paika* warrior, the Second Question."

He closed his eyes, and his jaw hardened.

Ruari stifled a laugh. She pitched her voice low and soothing, hazing the music of it around his senses like a magical mist. "This riddle is a very easy one, or a very hard one. The experience will be entirely your choice."

Lochaber's brown eyes snapped open, their golden depths lit with incipient panic. His cheeks sucked in. His whole body shifted minutely into a ready-for-action posture.

By the Old Ones, how this poor man makes himself suffer!

"My second question is this: have you realized that you crave the Highlands and Scots culture with a savage hunger? Perhaps unacknowledged until you visited the desolate, harshly beautiful Outer Hebrides."

Color smashed into Lochaber's face. Temper. Denial. "What sort of question is that?"

"There were no parameters set as to the nature of the questions."

She watched him flounder, tempted to put him out of his misery and ask another, more innocuous query. But she prized valor, drove herself to acts of fierce bravery. She would demand any man who stole her heart to match that.

Have you realized that you crave the Highlands and Scots culture with a savage hunger?

Ruari the Tartar's voice just got sweeter, the more provoking she became.

He sifted and sorted through possible answers.

Crave the Highlands. Oh, she was clever. Because *No* implied he hadn't realized, yet his *savage hunger* still lurked and tormented within.

He resorted to flippancy. "What I crave with every fiber of my being, since arriving in the harsh and beautiful Outer Hebrides and the Highlands, is a certain brown-haired, red-lipped, jewel-eyed, turbulent…"

Her lips snapped together in a line. Her eyes blazed fury and death. He shivered with desire. The memory flashed—her with a sword in hand…

"Don't you try to wriggle out of this by flirting, Lochaber Gordon! Don't you fall back of that luscious charm, to dizzy my senses, to accept a toss-away compliment instead of truth."

She inhaled noisily. "Do you know how much I *long* to hear you complete that sentence? But! *Answer my question.*"

Her lip curled in scorn, stinging him. She believed him afraid. He could not bear her contempt.

"Yes! Yes, then!" he shouted as he paced away across the churchyard, throwing words at her like a hail of arrows. He could not hold the shouting in, could not summon his lazy charm or his cold, hard decisive habitual manner. "Yes! I crave home like the verist opium eater. *Yes.* Scots Gaelic is balm to me, a lover's voice, the music of my soul. The sight of the tartan makes my heart kick in my ribs and my body swell with pride. I am Highlander! I am Lochaber Gordon, and I am *almost home.*" His voice cracked.

His breath hissed harshly in his ears. He sank down onto a mossy gravestone and buried his head in shaking hands.

A gentle palm rested on his left shoulder. The hand

began to soothe and stroke him, her touch sending messages of rest and safety through his skin and swimming in his blood.

"There is some mystery here, is there not, Lochaber Gordon? You crave home, and yet you reject your home with everything you have become."

He summoned strength from deep within. The words came muffled through his fingers. "You have your answer for today."

"And again, the answer creates a thousand more questions in my mind." She smoothed the hair back from his brow with gentle fingers. He pushed into her touch. *More.*

A smile floated in her voice. "Luckily there are hundreds of Pictish artifacts, here in Ross-Shire and over in your homelands of Aberdeen-Shire. Many questions. Eventually, many answers."

He replied with a groan.

Sineag returned with Ruari's drawing satchel. Ruari dived on her charcoals and crayons, alight with a mission to record the fascinating symbols. Lochaber walked around the church, examining the ancient graves and exploring the church's interior, finding some relief from his emotional storms.

Once he had established a safe distance, he glanced behind him. A tiny frown of concentration wrinkled Ruari's pale forehead; her body bent over the sketchpad. She was completely, happily absorbed in sketching the Dingwall Churchyard Stone.

Stray strands of hair tumbled free on her round cheeks. His fingers twitched. How he yearned to wind those silky strands around his fingers, grazing the warm, soft skin underneath. To kiss that tender neck.

Persistent woman. Once she had her teeth in a mystery, there was no distracting her or dragging her away.

But her question had reminded him. He could not marry. Especially not such a woman as Ruari MacDonald.

Her relatives would hunt him down and murder him.

No doubt they were on their trail already. And he mistrusted the earl's power on the mainland. He must make discreet inquiries.

****

A lunch of fish, potatoes, bannocks, and ale at the Dingwall Hostelry fortified them for the four-mile carriage ride to Strathpeffer. There, Ruari would set her eyes on the Eagle Stone—and ask her third question.

"I am so excited to see this Eagle Stone, which my little guide book says was carved in pre-Christian times. Its Gaelic name means Sounding Stone. The name alone makes me shiver!"

Lochaber grinned. Sìneag listened with an avid expression. The elderly maid was having the time of her life.

"Listen to this! Local tradition concerns the Brahan Seer: he said in the 1600s that if the stone fell three times, ships would be able to sail up to Strathpeffer—five miles from a sea loch—and be fastened to the stone. It has fallen twice already!"

Sìneag's eyes widened, and her mouth fell open. Ruari rubbed her shoulder.

"The Eagle Stone depicts a curling horseshoe and an eagle. Whatever can these carvings mean?" Ruari rapidly turned pages in her guidebook. "We know the theories regarding tribal boundaries or kin groupings.

Hmm…'the Picti markers commemorate the lives and victories of great warriors. Some suggest a magic caste, like Druids, wove enchantments with the carvings and stones.' "

Ruari felt her maid's shiver, echoing her own delicious thrills humming in her skin and tickling up and down her spine. She put an arm around the elderly MacNeil's shoulders.

Still no whispers that others had considered her own theories.

When she had collected sufficient evidence, she would startle Science and refute those women-haters at the Royal Society.

But she had lacked the fortitude to speak her ideas to a kind-hearted old professor. She must woman-up, practice, until she could call forth courage and fight as befitted her Norse-MacNeil blood, for the preservation of the sacred Lewis artifacts.

She had her third Lochaber question to ponder, too.

The poor man had had enough emotional shocks. She would ask a nice factual question at the Eagle Stone; a lovely plain query would restore his will to answer more puzzles. Later, she would express the riddle which fizzed in her mind. The soft embrace of evening twilight better lent itself to confidences and confessions.

A pang of fear bit her stomach: what if he decided he would answer no more? She had *so many…*

Ruari leaned her head back against the squabs and surrendered herself to the rocking of the carriage, the visions of delightful countryside streaming by outside the windows and her anticipation of feasting her eyes, building her knowledge, and wallowing in wonder at the esoteric Picts.

Her fierce, proud, warlike, artistic ancestors.
****

Lochaber led the way and Ruari followed behind him more slowly, supporting the arm of her elderly maid. They strolled the few hundred yards along a pretty hedgerow-lined lane which led up the hill from Strathpeffer village to the lichen-encrusted Eagle Stone, *Clach an Tiompain.*

The maid rested a hip on the low farm fence. Ruari rushed forward to the rough-hewn stone with a cry of delight. Lochaber relished her blazing jewel eyes and greedy joy as she studied the artifact. She stroked the weathered surface with a delicate fingertip, her face alive with wonder.

Jealous of a stone slab!
You fool, Lochaber Gordon.

The stylized engraving really was remarkable. A tendril of the old magic curled around even Lochaber's flinty heart, seducing him a little with its beauty and mystery.

The upper etching portrayed an arch or horseshoe decorated with discs and arcs. Below that, a fine eagle stood proud in profile with wings folded back and detailed feathers, talons, and beak.

"Extraordinary!" The accolade ripped from his throat. Perhaps Ruari's enthusiasm for these Picti pagan arts was contagious.

A ripple of nervousness possessed him as she turned to him, a wicked glint of humor dancing in those marvelous eyes. *Time for the third question.* He cut a glance to the maid, who still stared in superstitious dread at the Eagle Stone. The filleting wouldn't be too personal with Sineag present.

186

He hoped.

Ruari's luscious red lips curved in invitation. His cock gave a pulse. Could he steal a kiss with the dragon hovering nearby? Too late. The wicked wench was asking her question.

"I am going gently on you after your shocks of this morning, Lochaber Gordon."

He replied stiffly, "No need to treat me as though I am some puling weakling."

She laughed. "True? Then I will not hesitate with my petitions this evening."

Horror slammed him with the force of a broadside. Too late to retract or qualify now. Ah well. No doubt he would think of some defense by then.

Sìneag said, "Miss Ruari, I will make my way slowly back to the village now, and sit in that little teahouse and arrange a refreshment for you."

"Yes, Sìneag, get yourself out of this wind. We will not be long. Lochaber will answer a simple question, and then we will join you in a moment." Her voice sang with the happy music that seemed to spring from some unquenchable sparkling well inside her. That bright happiness called to him, called to his own black, withered heart like warm sun calls to a dying man.

Ruari faced him and took his large, hard hands in her own delicate, pale fingers. Those soft fingertips caressed the vulnerable skin of the underside of his wrists and explored the wiry auburn hairs springing on the top. His muscles leapt to attention. His blood immediately pounded in his veins and gathered throbbing in his groin.

He could stand so all day.

"Now, Lochaber. I give you a plain question, requiring only a simple answer."

"I don't trust your plain questions."

Her laugh trilled. She licked her lips, sucking in the top and then the bottom lip as she considered her query. His attention snapped to that wide mouth. While he gazed in helpless desire, she said, "Tell me of your roots in the Highlands. Does your family own property here?"

Chill swallowed him, as though he had been doused in a bucket of water from a Highland stream. He wrenched his hands from her grasp and turned away, gazing out over the charming green farmlands of Strathpeffer.

He could not refuse to answer. She would call him coward and lacking honor.

"My family...owns estates in the Highlands." *By Shiva.* "Major estates."

"*Major estates?* And the names and nature of these estates? Where are they located?"

"They are further questions. You have had your answer. You'll have to wait until the next Picti stone." And by then he would have a means to evade a precise response.

"No! You have given me half an answer only."

"Well, this stone is only two feet high. And broken. Half a stone. Half an answer."

She struggled, and then her face lit in a burst of laughter. "I'm going to punish you for this outrageous bending of the rules, Lochaber Gordon. The drawbridge is lowered. The guns loaded and the spiked portcullis ready to chop down."

"*Rules?* What rules? Perhaps we should—belatedly—agree on a few parameters for your investigations."

"Ha! Too late now, my friend. Just you wait for

tonight."

As he savored her bright face and lively eyes, gleaming with whip-smart intelligence, as he reveled in their feisty exchanges, which stretched and challenged his own clever mind, he realized—actually, he looked forward to more with every amused cell in his aroused body.

He leaned in and gave her a glimpse of the devil that lurked inside.

Her pupils dilated.

He said, tone harsh, grating the words over through the thick desire obstructing his throat, "Spikes and weapons? Bring them on."

****

In the tiny, cozy Strathpeffer tearoom, Ruari peppered him with so many direct and sneaky side-on questions about his family's mainland estates, he almost forgot his caution.

Ruari and the fearsome Sìneag withdrew to the ladies' retiring room for a few minutes, so Lochaber took his chance and sauntered into the tearoom kitchen. There a strapping, blond male cook, wielding a blade as though just emerged from a Viking longship, shouted at a scurrying boy to chop the vegetables.

"Aye," he informed Lochaber. "They are in a bustle at Ardross Castle. The Duke of Tuath arrives with a crony this week. Best you take this cleaver if you plan a visit yon. There's evil afoot."

"Crony? Do you know the name?"

"Some great earl or t'other. Chasing a runaway."

Lochaber's throat tightened. "The name of this earl?"

The cook thwacked his cleaver hard into the block.

"Doesna matter. Each titled English parasite bites worse than the last."

Chapter Sixteen

"Nonsense! It could be any earl. There is a scourge of English dukes and earls currently leeching on the Scottish Highlands."

"Ruari—"

"And I *must* see the Wolf and Deer Stones at Stittenham. Besides, Sìneag has a kinswoman at Ardross Castle. And my brave, uncomplaining, but elderly maid needs a comfortable bed such as a castle will provide. We will go to Ardross as planned."

A risk—but Sìneag wished to spend time with her relative. "The cook said the duke arrives this week, yes? We will be gone with the dawn. All will be well." She fixed Lochaber with her best glare. "That slimy earl and his dukish collaborator hold no terrors for a daughter of Callanish Castle."

"Your own castle may already be under Kilmore's greedy aegis. If this crony is the earl, and he knows Lochaber Gordon and a young woman have visited here—"

"Cease your bleating. Do not worry for me, Lochy."

The man's teeth ground audibly as he looked away from her.

They went to Ardross.

****

Close to Ardross, Lochaber delivered them to a little leafy clearing by the burn. "Wait here, please. I go to arrange our accommodation at Ardross Castle."

"So mysterious!"

When Lochaber returned, he refused to answer any queries, teasingly asking if she wished to use all her Picti stone questions in one gasp. He drove the carriage along a narrow road to an imposing gatehouse and though the grounds of a grand castle and estate. At the colonnaded entrance, servants ran out to take the horses to the stables and to collect the luggage.

A tall, lanky woman with hard gray eyes and dressed in neat housekeeper's black said, "Welcome to Ardross Castle, ma'am." She locked stares with Sìneag.

Lochaber's eyes glinted down at Ruari. "You shall see your Stittenham stones tonight. Built into an ancient wall there. Two miles hence."

"Perfect for an evening stroll in the twilight."

He nodded. His taut cheeks softened as he rubbed his jaw. "I hear there is a pretty river walk to Stittenham along the burn there, which you may enjoy. I know how you long to stretch your legs after being cramped in a carriage."

"Once we settle in here and refresh ourselves—not too many minutes, as I must see the Wolf and Deer Stones this evening!—I would be delighted to bear you company."

"With your maid, of course," Sìneag added in a stern voice which carried to all the company.

The gaunt housekeeper showed Ruari to a charming room with stunning views over the extensive gardens and extending out to the hilly countryside.

"You are interested in the Quiet Ones, my lady?" she asked. "The country hereabouts has many of their old roundhouses." She hesitated, then asked, "You are traveling through the Highlands with the Gordon?"

Ruari shot her a curious glance. The housekeeper had two spots of color high in her cheeks. She didn't seem the type to be merely indulging in gossip.

"We go to visit Lochaber Gordon's mother," she answered carefully, watching the housekeeper's every fleeting expression.

"His *mother*?" The housekeeper swallowed and launched into a torrent of words, as though to forestall further inquiries. "Well, anything you need, please don't hesitate to ask. We are proud to have you visit Ardross Castle, Miss…"

"Ardross Castle is one of the Duke of Tuath's residences, I understand. Is the family present?"

"No, my lady, they seldom are, preferring London society to the bleak Highlands."

"Nonsense! The Highlands are the most beautiful place on earth. Second only to the windswept beauty of the Outer Hebrides, naturally."

At last, Ruari had coaxed a smile from that chilly countenance. She pressed her advantage. "What did you mean about the Gordon's mother?"

But the strong face closed into a polite mask, and her lips set in a grim line. "I must be about my duties. Dinner at six, will that suit your ladyship? And an early breakfast, the Gordon says, as you mun be on your way by the dawn."

Ruari smiled her thanks. As she washed her face in the warm scented water in the ewer and basin and tidied her hair with the help of the small looking glass, she pondered the housekeeper's extraordinary reaction. Should she use one of her questions…? No. She thrummed with curiosity about Lochaber's answers to tonight's riddle. Not to mention the Wolf and Deer Stones over at Stittenham.

She brushed her dress down as best she could while still in it and straightened her shoulders for battle.

Sìneag arrived. "This is the rural Highlands, Miss Ruari. No sneaking off alone with a man in the dark."

"Surely a walk in the early twilight is unexceptional?"

Sìneag shook her gray head. "At least let me set off with you, and then I will peel back to the castle unobserved. I shall say you sent me back for an extra shawl." The maid eyed her. "You might show me the Picti stones tomorrow in the sun. I don't hold with calling spirits in the gloaming." The maid shuddered uneasily, then she rubbed her hip. "Besides, my old bones crave rest after all that jogging and jostling in the carriage."

"Oh, my poor faithful Sìneag! What am I doing to you?"

"Your mother was a worse trial, the old gods rest her beloved bones. Now, now. Squeezing me like that, you'll crack your corset."

"I'm not wearing one, my Sìneag."

The maid shook her head and muttered, "Of course you are not, Ruari the Turbulent of the Barra MacNeils."

Sìneag and Ruari collected Lochy, and the small party strolled along the sweet river path. The setting sun picked out every leaf blade, every green grass stem, and limned it in gold.

The old maid declared, "I'll leave you now, before the ghosties and beasties rise to torment my way back. Mind you return before full dark, Miss Ruari. They are a strange lot in this castle. Much unhappiness dwells here."

Ruari gave her a kiss, watched her tall form vanish into the twilight, and took Lochaber's arm.

The moon appeared low on the horizon, casting silvery-gold lights in the chuckling burn. Insects danced, making rings in the water. A squirrel chattered at them and skittered back up a tree.

Her heart picked up and her blood sang. "Question or stone first, Lochaber Gordon?"

"You delight me with your choices." Hoarse tone. A brave attempt at levity. His vivid hair caught fire from a stray sunbeam which had lost its way in the evenfall.

Everything took on an enchanted gleam. Shadows morphed into eerie shapes; a stump became a hunched dwarf; a shade slipped back behind a tree.

Ruari pitched her voice heavy and low, to blend with the present magic. "Lochaber Gordon, a question presses."

His strong hand grazed hers where it rested in the crook of his arm. She took that for encouragement. "A query about you hammers in my mind, from the time I first met you...and very much so since your dazzling display in the fight. All my notions of you—so cleverly created and fanned by you to fool the world, me included—have been so shaken up I hardly know which way is up."

"Are you attempting to slide in an extra question, using feminine charm and wiles?"

Ruari laughed. "*What* feminine charm and wiles? I only have myself, Lochaber Gordon. As you find me."

They walked on in companionable silence. Ruari wallowed in the sensation of his height and strength and proximity. Their bodies cleaved together as they walked.

At last, Lochaber said in a thick voice, "So ask your

question, Ruari MacDonald. This is your question for the Wolf and Deer Stones."

Wolf and deer. Oh, she could hardly wait to see them. But first—she must assuage her curiosity.

She halted them in their walk and drew Lochaber to a sturdy tree branch which grew horizontally out toward the stream, trailing leafy limbs in the shallows. She sat on the branch, and Lochy leaned against the tree trunk, eyes glinting. He put the unlit lantern on the ground and crossed his brawny arms over his chest. The burn leapt and glittered behind them.

Ruari inhaled and girded her loins for courage. The words rushed out before she could bite them back. "In India, you learned magical fighting techniques, which stir the blood and awe observers with your grace and self-mastery." She hesitated. The question would reveal her as much as Lochaber.

But the fresh Highland air, the magical twilight, lent her courage. "I wonder…did you also train in…*the arts of love*? Learn exotic movements, mastery of self? How to give and receive, heighten and extend pleasure?" *How* her heart smashed under her ribs! How her stomach clenched, waiting breathless for his response. Her thighs tensed and drew together under her walking gown.

Silence.

She whispered, "Lochaber?"

Did you also train in the arts of love? Learn how to extend pleasure?

This adorable purple-eyed wench was a pirate indeed.

A thief of his secrets.

His voice gritted as though he had swallowed sand. "What can you know of *the arts of love*? How can you even know such a phrase exists?"

"Perhaps my ancestors whispered it to me." Her tone firmed. "This is my fourth question." Her eyes blazed like dark pools, drowning him with their beauty and intensity. Her skin glowed alabaster. He felt like a ruffian, about to shatter that gentle composure. Stir notions he had no right to.

Blast this whole adventure! What could he admit to a gently bred young woman? How could he sully her virgin ears…?

"Lochaber. Remember my bright brain. Accord me the respect due to my fascination with other cultures, travel, experiences. *Remember my passion.*"

He did. Oh, he did. He swallowed. "Very well. Yes, I trained in *the arts of love*. Our bodies are intricate, clever, sensitive miracles. Using them for war or love, using them to the peak of their powers, is a form of worship, a kind of gratitude, for the gift of being alive…"

He had not meant to say so much. But her expression, the shape of her mouth! Her perfumed presence, blending with the sweet night air, ensnared him.

"You thrill my blood and send it racing in my veins, Lochaber." She stood up and moved close. His heart smashed like a war drum in his chest. The husk of desire in her voice tugged in his groin. So much for his vaunted self-mastery.

He burned to kiss her.

A small hand stroked along his stubbled jaw and slid down to rest on his chest, where his heart pulsed. "Show me," she whispered throatily.

He was undone. He must taste her again, this bright, passionate, rare flower of the wild, harsh Hebrides. He bent and brushed his mouth on those lips, wide and warm and lush. Her hands gripped his biceps.

He grasped her to him, feeling her trembling body shivering against his. Her desire lit a raging inferno searing in his blood. He kissed her hard, taking those plush parted lips offered to him so trustingly. He tipped her lips with his tongue, then slid inside her silky mouth, tasting her sweetness, demanding her response. His bold pirate maid darted her own slick tongue against his.

Her slender, vital form pressed against his body. Sparks lit over his skin. Her hands slid under his hair, down his neck, fingers dancing on his shoulders, his biceps and back. *Kamadeva!* He flamed for this woman. His cock strained against his trousers. She must feel it, pressing like an iron prong against her soft belly.

He touched a fingertip in the vulnerable skin behind her ear. Traced the pretty whorl down to her earlobe. Slid a seeking finger along her collarbone, stroking into her bodice. She whimpered delightfully.

He plunged both hands into her abundant, silky hair and cupped the back of her head as he leaned in for another kiss. He flirted with her mouth, touching, withdrawing, kissing that lush softness, enjoying the sensation of her body beginning to melt into him, to quiver and tremble with want and need. So passionate! So fierce in her response.

He burned to accede to her request, to show her *the arts of love*. With a supreme effort, he wrenched his imagination, and his hands, away. "Not here, my pirate. I want to love you in a room fit for a queen."

"Tonight…it's full of magic. The burn there sings of secrets and passion. Lochaber, why not show me…the preliminaries?" Her voice curled through him as seductively as the Dance of Veils. "Shall you kiss me at the castle, if outdoors is not to your taste?" Her eyes glowed like pieces of twilight sky fallen to earth, bright with desire—*Yes,* his brain and body shouted—but a pink blush bloomed in her cheeks and her eyes flashed with shock at her own boldness.

That hard resin of control deep inside reasserted itself.

He closed his eyes until he had achieved mastery of his rampaging desire. With deft movements, he smoothed her luxuriant hair and restored her person to a proper order. He growled, "Not this castle. Clàrsach Castle—my home—or the Gordon Castle Estate. The latter is closer."

She put a hand on her breast. "Two castles?"

He stared at the hand, his throat dry. "Several castles."

She opened her mouth to ask more, then paused, comically. "Ha! You have succeeded in distracting me most successfully, Lochy." Her voice wobbled, clearly still ravaged by passion.

His cock throbbed like a war horn, calling for action. *Lie down*, he ordered.

A surge of shouting echoed in the distance, far away. Lochaber's skin prickled.

She said, "That training in *the arts of love*. Who did you train with? Did you take exotic Indian ladies as lovers? Do you miss them, yearn for them still? Did you lose your heart, perhaps to an Indian princess, bedecked with gems?"

Did *jealousy* lace her tone?

"Those are questions five, six, seven, and eight. You will have to wait, thief of my blackened, worthless heart."

She tossed her head, her pretty lips in an angry line. "You adore making me wait."

He came closer, showing her a glimpse of danger, a promise of power and control. "And you will wait until the time comes to love you. Wait while I adore every inch of you, until you are screaming and ecstatic—and then will I satisfy you." He hesitated. *"I will make you mine, Ruari MacDonald. I promise you. I claim you. No other man shall have you."*

She studied him, rose mantling her cheeks. "The barbarian Highlander emerges." She gave him such a savage grin that his blood fired rockets once more.

He inhaled, collecting his shattered self-mastery. "Come then. The wolf and the deer await." With some difficulty, due to his still magnificent erection, he pulled the ancient, fraying map from his pocket. "Stittenham village is but a short step away."

As he turned to gesture the way, she reached down a hand and squeezed his left buttock. His blood leapt. His cock pulsed.

Kamadeva, but he loved her hands on him. "Stop that," he grunted, "or you will never see the wolf and the deer."

"I've already glimpsed the wolf. Now I want to see the stone pillar." Her hand slithered to the front of his falls, and she gave a mischievous giggle.

He coughed. He did not pretend to misunderstand her.

****

Ruari stretched forward to view the Picti-carved Wolf and Deer Stones, embedded in the ancient wall. Lochaber obligingly held the lantern closer for her, illuminating the clever design. His body heat slammed her senses. His warm breath tickled her neck. Her emotions whirled, and her thoughts scattered.

To anchor herself, she touched a fingertip to the wall and traced the curve of muscle and jaw in the image of the wolf. Different curves of muscle and jaw, looming just to her right, dominated her attention. *Wait while I love you. Wait while I adore every inch of you, until you are screaming and ecstatic...* She shuddered.

He jerked and looked up; she followed his frowning gaze. Away over the small hills, bright tiny pinpricks of fire blazed like a thousand fireflies. As she screwed her face to focus, a rumbling distant thunder shook the air. It sounded like angry, yelling voices. The pinpricks of fire grew larger.

She looked a query to Lochy. Before he could speak, she became aware of a thunder much closer—the clatter of a runaway carriage careening toward them.

"Watch out!" Lochaber pushed her behind him and bent his knees in a fighting stance, hand on the sword tucked in his belt. The carriage slewed to a halt, dust spraying around it in a cloud, horses rearing but brought rapidly under control by a firm hand. A cloaked figure pulled itself down from the coach with grunting effort and Gaelic cursing—in a panicky female voice.

The driver threw back her hood.

Chapter Seventeen

"Sìneag! By the Old Ones' grace, what ails you, woman?" Ruari blurted the harsh words more in fear than fright. She ran to her faithful maid and wedged a hand under her elbow. Sìneag bent over, her face an ugly red, gasping for air.

Lochaber was there in an instant, his strong arm supporting the choking maid, soothing her onto a low wall to rest.

She gasped, "The tenants are revolting."

He said suavely, "True. But most unkind of you to say so, Sìneag."

"Don't be a greater fool than yer mother birthed you, *a'bhalaich*." She heaved another breath, clutching Ruari's hand in a death grip. "A lad came—the duke arrives tonight—and the Earl of Kilmore with him! I've packed yer things, you and the lord's. Be gone!"

The maid half rose, gazing around wild-eyed at the flame-speckled country. "Ardross rises! They carry pitchforks and hammers, torches of fire."

"What do you mean, *lord*?" Ruari stared at Lochaber, whose brows snapped together. She left that mystery for the moment. "The tenantry protest?"

"Yes. Against the bitter clearances. This is the Duke of Tuath's castle, don't ye know it, and most of Ardross belong to him. He owns most of the north of the Highlands, now." The maid waved an angry fist. "The people have had enough cruelty. For decades, Highland families have been cleared for more blasted sheep, thrown on ships to the Americas, and Canada and Australia...some chose to cling to their homelands. Ten families are living in the graveyard, pulling weeds for sustenance, watching their bairns starve before them." Sìneag wrapped her arms around herself and rocked back and forth with a low, keening wail.

"What can we do?" Ruari whispered in horror.

Lochaber shook his head. "The Tuaths won't welcome my help. They don't forget the Jacobite uprising and which side the Gordons fought for—we marched for Bonnie Prince Charlie and Scotland. The traitor Tuaths sided with the English, goddamn their greedy, grasping souls, for it made them obscenely rich."

She swiped at his sturdy shoulder. "Not the Tuaths, you great *burraidh*! The tenants."

Lochaber's lips compressed. "This is not your fight."

Sìneag hissed, "Calm that fiery soul and get yourself in the carriage, Miss Ruari." She jerked her chin at Lochaber. "Take that buffoon with you—at least the man can fight—and be quit of here. Go, I tell you!"

"Sìneag, I'll help you into—"

"I'm not coming, Ruari, *mo chridhe*."

"*What?*"

Sìneag cupped Ruari's cheek. "The housekeeper— she is my kin. She came here when her son took a job with the factor yon." She smoothed Ruari's hair, in another rare display of affection. "I will stay and support the poor woman."

"Well, Sìneag, I must stay and support the MacNeils and the tenantry and strike a blow against wicked earls and dukes and all their evil, land-grabbing kind, making wealth on the broken backs of their starving people."

The maid looked to Lochaber. "Take her, and get out of here, Lochaber Gordon. She must not be discovered here. I fear for her life and safety—a bonny bargaining chip she would make between dukes and earls. She is the daughter of my heart, the womb and future of the MacNeils and the MacDonalds."

"*Womb of the MacDonalds?* Spare me! And don't be ridiculous, Sìneag, as if I'd leave—"

Whump! On a sudden, the world turned upside down. A hard arm gripped her across her rump, which poked out over a broad shoulder, her face dangling down a muscular back.

She gave a few experimental kicks to his hard stomach, which only clenched tighter, yielding not one iota. She punched him in the kidney.

He slapped her rump. "Behave." His voice was gravel.

Lochaber laid her gently on the carriage seat and pinned her with a brawny arm while he shuffled in close beside her. "Sìneag, tarry a moment."

The maid crept in and sat on the opposite seat, emotions battling for supremacy in her expression. Fear. Determination. Grimness. Overlaid with it all was a most satisfied glint in her eyes. "Ye need a man who can match your strength and will," the impossible woman declared.

"Not one, however, who mishandles me and gains his objective with physical strength rather than rational argument!" She struggled against that trunk-like bastion. As she did, her breasts pressed against the bunched muscles in his arm, sending thrills through her body.

With Lochaber, she could almost enjoy this close contact.

He snapped her a blazing glare. His arm shifted. Pressed. Heat shot to her lower belly. She gave him a hot stare from beneath her eyelashes. His lips snapped into a line. His eyes promised wicked revenge.

Lochaber cleared his throat. "My Lady Ruari, I give you a choice. If you must see more Picti stones, then we can travel through the night, northward to Tain, on the Dornoch Firth. There are many Picti artifacts in the region, and we should be far enough away to escape the trouble brewing here." He released his arm, brushed a hand over his face. "Or we can—"

They all waited.

"Yes?"

He mumbled into his hands. Ruari cocked a brow at Sìneag, who widened her eyes and shrugged, silently conveying a disdainful "*men!*"

Ruari ventured, "Or we can collect long, stout sticks here at Stittenham, for you to wreak your fighting havoc, or Sìneag and I can don men's clothes and wade into the fray, snatching swords, or perhaps I could find some bagpipes and play battle songs to stir the blood of the starving tenantry and make our enemies' knees quake in fear, or—"

Lochaber's voice overrode hers. Just as she was having fun. "Or," he said, fast and loud, "we can gallop fast to Invergordon, raise the ferryman, and make haste along the road through Nairn to…*Gordon Castle* on the Spey River. You will be safe there."

" 'Gordon Castle. You will be safe there,' " Ruari repeated. "You employ the same tone as one might when saying, 'There, you will have your head chopped off,' or

'There, you will be imprisoned for life, weaving flax into gold in a tower.' "

The maid glared. "Miss Ruari. Stop your frivolity. I know you have the soul of a warrior maid and fear no danger. It falls to those who love you to protect you. Go with the lord now, and I will see you anon."

Ruari was speechless for a moment. "Things must be desperate indeed for you to talk of love, my fierce friend."

The maid replied grimly, "That they are." A tear glistened on her withered cheek.

Shock speared Ruari's belly. Her throat thickened. The woman was invincible. Crying, now?

Lochaber fumbled in his pockets and pulled out a small purse. He opened it, gathering a handful of silver and gold in his palm. "Here. If you can join us in a few days, look for us at Shandwick or Rosemarkie. After that, try…Gordon Castle on the Spey. May your gods protect you, valiant Sineag of the MacNeils."

He poured the coins into her cupped hands. "I will protect your mistress with all the powers in my brain, my body, and my life."

The maid fixed him with a brilliant stare. "And you will give her the protection of your name."

Lochaber coughed. "There is no protection in that."

The maid looked mulish. "Promise me, for the bairn's sake. She is ruined else."

Bairn. Both Lochaber and Ruari spluttered. Ruari grabbed Sineag's hands. "Never mind that now. I choose Tain. I must see more Picti stones while I am in Easter Ross. Promise me you will not endanger yourself, Sineag MacNeil. Promise me you will come back to me. I need you, Sineag."

"Aye, well, we'll see what the Old Ones and the devil devise. Follow your heart, *mo chridhe*."

Lochaber leapt from the carriage in a smooth athletic movement and assisted the maid to disembark. He bowed. "I am honored to have met you, Sìneag of the fairies."

Ruari leapt out too and embraced her kinswoman. The maid dashed wetness from her cheeks with an impatient hand, smoothed Ruari's hair, then turned and walked away into the gathering dark, back toward Ardross Castle.

"Sìneag—the earl! He will harm you. Come with us."

The maid's pale face glimmered from the shadowy path. "That one will not recognize a servant. I'll be fine, Miss Ruari."

Lochaber clasped Ruari's elbow and assisted her back into the carriage. "Now, Miss MacDonald, make yourself comfortable. Try to sleep. We are going to gallop like the devil pursues us through the darkness. You may find it a little rough, but we must flee. Miss MacNeil is right. I learned something at Castle Ardross—the Earl of Kilmore's mother ran off with a Highlander when he was but a wee lad. He detests and blames us all. And you fleeing with me—"

"Oh! I see!—He is a slave to vengeance, then?"

He did not reply to her sally, instead plumping up soft tartan rugs and tucking them around her form. In the half dark, he froze, his gaze fastening on her lips. With a quick, soft movement, his lips brushed hers. A large, warm hand cupped her cheek. "You trust me so much."

"I trust myself, Lochaber, and all my instincts calm when I am with you. As though I am home in my spirit."

She hesitated. "And my blood thrills in my veins, and all my body softens and yearns for you."

He closed his eyes and said in strangled voice, "If you continue to say such things, my much-vaunted, finely honed self-control will shatter, and your maid—or the revolting peasants, or the Wicked Earl—will discover us still here at Stittenham, come the dawn."

She laughed, leaned forward and kissed him back, softly, deeply. She sat back and sighed. "How I've longed to do that!"

Lochaber groaned and ripped his body away from her. Before she had quite collected her wits, he had left the warm enclosed carriage interior and leapt up into the driver's seat high up at the front of the carriage. With a jerk and sway, the carriage set off at a cracking pace.

Ruari sat for a moment in the snug warmth, but curiosity and her hammering heart could not let her sit still. She squeezed her head and one shoulder from the window, wriggling with effort, the hard frame scraping fabric and the soft skin on her cheek. Her head knocked hard against the window frame as the carriage jolted. Ruari craned her head. Was that a last glimpse of Sìneag disappearing into the dusk?

Would she see that beloved face again in this life? This mad adventure of hers was changing more lives than her own.

She banged on the window frame. "Lochaber!"

"Yes?" The wind whipped the word back. Terse. Focused.

"I wish to sit with you up there."

"It's far too cold. Too rough. And you will distract me. It's dangerous, racing on unknown rough country roads in the dark."

"Well, I shall just climb up there then, through this window."

The carriage slewed to a stop. Lochaber jumped down, tore open the carriage door, grabbed a huge armful of rugs, and disposed them about her on the driver's box. When she was as well wrapped as a new cocoon, he took the reins and gave them an almighty crack.

Ruari snuggled closer.

This was a fine adventure.

****

Lochaber drove the carriage like a demon, urging the horses to their utmost, galloping over dark potholed roads. Pinpricks of light all over the countryside continued to rise and flare against the darkness, all weaving toward Ardross Castle.

A burst of fire in the distance. He called urgently to the horses to speed. He prayed he could get his fierce Ruari MacDonald to safety before she decided to join the fray—or before the fray joined them.

His eyes fixed on the road ahead. There—dodged a deep pothole. And narrowly kept to the sharp blind curve around this hill. Hellfire! Where had the road got to…There. He followed the thin ribbon of lighter-colored graveled mud which marked the track. It didn't deserve the epithet "road."

His companion was thankfully silent, allowing him to focus fully on his dangerous task. If the horses injured a fetlock in a pothole! If the carriage overturned, or broke a wheel, they would be in trouble.

He had the carriage lanterns lit, as two more fireflies of light in the landscape hardly counted for anything. They provided a weak golden glow of illumination.

A thunder of hooves shook the road ahead of their

escape. Lochaber looked around with frantic eyes. There. He slowed the carriage and pulled it into a clearing, sheltered from the road by a small copse of gnarly trees.

Not a moment too soon. He dismounted and stroked the horses to silence as a large troupe of uniformed soldiers galloped in the direction of Ardross Castle. Silver moonlight gleamed on polished buttons, boots, and long-barreled guns.

In the darkness, he and Ruari locked eyes. Their stares remained fixed on each other until the pounding hooves had passed.

"No, Ruari, we are not going back to the battle," he said before she could speak. "I swore to your terrifying maid Sineag MacNeil that I would protect you with my life."

"You could speak with the Duke of Tuath. Speak up for the tenants. Where is your courage, Lochaber Gordon?"

That stung. How he despised cowardice.

She tossed her head. "In fact, I am the cousin of the MacDonald. I too can advocate for the tenantry. Who better than me?"

Lochaber reached up, gripped her arm where it emerged tender-skinned from her tartan cocoon. "Ruari, no. They will not hear you. The Duke of Tuath, like his good friend the Earl of Kilmore, cares naught what you or anyone can say. They are determined to clear the land for sheep, and nothing will sway them from their fixation on gaining yet more riches."

He climbed up onto the box and embraced the large warm wooly heap of rugs, which somewhere within contained the woman of his most fevered dreams. "I know how this hurts you to leave them, my Ruari. I understand your pride and your bitter frustration. I understand your urge to justice and to protect your people."

"Do you? Excellent, we will be on our way, then, back to Ardross."

He shook her a little. "Listen, love. We play the long game. We will make ourselves safe and secure, then save who we may."

Silence.

Lochaber took a breath. "The very long game must be the better course. We could fight this battle here and now, maybe dying, maybe not, maybe winning, or not. We could lurk and loiter and assist the remaining, starving tenants to pick up the pieces and start again with nothing. We can assist what Highlanders and Hebrideans we can with bread and alms."

Ruari's cheeks shone cream in the near-darkness. Her night-violet eyes watched him gravely as she listened.

Fortified with the very sight of her, he let the urgent words tumble forth. "A better game is to support them with education and skills, to equip them to grow and change as the world changes. It is a terrible thing, to leave your beloved homeland and carve out a new place in a new world. But don't you see, Ruari, my angel, that we Scots are set up to accomplish just that? We are a tough, brave, determined race, with a strong streak of practicality that marries with a poetic imagination— exactly the traits needed to create the world anew."

She studied him, melting his bones with her caressing gaze. Her eyes flashed as the idea caught. He saw the moment his words seized her imagination and created a fire.

Her words came drowsy and thick as new honey. "I should have known you for a visionary and an adventurer from the first, Lochaber 'Lucky' Gordon, from what little I knew of you. You pretend to be a cool, unimaginative man of business. Yet you had the brains and courage to make your fortune in India. You are a man who sees and who dares. Very well then. Once more, I place my trust in you. Take me to Tain, though it shreds my heart to abandon these people."

Lochaber kissed her temple, a small piece of exposed alabaster skin peeping between dark braids and the tartan rugs. He clicked his tongue to the horses, jogged the reins, and moved the equipage from the copse out onto the road. He resumed their galloping pace, alert for soldiers and fleeing rebels in addition to potholes, blind corners, fallen trees and other road blocks, straying sheep, and any other threat which might disturb his Ruari's peace and safety.

His chest swelled. He felt like a warrior of old, protecting this woman with every skill at his disposal—including his most talented persuasion. Whew. Thank all her old gods of landscape and adventure. That had been close.

He expected Ruari to snooze and lean against him as they thundered through the night. She foiled his expectations. She sat tall and bright beside him, her quick intelligence analyzing the countryside, attentive to dangers, alert to the progress of the battle.

Fires flared up in the distance; shouting and battle cries peppered the air; the distant crack and boom of guns split the night; screaming wound like threads of terror around their senses.

He put an arm around her to comfort her. He knew

it tore her heart to leave her maid. Her courage astounded him.

In their silence, he had time to think, and unwelcome thoughts intruded.

He must tell her his secret, and soon. She trusted him, while he tricked her in the most underhand manner.

He was echoing the family pattern that he had left home to escape. Had sworn against ever repeating. And now, back on his native soil, he was doomed to mimic the mistakes of his father, as though the gods mocked him for his own harsh judgement of that roué.

He would tell her. At Tain perhaps. Or once they were safe at Gordon Castle. No, he must tell her before that. His stomach writhed in pain. He clenched his jaw. He could not bear to see her disdain, to witness her chagrin, to see the light in her eyes spark to fury when she understood how thoroughly he had seduced and fooled her.

Soon.

But not yet.

A terrible desire flickered through his brain. He would take her first, make love to her, claim her. And then she could not turn away from him, no matter the provocation.

He was such *a bastard*.

He smiled grimly, sick to his gullet with himself. He would deserve whatever punishment a furious Roderick MacDonald chose to mete out.

And with these lovely, agonizing thoughts, Lochaber beguiled the weary miles to Tain.

The carriage at last began the descent into the ancient stone village. Luckily, they were able to knock up a tavern with a stable and inn attached and gratefully entered the ale and pastry-scented warmth.

"Just the one room left, sir, our finest room, overlooking the grand bay. You and your wife will be most comfortable there. And shall you be wishful of a bath and meal? Here, Morag! Look after these travel-weary folk. Hot water. Pie and ale."

Lochaber agreed to it all.

Exhausted as he was—fully lusting after that pie and ale—his brain flooded with images of one room left, one bed between them. One bath before the fire.

Heat slammed into his chest and shot straight to his cock.

Chapter Eighteen

They'd finished their hearty warming meal.
Stretched their legs with a walk in the moonlight,
through the village and along the firth. Ruari was bone
weary, but her brain jangled with questions. And now, at
last, they returned to the warmth of the inn and climbed
the timber staircase, the risers worn hollow with age.

Lochaber shut the door to their room and turned to
face her.

Bagpipes immediately began blowing in her head. A
marauding flock of butterflies flipped and somersaulted
in her belly. She reached a hand behind her and lowered
herself into a tapestry chair by the fire.

A knock on the door. Lochaber hesitated, hand on
the doorknob.

"The lady's bath, sir," said a woman's voice.

Lochaber practically ripped the door off its hinges.
He opened the door wide, his eyes fixed on Ruari's,
blazing like one of the battle fires. The publican's wife
and a girl cast from the same mold entered, bearing
steaming jugs of water in each strong fist. A lanky youth
followed with a bronze hip bath, which he placed by the
fire, drawing fluffy towels from his shoulder and laying
them on the plump bed.

"Will that be all, sir?" the woman asked.

Lochaber cleared his throat. His voice husked.
"Wine. Fruit, if you have it. Scones. I thank you."

The procession departed. Ruari didn't move. How she longed for that hot water! But…

Another knock. The youth reappeared, focused entirely on his shaking tray, bearing wine, stewed apples, scones, jam, and thick cream. He placed the tray on a small table. The lad bowed and then smiled like a constellation when Lochaber handed him a coin.

The silence in the room thickened. Lochy rummaged on the dressing table. "Here. Small cakes of scented soap, with flowers pressed into them. A soft washcloth." He pulled a small table over to the bath and placed the items on it.

More silence. Lochaber said, tone gravel, "I shall go downstairs and wait in the bar. Drink an ale." His eyes had not left her face. His voice wobbled like the uncertain youth's tray. Sank to a whisper, threaded with need. "Or, as you have no maid at present, I would be happy to wash your lovely body, your beautiful form, your rounded arms…"

Perhaps it was her weariness. Perhaps it was the tremble in his voice. Perhaps it was this whole mad adventure, where all the rules changed every day. She trusted him this far. She yearned to find the inner Lochaber, and perhaps this would create the intimacy to give her the key to him. More than that. Simpler than that. She wanted to feel his strong, sure hands on her flesh. She needed touch for her battered, bereft heart. She sizzled and burned for him.

Ruari stood, and Lochy's eyes widened. She reached around and began to unbutton her dress.

"Wait." His hoarse tone scraped from his throat. He poured two small glasses of golden wine and handed her one. "Please. Allow me."

"I can manage. You can watch."

She took a swallow or two of her wine, then set the glass on the table next to the bath. Lochaber gulped half his glass. They locked gazes. Ruari started with the first button, slipping it from its hole and untying the ribbons holding the dress together. She shed the outer layers, tartan pelisse, dress, and petticoats, and flung them over a chair. Lochaber watched every movement with hot, hungry eyes, devouring her with his gaze. That incandescent stare called forth a response, burning fire under her skin, sending forks of lightning shooting to her most intimate parts.

She stood, shivering slightly, in her long semi-transparent lacy chemise, allowing his gaze to eat her.

And then, with a graceful, fluid movement, she stripped her underthings from her body, stepped to the bath, and lowered herself gratefully into its warm embrace. "Oh!" The sigh burst from her as the warm water lapped over and around the skin on her legs, bottom, waist, and chest. "Oh! Mmm." She closed her eyes in bliss.

Lochaber's voice rumbled bass. "You are exquisite. The most beautiful woman I have ever beheld."

A delicious trickle of warm, scented water ran down the back of her neck. She bent forward and parted her hair. More water. "Lovely!" she crooned. She should be embarrassed. Together, here, like this? It felt only special, magical, perfect.

A fat sponge dipped in the bath, then ran over her shoulders, sending scented bubbles dancing down her skin, down her arms, and over and between her breasts. The soft, warm rasp of the sponge was both soothing and enlivening. Lochy's warm breath tickled her ear as he bent closer.

"By all the gods," he croaked. "Your gleaming skin undoes me. Your sweet form, healthy and muscular with work and activity—a man's most potent dream." He cleared his throat. "Your bubbies, bobbing there on the water. Ruari. My Ruari. I cannot resist you."

From behind her, a long finger stroked circles on the round muscle of her shoulders, then tickled slowly down her spine to the cleft of her buttocks. She waited, breath hitching in her throat, her skin tingling with awareness.

The lazily stroking fingers circled the delicate skin there, then spiraled back up to caress her upper arms, front, and back.

His large hand brushed her bosom. Sensation sparked on the tender skin and forked straight to the apex of her thighs, softening and heating under her. A fingertip grazed her nipple, eliciting a soft moan from her throat. His hand enclosed her breast and softly squeezed. The other hand reached around from behind her. He held both bubbies in his large, tender hands, and gently jogged them in the warm water, the silky flow slipping through his fingers and adding a sensory slide as he caressed and explored the shape of her.

Those clever fingers slid silkily down her thighs. The whole of her sizzled and throbbed, her skin sensitive and lit with wanting. Lochaber reached over. His body rested hard and hot against her back. His fingers stroked up and down her legs, along her inner thighs, drawing them apart. Finally, his finger touched just where she needed him, aching with need.

"Lochaber. I know nothing about you," she whispered. "The more questions you answer, the greater mystery you become." His fingers stilled, resting on her rounded lower belly. "But my body trusts you. I trust you. With you, I feel safe. Home."

"Ruari," he murmured into her ear, the deep vibration singing through her blood. She curled her toes. He kissed her neck with soft, sucking kisses that speared desire racing through her veins. Her need, throbbing and pulsing in the core of her, increased in urgency with each kiss.

He shifted his hands again and stroked and caressed her skin, her shoulders, her bosom, her waist, her thighs. He came around the bath and drew her left leg up out of the water, kissing down its length. She jumped and shrieked with sudden, shocking sensory thrill as he sucked her big toe. He met her gaze, his eyes heavy-lidded, gleaming dark honey-peat with desire, and grinned like a shark. He licked over each toe, sending tiny delicious thrills from her feet stabbing into her groin. He carefully replaced her leg in the water, drew out the other leg, and repeated the process.

Ruari was coiling with urgent need now, close to exploding, or shrieking, or grabbing the man and pulling him in with her. He stood and took a mouthful of wine, handing her own glass. She swallowed a little, and he bent over her, kissing her mouth, sliding and exploring with an insistent, velvet tongue until she was boneless with wanting.

At last! He slid those clever fingers down her body, touched her intimate parts, pressed a hard, long finger inside her. Slick silk and warm water mingled, the beautiful friction of his sliding finger making her arch up in the water. The heel of his hand pressed her mound, creating an aching flare of half wanting, half satisfaction.

He held her strong against him with his left arm,

supporting her as he plundered and delighted her body. He circled his finger on her sensitive crest, and she jerked and cried out in wordless desire.

She was aflame, a lightning storm, a constellation of stars bursting into fragments in the night sky. And then she went entirely limp, gasping, resting against his strength.

Lochaber gathered her up from the bath and encased her in a soft fluffy towel. He rubbed her warm and dry, carefully patting dry her hidden places—under her arms, under her bosom, behind her ears. Then he wrapped her in a fluffy dressing gown and took her to sit by the small table.

"What about you?"

His trousers strained against the limits of the fabric. His cheeks were hollow and his jaw a monument to control.

"I can wait. Here. Drink some wine. Nibble a scone. Then sleep."

"I will. But then I must see you, Lochaber Gordon. Do not deny me."

The bump in his throat moved as he swallowed. His eyes burnt dark. "Eat first, my lovely. I can deny you aught."

Once she had repaired her strength, enjoying the soft crumbling scone, the thick silky cream, the fat dollop of raspberry jam, she pulled him up to standing.

She ran her hand over his jaw, enjoying the rasp of whiskers. His eyes glinted down at her, dangerous, enticing, yet soft.

"I am a pirate maid. I do not take kindly to being plundered so. Now, I take my revenge."

He laughed into her kiss. He stood obediently,

watching her intently as she slowly disrobed him. She pulled his jacket from broad, strong shoulders, running her fingers over their shape. Next, the embroidered waistcoat, the hint of exotic birds and flowers hidden in its embroidery, much like the secrets hidden within the man himself—hidden in plain sight.

Lochaber Gordon clad only in linen shirt and trousers was a magnificent sight. His muscular form pressed against the white linen, hinting at power and strength. The shirt narrowed where it tucked into his trousers, now pushed out at an angle like a half-raised castle portcullis.

She kissed his warm flesh with each part revealed as she undid each button, spread her fingertips through curling chest hair.

Lochaber groaned and took over the proceedings. He held her away with one hand, wrenching his shirt from his trousers and unbuttoning his falls with the other. Releasing her, he tore the shirt from his body and pushed his trousers over his mammoth erection and threw them across the room. He allowed her a moment to survey him in all his majestic naked pride, then he scooped her up and tumbled her to the bed.

He lay on top of her, taking most of his weight on his elbows, clipped on either side of her. He glinted down at her with a fiery gaze and gritted, "Now, my lady—"

But Ruari hooked a leg around his, and using her body weight as leverage—and the gift of surprise—she flipped him onto his back, with her on top. She snarled down at him. Then she smiled saucily and slid her body experimentally up and down the length of him.

Lochaber's eyes widened, and his whole face softened in shocked, grateful astonishment.

Excellent. Despite all his unknown romantic adventures with exotic princesses in hot climes, she could surprise him. The trouble was, she had no idea what to do next. She laid herself gently along his length, reveling in her softness sinking into and resisting his hard, honed weapon of a body. Her fingers explored him, lightly caressing small scars and notches here and there on his skin, white and soft in places, and harder and freckled where his pale Scots skin had been exposed to harsher suns than he was born to.

For a while, he lay under her ministrations, groaning under his breath as she touched secret, sensory parts of him: his soft pink nipples, the hollow in his throat, the shadow where hips met belly. She slid a cautious, wondering palm along his hot silky shaft, and he jerked and bucked, an oath splitting from his throat.

He writhed a little under her touch, only muttering, "Yes, yes, more."

Suddenly, he had had enough. All pretense at her physical mastery and control disappeared as he gripped her hard and flipped her onto her side, lying alongside her. His kisses burned like fire, inflaming her already engorged intimate self. He stroked and rubbed until every muscle was jelly, then circled and stroked her cleft until she jerked her hips up in invitation, crying out with inarticulate noises of desire.

"I want you, Ruari MacDonald," he whispered.

She could only nod. When it became clear he would not proceed without her express consent, she summoned words from some deep part of herself. "Then take me, please, Lochaber. I want you. I want only you, to show me what love is between a man and a woman. My body knows you, trusts you, *desires* you. Yes, *yes*!" She shrieked the final yes as Lochaber drove himself on top of her, his large hand squeezing her buttock tight.

His mouth lowered to hers. His kiss was soft as a new spring breeze, then warm as mid-summer. He rubbed his hot, silky, engorged manhood over her seam. She spread her legs, opening for him. He slid in a section, waited while her muscles strained, then flowed around him. Carefully, he slid within her.

"So big!" she murmured and his manhood pulsed.

"How are you faring? Does this hurt?"

"No!" she lied. "I want you, Lochaber. This feels…marvelous, a miracle, so…joyful."

They moved and rubbed each other until they had the right position. Lochaber began a rhythm that made every cell in her body shriek and clamor with sparks, with joy, like a band of bagpipers blowing hard in a red-gold dawn.

The friction was like every dream come true. The size of his body, his manhood, his taut muscles, the athleticism of his body. The relentless tension built and coiled inside her. Her heart swelled. Then her mind filled with starbursts as a momentous climax took her. Lochaber shouted, pumped twice more, then tensed, making to withdraw from her body.

"No! Stay!" She gripped him hard.

He said, "Ruari!" and then his body wracked as he pulsed inside her. For a moment, he collapsed on top of her, almost too heavy to bear.

She wrapped her arms around him and held him tight. She felt him shake in her arms, overcome with a strong emotion. She held him and let him ride out the storm. Together. Warm, loving feelings poured through her like warm honey-peat whisky on a brisk day.

Then the infuriating man pushed himself up, sat on the side of the bed, head in his hands, his whole body slumped as though defeated.

Hurt and rejection smashed through her, as though she had been downed by a wave she didn't see coming.

"You don't look like a man whose dream just came true." She tried to keep the pain from her voice, but the words emerged from her mouth like a whip.

"Ruari. God, what have I done?" He turned to her and hissed, "I spent my seed inside you."

"And it felt so right. Perfect." What ailed him?

"Don't you know how children are begotten, my Ruari? Women are cocooned in shocking ignorance, but you are a countrywoman, and—"

"Don't be ridiculous! Of course I know." She put a tentative hand on his shoulder. His skin jumped as though bitten. She took her hand away. Put it back. Curse the stubborn man, with all his secrets. "Like all men, you believe your seed so powerful, so indestructible, that one lovemaking is all it takes to create a life? Ha!"

He faced her then. She shrank back when she saw the anger blazing on his countenance.

"Once is enough, do you understand? Once!"

She screwed her eyes up. "What is this scene all about, Lochaber Gordon? What has happened to you?" She hesitated. *Courage, daughter of the MacNeils and MacDonalds.* "Do you have a child out of wedlock already?"

His back stiffened to ice-block rigidity. His neck and jaw clenched so hard he might pull a muscle.

She thought for a long moment the answer to her question would have to wait for the next stone, but then...

Muffled words. Muttered curses.

Then he raised his head and looked her square in the eye. "No, Ruari. You see, *I am that child.* And I have vowed never to inflict my circumstances on another living creature."

While she gaped, he rose from the bed and stalked back and forth across the small bedroom. "I apologize for being so uncontrolled, so rude and uncivilized as to so completely lose all self-mastery. Clearly, I am not myself with you, Ruari of the MacDonalds. *We must never do this again.* I pray that nothing has come of this night." He rubbed his hair, said as if to himself, "I'm tired, that's all. Tired."

I pray that nothing has come of this night.

Except one foolish woman's broken heart.

He pinned her with a golden-eyed glare. "We will not do this again, we will not speak of this again, even at your bedamned stones. I curse myself. I'll sleep in the tap room."

"Lochaber—" she pleaded.

But the door slammed behind him.

In a small eddy of air, he was gone.

****

Ruari hugged her knees to her chest, hurt and dazed. She couldn't deny it. She felt most cruelly used. Ravaged, afloat with love and desire, and then cursed and abandoned. Treated as though she were the villain in the piece, rather than a longed-for lover. And men said *women* were mercurial creatures.

She half rose—she could face him down, now in the taproom. His explanation had been worse than useless. *I am that child.* His hurt and anger had shredded the air.

They could have it out, here and now. Don't the let

the sun go down on an argument.

But by all the old gods of sea and land, she was so deathly tired.

Maybe if they both slept, they could discuss it with clearer heads. His words snapped back like a whip in the wind. *We will not do this again, we will not speak of this again, even at your bedamned stones.*

She should respect that.

She listlessly picked up her dress and arranged it tidily over the chair. Smoothed her underwear. Hung his so-hastily discarded garments and placed his boots neatly together under the window.

As she handled his clothes, inhaling their unmistakable Lochaber scent, her private parts twanged with a pleasant ache.

Wait. His clothes?

A feminine shriek sounded in the passage. The door flew open.

A bubble of happiness welled in her chest—he'd come back—but no.

Lips set, a mad flush on his cheeks, Lochaber snatched shirt, trousers, boots and flung out again. The bang of the door shook the hotel to its foundations.

Bitter humor swirled in her belly. She hoped he'd actually stepped naked into the taproom.

She glared at the door. *Never discuss the most important night of her life?* Well, pirate maid Ruari MacDonald had not agreed to anything so meek and cowardly.

She brightened. *He* might be used to throwing his weight around with his minions, but he did not fully understand a warrior woman of the Scottish Hebrides.

A fierce grin enlivened her countenance, and her

heart jerked in her ribs. The battle lines could be drawn anew.

Her life and her heart were at stake. She would not lie down meekly for anyone, not even the man who currently turned her whole life upside down, until she was living the most shining adventure she had ever dared to dream.

Draw your best weapons, Lochaber Gordon. Ruari MacNeil MacDonald of Leòdhas is coming for you.

Chapter Nineteen

"These bannocks and local honey are delicious, are they not?" The truth was, they stuck in her throat. She swallowed down another yeasty lump of bread and honey.

"I am delighted they meet with your approval." Stiff. Cold. He still would not meet her eyes, apart from one swift, melting, assessing stare as she walked into the tiny breakfast parlor. He cleared his throat. "Are you well, this morning, Miss MacDonald, after the alarms and rough ride of yester evening?"

Her knife clattered to her plate. She stared at his tense, averted countenance in disbelief. "I did enjoy our *wonderful* ride last night." She waited. Nothing.

Fine. Get out the sharp swords. "It was my first such mounting." She softened her tone, laced it with sweetness. "And my heart leaps that I shared my first wild gallop with you Lochaber Gordon."

A burning flush crept up his neck to meld with his flaming hair. His gaze remained fixed on his plate. A tiny pulse twitched in his tight jaw.

She summoned her courage and fired her final thrust. "But being my first, perhaps I am more prone to hurt than one should be. Perhaps it is usual for a gentleman to depart in moody anger after the event. Leaving the damsel distressed and confused."

He did regard her then. Wounded deep brown eyes.

His expression! One part guilty regret, one part angry pride, all overlaid with simmering, urgent desire.

The sweet honey suddenly rocketed around her veins. She spiked with mad energy. He cared!

His gravel voice melded with the sugar racing in her blood. "I beg your pardon. I have misused you in an unforgiveable manner."

"I don't want your apology, you great *burraidh*!"

He ignored her. "This morning, I'd best take you to Inverness and your brother. The long way around, via the Black Isle. And hope no lasting damage has been done from last night's work." His nostrils flared. His lips compressed in a bitter line.

She licked a finger with the tip of her tongue and slid him a smirk. "*Last night's work.* You refer to the naked apparition in the taproom, I surmise?"

He ground his teeth. "Don't be a fool."

Her playful energy left her, replaced by roiling, restless fury. "So. Like all the best rakes, you would take me and then abandon me. Like all the foolish women before me, I believed your words of love and desire..." She stopped. There had been no words of love. No promises. He had not betrayed her or lied to her. She grabbed a bannock from her plate and stumbled blindly from the room, down a long hallway and out the back door of the inn. She needed air, and solitude, and— really, she needed to play her bagpipes on the battlements of Callanish Castle, watching her seal-sisters play and leap in the dawn.

For the first time, she was assailed by such an overwhelming wave of homesickness for her island home, her brother and tenants, and her familiar misty horizons between sea and sky, that she bent over, gasping for breath. Hot tears sprang from her eyes, stinging their way down her cheeks.

She marched smartly away, dreading now for Lochaber to find her and wheedle and coax her around. Her pain was too great. She race-walked through the village, all her instincts taking her legs toward the loch, the Dornoch Firth. The brisk air and rapid movement eased her breaking heart, a very little. She rubbed the salt tears from her eyes and cheeks, loath for any morning walkers to see her so vulnerable.

At last! She feasted her eyes on the sea loch and the stretch of blue ocean beyond. Not *her* sea, but in her desperate need, she told herself that all seas were one, and perhaps those seals and dolphins knew hers…

Ruari sat by the gently lapping loch, basking in its soothing, familiar music. Her mind circled to her predicament and lurched away in pinpricks of pain. Fingers tight on her thighs, she fought the hurt. In the distance, the smooth heads of dancing dolphins sparked a tiny flare of wonder. Her breathing slowed and calmed.

You can't give up now. Just like the mystery of the Picti stones, she must persist, she must unravel the secrets of the man she had chosen. The gentle waves spoke in their soft sea words, infusing her with determination and fresh courage.

He had admitted one fact, as large and looming as Callanish Castle. He was a bastard, and that had cast a great shadow over his whole life. Perhaps his admitting that fact to her had torn something open within him that he had kept locked away, and now he floundered in a world of dark confusion and panic. His rejection issued from an old, deep hurt.

Come now, Ruari MacNeil MacDonald. This is the

fight of your life—and you retreat at the first defeat? Disgraceful! She even found a grin. She called up, loud and clear in her mind, the rousing song of the Highland pipes calling the MacNeil battle tunes. Her flesh pricked out in goosebumps, and small hairs stood up along her arms and the back of her hairline.

March on! She leapt to her feet with the belting battle chorus of her imaginary bagpipes.

In the center of the village, silhouetted against the pink-streaked morning sky, rose the unmistakable peak and spire of the village church. Didn't Lochaber mention something about a Picti stone in the Tain churchyard?

****

Ruari bent over the stone, suffused with the wonder and awe always generated in her by Picti artifacts. The Ardjachie Stone bore, intriguingly, more than thirty irregular cup marks, a spoked wheel, and an inverted L-shape. *Yes.* The carvings could speak of a radiant planet in a star-filled sky, a defined arrow showing direction.

"Is this a star map, my ancestors?" she whispered. She clenched her fists. "But I need more! I must see the Picti beast, on the steles near to Aberdeen. What can that be, but a stylized constellation?"

A shadow detached itself from a dark stone buttress of the ancient church and covered part of the stone.

"I guessed I'd find you here. Eventually." The rich deep voice vibrated through her body. Her skin sizzled with tiny needles.

She whirled to face him. Clenched her hands by her hips. Jerked her chin skyward and pursed her mouth in a challenging twist.

"It's not just the potential child," he said. "I have a mission. An ugly mission. *Vengeance.*"

231

She blinked. Lowered her hands. Frowned. "Revenge? On whom, and why?"

Lochaber gestured to an old wooden bench curving around an alder tree, scented with flowering herbs growing rampant underneath. She sat, far enough away from him that she could study his countenance. And just beyond his reach, should he try to flummox her with physical caresses.

"The next place I had intended to take you, Castle Gordon, on the mouth of the Spey River. The estate is owned by the Duke of Gordon." He fixed an intent dark stare on her. "My father."

Her eyes jolted wide open. "You are the *son of a duke*?" She rose and gave him an ironic bow. "Your Grace. Of course you may deflower the daughters of lesser Scots nobles. That is your *droit de seigneur*, is it not, the alleged right of a feudal lord to have sexual congress with a vassal's bride on her wedding night, except you got one thing wrong, *Your Grace*, it was not my wedding night. Was it? Just like the bloody English, your model—"

"Ruari!" He jumped to his feet. Gripped her upper arms.

Her chest heaved as she battled to suppress the scorching tears.

He shouted, no doubt to penetrate the clamoring in her ears. "I am *his natural son*. My mother is his housekeeper."

The noise in her ears dimmed. "His natural son. Yes, of course. You said you were a bastard. And you are."

Lochaber snorted in bitter amusement at her sally. "His eldest son. My father has not married, will never marry. He refuses to bring my mother to wife, even though she has been his mistress for more than thirty years and borne all his four children."

"Oh, Lochaber." His pain pierced her anger. Pity wrenched her stomach.

He still gripped her hard. "The dukedom will become extinct on the death of my father. Most of his wealth and estates will devolve to my cousin. That puling wretch is legitimate, but via the female line. No title for him." His face paled, and his eyes glittered. "I mean to see them both ruined before my father goes to his much-deserved end."

A pang smote Ruari. She did not know this embittered man that faced her in the little churchyard. This was a new creature, possessed with the flame of vengeance.

"You cannot blame your father," she ventured. "Look how it happened with us! You are a child of love, Lochaber Gordon."

He twitched, but the pale, desperate, set expression on his face lingered.

Certainty flared within her. "As will ours be created from love, if I was lucky enough last night to conceive *your child*."

He jerked as though struck by a sizzling bolt of lightning. "You cannot wish for that! I tell you, the life of a bastard is a most miserable one, disdained by even the meanest stable lad who was actually born in wedlock, subject to taunts and bullying, and then when grown! Passed over for any preferment or promotion, tainted by the shame of my getting, when that had nothing whatever to do with a man's talents or abilities! I am akin to those born with a hideous birthmark or harelip or crippled limb that is not one's fault—I was branded by that stain for my entire life!"

"Yet look at the man that has made you!"

He shuddered and knocked his forehead with the palms of both hands. "I had to learn everything, gain everything, the hard way. And now all that childhood ill-treatment, all that adult discrimination, has cracked and blackened into a powerful call for revenge on he who willfully created this situation—my father—and he who will benefit through no effort of his own—my cousin."

"Lochaber. All this has made you a fighter. A man with pride and strength and compassion. A man with imagination and entrepreneurial spirit that leaps into the wider world. A man who…who I can love. Be proud of the warrior you are—for you have made yourself into a work of art, Lochaber Gordon."

He stood tall, there in the churchyard, gazing at her in stunned disbelief. His eyes glittered—*with unshed tears*?

"*Take me*, Lochaber Gordon," Ruari whispered, in a deliberate echo of last night. "Take me to meet your father, your mother, your siblings. I long to meet your family. This is Scotland. We hold all our family dear, within wedlock and without." She stepped close to him, ran her cool hand down his flushed, heated cheeks. "You have made of yourself an exceptional man, a fine man. But you are made from the Scots Highlands, and I know that part longs to be acknowledged too. Recognize your history and your blood." She stroked his hair. "I will be with you, when you do."

For a moment, he relaxed into her soothing, stroking touch. Then he marshalled all his anger and pulled away. "I am determined on my vengeance. We return to

Inverness this day. You will go home from there."

Anger pierced her diaphragm. "Have you forgotten why we ran? Would you have me married to that slimy cold earl?"

"Your brother will protect you."

"He cannot, if my cousin is determined on selling me."

He closed his eyes. His face was all hard bone: cheekbones, jaw, forehead. "You cannot marry a bastard." His voice cracked.

Ruari laughed. Victory! He had finally uttered the unspoken word which hovered between them. *Marriage.* "The Earl of Kilmore is a greater bastard than you, any day. Come, take me to your sisters. I yearn to meet them."

"It would not be suitable."

"I am not a *suitable* woman, Lochaber Gordon, or had you forgot? I interest myself in unwomanly, intellectual pursuits—the fascinating Picti. I give my maidenhood to a man who captures my heart but does not dignify our love with any offer of marriage. How can you recommend convention to me?"

His harsh features had softened, just faintly. She aimed another shaft at his flinty heart. "You are the only man who has understood me, at all. The only man who has enabled me to indulge my burning curiosity, my need to research and understand Scotland's mysterious and vibrant history. I will not leave you in your hour of need. I will stand by you, while you seek to reconcile these divided parts of you."

He swallowed. His voice gritted. "How can you be so wise, my friend?"

My friend.

And they were. Friends. Lovers. Kindred souls.

The Highland pipes in her heart blew a rousing chorus. "Because I too have suffered in my bid to find selfhood. All of us who seek our own path, who hear the skirl of different bagpipes, we all suffer exclusion by the group. It activates our deepest fears. The human left out on the dark and cold will surely be eaten by predators."

"Unless he becomes one."

"No, Lochaber. He might just create a new path, that serves humanity. He creates it alone, but then those that follow after are healthier, happier, and stronger." She cupped his cheeks. "Would you trade your years in the East India Company, then, for the conventional, comfortable life as the legitimate son of a duke?"

Suddenly, his whole expression lightened. "Our positions are reversed. Now who advocates for a shining future!"

How good it was to hear his laugh ring out, joyful and merry.

He rasped, "You are a witch!" And then he held her as though she were made of delicate, painted porcelain and lowered his lips onto hers.

Ah, this kiss. His warm lips stroked hers, saying all the passion and love he could not. She kissed him back, glad and grateful and smiling into his mouth, stroking and tangling her tongue with his. Maybe nobody had ever said words of love to this proud man, so he did not know how. He might know how to *make* love, *express* love with lips and hands, body and strength, but not *say* the words of love.

"I will teach you," she murmured into his willing mouth.

He scooped her up, nestling them both back on the

bench under the alder tree. He placed her on her lap, his mammoth erection pressing hard into her soft bottom, and plunged back into a sizzling, passionate kiss. His clever fingers pulled at the lacings of her bodice, and then trailed inside over her tender skin, until they circled and flicked the aching peaks of her nipples.

She ran eager hands over his bulky arms, his shoulders, down his back. Tickled the soft skin at the nape of his neck and welcomed his shuddering response.

His mobile lips closed on her once more, demanding, plundering, calling her own passion thrumming and thundering in her veins as she kissed him back.

"Hm-hmm." The sound of a manly throat clearing penetrated Ruari's dazzled consciousness. Lochaber broke the kiss. She pressed her face into his body, peeping over his shoulder as her hands worked fast to reassemble her disordered front lacings.

Oh dear! The priest. The Church of Scotland ministers were notoriously Calvinist and strict—would he assault their ears with a fire and brimstone sermon? She was accustomed to the high-spirited Catholicism of her beloved islands, and many Presbyterians dwelt there too. All priests, regardless of denomination, would frown on such a scene of love disgracing their churchyards.

Some reverends were appointed to their ministries by big landowners. Could Lochaber act the duke's son and extricate them from this embarrassing tangle?

Oh! This minister tactfully turned his back, rather than raking them with a brimstone stare and consigning them to a dreadful hell.

Lochaber cut a glance to check her lacings were

once again functioning and demure. He gently put her away from him and rose.

Ruari danced to her feet, and before Lochaber could utter any fatuous remark, she trilled, "Hello, Father." She racked her mind for the correct term for Church of Scotland ministers. "Minister." She added, for good measure, "Reverend."

The minister whipped around. His alarmed gaze darted to Ruari's bodice, and then he smiled in relief to see she was buttoned up once more.

She gestured to the stone. "We have been examining that most fascinating Picti stone here in your adorable churchyard. Can you tell us aught about its provenance and history?"

The minister, a young, bright-eyed man with chaotic hair and dark, disheveled religious clothing fixed her with a gleaming regard. The smile lit his countenance. He tugged at his white cravat and adjusted his dark suit, muttering, "Blast this infernal garb," in a thick Highland accent.

He said, "You are from the Islands, then? You have their rare music in your voice. Lovely. Lovely." He tugged his white cravat again, until the fabric sighed and the loose bow flopped sideways. Ruari longed to reach out a hand and straighten it for the poor man.

The minister waved his arms rather wildly. "Yes, yes, most intriguing, these old slabs and carvings. My predecessor would have it that the stones are ancient, evil paganism. He wanted to remove the artifact, but the parishioners rose up and refused to permit it. Refused! And yes, the stone welcomes new visitors to Tain and to the church, and for that we must be grateful, aye?"

Ruari blinked furiously, wide-eyed, while she tried

valiantly to smother the laugh burbling up irresistibly from inside. Her lips quivered. Did the minister talk so much to cover their mutual embarrassment? His sallow cheeks bore pink highlights, and his eyes shone very bright. Or perhaps he was always like this.

He went on, "Did you have the chance to study the stone before you needed to, er, rest on yonder bench?"

Oh dear. A smothered nervous giggle trilled out. "Are you able to tell us about the Picts?" Ruari answered quickly, as though her laugh was part and parcel of overweening excitement.

Lochaber put a steady, warm hand on her back, anchoring her. She calmed instantly. She found her sensible self with a big inhale of breath and gestured over to the Ardjachie Stone. "I'm so fascinated by the mystery of the Picts. Whatever can those cup marks mean? What, there are…at least twenty or more? And the wheel design? I have not seen that one before."

The minister was so excited, he practically flapped his garments and took off, like a peculiar but friendly raven. "More than thirty cup marks." His voice radiated deep pride, as if he had painstakingly carved each cup mark himself. He stalked long-legged over to the stone, talking all the while. Ruari followed, Lochaber sauntering along behind her.

The minister extended his arm like a showman and proclaimed in ringing tones, "Aye, the spoked wheel. A most unusual pattern. Unique to Tain churchyard."

Ruari's giggle was lost in the wave of wonder which crashed over her as she bent to study the stone. "The spoked wheel is fascinating. And that inverted L-shape below. So different. Can they be of the same period as the other Picti stones? So far, I have seen the Boar Stone, the carved eagle, deer, and wolf. The curious crescent shapes, lightning bolt, Z-arrow. They have a very different...feel to them."

Oh no. The minster's long face crumpled. His brows came together, crestfallen.

She added hurriedly, "But the Ardjachie Stone must be a vital part of the story, of the compelling mystery of lost Scots history. Does the spoked wheel denote a more recent civilization? Or is it some kind of stylized sun pattern? *A star map? Why* are the symbols different here?"

She uttered this stream of words to bring the happy light back to the minister's face. But as she spoke, the old compelling sense of fascination stole through her, curling and tickling in her blood like aged whisky, mellow with flowers and honey and peat. She yearned to plunge into study of the past, like diving into the cold, exhilarating seas that lapped and beat around her castle home.

The minister stared at her. And he said a most surprising thing. "Are you a Picti scholar, then?" Color mounted his cheeks once more. "I will write you a letter of introduction to a professor who normally works from the University in Edinburgh. He abides currently at Rosemarkie, a wee distance along the road. He studies the cross-slab there at the Rosemarkie museum." His shoulders rose and he closed his eyes for a moment. "You must see it! Magnificent. *Magnificent*."

Ruari's mouth opened, but no words came.

A Picti scholar. Could a woman be such a thing? Imagine that.

The friendly minister turned and took a step, but then turned back. "I suggest it may be best—" He coughed. "To…ahem. If you must take your… *relaxation* out of doors—"

Ruari emitted a small, awkward shriek. "By all the gods!" It was her turn to cough. "Oh dear, no blasphemy intended."

The minister waved his hand, indicating forgiveness. "Perhaps not in the churchyard, aye?" He frowned, considered. "But then again, all love praises God." He bowed. "I will write the letter. Tarry one moment, one moment." He departed in a purposeful bustle of black.

Ruari and Lochaber finally met each other's eyes. Their gazes locked. A quiver tickled in Lochaber's lips.

Simultaneously, they burst out laughing.

Chapter Twenty

Lochaber flicked the reins. This visit to the professor at Rosemarkie was both good and bad. It delayed his plans for vengeance. He was so close now. So close that all his bitterness and darkness welled up and battered at his soul. The picture of his haughty, proud father's face floated in his mind's eye. He curled his right hand into a secret fist. Not long now. Not long.

His cousin's long-nosed, complaisant, equally hated face shimmered in memory. He imagined that smug complacency turning to pop-eyed horror and then anguished pleading, as he realized that Lochaber had systematically bought up all the land around him and all his gambling debts. Lochaber's last slash of the sword would be to possess the Gordon Castle and estate, beggaring his cousin.

But he hardly wanted anything to do with the castle and lands, once he possessed them. He would sell them cheap to some niggardly, absentee lord who would wreak misery and hardship on all that branch of the Gordon family. On the *legitimate* branch.

How dare they brand a man as less than human through the simple accident of birth? How dare they torment and bully, restrict and discriminate, by birth rather than ability?

He shifted in his seat. All those years fighting his way up in the East India Company. All those years, leaving his homeland, leaving his few friends and his sisters, fighting to survive in a foreign land, far away. Ruari MacDonald was right. Of course. The Highlands were part of him, a deep, secret part. His heart cracked now with futile grief that he had spent so many years away. Vowing not to return until he could wreak vengeance on all those who had wronged him.

He looked over to her, snuggled in her blanket, reading and rereading with wide eyes and an endearingly absorbed expression the pamphlet the mad minister had given her, all about the Ardjachie Stone.

Her shining hair danced around her round, rosy cheeks. Her strong brows and long dark lashes framed her glittering amethyst eyes, shining with leaping intelligence. The warmth of her body as she nestled next to him sang a song to his blood. But not a song he wanted to listen to: a song of love and gentleness, peace and happiness.

His mission had no place for hot-blooded, fiery damsels with the power to move him from his life's objective. To deflect him from his path. He must have his revenge.

He must.

But he would gift her this time with the Picti professor. There must be some way a female could participate in scholarly pursuit? Perhaps correspond as a man? Could he loan her his name and identity—but then what would become of his vengeance? He could not sully his name if he wanted to offer it to her.

A bolt shot through his blood. *Offer her his name.* How he burned to do that!

But he would not wish on her the stain of allying herself with a bastard. *Bearing that bastard's children.*

A pang of fierce, painful longing coruscated his heart and lungs. A vise imprisoned his chest. He struggled for breath. The longing was so intense, he reached out an arm and pulled her closer.

She smiled up at him. All thoughts ceased. A wild joy rippled in his veins. *She could be his.*

But no. Impossible.

Focus, man.

****

"How quaint, Lochaber! What a darling house." The Picti collection at Rosemarkie was housed in two-story, whitewashed Groam House, which functioned as a residence and local museum. A sprightly, gray-haired woman bent over in the tiny rose garden, pulling weeds.

She sensed them and straightened, holding out a work-roughened hand. "Welcome to ye. I'm Lizzie MacLean. I look after the house and the collection for Himself."

Ruari introduced themselves, giving their first names only. The woman's eyes lit with curiosity. She spent a few silent seconds studying Lochaber's features. "He'll be a Gordon, then, this one?"

Ruari laughed in delight, and turned to see a thundercloud descend on Lochaber's brow.

"Is the professor here?" she asked quickly, secretly thrumming inside. See! Even the country folk recognized Lochaber. His lips formed a white line, and his jaw tightened enough to chew the Picti stones to flinders. But his hidden, deep feelings for his own country called to him, began to possess him—and *his country recognized him.* If only he could be at peace with these warring, wounded parts of himself—he could become the merry, intelligent man he was born to be. The

244

man she might spend her life discovering.

"You mean my Professor Malcom, or the visiting professor from the university?"

"Two professors! A luxury of information about the Picti stones and fragments then."

Lizzie MacLean grinned. "Ooh, my love, I'm not sure you want to get them started. There's no brake lever. Best you have something to eat and drink first, else I'll find you there, hours later, with a raging hunger and thirst on you, lying unconscious on the floor, with the learned professors arguing over some tiny useless fact about the Picts."

Ruari hesitated. "I believe I'll take my chances, Mrs. MacLean. I understand you house a most astonishing stone here, a great cross slab with the most intriguing carvings."

The caretaker swelled with pride. "No finer in the country. This way, this way." She escorted the pair to a small room, filled to capacity with small tables and display cases. In the center, a tall, magnificent Picti stone dominated the room.

With a cry of astonishment, Ruari ran forward. Two men were deep in earnest discussion, bent over a table, studying a pottery fragment with the aid of magnifying glasses.

"Leave them, Lord Gordon," she barely heard the caretaker say. "I've hot scones and jam…" Dimly, she was aware of the caretaker taking Lochaber somewhere. She felt his absence as if warm air had been suddenly sucked out of the room.

But she only had eyes for the tremendous, marvelous, cross-slab stone which towered before her, like a figment of her most vivid, miraculous dreams.

The top carvings depicted a bird and ovoid shapes full of raised dots mirroring each other. Below that, a crescent engraved with inner knotted designs stood above an ornate, engraved square, reminiscent of images of the ancient engraved texts, with a stunning cross inside. Other images included crescents and V-rods, double-disc and Z-rod, comb, mirror, and mirror case. Or perhaps stars and planets and seasons, if her ideas were valid.

"Astonishing!" she breathed. She whipped around to the other side, to view one thick cross and many twining spirals and curlicues. "Fascinating." She groaned audibly in a kind of intellectual ecstasy. The carving was exquisite, refined, delicate. And deliberate. She whispered, "Star maps! They *must* be. But how to interpret?"

A deep voice said, "Pardon me, interrupting your reverie."

She jerked back with a jump. "Oh, not at all."

A tall, bright-eyed man in his thirties stepped from behind the stone. "We think perhaps the symbols represent clan delineations and land boundaries—"

"Don't fill the young lady's head with your nonsense now, Ross! It's perfectly clear to anyone with an ounce of scholarship that the markings are related to seasonal incidents and recording natural stimuli, with a sprinkling of map markers superimposed in a stylized rendition."

Ruari opened her mouth. "Oh—"

"Definite traces of ancestral lines, MacGregor. Don't be confusing this young miss with your infernal codswallop about nature and maps."

Maps! Her gaze swiveled from one to the other,

entranced. The men interrupted and spoke over each other, their Scots accents thickening as their discussion heated. She followed their learned language as best she could. Clan markings? Land boundaries? Aerial maps! How incredible.

Seeking an interpreter, or someone to share her amusement, she glanced around, wide-eyed. Lochaber leaned against the door jam, his mouth twisting in a sardonic grin. He straightened and gave her a short bow in one elegant motion. He stepped closer, his height and warmth commanding her attention, until he murmured in her ear. The deep tones rumbled right down to her toes. "I give you your natural element. Picti scholars."

He was correct. Her heart had picked up, beating in excitement. She endeavored to suck everything in, to absorb the fascinating information they threw out with such enthusiastic abandon, as though she was a human sea sponge swallowing life-giving water after years of drought.

She tuned into the professors' conversation.

Ross said, "At least we are in agreeance of that, MacGregor. The Picts were distributed across Ross and throughout the east of the Highlands, over Aberdeen region, why, the very name, Aber, prefixes a Picti community—"

"You are wrong." The high, commanding tone issued from her throat before she could repress it. Oh dear, what a thing to say to learned scholars. Lochaber laughed and nodded encouragement to her, returning to lean back against the entrance, as though to enjoy the show.

Both scholars turned to her with intent, excited expressions.

"*Wrong?*" said MacGregor, in tones ringing with disbelief.

Ruari squared her shoulders. She was used to doing battle with her fierce brother. These men could be little different. She flicked a glance at Lochaber to draw courage. His grin warmed her.

"Quite wrong," she said in her best confident, carrying Daughter of the MacDonalds voice. "In my own island home—" She paused to swallow a sudden lump of homesickness. "In the majestic Outer Hebrides, Picti remains abound."

"You must be mistaken, Miss." Ross.

"You are confusing Norse remains with Picts." MacGregor.

Both men stood with alert faces, happy as hound dogs pleading for a pat. Perhaps few people ever disagreed with them, and they were as thrilled as fishers in herring season.

Ruari smothered a happy giggle. "Gentlemen, I know my Neolithics and Norses from my Picts. I have been studying their artifacts and remains since I was a wee lass. In fact, on a coastal dune near to my home, a grave houses the remains of a Norse warrior with a female Picti warrior. Buried together. With all honor."

"Impossible!" both men declared in one voice. They appeared as stimulated as young boys on Christmas morning. Perhaps they had become wearied of incessantly arguing with each other and now sparkled with delight at this new intellectual sword fight.

"A female warrior?" said MacGregor. "Ridiculous!"

"Buried together? Picts in the Hebrides? But this throws all out theories to dust!"

Both men inexplicitly appeared overjoyed at the

prospect of overturning all their careful research and findings.

Professor Ross said in eager tones, "Would you care to partake of a nuncheon, to discuss these weighty matters further?"

Ruari's heart arrowed into the sky. She sent a glance to Lochaber. Would this entertain him?

Look at her radiant face, lit like an angel's. As bright and rosy as when he had caught her swimming in the seal skin in her own turbulent, stimulating seas. Cold to most others. The balm of life to Miss Ruari MacDonald.

Pictish studies was another such.

He peeled himself into a standing position and rearranged his features into a polite, interested mask. He would endure worse than a lunch filled with talk of ancient stones and moldering remains to see her so animated, so thrilled, so engrossed with life.

Ruari always was engaged with life, leaping in with her whole delicious body and whip-fast mind into every situation and all the folk who were lucky enough to cross her path.

But this? Study of the Picts and ancient Norse nourished her, delighted her. Powered her up. She was in truth a kind of vibrant, laughing, female professor. These strange men were her true kin.

A fierce stab of jealousy flayed him. He manfully squashed it down and uttered his delight to attend luncheon.

They followed the professors, who stopped for urgent debate every few paces, to a small upstairs dining room in Groam House. Tiny windows opened to sparkling Rosemarkie Bay. Shimmering in the distance, less than two miles across the Moray Firth, lay the

Scottish mainland.

The shudder caught him. Laid waste to his fortitude.

Forty miles to the duke's estates on the mouth of the River Spey. The estates which his cousin would inherit.

Or three fast days travel through the mountains to Castle Clàrsach, his father, and his family. His childhood home, that he not seen since he was a foolish green lad fired with ambition and vengeance. Those hot fires of revenge had cooled to a continent of ice over the years. Solidified to unyielding granite. He could not change his trajectory now.

"Sit you down, sir." The caretaker Lizzie MacLean's voice buzzed in his ear for the second time.

"Lochaber." Ruari's soft tone recalled him with a jerk. He plastered a civil smile over his face and pulled out her chair. He chose a seat for himself facing away from the window and that shimmering, hazy view of northeast Scotland. Away from his torment. And his revenge.

Lizzie MacLean piled food on the professors' plates. "There now! I canna trust ye to feed yourselves, grown men as you are supposed to be. Eat that. You need your strength." She quirked a humorous, gray-threaded brow at Ruari, who laughed in response.

Professor Ross took an absentminded bite and leaned forward. "Please, Miss MacDonald, are you able to describe the grave in detail? Whatever you can remember. The positions of the remains. The accoutrements. The choice of location." He smacked himself in the forehead. "Oh, I do apologize. Please don't strain yourself. Enjoy your repast."

How Lochaber loved to see her laugh so. The bitter, vengeful part of his spirit warmed, and his eyes narrowed. These men invited her to converse with them—a credit to them for that—yet they expected a hesitating, rambling, imprecise feminine discourse.

A harsh grin quivered to life on his lips. Right about now...

Ruari put down her fork. She finished her mouthful, chewing carefully, fixing each professor in turn with her proud, amethyst gaze.

Lochaber's heart swelled. *She is magnificent.*

Ruari MacDonald lived the courage born of her wild islands. No bowing to expectations of female intellectual inferiority. She let them have it.

She launched into a precise description of the site, the remains, and the artifacts accompanying them. Measurements. Details. And then she smacked them with her own ideas and theories about Norse travelers and Picti warriors. About the matrilineal nature of the Picts. About the freedoms of their women as compared to the present day. And finally, her intelligence blazing like the sun itself, she spoke of Picti steles as star maps to navigate deadly sea travel back to their ancient homelands.

Professor MacGregor gaped, mid-chew. Professor Ross appeared to be in the throes of an apoplectic excitement. Lochaber himself was torn between mental amazement and an overpowering urge to stand up and *claim* her, to rush her from the room and *take* her in a savage bid to merge with all that passion and fire.

Professor Ross regained his capacity to speak. "But you must come to Aberdeen, Miss Ruari. Together with our learned colleagues and friends, we are reviving the Aberdeen Philosophical Society, known fondly as the Wise Club, that bastion of the Scottish Enlightenment.

We have archeologists, philosophers, historians. We Scots number among the brightest brains in the western world."

Ruari said, "There would be interest in my claim to Picti artifacts in the Hebrides? And my theories as to their interpretation?"

MacGregor waved his wine glass, not noticing a spray of airborne claret droplets. "Interest? If we present your findings to the Society, we will create an uproar. Uproar!"

Lochaber frowned.

Ruari speared a glance at him. Quick shake of her brown locks. *Don't interrupt. This is my fight.*

"There is more," she added, silk-voiced, weaving a charm around and over every man present. "A settlement. A longhouse and smaller dwellings. The paraphernalia of daily life in ancient times."

Ross's glasses slipped down his nose. MacGregor swept an agitated hand through his hair, rendering it into ragged peaks.

Lochaber inhaled. Squeezed his fists. He wanted this woman as his own. His cold inner businessman, so carefully grown and cultivated over so many years, had morphed into an adoring claimant for her attention. Just by the musical lilt of her voice casting her spell over all.

The Wise Club had no hope. He grinned like a shark.

Ruari took a small sip of wine, studying the professors, some kind of plan brewing behind those beautiful eyes. "If the Wise Club wished to study the remains, would it be likely that the tenants and land would be cleared for sheep or industry?"

Ah. Clever lass.

Ross flushed red. MacGregor paled. They both

spluttered. "Impossible!" Ross hammered his point home with his fork. "We will gain an order from the Royal Society and the queen that all such activity must cease in the interests of Science."

Ruari looked fully at Lochaber then. Triumphant. Sparkling. Like a barbarian queen riding to victory. Imaginary battle drums pounded loud in his ear.

She pushed her chair back and rose to her feet. The men all rose with her—no doubt in kinship rather than mere manners.

Ruari MacDonald held up her own fork and proclaimed, "We shall attend the Wise Club symposium, and *I* shall present my findings." Flags of bright color mounted her cheeks. Her lips parted in evident excitement. "I know the sites and artifacts best. I know the details and can answer any questions. I shall inspire the Wise Club's patronage and interest. *I must.*"

Awkward silence resounded. The men folded back down into chairs. Ruari resumed her seat. Her gaze snapped between Lochaber and the professors. "What?"

He raised a brow. "This Wise Club may be sadly misnamed. It is likely to lack wisdom—because no doubt women are excluded from its hallowed halls."

Silence slammed like a fist around the table.

Ruari's face lost all its vibrancy. "No!" She sucked in air. Grabbed the table edge. "The chance to share ideas with fellow scientists—within my grasp, and yet—so cruelly denied?"

Ross said, "I must profess, I did forget your gender for a moment there, Miss MacDonald. Your ideas…"

Lochaber snorted. He should be so lucky. Or maybe he had that wrong. So unlucky. She excited him all ways: mentally, spiritually, emotionally. The urge to possess her simply grew more intense. As she leaned forward, a silky dark curl spiraled over her shoulder, emphasizing the soft white skin on her neck and swelling gently into her bodice…

Stop that! he ordered his groin. His cock ignored him.

MacGregor said in halting tones, "The original Wise Club corresponded with great female minds such as the Russian Princess Yekaterina Romanovna Vorontsova-Dashkova, first president of the Russian Academy. There is certainly debate among our members about the capacity of the female intellect, this is true, but then we interrogate every subject with vigor, do we not?"

More awkward silence.

Temper darkened Ruari's face like an imminent storm brewing over the Hebridean sea. She said in challenging, ringing tones which sent spears of excitement stabbing down Lochaber's spine, "Well, gentlemen? I demand the right to present my own findings. Even if I must cut my hair and don the garb of a man! A kilt would do, no?"

Cut her beautiful hair? Loss pinged through him. "No!" The word forced itself through stiff lips. "There will be an exception or loophole written into the rules. We will find that exception and exploit it." He snapped his gaze around the table. "I am well accustomed to reading contracts."

The professors beamed at him. MacGregor pointed his knife dangerously close to Lochaber's nose. "A man of business! Excellent, excellent."

Professor Ross added, "Let us bring Miss MacDonald, to present her findings and her theories. Ha! We shall challenge that boor Erskine, and it's time

Hamilton had his come-uppance. His theories of the Neolithic history—tainted by his own narrow lens, completely unsupported by the evidence…"

The professors leaned in, spouting a hail of learned terms like bullets in an Indian mutiny. The remains of their lunches lay untasted on their plates.

What had he done? A blazing choice lay before him.

He could proceed to the duke's estates and the Gordon ancestral castle at Cluny. He could fulfil his life's dream and take his revenge. Revel in the supremely Scots satisfaction of long-awaited, long-anticipated vengeance. For all those blood crimes wrought on his family in the aftermath of the Jacobite tragedy. For all the hurt and abuse of his youth, all the extra work and effort required in his working life as *a bastard*.

Ruari's features shone, utterly entranced as she listened to the professors. And then—she butted in. No fear. As engaged in debate as the men. She said her piece, logically, eloquently. Argued, using evidence as fluently as he used the *khanda* and *patta* swords, slicing their research into shreds.

Pride for her swelled in his heart.

He could wreak his vengeance. *So close now.* Bitter yearning twanged through him.

Or—*he could swap his life's dreams for hers.*

Take her to Aberdeen. Fire her into the smug, unsuspecting male Wise Club like a great monsoon rain flooding the arid desert. Powerful. Unrelenting. Life-creating.

Support her to be the blazing, proud Ruari MacDonald of her future.

He might be a bastard.

But he was a clever, unrelenting, determined

255

bastard.

He was a worthless lump of cold, bitter anger—but *she* deserved the sky and stars. A king's ransom.

Yes. He would use it all for her.

He asked, "When does this Wise Club, the Philosophical Society meet?"

Ross replied, "In five days, lad. MacGregor and myself will take four days to travel the ninety miles. It may be done in less, with several changes of horses."

Four days in a carriage with the adorable, sensual, ferociously brave Miss Ruari MacDonald. His better self battled hard with his base desires. Achieved a very narrow victory. "We will summon your maid Sìneag," he said hoarsely and then snapped his lips shut before his aching lust could countermand his noble words.

Ruari gripped both fists and stuck out her bottom lip in a hard pout. "I'll save all the MacDonald tenants yet!"

The professors were oblivious, deep in argument.

Ruari's dark brows quirked and her sparkling eyes locked with Lochaber's gaze.

They both laughed.

Warmth stole through his belly.

Chapter Twenty-One

"The Picti stone at Rosemarkie was huge. Worth at least three questions." Ruari flung the challenge, her eyes dancing and teasing. Her words bounced around the carriage, in counterpoint to the rocking and rolling motion of the light conveyance jogging fast toward the mountains. A thick plaid wrapped most of her form, as she sat on the inside seat facing him. But under that warm blanket…his brain *would* conjure delicious, tormenting images of that jiggling effect on her soft curves…

He swallowed. Fixed a virtuous stare out at the passing scenery.

Sìneag and the young hired groom perched outside on the driver's seat. Lord only knew what they found to talk about. Perhaps the maid slept.

He had sent for Sìneag immediately after luncheon, and she had arrived that evening, in time to grumble her way through restoring Ruari's person and clothing to rights.

Sìneag related a dreadful tale. The Ardross tenants had risen and were brutally put down by the Duke of Tuath and his friend the Earl of Kilmore. The protest leaders had been rounded up, slaughtered or arrested, their homes and possessions burnt to ash, and their families thrown onto great ships bound for the Americas, Canada, or the Australian colonies.

"Best keep running, *mo chridhe*, until you are safe

in the Gordon fastness." The maid rattled her teacup in its saucer. The earl is a jealous man, and you have humiliated him."

"Sìneag, I am not *running* from any earl. I am rushing to embrace my glorious future! I did not consent to a marriage with that man. I am not in his power—even if my useless cousin has sold the MacDonald lands."

Miss Ruari MacNeil MacDonald—courage and passion flamed in every cell. No Plan B for her. And yet, that sparked an idea in him…

The maid bent her fierce stare on Lochaber. "That Kilmore might do anything. Clever of you, my lord, to summon me in yon professor's name."

As dawn pinked the sky, the little party had set off for Aberdeen. They would travel through the spectacular Cairngorm mountains, via Grantown-on-Spey with a short detour to Rhynie. The professors would follow more slowly in their own equipage, following the longer coastal route.

The mountains! Almost there.

The passion to set foot in them once more throbbed in Lochaber like a fever. He wanted to imbibe that unique soil-rich, green mountain air. He longed to run, as he did as a lad, through the high green forests dappled with bands of slanting sunlight and down into rocky, misty glens, rushing with brown burns.

He could eat game pie and pheasant pâté, smoothed down with the finest peat-infused whisky in the wide world.

Home! His whole being shouted with it. The call of the mountains sang to him like a trumpet of angels. He clenched his thighs.

"Soon," he said to Miss Ruari, "soon, we will relieve

Sìneag and Hamish on the driver's box. Should you enjoy watching the countryside? Your first sight of the justly famous Cairngorm mountains?" Even he heard the stupid yearning in his voice. He added in a cold tone, "If it amuses you."

She turned her eager face closer to the window. Blast! Why did he say that? He missed her teasing, her sparkling attention, even to gaze at the green farmlands beyond. Jealous of a field now. *I'm in a coil of trouble.*

"Mmmm," she replied, the sweet vibration of the sound calling forth an answering throb in his chest. "Yes—the mountains. I long to breathe their sweet air, so different from the salt-laced fresh breezes of my home. Tall trees thronging together, shady walks underfoot, soft with leaves, burns tumbling and tinkling, reflecting the forest above—oh! It all sounds so lovely."

She turned to him again, her face lit. That wicked sparkle presaged something to his detriment, no doubt, but like the verist love-struck fool, he could only wait for her next sweet torture.

She smiled, glinting at him from under her ridiculously curling dark lashes. The warm bundle of tartan-wrapped woman leaned closer across the carriage. "In the meantime, Lochaber Gordon, perhaps we may beguile our journey. With secrets." She drew out the "ss" sounds, hissing and sibilant. "Give me another of your hidden talents, for the Rosemarkie cross-slab. A big, fabulous, stunning secret, to match the wonder and glory of that stone."

Danger! All his instincts forbade him. And yet—a traitorous tendril of wanting curled within him, a viper of need waking. He wanted to tell her…everything. He had never had another living soul who knew the whole of him.

The realization slammed him back against the squabs. He was his own Castle Gordon, drawbridge up, chilly moat all around. Built stone by stone with cold ambition.

The edifice shook. The drawbridge ropes frayed, a very little.

He countered, "What of your own mysteries, Miss MacDonald?"

Her scorn shredded him. "I'm about to share my 'mysteries' with all the world. I'm terrified, actually." Her cheeks sucked in. Then her wide eyes flashed fire. "There is nothing I would not do to save our unique Picti heritage. I am becoming convinced that the Island artifacts differ substantially from those of Easter Ross and perhaps Aberdeen...I must view the marvelous Picti Beast at Rhynie to confirm my theories..." She tossed her braids. "My apologies. I am quite obsessed! In any case, you already know all my private concerns."

The impulse swelled within him. "Not *all* your private business, Ruari the Turbulent." His voice came dark. Gravel with greed.

He moved, stealthily as a cobra, to sit beside her. Allowed the movement of the carriage to gently bump her body against his. "Put down that tartan rug a little." His voice croaked like a pond full of frogs. "Let me see your flesh quiver."

The rosy flush mounted in her cheeks. Her gaze sparked at him. Her right hand reached up. Fingers tangled in the fabric. Slowly, she drew the plaid rug down, exposing her bodice to his hungry view.

By all the gods. White mounds of breasts jogged and vibrated with every rock of the carriage. He licked dry lips. His cock leapt to attention.

She pulled at her bodice. A tiny slice of pink nipple peeked through the lace at her neckline.

His throat thickened.

"So beautiful." More anguished moan than words. "Ruari MacDonald, I must kiss you. I want my mouth on those soft, enticing tits. I'm so hard for you."

Just then the carriage made a lurch, landing Ruari almost into his lap. Lochaber prided himself as a cold, deliberate thinker, and he was ever the opportunist. He seized the moment—and the woman—and lowered a hot, demanding mouth on hers. So sweet! So plush. Such softness, such fire!

His large hands gently caressed her neck, behind her ears, her hairline, until she cocked her head, silently demanding more. He bent his head to her exposed neck; the carriage jolted. His mouth slipped—straight onto the top of a wobbling breast. At the same time, his massive, aching erection nudged her soft thigh.

He held her tight, to keep her safe from the swaying. He pressed her body against his. So good. So lovely. He moved back a little. Put his lips to her nipple, breathing warm air on her sensitive tip. Flicking the tip of his tongue over and around the ruched peak. She moaned, deep in her throat.

Then, dammit it all to hell and back, she pulled away from his seeking mouth.

He was bereft, lonely, robbed.

With an athletic movement worthy of a *paika akhada,* this courageous, fiery woman straddled him. Knelt, knees balanced on the carriage seat on either side of his lap, facing him.

Experimentally, she sank gently down onto his lap.

By all the gods! Just then, the carriage lurched and rocked over a bump, airborne momentarily and coming down with a thump. Straddled over him thus, her parted legs, her secret softness, landed down hard right on his throbbing, aching cock.

Again, he prayed.

"Ooh!" Ruari said. "Nice." Her throaty, sultry whisper extended his staff by at least another two inches.

He gripped her upper arms, enjoying their slim strength. Bagpipe-playing arms. That image was a mistake. Now all he could picture was her plush lips gathered around the pipes' mouthpiece…

An internal war raged. Honor won. By the slimmest of margins.

But first…one more bump in the road…

He lowered hungry lips on hers. Tasted her top lip. Brushed a kiss over her plump bottom lip. Flicked a tongue tip where they joined. She parted for him.

As his mouth explored her, his arms held her from falling backward. He loved the feel of warm, strong woman, pressing hard against his strength and agility. He adored her fire and passion, as she kissed back, growing savage now, a pirate queen indeed.

Now she plundered him, stealing kisses, tasting him with her lips and tongue. He surrendered to her, allowing his head to fall back while she licked and kissed and gently sucked on his bottom lip.

The carriage jolted again. They met, hard and close, where they most wanted to be. Oh sweet heaven!

Enough. He must stop, or tear the garments from her body.

With main willpower, he grasped her hips with both hands and lifted her away from him.

Her lovely face hovered inches away. Her wide mouth, reddened and swollen with kissing, begged him. He hated the hurt and confusion lurking in her beautiful eyes.

He never wanted to hurt her. And that's why he must stop this damnably compelling lovemaking now.

"Secrets," he croaked. "Very well. Ask me your question." He could only hope her question would be so devastating that she would douse his lust to a mere inferno. Instead of a near-erupting volcano.

His closed his eyes. Mentally repeated a few *paika akhada* mantras to regain some semblance of control.

"Can one not make love in a rocking carriage?" she asked.

"Yes!" the answer burst from him. All his hard-won control, the closed portcullis of his emotions, was splintering. "But we are not making love today."

"What if I wish to, Lochaber Gordon?"

Whatever you want, most beautiful of women! his cock clamored.

"And risk a child?" He allowed his anger to rise. Perhaps fear and fury would overtake his lust. "The last thing I can ever countenance is an illegitimate child. You understand me."

"But Lochaber." The sweetness and wonder in her voice called deep inside him. "A child of ours would be a child created of love. The best beginning for any child."

He turned away, struggling. "The things you say, Ruari MacDonald. You must have a large amount of uncivilized Pict-Norse blood running in those fierce veins."

"Take what you want. Fight for it," she answered. "*Victory or Death.* And I want you, Lochaber Gordon."

She climbed back over his lap. Braced her hands firmly on the carriage squabs to either side of his head. "I saw you fight, Lochaber. I watched you wield your limbs and body like a weapon, a glorious, thrilling song of strength and power. A victory song of mental strength—for every move revealed many years of determined practice, of working muscles and honing your will until they could sing a song of deadly joy."

She brushed a kiss over his lips. "And I imagine those hands, your brilliant mind, your extraordinary body, put to the service of love. Of loving me. Will you teach me love, Lochaber?"

The carriage lurched. He seemed to bury himself in her, despite the layers between them. He could not withstand her.

"I know little of love," he replied hoarsely. "But I can offer you pleasure. Will that suffice?"

She smiled like a mermaid, full of mystery and tricks. "Mmm. Pleasure. Tempting." Her drowsy voice played on his senses. "For now. Perhaps later, I will require love. I will take what you feel you can give me, Lochaber. For now."

He could resist no longer.

He ripped the plaid from her body and cast it away to the opposite seat. He took her hard in his arms, crushing her against him, feeling the proud beat of her heart, the delicious, tormenting curves of her flesh.

He reached around them and spread her skirts, until there was bare woman resting and rubbing against the falls of his breeches. With every bump and lurch of the carriage, she slid and kneaded against him. Even through his breeches he could feel her slickness, her desire. *For him.*

How was she even possible? Maybe he had dreamed her from the sea, and she was in fact a selkie, enchanting him.

If that was so, then he could ravage her. When a magical being requests your body in the act of love, you give it. Give the mermaid as much as she demands, as much as she wants.

He kissed her softly; he kissed her harder. As he ravished her, one hand strayed across her silky skin, playing and teasing. The other hand drifted down to her skirt-covered thigh, tickling and tormenting. He pulled those layers and layers of fabric and petticoat aside.

Bare soft skin on her thigh. Both resisting and giving under his touch. He traveled the fingertip around to her inner thigh. Touched, caressed the tiny curls lacing her entrance. Hot and slippery for his touch.

She inhaled sharply. Jumped a little, then regarded him with an intent, dark-jewel stare that made his insides melt and fire.

The finger moved down and rested there, lightly on her seam. Waiting.

There! The carriage bucked. Her body rose up and landed down hard, his finger deep inside all that tight, slick heat. She squeezed her intimate muscles. By all the gods of hill and burn!

He gripped her buttock with one hand and began to stroke and caress and plunder with his finger. Each time the carriage obligingly bumped and jolted, she came down hard on him. Her half closed eyes glowed. Color rioted on her plump cheeks, and her breath rushed hard and fast.

"That's it, my Ruari, that's right." He circled her sensitive peak there, rubbing and tickling, faster and faster, allowing the carriage movement to bolt and buck her toward her climax.

She moaned out loud now, uttering small cries and writhing in uncontrolled ecstasy, her head thrown back, whipping him close to his own climax—and he hadn't even undone his breeches.

How he longed to. But this was for her alone. Him too, if he was honest. The passion wringing her features made him greedy. He wanted her in a bed, laid out naked and gleaming before him, with hours to dedicate to their lovemaking.

Ruari bucked and gasped in her climax, shuddering and clenching around his fingers, plunged deep inside her. Then she melted against his chest. He loved to feel her there. As though she belonged nowhere else.

"That was just a taste, my Ruari," he whispered in her ear. "Pleasure for now. Later, you shall have—" He couldn't make himself say it. He didn't deserve *love*. But pleasure? He would dedicate every bone and muscle in his body to give her joy and satisfaction. "Later you shall have…*more*."

For minutes, Ruari nestled against him. Her thudding heartbeat gradually slowed. She shifted off him, arranging herself next to him, and snuggled into his side.

Ruari's cheeks flushed again. She looked delightfully embarrassed and shy. Blinking in surprise and delight. This soft Ruari could not last long.

"And now you," she said.

His staff strained toward her. "Not this time, my darling," he managed. "This was for you."

She stretched out a hand. Hovered it above his straining breeches. Lowered it a little more. His mouth dried.

She waited. The carriage jolted.

Her hand met his aching cock. She rubbed.

Lochaber groaned aloud.

He slammed back against the carriage seat. "Take me as you will."

Delicate fingers dexterously flicked open the buttons on the falls of his trousers. His entire body pulsed with fire, with need. His blood hammered fast and urgent in his veins.

He should tell her, no. He should lift her aside…

"Oh!"

His cock sprang free. Her gasp built thickness and length in his engorged organ.

She ran a hesitant finger up and down his length. He quivered and bucked in response. His hands clenched on the carriage seat, resisting the overwhelming urge to *take*.

Her plush lips were parted in a rich bow of astonishment. "Show me how to pleasure…?" she whispered.

Those fingers that stroked and caressed music from the mighty Highland pipes now brushed the length of him. Cupped his stones. He closed his eyes in an agony of desire. He opened his eyes a slit and studied her.

The hoarse words sprang from his throat. "Ruari, my brave, undaunted warrior. You don't have to do this. We can stop now, if you wish. Or resume later. *Your* pleasure was *mine*, I assure you." He forced a grin. He practically blasted from his trousers with the image flash of her body writhing about his stiff fingers.

"Do you deny me, Lochaber? I want to share pleasure with you. Not take." She tickled a trill with dancing fingertips around and up and down to the root of his straining organ. When the carriage swayed, she caught him in a warm, firm clasp.

Oh, by the mountain peaks, this woman was lovely.

"Very well," he gritted. "Like this." He took her small, clever hands in his own and wrapped them around his staff. "That's right. Oh yes. Like that." He guided her fingers and hands into a fast friction, watching to check for her comfort, while pressure grew in every cell of his body. As they pumped together, she leaned in and kissed him. He met her with savage desire, tracing the lush shape of her lips, testing their bouncy resistance, then tasting and claiming her lips, mouth, tongue.

His cells detonated. He wrenched his body away and finished the business himself, while she stared brilliant-eyed and rosy-hued over his working arm. The warmth of her hands sank into his back and shoulders. He reached his own climax, shuddering and jetting onto the carriage seat beside him, and she clasped him in a tight embrace from behind.

For a timeless, splendid moment, they rested in each other's arms, replete. Emotion filled him: a fierce urge to protect, to cosset. To empower this magnificent, generous-hearted woman.

"Lochaber," she said in a drowsy, drugged tone.

"Mhmm?" He gently tucked a stray shining lock back behind her ear, as sweetly formed as the rest of her. A walking miracle of nature. "Whatever your heart desires…" *Hell.* Did he say that out loud? Danger prickled lightly on his skin.

"My Picti stone questions."

He hesitated. Brushed her cheek. "Not a few minutes ago, you asked a question about—" He cleared his throat.

"No, I did not!" She drew back, laughing. "I suggested. I pleaded. No questions."

The sense of danger stabbed him outright. Hamstrung, trussed.

"Did you think I would forget?" she asked, amusement dancing in her tone, as golden and uncatchable as a sunbeam. A gentle hand ran up and down his thigh. A sensory shudder racked him.

He grinned, conceding ground. "I knew you would not." All of him waited to see what she would tease from him next.

Chapter Twenty-Two

Could he be actually enjoying this masterful dissection of his emotional fortress?

While she prepared to slice him neatly open, he plucked a handkerchief from his pocket and collected up the evidence of their tryst, scrubbing at the damp spot. He raised the carriage window an inch and disposed of the sticky item, praying the alert maid on the box would not see it fly into the wind.

He prepared himself to rebut and tease away any attack on his inner walls.

"My first Rosemarkie Stone question." Her brilliant lavender gaze pinned him to his seat, lashed him to her will. Her words came lazy and sultry, curling in his blood like smoke. "That training in *the arts of love*. Did you take Indian princesses, with long black shining hair to their feet, trained to pleasure men?" Her voice hardened. "Do you yearn for them still? Does India own your heart?"

His heart smashed in his ribs. "That's three questions," he teased.

"It was a big stone," she retorted, cocking her arched brow in such an adorable quizzing manner that he itched to rip the fabric from her body and pleasure her properly. Those words. *It was a big stone*. Desire ripped through him like wildfire.

He considered her questions, Again, he found he

wanted to tell her. Yearned to share this secret, vital part of him. Could deny her nothing. How best to explain?

"You have your Picts," he began. He stroked the soft hair springing joyfully around her hairline. "India is like that with me. Endlessly fascinating. Strange and different. Harsh and beautiful, rich and colorful and magical."

He pinched her chin lightly in his fingers. Traced a fingertip over her plump lower lip. "India made me, saved me. Enabled me to find the man inside who belongs to the world, not this lonely, mist-drenched northern outpost of the civilized world."

She looked down. He waited, dreading her answer.

When it came, it seared him with its intelligence. Its clever, penetrating depth. "And like a man, you plundered India, took all she would give you and more. Made love to the women, battled the men, wrested the country's wealth for your own. Conquered."

Her cold tone froze him.

He gripped her hands. Crushed them, desperate to explain. "You are correct," he replied, his tone curt. "The Company began to commit acts which were reminiscent of the Culloden genocide. Too brutal, too corrupt for my taste. *And yet not*. India was not laid waste, not completely. She stands proud and unconquered. She will be a power still."

Ruari stroked his hair. *How good that felt*. "Did your princesses do this?" she hissed. "You have such splendid bright hair, the women would not have before seen such a blazing richness. Did you let them do this while you bent to their breasts? While you plundered them below?"

"Is that *jealousy* adding savage spikes to your words?" He challenged her with his gaze, teasing her skin with a fingertip.

Her lip quivered.

He sought for truth. "They taught me much, my lovers. But I swear to you—my heart stayed my own. Cold, lonely, and bitter. No matter where and with whom I sought to melt it, lose it, repair that frozen organ, I remained an unloved Scots bastard."

She didn't laugh. She whispered, "You are not an unloved Scots bastard, Lochaber Gordon. I…" She swallowed. Changed what she was going to say.

So. *She couldn't love him either*.

Instead, she said, "Will you show me more? More of bodies and pleasure?" She blinked, waiting for his reply while he choked on his words. But only for a moment.

She drew away from him and laughed. Changed the atmosphere as though she feared his answer. "I long to learn many things you learned in India. Most of all—the *paika akhada* fighting! My brother nor the MacDonald men would not stand a chance fighting against me."

"Ruari."

A hurt expression shadowed her face. She raised her chin, wrinkled her nose, snapped a saucy grin at him, and turned her attention once more to the passing scenery.

****

He had closed himself off from her. Again.

He elicited the most urgent and exquisite sensations from her flesh and body, demanding and claiming her pleasure, until she writhed and moaned under his touch. And then him! A revelation. That silky, firm length, pulsing under her touch…a thrill of feminine power leapt in her veins.

And then her Picti stone questions. He did gift her

an answer, of sorts, ringing with honesty, but a response which pained and hurt him—and then he shut right down. Brought down the ice and snow, to encase the essential, warm, loving, funny man inside, leaving only brittle permafrost for others to slip and skate over.

He had bequeathed her glimpses now. That Highland lad still dwelt inside, hurting and yearning for family, acceptance, and love. She had held a proud man in her arms, with endless love and care to offer.

Just like her Picti studies, she would unravel the meaning of the hints and symbols thrown outward, melt the layers of ice which encased this man, and free him to the world. And to her.

Typical man! He was covering the awkward moment by reading a document, covered in close-printed text. The paper rustled in his hands. She craned her neck to sneak a glimpse of the content which had him so engrossed.

His entire body went rigid. An oath ripped from his jaw. His brows lowered into thunder. "Never!" he muttered. "Not while I breathe!"

He saw her looking and abruptly folded the documents in half.

She met his gaze. "What are you reading?"

"It doesn't matter."

"Apparently it does!" She smiled sweetly.

His eyelids lowered over glinting eyes. His jaw set. He reached for the leather document satchel. She put a hand on his arm. They both froze.

Would he rudely shake her off? Instead, he lowered his gaze to her hand. Color rose in his neck and cheeks. The man actually blushed! No doubt remembering where her hand had recently plied flexible fingers.

He looked over her shoulder. An unholy joy lit his face, rivaling his flaming hair. "The mountains! Look, Miss MacDonald, we arrive in the foothills." He grasped her waist with large, warm palms, and used his strength to shift her to face the window.

She sang a gasping croon of joyous amazement. Rose, rushed to the window, knelt before it. "So green! Those misty blue peaks, marching away in the glorious distance. Trees, forest, burns. Oh, Lochaber!"

He squeezed himself to the edge of the seat and placed his hands at her shoulders, looking over her at the view. His clasp gripped, then softened. When she sensed he had immersed himself in the scene unfolding before them, she ducked under his arm, wriggled from his clasp, and made a snatch for the satchel.

He snaked out a fast arm and grabbed a corner.

She tugged.

Narrowed her eyes. Gave him a dagger stare.

His lips twitched. He loomed over her.

Their gazes locked. When he least expected it, she aimed a short, sharp kick at his shins.

He did not react. At all. Completely master of himself. A slow, wicked grin stretched his mouth. His eyes flashed challenge.

She tugged the satchel. He tugged back.

She stretched up a hand. Dipped a finger into her bodice, gently traced the edge of her cleavage. His Adam's apple bobbed. Dark whiskers stood out on his jaw.

She pulled the satchel a little closer with one hand. Her other hand, currently tickling her cleavage, danced down her bodice, her waist, her skirts. Without breaking their gaze, she hiked the silky fabric higher. Higher again. Cool air kissed her ankles. Her calves.

His gaze slipped. Snapped on her bared ankles, back up to her face. His face clenched like granite. The ice man blazed with cold determination.

She allowed her head to flop back, exposing her neck to his burning gaze. She bunched her skirts around her hips. His gaze shot to her thighs. She parted them for him, exposing her bared sex.

And then she grabbed the satchel and scooted to the other side of the carriage.

She stood bent on the swaying seat, leaning her weight against the side wall, adjusting her balance as though trawling high seas in her rowboat.

He made a grab for her. She flung the empty satchel at him and browsed the paperwork, quickly leafing through while evading his grasp. She jumped from one side of the carriage to the other, landing on the opposite seat with bent knees.

Lochaber's voice rang with command. "Ruari! Stop this mad game, now. You'll harm yourself."

"Nonsense," she retorted. "I grew up jumping off high castle walls into unsteady seas. Racing my brother and kinfolk in small boats tossed by storms. Ah ha!" She squinted at him in confusion. "These are the rules of the Aberdeen Philosophers' Society, aka the Wise Club. Whatever can have upset you in here?"

Lochaber subsided onto the seat. His glower could have ignited a cold Hebridean sea in winter. His lips thinned to a pale slash of fury.

She sat opposite, riffling through the document, casting him an occasional glance to check he wouldn't make another grab for them. Apparently, risking her person was sufficient to make him obedient. She watched carefully for the flicker that told her he would move again—and the man could strike as fast as an enraged serpent.

"Oh! *Oooh*! I see." She rested the document on her lap. Stared at him. Cast her eyes back down to the tiny print.

" 'Those of the Female Persuasion are excluded from the Aberdeen Philosophers' Society (the Society) in order to save them from Risk of Disordered minds and Unnatural impulses.' " She made a comic grimace at Lochaber, but he merely simmered. She waited, then read on, " 'Exceptions to this firm Rule, may be made only and solely with the express written imprimatur *or verbal announcement in the relevant meeting* of a local Peer of the Realm.' " There was far more archaic, hedging and qualifying language, but she had covered the salient point.

"Peer of the realm," she repeated. "Someone like a...duke?"

"Yes. To get you into that symposium, and certainly if you mean to present to that thick-headed bunch of pompous fools, we will need express written or verbal permission from the duke. From my hateful, irresponsible *father*. The man who gave me life but refused me the protection of his name."

Silence. Awkward, echoing silence.

Shattered suddenly by the upside-down face of the hired driver, the youth Hamish, filling the window. He knocked on the glass. "My Lord Gordon, you said ye wanted to sit the box when we get to the mountains. We'm here now, my lord. Not long till Grantown-on-Spey, the north edge of the Cairngorms."

The face disappeared. The rocking pace slowed.

Clatter sounded under the horses' hooves as they hit a stretch of gravel and scree. The carriage door wrenched open, and Ruari stepped out into the fussing care of Sìneag. The horses grazed the roadside grasses and lipped up water from a shallow pool. The two women strolled off to a nearby cluster of shrubs.

When they returned, the maid and Hamish plunked themselves in the carriage. Lochaber assisted Ruari up onto the high box. His set jaw and cheeks of stone radiated grimness. He took the reins and clicked the horses into motion.

He had still not uttered a single word. A pulse jumped in his cheek.

Ruari gazed around her in wonder. "Lochaber, it's all so lovely! The great granite tors rising so steeply. Foothills fringed with white-trunked, dapple-barked trees with those bright leaves."

"Birches."

She hesitated. Couldn't resist a tease. Everyone took this man too seriously, including himself. More sibling time would have cured that. "So. He speaks."

His frown jumped down at her. Nostrils flared.

"What are the other trees, Lochaber?"

His gaze flashed to the scenery. "I left the mountains when I was but a lad, believing myself a man. I think the English common names are pine, birch, rowan, aspen, and juniper. Willows, alder." The harsh planes of his face softened. "We called them birk, caorann, fairy trees, and old man willow."

"And wildlife?"

His eyes lit. "Keep your eyes open. We might see mountain hare, pine marten, red deer, fox, squirrel, roe deer, Scottish wildcat, the capercaillie, crested tit, and crossbill. Grouse, goosander, siskin, long-eared owl, osprey, red-breasted merganser, redwing, stint, wood sandpiper, horned grebe, and golden eagle. Wildflowers…"

The years fell from Lochaber. She sat nestled into his warmth on the box. Once more he was that bright flame-haired lad, springing from cliffs and leaping wild, tumbling burns.

The mountains unfolded before them, towering blue-gray into the sky. The air kissed her cheeks, colder than the coastal, salt-laden breezes, and redolent with the enticing scents of green growing things and rich soils. The wind whispered through the forest, and the horses' hooves thudded softly on the leaf-strewn road.

An eagle soared overhead, wings outstretched, hovering for a period, then diving for prey. "Magnificent!" Ruari breathed.

Lochy released his left hand and put his arm around her, squeezing her tight. Palpable emotion flowed from him—grief, regret, the joy of homecoming, the pain of a cracked, hidden heart opening to the sights and smells of his childhood home. She leaned into him, content to allow the man to alchemize all his complex, contradictory feelings.

A pulse of excitement hammered in her veins. Travel! New sights, new people, different food, words, and customs. And that was just the Highlands! She snuggled into Lochaber's warmth, drinking in the scenery, allowing her mind to float free on a happy dream of traveling with him to distant countries, secure in his protection and wealth, experiencing life at the edge. They would visit the ancient stones and artifacts of all the cultures of the world…she would become a kind of female archaeology professor…

The horses picked up the pace as they neared a tiny town on the mountain frontier. The sun sat low in the sky now, heralding evening with bright beams shining slantwise. The carriage drew under an arch and into the yard of an ancient inn, wrought from the grey stone of the surrounding mountains.

"Grantown-on-Spey. The mountain frontier." He turned to her, his voice as rich and fruity with emotion as Christmas pudding. "Tomorrow, as we venture into the heart of the mountains, you shall see wonders."

He smiled then. "But now, my intrepid, brave, dauntless pirate-witch, for now you will rest, eat game pie, and quaff fresh mountain ale. Perhaps enjoy a local song or two by a roaring fire, enlivened and softened with the finest *uisge-beatha*."

She could almost feel the smooth burn of heather-laced whisky sliding down her throat as she warmed herself by a leaping fire. "Bring it on, Lochaber Gordon."

Tonight, she would consider everything. And soon—after they'd traveled to the ancient market town of Rhynie and seen the Picti wonders there—soon, she would broach the question of talking with the duke.

She was becoming more and convinced that that was something Lochaber needed to do, to heal those childhood wounds.

That, or punch the man fully in the jaw.

Chapter Twenty-Three

The long, weary drive from Grantown-on-Spey to Rhynie faded fast from her mind and muscles. The professors at Rosemarkie were right. The ancient market town had once been a Picti stronghold.

In Rhynie, she'd woken early but couldn't wait for the others to emerge. Walking off her restlessness in the early morning, she tagged onto the edge of a lecture group of some kind—discussing Picti stones!

"As we see here, the mirror and comb—" The historian's plummy vowels rolled among the small but avidly listening crowd like bowling balls.

Ruari's heartbeat smashed in her ears. *Now!* Ask your question. Make your statement. This is a tiny crowd compared to the audience numbers attending the Aberdeen Wise Club symposium. Best to practice now.

The old professor Alexander Ross at Inverness—despite his kindness, she'd been unable to contradict his ideas. She opened her mouth to speak.

Her legs went rubbery, and her stomach tried to squash itself into her neck. An invisible hand tightened her throat. A croaky sound emerged.

Ruari envisioned the sword of her ancestor clenched in her right hand, the fire of her Norse kin flaming in her veins. *For you!* She found her voice. "On what authority are they always termed mirror and comb, sir? Perhaps they represent the sun or moon, or—"

The man spoke on, utterly ignoring her. Good thing she didn't have the warrior's sword in reality, for she'd smite the pompous fool's head from his shoulders.

She pushed her way to the front. Smiled at the people next to her on either side. Repeated her statement, loudly and clearly. "—or astrological symbols."

The tall man stared at her as though she'd grown two heads. His mouth puckered in like he'd swallowed a lemon. Oily, patronizing tones oozed from him. "Wise men who have studied the mysteries of these artifacts for decades have pronounced these *mirror and comb*." He uttered a falsetto laugh. "I think we can rely on their authority." The crowd obediently tittered with him. He dismissed her in an instant. "Now the fish symbol…"

Ruari! Courage! This is just one man—soon you will address many such. Deep breath. "I too have studied these artifacts for many decades—"

Mocking laugh which seared straight to her marrow. "Oh? At which university?" He glanced around the crowd, sharing the joke. Of course no female was permitted to attend those hallowed halls.

A woman's scornful voice cried, "Ignorant Islanders—they never know their place."

Embarrassment prickled and rose like a hot red tide over Ruari's face, neck, chest and down her legs. Fury churned in her belly. A thick lump choked her throat, preventing speech.

The lecturer gestured to the stele behind him— "Shall I talk? Or do you wish to proffer your learned remarks on the Picti Beast, miss?"

She shook her head, silent with mortification.

Her brain whizzed in a panicky loop. This must not repeat when she presented to the Wise Club. Or all of this grand adventure—her wronging of Alasdair MacLeod, her flight from the wicked earl, this reckless, mad journey—would have been in vain. Her reputation shattered. Left with nothing. She would have to become her cousin's pensioner. Her precious, unique Lewis histories and artifacts cleared and lost forever.

Her heart yammered under her breastbone. Fury and humiliation welled as the lecturer's scorn—and her pathetic response—replayed over and over in her mind. Hot tears pricked at the back of her eyes. She pressed her lips tight and willed this weakness away.

Courage, lass! Keep your gaze on your star. Persist. Survive.

When the historian and the crowd dispersed to the next site, Ruari stepped forward to examine the stone alone.

At last! The mysterious Picti Beast. A strange dolphin-like sea-beast, with a long, curved bill and curling limbs. Excitement buzzed gently in her veins again. *Yes!*

A constellation rendered in stone, indicating a specific time of year, positioned to a particular angle to the horizon.

Star maps.

She had enough data to posit her theories. Enough evidence at least to clamor for more research. The Wise Club *must* listen to her now! She must find courage and clarity. Be empowered to present her ideas.

A vivid fantasy unrolled—not only would her star-maps theory gain traction, but the Royal Society would apologize and recognize her science. She would write learned papers. She would attempt to recreate the ancient journeys undertaken by the Picts, by reimagining their unique star maps of the skies...artifacts would be protected all over Scotland...

Her brain sparking like a carnival, Ruari followed the distant lecture group to the next site. Lurked behind a huge old oak tree until they left.

She stared, open-mouthed, at this ancient wonder: Rhynie Man, a clearly etched warrior with a large head, long hair, beaked nose, sharp teeth, and a pointed beard, wielding an axe. "A guard," she whispered, reading a small sign. "To an ancient fort which may have numbered hundreds of roundhouses and thousands of Picts. How *utterly* extraordinary."

"There you are!" Sìneag appeared and tugged her elbow. "Come, Miss Ruari, to your breakfast. Ye'll addle your mind and starve your body with this mad obsession with the Quiet Ones. The verra body I've taken such care of since ye were a wee bairn—"

Ruari laughed. "You go and sample the breakfast and order what you like for me. I promise I will consume it—just as soon as I have seen and copied the Picti stones in the Rhynie kirkyard. I am too excited to eat just yet."

Lochaber stood back, quirking an amused brow. She smiled at him. "You appear half famished too. Go and eat. It's far too early in the day for wicked earls to accost me or other strange adventures to befall me."

Alone once more except for her notebook, Ruari followed the spire to the kirkyard. Wonder possessed her in a kind of ecstatic glee. The Rhynie Picti stones were fabulous, in every sense of the word.

Three Picti steles. Carved with the double disc and Z-rod, and a "mirror and comb"—all of which could be planets, star constellations, and directions. The mirror, with one large circle and two small circles depending from it—in her theories, the design represented alignments of the sun and planets, an eclipse, or the solstices.

A moment of corroding doubt snaked through her. Was she after all, misguided…?

No! The professors at Rosemarkie swam into her mind. They supported her. She *would* present her findings to the world of science, as fearlessly as her Norse and Picti ancestors had once navigated unknown seas to reach a safe new homeland.

Ruari hastened back to the inn, bubbles of victory popping and coursing through her veins. Under Sìneag's watchful eye, she choked down some breakfast.

"Aye, the clearest Picti Beast is just south of Rhynie on the road to Aberdeen," the inn maid told her as she poured more hot tea. "Etched on the Craw Stane."

Ruari hurried them all with their packing and departure, and in very few minutes, the carriage drew up to the Craw Stane. The stone stood six feet high, etched with a graceful shark and, directly under that, a perfectly engraved Picti Beast.

Familiar wonder engulfed her as she sketched the designs in her notebook. Behind her, Sìneag uttered a prayer and the lad Hamish crossed himself.

"I lack one vital piece of evidence," she said to Lochaber. "The Picti were clearly unique. No one can interpret their mysterious carvings and purpose. Yet I arrived at my ideas from an experience long ago in my girlhood."

Lochaber assisted her back onto the driver's box and wrapped her in plaids. Once Hamish and Sìneag were tucked safe inside, and he had taken the reins in his calm, strong hands, he asked, "Yes?"

She studied him. His gold-peat eyes shone bright and intent. He really wished to know.

"When my uncle lived, he sent me to a snooty finishing school in London. I mostly detested it—the headmistress refused to let me play the bagpipes—hated it except for the education itself and visits to London museums."

"No bagpipes in a crowded girls' school. Very sensible. Imagine if you had roused their savage blood with your music?"

"Ha! No chance of that. Most of those English misses had whey in their veins in place of fierce blood."

Lochaber held the reins in one hand and stroked her cheek with the other. "Tell me."

"They took us to the British Museum, and there I beheld the most extraordinary collection of art and objects created by the Aboriginal peoples of the Australian colonies. While my group of girls wandered away, bored, I was transfixed by several dot paintings, which the curator—I am forever grateful he deigned to speak with a hurly-burly schoolgirl—explained were geographic visual maps of waterholes and travel paths, star stories and star maps. My brain must have made a jump to my strange Lewis Picti stones and fermented internally ever since. One day, looking at the Picti artifacts on MacDonald lands, the idea simply exploded in my mind. This whole journey is an exploration of that."

****

The disaster happened as the late afternoon sun gilded the mountain peaks and cast long purple shadows in slanting lines. Lochaber and Ruari were taking their turn inside. He estimated they were a mere few miles before Sauchen. Of the all the damnedest luck! He had hoped to rattle through, closing his eyes on the familiar peaks and forests of his childhood land.

Two nights ago at the Granton-on-Spey inn, they had filled themselves with ale and whisky, game pie and grouse pâté, laughed at local jokes and nodded their heads to mountain music.

Home! Sang his blood. When he had bitten into that first bite of game pie—a torrent of memories exploded in his brain like a spring flood.

And Miss Ruari's face as she listened to the fiddle and pipes, her eyes like stars as she tapped eager hands on her knees. And taking the whistle and joining the locals in stirring tunes…his heart had turned over, leapt up, announced a rush of emotion as bright as sunshine after rain.

And then Rhynie. Ruari blazed like a beacon of happiness beside him.

But now! The conveyance shuddered and jerked— had a wheel caught? The carriage, with him and Ruari inside—locked in a delicious embrace—rocked alarmingly, then teetered and crashed on its side.

Outside, Hamish's Gaelic cursing overlaid Sìneag's blistering dressing-down of the lad for a green fool. The horses kicked and neighed.

Ruari's soft form lay on top of him.

Her dark eyes held amusement rather than ladylike distress. "Well, this is a surprise," she said.

His hands came up to run along her cheeks, slide down her arms. "Are you well?" A spear of terror lanced him. If she had been hurt! Luckily his whipcord reflexes enabled him to fling his body beneath hers as they toppled.

"I'm fine! And you?" After his nod, she added, "We must clamber out and see to the horses, and Sineag and Hamish."

"We are currently lying on the door. The carriage has capsized. Flexible as I am, I cannot fit my frame through that window."

Ruari screwed her face around to examine the window. Looked back into his eyes and graced him with a dancing, mischievous grin. "But I can. The three of us should be able to push the carriage to rights and release you. But you must wait until I see to the horses."

Lochaber nodded, sick to his toenails. To dwell here, useless, while Ruari, a lad, and an old, though feisty, maid freed them. It was too much.

As though she heard his thoughts, Ruari stared at him. "Bide here, Lochy, and we will free you anon."

He supported her while she thrust her head and shoulders out of the window, now the ceiling of the carriage. The floor was the door side. "Are you all right out there?" Urgency laced her voice.

"Aye, we're fine. I've cut the horses free." Hamish's panicky tones floated back.

Lochaber said, "You'll never be able to right—"

"Blast! Lochy, I must remove my dress to be able to get through this window. Too much fabric. Here, help me, can't you?"

"I'm always glad to remove your dress." A tinkling laugh rewarded him.

He gripped her. "But Ruari, sweet lass, you'll freeze in this mountain air only clad in your chemise."

"Come on, get these fastenings undone! Stop your maundering."

Lochaber obliged and watched as Ruari's round

bottom, covered only in thin, soft white linen and lace, wriggled and contorted. By the time she had squeezed half her body through the aperture, he had a rod as stiff and hard as a fire poker. Damn, he was an evil man.

"Loch, I'm…stuck."

Her bottom poked at him, round and luscious. Her long shapely legs bunched and pushed. And underneath all that…he swallowed. Underneath, she was bared naked to his gaze.

He stretched a fingertip up. Traced it up her thigh. *Grazed her cleft.* She jumped. Froze. He stroked again. She wriggled. He reached both hands and cupped her lovely round bottom cheeks. Squeezed.

"Give me a little push, will you?"

And finally, despite the roaring, clamoring of his inflamed blood, he held both those plump cheeks and pushed her from the carriage window.

He gathered her dress and shoved it after her. "Put your dress on," he shouted. "Before you catch a chill. *Sìneag.* See to your mistress."

He pressed his head to the window, trying to ascertain what was happening. Never had he felt so powerless. So frustrated. If that whelp Hamish had caused this accident, he had better be running now.

Suddenly the carriage began to tilt. How on earth? A man's voice, thick and gravelly Highlander, threaded through all the other sounds. Help had arrived.

Lochaber waited in the carriage, simmering with frustrated fury, while slowly the carriage tipped the right way up, but slewed down to the left. A broken wheel perhaps.

"All right! I'm getting out! Hold on." He slammed and kicked at the carriage door until it wedged open, and he burst from the carriage.

The horses were free, two grazing by the side of the mountain road and two nose-deep in a peaty burn drizzling from the hillside. A skinny sharp-ribbed nag grazed alongside them.

A large man clothed in dirty, ragged plaids stood by Ruari and Hamish. He smiled and nodded at Lochaber. "All's right, my lord. A wee repair and ye'll be on your way agin."

Ruari still stood in her chemise. Lochaber scooped up her dress and held it to her. "Miss MacDonald," he grated. He glared at the man, daring him to watch, while Sìneag assisted her mistress to become decent once more.

The man cocked an eyebrow at Lochaber, opened his mouth.

Lochaber grated, "Make one joke about scantily dressed women, and your life is forfeit." He stepped forward and loomed over the man.

Typical Highlander. He didn't quail, instead grinned cheekily, revealing a mouth of blackened teeth. "I'd say a scanty woman is an opportunity, not a joke, sir."

Lochaber's snapped reply could have frosted the fires of hell. "Miss MacD—the *young lady*—had to remove her dress to squeeze from the carriage." He shook his head. "I don't need to explain myself to you. Tell me, where is the nearest inn? The ladies need to warm themselves and recover while we check this infernal carriage."

The Highlander smirked. "Just yester night, I stayed in a braw accommodation. The vittles, so delicate; a mere three spots of blue on the hard bread, bursting like spring flowers. The ale, it's true, was more of the brackish water variety, but then, it's all about the company, is it not? Such witty conversation and informed parley. An old lag, a drunk, and a highwayman—aye, quite the crush in that establishment yester eve. The best steel manacles, wrought of the heaviest metals. Even the towel was stamped with the duke's crown."

Lochaber's hands twitched, but he managed not to strangle the decrepit jailbird. "I want an inn, not a jail."

But the man spoke in the accents of Lochaber's childhood. The Highlander's humor and dignity, despite desperate circumstances, rang a chord deep in his belly. And the lag had stopped to help them.

"Here," said Lochaber. "I thank you. Perhaps this will ensure a comfortable bed, game pie, and proper ale, for a night or two." He tossed him a sovereign. The man snapped out a fist and caught it deftly. Bowed.

"Thanks, freen. Dinna fash yersel, I'll be on me way then." He quirked a hairy brow. "Look after the lass. She's a fine, feisty one." He mounted his skinny old horse and ambled off.

Look after the lass.

His childhood home, Clàrsach Castle, the seat of the Duke of Gordon, could be less than two miles hence. With a quick visit, he could warm the ladies and ask the duke to sponsor Ruari at the Wise Club.

Ruari could save her artifacts and lands and begin on the path toward her dream. A female Picti professor. The fellowship of bright minds that would inflame her own brilliant intellect. The company and life that she deserved.

A tearing feeling lanced his heart. His innards were being carved up with the sharpest, wickedest *patta* sword. Shrieking echoed in his brain.

Humble himself to ask the duke for his patronage?

The man who had wronged him, robbed him of his name, deprived him of his rightful inheritance, through willful negligence?

Lochaber choked on nausea. His life's dream. His vow of vengeance. The fire of ambition that had driven his success in the world.

By Shiva!

He would find an inn in Sauchen to succor the ladies. He would revenge himself on the bastard duke. And think up another way for Ruari to present at the Wise Club in Aberdeen.

He had two days.

One day to travel to Aberdeen. One day to find a sponsor for Ruari.

That would have to do.

Chapter Twenty-Four

"Yes, His Grace is in residence at Clàrsach Castle, my lady." The maid in the pretty inn finished pouring blissfully warm water into the hipbath by the fire and bobbed a curtsey. She lowered her voice to a confiding whisper. "And his housekeeper with him. He will not marry her, although she bore him seven children, three living."

Ruari wrestled with temptation. Failed. "How many sons?"

"Just one, miss. Lost. Gone away. When he was barely grown from a lad, my mam told me. 'Tis said the duke pines and grieves his wicked old heart for his only son. He spent *years* combing the world for news of him. But the old duke is a proud one. He waits. Waits and laments. All those riches, all that power, and he chooses, out of bluidy-minded stubbornness, to not lift a finger for the thing he wants most. His only son."

Ruari peeled off her dirty, damp clothes and tested the water with a curving foot. Oooh! Gratefully, she stepped into the tiny bath and immersed her entire body, sighing with pleasure. "And his sisters?"

"The younger one married a farmer, gone to live on the Borders." The maid tossed her head and sniffed, conveying her poor opinion of the Lowland Scots. "Even though they were duke's daughters, they could only hope to marry a man who needed wealth. Plenty of that type of man in society, of course. But no lords as befitted their station. Stained, they are. 'Twould have been better if His Grace married his housekeeper, scandalous though that would ha' been."

The maid soaped Ruari's hair, massaging her scalp with strong fingers. Ruari wallowed in bliss for several minutes.

"And the elder sister?"

"Gone away to France. Distraught when her brother left. They were close, all the castle folk say."

A plan began to tickle in Ruari's mind. Lochaber hated families. He was bent on his revenge. But mad though they might be, impossible and crazy and reckless and completely maddening on top, well—family was family.

Lochaber was grown now, rich and talented and clever. And he had built all that himself. His desire for vengeance was a lad's bitter ambition, stunted and thwarted, never shaken out into the light.

She must somehow show him that as a man now, he didn't need all that fiery craving anymore. His own remarkable skills and talents could propel him forward.

The duke had grieved bitterly for all the years of his son's absence—surely that was revenge enough?

Lochaber was fine alone. He didn't need his family to support him, or guide him, or shape him. He had done all that as a lonely, clever boy, all by himself.

But he needed his family for something.

To love him.

Ruari thoughtfully washed one foot, then another.

Perhaps if he forgave them, welcomed them, that bitter ice inside him could thaw. If he forgave them, accepted them, he could free up space to love with a whole heart. He could love his own family—and know the healing, joyful power of loving others.

Could she employ Lochaber's regard for her as a lever? Could she plead with him to ask his father to sponsor her at the Wise Club?

Everything in her revolted. *No.* He must make the choice himself. Not be tricked or flattered or manipulated into greeting his father.

Ruari splashed water on her face. By all her warrior ancestors! This lovely warm bath was making her maudlin and fanciful.

But it also gave her ideas. She revolved a scheme in her mind to ensure her entry to the Aberdeen Philosophical Society. She didn't need Lochy to sacrifice his fine revenge. He must do that for his own sake, not hers.

She wouldn't ask her Sìneag to help, either. She'd ask this friendly, gossipy inn maid.

Ruari grinned and submerged herself in the water before stepping out into the folds of a giant soft, warm towel.

She recalled line by line that appalling letter from the Royal Society, adding fire to her purpose.

****

"Are you sure, my lady?" The maid, Osla, held the scissors, wide-eyed. "You have such pretty hair." The maid's gaze raked Ruari from head to foot. "The footman's wee brother's clothes look well on you, if verra strange. But if you cut your bonnie hair, ye'll look like a lad, and no mistake."

"That's the aim, Osla. Quick now, before my Sìneag decides to check in on me."

"I'll get in trouble for not fetching her first, my

lady."

"Nonsense. I'll pay you..." Ruari mentally reviewed the sad contents of her purse. "Nay, I'll give you a—" She swallowed. Marshalled her courage. Pirates took with daring and dash. And they gave with impunity. "—an old and very beautiful brooch, which you must treasure always. Owned by a warrior maiden from the islands. The brooch will lend you her warrior strength."

Ruari closed her eyes against the pang smiting her heart. Compressed her trembling lips. The brooch was *just a thing*. She would give the jewel in one of the greatest acts of courage in her life. She felt in her bones that the warrior maiden of Tolstachaolais would approve.

The maid's voice, low and sweet, answered, "Very well, my lady. The quality does ask for unusual things, but I've never shorn a lady's hair. Do you want to watch in the mirror?"

Heavens, no.

"Quickly now, Osla."

Ruari sat stiff and tall as the heavy scissors pulled and tugged at her hair, making chopping, lopping sounds. All around her, long shining hanks of brown locks dropped onto the floor.

As Osla chopped, Ruari began to get the strangest sensation. Her head lightened. Her neck flexed comfortably. Her entire spine rose up, straight and free.

She had sacrificed her hair so she could pretend to be a man, so Lochaber did not have to demean himself to his father. But instead—!

Her head felt light and open, the better to think and plan and analyze. Blast men! Why should they enjoy all this liberty of short hair and comfortable clothing?

When the maid had finished, she solemnly handed Ruari the mirror. As Ruari gazed on her new appearance, a little shock traveled from her stomach and flip-flopped in her heart. Squeezed her throat until she choked.

Pride steeled her jaw and squared her shoulders.

Not bereft of beauty.

Free.

Before she lost courage, Ruari went to her belongings and rummaged in her pack. She drew out the brooch and stared at it longingly, then kissed it, uttered a silent prayer, and gave it to Osla, who held it, open-mouthed with wonder.

The maid thrust it back to Ruari. "Oh, my lady, it's too beautiful. I'm verra glad to do you a service. That brooch is wasted on a tumshie maid. Here. You keep it."

Yes! How her heart leapt!

But no.

Ruari folded the girl's fingers over the brooch. "The brooch is yours now, Osla. Let it inspire you and lend you courage when you most need it. And think of me when you wish to do something a little mad." She smiled reassuringly.

Osla clutched the hand holding the brooch to her chest. A flush spread over her cheeks, and her eyes blazed. Apparently, she had finally run out of words. She nodded, curtsied, and departed, her new talisman held tight against her ribs.

Ruari rummaged through her clothing and picked out her fussiest petticoat, adorned with fine lace and delicate embroidery. She studied it for a long moment, and then in her second grand, symbolic gesture, pitched it from her window.

The white flounced petticoat flapped and

somersaulted in the wind, like a strange white seabird delighted to be freed.

And now to dinner.

****

Lochaber nodded to the young lad who slid into the bar, dressed in tweed breeches, waistcoat, and cap. Something familiar about him. He quickly looked away. This place could be filled with Gordons, relatives, old retainers, their families, people whom he had known in his youth.

Took a large sip of ale.

And then spat it over the counter.

His gaze snapped back to the lad.

God in heaven, the lad was mad, bad Ruari MacDonald, blast her shining violet eyes and wicked, saucy smile!

A blast of realization shook him to his core.

The wench had done it for him! Disguised herself as a man, all so he did not have to speak to his horrible father.

The world tilted. Turned upside down.

He was only a coward, and she the fearless warrior.

Lochaber Gordon, you yellow-bellied, lily-livered selfish fool.

"There's no need for that *amaideachd*," he snapped. "I'll speak to my father this evening. He'll sponsor you if I have to—"

"—Tell him you missed him?"

Pain slashed Lochaber's chest. "I shall do nothing of the sort. I'll tell him—"

"—That you love them all?"

Lochaber spluttered. His cheeks flushed red, then he blanched alarmingly pale.

He battled shock already. She may as well show him the worst.

With elaborate casualness, Ruari pulled her cap from her head and shook her chin-length shorn locks. "Fetch me an ale," she grunted in a deep voice to the barkeep. "Please," she added. Just because she was a lad, didn't mean she would be rude.

She slid a curious glance to Lochaber, who held his glass suspended midair, his eyes starting from his head. "You didn't," he breathed.

"I certainly did. And I feel light and free and marvelous."

"Your lovely hair."

"Don't start weeping, for Chrissake, Loch. It's only hair." She shot him the cheekiest grin she could manage. "Oh, such fun. Cursing and blaspheming. Bloody. Bollocks. Tits!" The last word sprang from her lips as a squeak, for Lochaber had risen, taken one firm pace, crowded her against the bar, and pinned her with a ferocious glare.

Her heart didn't yet know it was a lad, for it raced in a rather fluttery, maidenly fashion.

He growled, "What else have you done, Ruari the Tartar?"

She was almost afraid, he appeared so severe.

His eyes flashed, deep in their sockets. His cheekbones and jaw could have been mined from the granite mountains outside. "You did it because I am too spineless to speak with my father. Didn't you?"

"Lochaber, I—"

"Well, I won't have it! Don't do anything else, because I'm going this instant."

He slammed down his ale, slopping amber liquid

over the bar. His hand actually shook.

"Fine then. I'm coming with."

Lochaber froze, his expression a picture of seasonal change compressed to a moment: the light of summer, the dour gray freeze of winter, hope springing forth…

Ruari rose from her stool and hooked her hand in his arm. "And no, I'm not changing to meet your father, the grand duke. You won't wait while I don a dress. So, we go like this."

And then, just like a miracle, a slow smile tickled at the corner of his mouth, wiggled a little of that sternness away, and then the smile spread: wide mouth, bunched cheeks, laughing eyes, brows lost in the blaze of his hair.

"You wench," he gasped. "You clever, brilliant, unique, mad pirate. That will do nicely."

And then the laugh burst from him, bellowing and filling the room. Ruari couldn't help but laugh too. The barkeep grinned, adding a few unlikely high-pitched snorting guffaws, and the cook rushed in to see what all the fuss was about and joined in the laughter, flapping a serving cloth. Three maids belted into the bar and giggled and sniggered. Soon the whole bar shook with the uproar.

Hamish rushed in, followed by Sìneag, and was engulfed in a great Lochaber hug.

Hamish peeled himself away. 'My l-lord," he stuttered. "We must make haste."

Lochaber cuffed him on the shoulder. "What ails ye, lad? Relax, have an ale."

"Nay, my lord." Hamish shifted his feet. "The Duke of Gordon is not in his castle—he went to Aberdeen two nights past."

Sìneag interjected, hands on hips and surveying the

mad, laughing throng with profound disapproval. "Those addle-pated professors had their dates wrong. The duke will open the Aberdeen Philosophers' Club Symposium—*on the morrow*."

Tomorrow? But she wasn't prepared! She gripped Sìneag's arms. Her faithful old friend set her lips and nodded.

Lochaber blazed with purpose like a momentarily arrested comet. A pillar of fire. "Hellfire and damnation! We must get you there in time, Miss Ruari MacDonald, to present your findings, to those who can create change." He whirled on Hamish, who quailed under that flaming gaze. "You are sure of your facts, whippet? We would not want to hasten through the night to mighty Aberdeen town, only to discover the duke snug back here within the walls of Gordon Castle. Your head would not stay long on those spindly shoulders."

"Leave the lad be," commanded Sìneag, with all the vigor of a lifelong maid of a riotous Hebridean family. "You should be ashamed, Lochaber Gordon, to bully a wee lad who is doing you a service."

Lochaber's face was instantly contrite. "Indeed. I apologize unreservedly, young Hamish. I thank you for uncovering this urgent truth."

His gaze shot to Ruari, who leaned on the bar, admiring this inferno of energy and decision. She might be dressed as a lad, but all that magnificent male possessiveness, that remarkable, honed physique and high-powered brain, all functioning at her service…well, it made her *lust* for him in the most female fashion, from her hairline to her toenails.

"I will be ready in fifteen minutes," she said. "How long will it take to get to Aberdeen?"

"Four hours," called one of the farmers avidly observing the drama.

An elderly man with a pipe tapped his cane. "*Breislich* nonsense! Not less than five, by the stars."

A feisty lad called, "Not more than three hours in a carriage. I've done it in two, with a fast transport. I'll drive you, for two gold sovereigns."

Men and their equipages! If these Highlanders were anything like her brother and the MacDonald men, the debate might rage for hours. Ruari turned to Sìneag, who forestalled her.

The maid said, "I'll order dinner in a basket from the kitchen, to be eaten on our way. Hot drinks, rugs, hot bricks." Ruari nodded, and Sìneag bustled away.

She said to Lochaber, "It might be a good idea to get a local to drive us. They know these treacherous mountain roads."

"These yokels? Probably never left Sauchen in their lives."

Ruari considered him. The man burnt with energy. She knew that fire—she burned with the same flame whenever she examined her artifacts, ancient burials, carved and engraved stones. "And where will we stay, once in Aberdeen?"

He regarded her grimly, all light and laughter vanished from his face—now a hard, blank granite slate. "We will stay with the duke."

"No, Loch, not at all necessary—

"You will rest in comfort with what remains of the night. On the morrow, you shall present your remarkable findings and, more importantly, your theories and ideas, to the Wise Club of Aberdeen. Presenting as yourself, Miss Ruari MacDonald, under the patronage of the Duke of Gordon."

He radiated determination, force, will. His body vibrated with purpose. He lowered his voice, warmth creeping in. "Please. Allow me to do you this service, my Ruari. I will carve away any obstacle that stands between you and your dream. I will employ every scrap of grit, lever open every option that I have, and many that I don't."

"I will be presenting as myself, male or female. Ruairidh is more often a man's name."

He sank warm hands onto her shoulders. Teased the hair ends bouncing at her chin. "I recognize you now." Hoarse. "Curse me that it has taken this long. From the first, I wanted you, so beautiful and desirable. I soon knew you are a woman in a hundred, a million. But now? Almost too late, I've had a blast of realization: within that beautiful, determined, curious woman beats a heart that thrills to destiny and adventure. *Like mine.* Full of courage, though driven by love and loyalty. Not by bitterness and a savage drive for vengeance."

Lochaber gazed at down at her, his brown eyes vulnerable and open. "I…love you, Ruari MacDonald." He lowered hungry lips onto hers. She sank into his desperate embrace, kissed him back with the fervor swelling her heart. The room shrank and disappeared. There was only her Lochy, the heat of his body, his passionate kiss, the words beating in her mind in time with the pulse of her blood. *I love you, Ruari MacDonald.* She must answer him. The moment they stopped kissing.

"No time for that, my lord and lady!" The ribald accents finally pierced Ruari's consciousness. "If ye want to make Aberdeen. What say I drive ye, and ye can

302

kiss and canoodle all the way in yon carriage?"

Lochaber ripped his mouth from Ruari's but kept her gripped firmly in his embrace. "I will drive her, and no one else." He looked down at her. "Outside then, in fifteen minutes. If you will permit this *bastard* to serve you."

"Lochaber, I—"

"Shh. Later."

Ruari quirked the left side of her mouth at him. Wriggled her breasts a little, just to see lust spark in his warm gaze.

She nodded. "To Aberdeen."

And to both our epiphanies.

Mine, presenting my ideas to people who will embrace and debate them. Save the MacDonald lands and their unique Neolithic and Picti artifacts.

And Lochaber will speak to his father, the duke.

She rushed away to her rooms, mind whirling with lines of argument, possible questions. Mentally shoring up her facts and evidence about Picts and Norse, warrior maidens, and selkie legends.

I love you, Ruari MacDonald.

She hugged his words to her like a talisman. They would keep her safe and warm, while she stood in front of a crowd of learned men, alone on the podium, with only her knowledge and passion to impress them.

Chapter Twenty-Five

Ruari refused to sit in the carriage alone while Lochaber drove them. Instead, wreathed in rugs, exulting in the brisk, clean air, she huddled next to him, watching his large capable hands with fascination as he handled the reins with dexterity. Imagined those hands on *her*…

Lochaber had hired fresh horses, the fastest the inn at Sauchen could provide, and a light, fast phaeton from the lad at the inn, the better to get to Aberdeen with all speed. Hamish and Sìneag would follow in another vehicle.

This night was one of the most magical of Ruari's life. In the speed and darkness, alone with Lochaber, rushing through a starlit night toward the greatest dream of her life…

"*Lucky*," she murmured.

"Yes. You may call me that now. For I have had the great luck to find you, Miss Ruari MacDonald, pirate maid. Thief of a man's worst characteristics, leaving him…No. It's not possible." A flash of surprise animated his expression. He turned to her in the darkness, moonlight gleaming on the harsh planes of his face. "I feel…happy!" His brows disappeared into his hair. "How utterly extraordinary."

She laughed. "I'm happy too," she answered softly. "And lucky too. I love this night, under the sparkling stars, here with you. Rushing toward our chosen destinies. The great mountains in jagged silhouette against the floating silver moon. The fresh smell of the mountains. Unique, is it not?"

Lochaber shot her a quick look, before studying the rough road before then once more. "That smell is the scent of home for me. Brings happy memories crashing back. I had forgotten joy dwells in these peaks and valleys too. And you are energetically like home for me. We belong."

Cold wind whipped her cheeks. The rhythmic clatter of the horses and the solid warmth of Lochy next to her lulled her into a doze. The mountains rose and parted as the view changed in a series of majestic, breathtaking views, under a velvet sky studded with stars.

All too soon, Lochaber steered the team through an imposing arch and up a wide gravel drive lined with elegant trees. In the distance, a palatial manor blocked out the night sky.

"My father's Aberdeen residence," Lochaber gritted. The cold mask had slammed down over grim features. His lips curled in a snarl. His nostrils flared in disdain. For his father? For himself, for adjusting his vow of vengeance?

That had to hurt. He needed to reunite with his family. But could she be the cause of it?

"Lochaber. We can stay at an inn in Aberdeen. Do this when you are ready. Not for me. Not tonight."

Finally. A tiny, glinting smile, like a dragonfly alighting on a pool. "I will never be ready to reunite with my horrid father, my Ruari. So permit me to do it for unselfish reasons. The novelty alone of acting in an unselfish manner amuses me sufficiently to keep going."

They pulled up at the grand entrance of the towering

mansion. Pillared and terraced and staired. *Blast*. Was she ready for this? She was of noble descent, but of the islands, accustomed to great crumbling castles, impertinent, opinionated servants, and machair-laced landscapes. Not this…this edifice, this scream of centuries of wealth and privilege. How would these mainland royals take her, a forthright island maiden, long lost to propriety and refined manners? She'd been so concerned about Lochaber, she hadn't thought…

Pull yourself together, Ruari the Turbulent. This man needs you. Victory or Death. By sea and by land. The blood of both her clans beat strong in her veins.

Lochaber hammered and bashed on the heavy front door.

The door finally opened. A tall, stooped elderly man stood there, holding a lantern high. Coat thrown over pajamas.

Silence.

"Is it you, wee Lochaber? Is it yourself, come home?" The lantern shook, casting rippling light over the scene. Flash. Lochaber's jaw working. Flash. Polished floor. Paintings. Flash. The old man's face, trembling. Tears running down his whiskery cheeks.

Ruari grabbed the lantern. Lochaber stepped forward. "Currie. Yes, it's me." He embraced the man, while snuffling noises emerged from somewhere within Lochaber's waistcoat. "Miss MacDonald, this the Gordon family butler, Currie. It's very good to see you, man."

The Gordon family. Not *our family*. Not yet.

"Is the duke within?" Ruari asked, when the old butler seemed like to leave them standing on the front steps while he stared as though piskie-led at Lochaber.

"Nay, lass, Miss MacDonald. Soon, perhaps. But the mistress…! Her old heart will crack with the joy of it. Come ben, come ben." As he mentioned his mistress, he woke from his enchantment.

He shuffled inside, muttering, "I'll call the stable hands to care for your team. They'll be fed and groomed this instant, young Lochy. And the good whisky to warm you, after that cold ride."

Soaring ceilings. Walls covered with huge oil paintings and ancient weapons. Creaking suits of armor. The scent of beeswax and linseed oil.

And then, the library. A huge, book-lined room, large comfortable chairs by the fireplace, and a gleaming table under the windows.

The old butler handed out exquisite carved crystal glasses containing an inch of glowing amber whisky. He bent and touched the flint to the wood arranged in the hearth, and soon a roaring fire crackled and danced.

In moments, a blushing maid appeared, curtseying and staring bug-eyed at Lochaber, while she handed out shortbreads. "I'm to take ye to your room, now, ma'am."

Ruari looked to Lochaber. "Go then," he said. "Rest. I'll see you in the morning." He cupped her chin in his warm hand and brushed her lips with a kiss.

She followed the maid up a tall curving staircase and along a dim corridor, lined with more paintings and scented with flowers. The maid showed Ruari to a richly decorated room, fire already taking the chill from the room, plush covers on a high bed invitingly turned back.

"There's warm water in the jug and tooth powder and brush, all you need there on the dresser, my lady." She curtsied again. "Shall you be needing anything else?"

"No. I thank you. My maid Sìneag will arrive at some point. I have no need of her tonight. You can show her a bed, and I'll see her in the morning."

"Aye, my lady."

And then she was alone.

Ruari's mind whirled. Voices and words slammed in and out of her brain. All these new experiences, new emotions. Suddenly it was all too much. That soft bed called. Ruari washed her face and body using the jug and bowl, cleaned her teeth, plaited her hair, and donned the delicate lace nightgown laid out on the bed.

She gratefully climbed under the covers.

A knock at the door.

Ruari sat bolt upright. Had Lochaber come...?

The door opened.

And then, a tall, grim woman with Lochaber's golden-peat eyes entered the room.

Ruari leapt from the bed and wrapped herself in the over-gown draped conveniently over the back of a chair.

"Please, sit." The woman gestured to one of the chairs by the fire. "I know it's very late."

Oh-oh. Would she be ejected, as unsuitable for the son of the house? Was she in for a reprimand? Fury began to coil in Ruari's stomach. This woman, clearly his mother, had betrayed her son by allowing him to be born a bastard. Staining his whole life. Embittering the generous heart with which he had been born.

Lochaber's mother produced a glowing bottle of whisky from within her dressing gown. She treated Ruari to a wicked grin. It was so much like her son's that Ruari's fury abated a little.

The woman took two small glasses from a cupboard and poured them both a dram.

She studied Ruari. Ruari studied her right back. Lochaber had much of this woman in him. The height. The imposing dignity. The determination radiating from her like waves. He must get his beautiful flaming red hair from his father.

The woman's low voice rang deep and resonant. She probably had a lovely contralto singing tone. "So. You are the means of reuniting me with my only son. I began to think I would die before setting eyes on him again."

Oh, my ancestors. The poor woman. Ruari's fury faded some more. A mere tickle on the edge of her brain.

"I understand from Lochaber—" His mother gulped. Smiled with down-turned wobbling lips as she dashed a tear from her cheeks with impatient fingers. "When I discovered you were the means of reuniting me with my only son, I had to set eyes on this extraordinary woman."

She held out her glass. Ruari clinked it. "Tell me about yourself. From the lonely islands."

"I'd rather hear about your family. Lochaber as a child. You must long to talk about him. And I am very ready to hear it."

"Oh, your voice. The music of the islands sings in your accent. No wonder my son is bespelled."

Ruari narrowed her eyes. Was that a jab, after all? Pretend friendship and then spike her to death?

She'd had too much whisky. And she may never have another chance like this one. Ruari the pirate sea-queen demanded answers. "We aren't ready to have a friendly chat."

"No? No."

Ruari gulped her drink. "*A bastard*? You profess to love your son, and yet you allowed him to be born *a bastard*?"

The woman slopped more Glen Garioch in Ruari's glass, eyes fixed on the act of pouring.

Ruari said, desperate to know the answer, to understand this enigma, "Being a bastard has embittered his entire life. It's why he left home. It stung him to become a driven success, so he could wreak vengeance on all who had wronged him. Can you see how that would corrode a man's heart?" She got up and paced. Swallowed whisky.

"And I want that heart, do you understand me? Not black and corroded and desperate and bitter. But able to give and love, to permit himself happiness. And you have—maybe—robbed me of all that! The finest, best man of my acquaintance. Poisoned by his birth. You remain with his father, do you not? Then why not marry the man? Surely you have some sway with the duke?"

Lochaber's mother's mouth twisted. "That fire, that ambition? That determination? He gets it from me."

Ruari sat. Put her hands on her thighs. Listening, with everything she had.

"Lochaber and his sisters were born bastards, out of love."

What?

The woman smiled gently. "The duke, he is a foolish, vain man, who lives for silly hopes. He likes to think of himself as a young, fiery buck. He lives to believe the gorgeous, impossible woman of his dreams is just around the next corner. He hates to feel trapped, to feel tied down. He wants to feel he has options."

Ruari waited, staring into the dancing flames. In the strangest way, this was starting to make sense. Everything rebelled. She wanted to revile and hate this woman. But instead, a blossom of admiration unfurled a little in her heart.

The duke's elderly lover said, quiet-voiced, "You are an unconventional woman, or I could not say all this to you. I am sorry Lochaber was so bitter about being a bastard. But he was a bastard from love. His father the duke needs me, as he needs no other. I ensure him a happy existence. I shield him from unpleasant reality. I allow him to see himself as a hero, the man in his imagination. He loves me, in his own way. And I am content. To be with him in any way I can. Because my love for him is fierce, and honest, and unblinking. Ageless and timeless and as deep-rooted as the Cairngorm mountains. There is *nothing* I would not do for him."

She sipped her Glen Garioch, eyeing Ruari with those hot brown eyes. Everything else—her night rail, her smooth plaited hair, her composed features—spoke of grace and decorum. Only her eyes revealed the ferocity and focus inside.

Just like her son's.

She said, "Do you love my son like that?"

Ruari met her fierce gaze with one of her own. Uncowed. "Do you know," she said, "I believe I do."

They locked gazes. Clinked glasses. Drank.

Lochaber's mother nodded once and departed in a whisper of skirts.

Well.

****

Ruari woke before the dawn, just like every morning of her life, despite all the shocks and surprises yesterday wrought.

Need buzzed in her skin, hungered in her guts.

She pulled her MacDonald plaids from her trunk and

donned them. Skirt. *Earasaid*, which she could wrap over shoulders and head.

Time to go searching.

Ruari tiptoed down regal staircases as wide as her father's smaller hall. She peered into rooms filled with elegant furniture, history, luxury, all maintained to perfection—the legacy of bearing children with your housekeeper, she surmised.

At last! Near the grand library, she opened the door on a small pretty room containing harp, piano, baskets of whistles, racks of flutes, stringed instruments, drums and percussion. She pulled open a large, polished cabinet. There!

Seven different sizes and styles of bagpipes, including two she had never seen. For a few moments, she fingered their elegant red bags and short chanters, ablaze with curiosity.

Pink fingers of light crept around the curtains. The Gordon piper was most remiss. Still abed.

Ruari gathered the largest, loudest, most impressive set of Highland pipes, brash with Gordon tartan. She staggered under their weight, then distributed it around her body. The strap diagonally across her chest, firmly holding the instrument to her body, she went up and up— and up.

Mountains stretched to the west, shades of blue and gray overlying each other and blending with the pale sky. To the east and below, the great city of Aberdeen spread before her. The Gordon mansion sat in ornate pleasure gardens. And farther toward the rosy dawn...the heaving, calling, sparkling sea.

Ruari hoisted her pipes and gave a preliminary blast. Not as bottomy as her own set, but strong and fearless.

She blew another blast, to greet the day.

And then she played, blowing free and wild—a song of her heart, of her island home, of her much-missed, beloved family, of ancestors and seals and warrior maidens long turned to dust, leaving only their sword and their brooch for their kinswoman to discover.

She played hard and loud and long, the wind whipping her hair and tears streaming down her cheeks, arms and lungs aching.

But still she played on, as the dawn turned the sea to molten, moving gold and ruby, and far out to the ocean a pod of seals bounced on the waves.

I will swim with you again.

A great cheering echoed from the castle yard. As her song died away, carried over sea and land to her heart's home, she looked down. The castle yard was full of people—servants, stable hands, townsfolk. The housekeeper-duchess, tall and proud, lifted a hand in greeting. Or perhaps benediction. The entire crowd cheered and waved once more.

And then a shadow detached itself from a pillar, here on the rooftops. Lochaber.

He came to stand next to her. Put his arm around her, pulled her close. Claimed her, in the sight of all his people.

"What will you wear, this day, my Ruari?" he asked her, brushing a tear away with a fingertip. "For the day you claim your right to speak with learned men, professors, historians. Will you dress in your breeches?"

She smiled slantwise up at him. "I will not wear borrowed garb this day, Lochaber Gordon. I go as myself, Ruari MacNeil MacDonald, daughter of the Islands." She raised a fist to the crowd milling below. "I

313

will wear my own mother's MacNeil tartans. *Victory or Death*."

Among all the fists raised back, the duchess held her clenched fist high, a jeweled bracelet shining in the morning sun like a promise.

A sound like thunder split the fresh early air. A high crested carriage, pulled by a thundering team of horses, careened through the gateposts, spraying bystanders with pebbles and mud and sending castle servants diving into the shrubberies for cover.

The entire equipage shuddered to a mad, swerving stop in the center of the yard.

Servants hustled forward but too late.

The door banged open. A small sprightly man with a crest of blazing red hair alighted from the carriage. Fisted his hands on his hips. He stood, legs well apart, staring up at the rooftops, where Lochaber lurked, arm tight about her waist.

In the booming voice of a much larger man, the duke—for surely it could be no other—cried, "Is that my son up there? Lochaber Gordon. Is it finally you?"

Lochaber's body stiffened against her.

Chapter Twenty-Six

Thank all the gods he had his arm tight around Ruari. The world tilted and spun in a multi-colored vortex. High-pitched screaming rang in his ears. Spears of lightning scissored in his blood.

"Lochaber. Lochaber." Ruari's whisper came from far away. "I have you."

There. Down below. Staring up at him. His hated father.

His beloved father. As a wee lad, he had adored that man. Before he knew what *bastard* meant to the world. Before he knew illegitimacy as the laziest of betrayals.

The man vanished. Lochaber took moments to calm the trembling of his muscles, to discover the solid bones supporting his frame, strong and sturdy as he had built them with many hours of physical practice.

His whirling mind, also subject to many hours of disciplined meditation. Yes. Breathe.

Oh. How long had he been leaning his considerable weight against Ruari the Great-Hearted? She held the heavy Gordon Highland pipes in her other arm, unwilling to release him so she could put them down.

"Ruari, forgive me. Here, give me those." He held the weight of the instrument while she hefted the strap from her shoulder. He stretched out a finger, pulled the tartan back from her shoulder. A blazing red brand had sunk into her soft flesh.

He held both her shoulders tight. Bent his head to kiss the mark of her care for him. To his horror, a hot teardrop fell with his kiss. *His tear.* By the gods, he was all about in his head.

He rasped, "Ruari, my sweet mountain burn, eat, drink, prepare yourself. Little more than four hours remains until the symposium opens at ten."

"Your father?"

"I will find that curmudgeonly, that *aingidh, fèineil,* thrice-damned, *useless* duke, and give him the thrashing he deserves."

"Ah, Loch, was that the plan? Or was it to ask him to admit me to the Wise Club?"

A low chuckle floated over from behind a pillar. A door slammed somewhere behind them. "Lochaber, my only boy, is that you, come home?"

"I'm not leaving you!" Ruari hissed.

And then his father stood before him.

Why, the man was barely larger than a bantam rooster. A pang smote Lochaber. Age had creased and spotted that once-loved face. The brilliant red hair he had bequeathed to Loch was now muted with gray. His fitted, elaborately embroidered garments shrieked indolence and wealth.

Smiles wreathed the man's countenance. He stepped forward, made as if to embrace his son.

Lochaber stepped out of reach. Summoned his most ferocious glare. The smiles dimmed somewhat.

All his attention riveted on his parent. He sensed Ruari's clutch on his fingers, like a lifeline holding him to his purpose.

"My son!" the man bleated. Tears shone in his eyes. Trickled down his cheeks. "How long I have hoped and yearned for this day. Your absence has been a rusted sword plunged in my heart."

Lochaber's lips quivered. The rush of emotion disoriented him. He longed both to embrace the old villain and to deck him with a swift uppercut. "I should throw you from these battlements." His bitter snarl would not be choked down. "At least nobody would believe I did it for your riches, as I *inherit nothing*. Given I'm *a bastard*. It all goes to my *legitimate* second cousin, because you refused to honor my mother with marriage. I may as well have been born a Fraser or a Grant, for all the use the name Gordon has done me."

He may as well have struck the old man, who flinched with each one of his accusations.

He wiped his forehead, surprised to find himself sweating. "Oh, what does it matter now! It's done, I'm a man and have made my way in the greater world. Freed myself from—" He gestured at his father's clothes. "—fussy coats and mincing manners. Tedious dinners. Murderous battles with adjoining landowners about mere inches of land. Perhaps you did me a favor, at that."

Ruari squeezed his fingers and smiled up at him.

The duke beamed. "And now you are home where you belong. And lad, I need your wisdom and worldly knowledge…"

Lochaber suddenly came to himself. Ye gods, all those years of training in calm control of body and mind, the harsh discipline of Indian *paika akhada*, and he lost it all at the first sight of his old man. His old master would have ordered extra physical training and solitary meditation for a sennight.

He smiled down at Ruari the Pirate. She kept him earthed when everything else on heaven and earth had abandoned him. Time to assist her, now.

Lochaber held out his hand to his father. "Later, tonight, we will talk, yes?"

The duke nodded and grasped Lochaber's hand in both of his. Bent his head and kissed it.

"But now, this morning, I need…" His voice stuck in his throat. Strangled by fury, by his vow of vengeance. His pride. He cast a glance at Ruari.

She said, "Don't do it, Lochaber. I was wrong to permit you to even consider it. I'm as proud as you, and I'd cut out my tongue rather than release a vow. We'll find a way. Come now. We must find an inn in this city so I can prepare."

Yes!

How he wanted to! How he longed to shove the duke to the ground and go his own way once more. His blood hammered a war dance in his veins. A pulse thrummed madly in his neck. He inhaled.

No.

Ruari MacNeil MacDonald must have her day.

He opened his mouth and said the words in a torrent, before he could call them back. "This morning I need the benefit of your grace. You are opening the Aberdeen Philosophers' Society, the Wise Club. It is in your power to sponsor a female to attend. And you will. You will sponsor this woman, Miss Ruari MacDonald, amateur archaeologist, philosopher, scholar of the lost histories of the Norse and Picti."

He could no longer regard his father's countenance. Lochaber turned abruptly, chest heaving as he sucked in air. "Come," he said to Ruari and began to drag her away.

"I cannot admit a dim-witted *female*." The duke's voice followed them. "The members would riot, lad."

Lochaber released Ruari's hand, turned and in one swift movement, punched the old reprobate hard in the jaw. The duke's head snapped backward. His face showed astonishment as he toppled hard to the ground. "Guards!" the duke shouted weakly. "Guards!" He slithered back on elbows and haunches. "Where is Ceitleen? Where is the duchess?"

Lochaber stood over him, fist raised. "She is no duchess, because you refused to make her one, you a*ingidh* old miser."

He had longed to smite, strangle, murder his father. Fantasized this scene, playing versions over and over in his mind for as long as he had been a man. But strangely, looking down at the decrepit old fool, he suddenly felt there was no honor in it. His father was too old, too foolish, too vain and feeble. No longer a worthy opponent for Lochaber's ferocious talents. If he ever had been.

With that punch, he'd smacked out his vengeance. *Success is the best revenge.*

He toed the sniveling man with his boot. His father spat Gaelic at him. A torrent of curses.

Lochaber waited until he had finished, then helped him up. Brushed the swelling bruise on his jaw with delicate fingers. "Come, then. I'll take you to my mother." He bent a glare on the duke. "And since when did you care about the opinions of lesser men? You will admit Miss MacDonald to the symposium."

He glanced at Ruari, hovering by the roof edge, smiling sardonically. No male antics upset her. She must have had years of them with her brother and kin.

"She will have a battle anyway, even with your permission to attend. She wants to present her own research, to challenge these scholars with their baked-in theories. She has my mother's support in this undertaking. My mother says she has not seen such courage since she herself agreed to be your mistress."

The duke halted. Bent over.

Lochaber hesitated. Had he hurt the old man when he punched him?

The duke began to shake. Laughter erupted from him in a volcanic explosion. He bellowed with laughter, tears pouring from his cheeks. "My son, my son," he gasped. "What a fine man you have made of yourself."

The duke turned and regarded Ruari—for the first time. Strode over, reached out a gnarly old hand. Pinched her cheek.

Ruari jutted her bottom lip. Eyes flashed. "I don't care if you are a duke, and Lochaber's sire," she said. "Do that again, and I'll punch you myself."

The duke laughed again. "A MacDonald, did you say, laddie?"

Ruari snapped, "A daughter of Castle Callanish on the Islands. My mother's people are the MacNeils of Barra. The Royal Pipers."

The duke grinned. "Well, that explains it then. MacDonald and MacNeil. Famous pirates, the lot of them. I'd nae refuse a MacNeil of Barra. She'll go to the symposium, and the lord help those scholars."

Still chuckling, he permitted himself to be escorted to the low door which led to the internal stairways. Just then, a mass of liveried guards burst onto the rooftop, swords bared, heads swiveling for danger.

"All is well!" said the Duke, his booming voice restored. "More than well. My son is returned to me."

****

320

Men crowded the streets of Aberdeen, many dressed in the Scottish tweed woven in her own Leòdhas. Others rushed about in flapping black professorial robes or strode importantly forward with bulging briefcases. Deep voices flowed around her like a river, earnest, arguing, talking over and above each other. The fusty, smoky, whisky smell of many men crowded together assailed her nostrils, as exciting as landing in an unknown country.

Ruari's heart leapt and danced. All so new. So strange. So different. Part of her wanted desperately to cling to Lochaber's hand, but most of her trilled with bubbling excitement. She would hear such wonders!

And all thanks to Lochaber, breaking his vow for revenge. She owed him everything for creating this chance.

She wore a cloak and hat to cover her obvious female person. Thus far, all the men were too busy engaging in learned dialogue and diatribes in the street to notice her. Some men bowed to the duke, resplendent in embroidered velvet. Several women loitered, bidding goodbye to their menfolk at the entrance.

She inhaled, straightened her shoulders, and summoned the blood of her ancestors. A vision of the Picti warrior floated before her. "I do this for you," she whispered. "Lend me your courage."

Once inside, she took her seat alongside Lochaber, her heart almost beating out of her chest. The duke had hustled her through the entrance with a frown and a wave.

The room dimmed. The deep hum of male voices lowered, except for a last whisper or two from men unable to leave their argument be. She sneaked a glance around the room, under cover, hoping to see the professors from Rosemarkie.

The duke stalked to the podium and formally opened the proceedings, with the speech written for him by Lochaber's mother.

After that, one by one, the men were introduced, bowed to scattered applause, and gave their presentations on a podium on the stage at the front of the room.

Ruari's entire attention was focused on their speeches. She greedily absorbed it all. The language. The facts. The theories, discussion, questions. Never had she felt so alive! Her mind careened and soared, as though she had flown off the battlements of Castle Callanish and flew high over tumbling seas.

And then the duke rose and possessed the podium once more. Oh, what a speech! He announced a special guest presenter, not on the compendium for the symposium. A special Picti scholar, newly arrived in Aberdeen. Ruari glowed.

With a grand flourish, the duke concluded with, "I bring you—Miss Ruari MacNeil MacDonald of Lewis!"

Ruari inhaled. Rose from her seat. Walked proud to the podium. Her ears rang with noise, so that she didn't at first hear the sound swelling in Aberdeen's great conference hall.

Clapping as thin as the duke's hair dotted the auditorium. But beneath that, a groundswell of deep noise thrummed. Like a swarm of bees. Like a giant wave far out at sea, moving fast and relentlessly into shore.

The sound of shocked male disapproval.

A balding man with a beaky nose stood up. "Outrageous! Who permitted this travesty?"

Another man, his kindly red face twisted now, shouted, "Polluting this respectable hall!"

Ruari had never permitted her brother to treat her with less than respect. This situation was no different. Just like her menfolk. Except two hundred of them.

She could wobble down, give up, let them win. Or she could find her sword, the sharp edge of her intellect, and smite them with it.

She gripped the podium. "Sit down, and shut up!" she roared, with lungs expanded from years of playing the Highland pipes. "I've had the courtesy to listen to all of you—despite your incorrect assumptions, your paltry lack of evidence, your mainland-centric research! Here is your chance to glean new information. *Call yourselves scholars!*"

She ignored the burgeoning noise in the room. Her cheeks burned red. Her stomach somersaulted into her throat and tied itself into a knot. Nausea swirled. She thought she'd be sick.

But she would not let them win.

Ruari shouted over the noise. Steadily, logically laid out her findings. Explained her ideas. Ignored the yells and taunts of "feebleminded," "blue-stocking," "softening in the brain," and "sin against nature." Dodged a notebook flung hard at her head. Kept talking.

The duke's guards dragged three men from the hall, kicking and protesting.

She talked on, hands waving to try to describe what she had seen. Now some of the hurled abuse was in response to her findings.

"Outrageous!" yelled a professor. "Quite wrong, quite wrong."

"You mean, you are, sir?" she asked sweetly.

Laughter sprinkled through the hall. Winning! She was winning.

A man stood, asked a question. Her friend from Rosemarkie! The hall quietened. Listened to her answer. More questions. She had them now.

So into the silence, she made her pitch. "These graves, these artifacts are at terrible risk of disappearing." They listened now. Yes, she had them. Learned brows frowned, bearded mouths pinched.

"These unique artifacts can be observed. Your research deepened. Questions may be answered. Distinguished scholars can review my findings. But only if the land is saved from unbridled development or clearing!"

Echoing silence, then that growing murmur like a swarm of angry bees. They were Scots, in the main. They knew what clearing entailed.

And just in that precious moment, when the world changed. When she had the respect—or at least the ears—of scholars, of people like herself who lived and breathed the mysteries of the past, just then…

The doors crashed open. A horde of wild men dressed in MacDonald tartans stormed into the Aberdeen Philosophers' Society. "There she is!" shouted a MacDonald liegeman, pointing a hoary finger at the podium.

At this most inauspicious moment, her cousin's men had finally found her.

The clansmen pulled out swords and clubs and waved them with menace, shrieking a heart-pounding MacDonald war cry.

The duke's guards waded into the fray and clashed swords with the mad MacDonalds. A man in the audience leapt to his feet and yelled, "Summon the Aberdeen militia!"

All around her, the room erupted into utter chaos.

Chapter Twenty-Seven

Oh, my pirate ancestors, was all she could think, as Lochaber vaulted five rows of seats and landed athletically onto the stage. *They'll never allow another woman to present for a hundred years.*

"Ruari!" he said, and hugged her in a desperate embrace. "There's only one way to protect you now. Hmm. Perhaps not only one. I'm an inventive man." He wiggled his eyebrows suggestively.

In the midst of this madness, he offered *banter*?

Despite herself, the giggle squeezed from her throat. "Do it, then."

Lochaber turned to the heaving fray.

What had she done? "Loch, I've reduced a respectable assembly of learned men to a pitched battle. In a matter of minutes." A quavery cackle bounced in her stomach and erupted from her lips. Wild laughter hovered just behind her teeth.

"That's my adorable Pirate Queen. Never a dull moment." His dark gaze raked her, promising sizzling times…soon. "Stay here, one second."

In two paces, he reached the side edge of the stage and nabbed a portly man making a rapid exit from a small side door. He murmured something in the man's ear. The man blanched, chins quivering. A little more persuasion from Lochaber and his victim nodded, albeit most reluctantly.

Ruari snapped her attention to the fighting. "Loch! I'll have to flee in a moment!"

He dragged the portly man onto the stage with him.

Lochaber faced the room, tall and commanding. "A moment of your time, sirs!" he bellowed authoritatively, in a clarion voice obviously used to summon armies across the vast distances of India. "Your attention. Now!"

To a man, the hall responded. All activity ceased, all speech, threats, actions froze in the moment. Clansmen stood brace-legged, swords high to strike. The liveried duke's men held MacDonalds in headlocks and armlocks. The disdainful Rhynie lecturer, purple-faced, stood half strangled by a hairy MacDonald forearm. The uniformed Aberdeen militia had taken up arms against all comers.

"I am Lochaber Gordon." He licked his lips. Squared his shoulders. Only Ruari could see his fists, clenched white-knuckled behind his back.

"I am the bastard son of the Duke of Gordon. I am Colonel Lochaber Gordon of the East India Company." Murmurs exploded like gunfire.

He had announced he was a bastard to this entire company? "Lochy, what are you about?"

He kept talking. He turned to Ruari, took her hands in his. "Do you, love of my life, daughter of the great MacDonald clan, kin of the MacNeils of Barra, take my hand in marriage, to bear my *legitimate* children, to love and cherish from this day forth?"

"Lochaber!"

"Say I do," he hissed. "Please. And then only I can claim you. No one else." He pressed her hands, hard. Begged her with his melting gaze. "I can keep you safe.

Cherish you as you deserve."

"But I don't want to be cherished, particularly, Lochaber."

One of the MacDonalds called in a piercing yell, "Well, are ye marrying the man or not, lass? This sword arm wants to know if it's wielding a weapon or a whisky."

Half the hall laughed. Others hooted. Several of the Wise Club frowned. But they stayed glued to their positions.

Her man said, "I will aid and support you to be the woman you long to be. A true scientist. A generous, brave-hearted woman with boundless courage. You will aid and support me to become a man I never expected. With your grace and wisdom, and your huge, bonny heart." He brushed a soft kiss on her lips.

"Marry me now, my wonderful, extraordinary, remarkable Ruari MacDonald. From the very first, you cracked open my heart. Look at me! Reunited with my father, made my mother happy, proud of a pirate wench who stole convention and gave it back on a platter."

A MacDonald accent from somewhere in the hall: "Ye canna kiss the lass yet, man. She hasnae said yes!"

Ruari regarded him solemnly, then turned to the hall. Everyone was frozen, waiting for the next scene in this drama. Swords dangled down beside relaxed arms. The neck holds had morphed into loose embraces.

She said in her clearest, most carrying voice, "But you hate family, Lochaber Gordon. I want to bear children. Fierce, feisty MacDonald, MacNeil, and hopefully Gordon children. Lots of them. I will not bear them to a man who denies my family—nor his own!"

Agreement sounded through the hall. Silence

descended once more, as every soul present waited for his answer.

None more so than Ruari.

What a gamble.

Saying all this before the duke, before Lochaber's townspeople. Before men she had hoped could be her friends and colleagues. Risked the withdrawal of his offer and his affections.

Gambled it all away to ease one man's bitter, broken heart.

For she knew, now, that Lochaber's lifelong desire for vengeance quickened not because of parental neglect, but because he loved his family deeply. He had loved them for years, so much so, that when he discovered he was bastard-born, it had hurt in the deep, unreasoning, uncomprehending way of a hurt child.

Could he accept that truth and be a whole man?

He swallowed, the bulge in his throat working. She reached for his hand. Lochaber met her gaze. The pain in his eyes nearly unwomaned her.

She bit her lips to keep from retracting her words, from offering soothing phrases of comfort in their stead.

Lochaber inhaled. Exhaled. Shot out a fist and grabbed the large gent, who had stolen the opportunity to try to sneak off the stage.

"Not only do I love you with all my heart, Ruari MacDonald of the Islands. I love your family. And I love mine. I thank you for being the means of reuniting us, over my stubborn foolishness."

"My son!" called the duke. Good gracious, the man was crying all over his embroidered velvet.

"And now, my Ruari, enough prevarication. Answer me: Will you marry me, bear my children, and love us all with all your glorious, piratical heart and soul?"

"Yes, I will marry you. *I do*." The duke wasn't the only one with silly tears pouring from his eyes. Her Lochy stretched out a gentle finger and brushed the tears from her cheeks.

"And now," he roared, "Bishop of Aberdeen, you will marry us here and now, on this stage."

"Sir, the banns must be read for three weeks—"

"Pish and podsnappery! Not in bonnie Scotland!" Lochaber's curved sword flashed as he pulled back his plaid.

The bishop's chins wobbled. "The documents. I must away to the church offices—"

"Marry us, fool! You may complete all your officious paperwork later, I care not. I have MacDonalds waiting to carry my beloved away. Make it snappy. Forget the preamble. The vows, now."

The MacDonalds obligingly gave a threatening roar to underline Lochaber's point and subsided to watch the action once more. The giggle tickling in Ruari's skin turned to a sizzle of burning lust. Her man was magnificent.

She said sternly, "The vows, now."

Thus overruled, the Bishop of Aberdeen rattled through the wedding ceremony while Lochaber and Ruari held hands, gazes locked, wonder simmering in their veins. He said the vows, and then she.

The world fell away. There was only Lochaber. His bright hair. His hot gaze. His remarkable, agile body. His quick, alert, flexible brain. And his heart—as brave, generous, and strongly rooted in history as the Cairngorm Mountains.

And then they kissed.

Husband and wife.

Every man in the hall—and plenty of women now, for somehow the news had filtered into streets and homes, shops and kitchens that the duke's son was finally come home and was marrying his lady in the Aberdeen Hall—yelled, cheered, applauded. Threw their hats and caps in the air. Waved their tartan shawls. Spontaneously launched into Scottish reels, professors hooking arms with dairymaids, MacDonald warriors dancing with Gordon men-at-arms.

"Everybody back to the Gordon estate!" called the duke. "My only son is married this day!"

The cheering shook the roof beams, and then a tide of people flowed out of the hall and into the street.

Back at the duke's mansion, people filled the gardens. Tables were set up, foodstuffs hastily fetched from homes and shops all over Aberdeen and beyond. Barrels of ale and whisky were rolled from the Gordon cellars. Musicians tuned their stringed instruments, and the pipers played experimental blasts on their bagpipes.

In the middle of the celebrations, Lochaber's father stood on a makeshift stage, his housekeeper and mistress standing to one side, her hand on his shoulder.

"Here ye this!" shouted the Duke of Gordon. He went into a long speech outlining every one of his son's brilliant achievements.

"Apparently," Lochaber murmured in Ruari's ear, still holding her around the waist from their dance, "the duke has been following my progress and posting newsletters about it around the countryside, for my entire career. Every achievement. Every award. Every advancement." He snorted with bemusement.

"He loves you," she said. "As do I."

"He takes after his mother, clearly," shouted the duke. Everyone laughed with good-humored abandon. "And as I have not done the right thing by the woman I love best in the whole world, better than I love the breath in my body, I will make her happy now." He took a large swallow of whisky to moisten his throat.

"Lochaber Gordon, you have grown yourself into such a man! A man I am proud to call son. I declare before all these witnesses that you are the child of my body. The dukedom will expire on my death—it too late to remedy that—"

Groans from the crowd.

"—I herewith I name you, Lochaber Gordon, my son, my heir to all my estates and properties which are unencumbered by title and primogeniture. That is almost all my wealth and lands. And it is in my power to knight you, Sir Lochaber Gordon, Baron of Aberdeen, Lord of the Cairngorms."

Ruari gripped Lochaber's fingers. His lips twisted in a kind of pain she had never seen in him. His eyes darkened. He kissed her with a hot, desperate, blind kiss.

And then he flung away toward the makeshift stage. Oh no...

She walked with a dignified hurry after him. She was his wife now.

Lochaber mounted the stage and hugged his father in an enormous bear hug, tears running rivers down both their faces.

Over their shaking shoulders, his mother's brown eyes locked onto Ruari's. She nodded, once. Sent Ruari a jubilant smile. And then turned her attention back to her men.

****

Much, much later.

The townsfolk and Wise Club still danced Scots reels out in the gardens and grounds. The MacDonalds filled the Gordon mansion, sleeping wherever they could lay their heads, after their long march to capture Ruari.

Her brother, Roderick, and his new wife Flora had somehow appeared in the midst of the celebrations, having traveled hard across country in the wake of the MacDonald army.

Ruari kept patting Roddy, to reassure herself he was real. When she wasn't touching, hugging, ogling, and kissing her husband.

"We went home to Callanish," Roddy informed Ruari, Lochaber, the duke, Lochaber's mother, and Murdo and Donald MacDonald. He took another sip of Ardmore. "Aye, a grand drop this," he said to the duke, who leaned over and poured another inch of amber fluid in Roderick's glass. Ruari privately thought that no whisky could top the Island single malts. A small pang of homesickness stabbed her belly.

She glanced at Flora, who glowed like a queen of the islands, leaning into Roddy as though he was her lodestone. She had definitely shed some of her frostiness!

Roddy rolled the whisky around in his mouth. "The strangest thing. Our cousin the laird has somehow become fast friends with the Wicked Earl. And the foolish man—our cousin—has gambled away his castle and lands. But!" He held up a hand to cut short Ruari's stormy response. "The Wicked Earl is well served. He has made Balgair his factor. I suppose a more troublesome, meddlesome, disobedient factor never lived! They appear the best of friends, with my cousin willfully disobeying the earl's every command, and doing just as he pleases. With the earl's fortune to back his excesses."

"But Roderick, your farms! My lovely home."

"Do not distress yourself. The earl and Balgair gamble every night. In due course, the laird will win back Callanish Castle. I will claim my inheritance early and force the laird to release the properties and lands to me."

Flora added, "And if the castle remains lost, my brother the MacLeod has offered Roderick two of his estates, on Skye and Harris. Alasdair will revive an ancient title. All will be well." She blushed prettily and glowed at her dark-visaged husband.

Ruari squeezed her own husband's hand. "Your mentor, Billy Bentinck. He must come to Aberdeen."

Lochaber's glinting smile hitched her breath. "That happier letter is already sent, my beautiful wife. We will show him Picti stones and ply him with whisky until he agrees to all you propose."

Her handsome husband smoothed a tendril of hair from her cheek. "Do not fear for your Picts and Norse ancestors. The professors will petition Parliament tomorrow—for tonight they celebrate our marriage—to place a stay on any clearing, until the remains and artifacts are fully examined. And you know how long professors take to study and agree on any matter…more than a lifetime, I'd wager."

He smiled into her eyes. "The Royal Society will grant you the first female membership."

"Oh! The first of many women, I hope! My campaign will begin as soon as the ink is dry." She leaned into his caress.

The duke had been frowning all this while.

"What ails you, *Father*?" Lochaber asked, with a husk in his voice. "No, no, don't start crying again. Please."

The duke said, "I hate to concern you on your wedding day. But your inheritance, significant though it is, could be more. An unknown agent has been buying up every available property through all the lands of Gordon, Fraser, Grant, Ogilvy—"

Lochaber's laugh echoed through the hall. "That's me, my duke. I own them all. I planned to harry and press you, buying properties and lands where I could, through your territories and borderlands. But now I see I merely shore up *our family lands* with additional properties and investments."

The duke choked. "You are your mother's son, my boy."

"Now," said Lochaber in a dark, determined tone. "Such a family reunification means almost everything to me. But it is my wedding night, to the most beautiful woman on earth. The bravest, to choose me. Strong and unique. You'll pardon me."

And with that, Lochaber leapt from his chair. Before Ruari had a chance to so much as squeak, he scooped strong arms under her back and thighs and pulled her bodily to him. His heat and strength surrounded and supported her as he carried her to the staircase.

"My love," he said in her ear. "My sea-witch, my pirate. You will open all your treasures to me." One of the MacDonalds blew a triumphant, rousing bagpipe tune as he carried her up the endless, steep staircase.

Lochaber crashed into the suite prepared for them, slamming the door closed with his foot. He turned her so her back rested on the door. Framed her body with muscled arms. Her heart drummed a rapid tattoo in her breast.

"Ruari MacNeil MacDonald Gordon. I'm going to slowly peel away your clothes. I want to see you in your pearly, creamy glory." His voice rasped.

She trailed fingertips over the red stubble on his jaw. "And I will see you," she whispered.

He took her in a searing kiss that spoke of all the tumult of emotion they had been through this day. His hurt. His lost vengeance. His joy. He gently sucked her lower lip between his own. Took her upper lip. Plundered her with his tongue.

And his hands! They ran all over her body, tickling, teasing, stroking. Arms, shoulders, neck. Hairline. He groaned in her mouth.

And then he undid the MacDonald brooch on her tartans, stripped her family plaids away. Yanked at her blouse, loosed the light stays she had donned for her day of victory, ran hot hands over her soft linen chemise, plucking and tweaking her nipples under the fabric until they peaked and tingled with wanting.

How she wanted him. Her hands traveled all over his incredible, superb body. His hard, honed flesh, his muscular frame. She wanted to feel, to kiss, to lick all of him. His broad shoulders. His wonderful, flexible, toned muscles. Biceps, forearms, fingers. Buttocks.

He grabbed her by the hips and pulled her hard against him. His shaft bulged as straight and strong as a *khanda* sword.

"Lochaber," she groaned, and then his mouth met hers with passionate violence. The kiss—hot heavy and intense. "More," she said into his mouth.

Lochaber hoisted her against him. Jolted her body

so her sex met his shaft. Rubbed hard against him. "Yes. Oh yes," she moaned.

He moved from the door, still holding her body against him. She wrapped her legs around his hips.

And then they were on the bed. He kissed her mouth, her nipples, ran trails of sweet kisses over her skin until she writhed beneath him. And then! Oh goddess! He kissed her *there*. She bucked and jumped. He held her firmly, kissing her cleft, teasing her silky folds with a fingertip. Never had she felt anything so exquisite, so... "Lochy. Lochaber."

"That's it, my Ruari. Open yourself to me. Take your pleasure, my pirate queen."

And he kissed and stroked and caressed until sparks exploded her mind and her body shook and convulsed, by a giant, marvelous wave...

Lochaber tore the clothes from his own body. She ran eager hands and fingers over his bare chest, his lovely long legs, his ribs...his enormous erection. She clenched her hand around his silky length. Squeezed. Luxuriated in his groan. "My Ruari," he croaked. "Later, we will linger and explore. But now, I cannot wait. I must take you, do you understand? I hate to hurt you, but its only your second time—you may sting a little."

"Pain and pleasure? That is just life, my Lochy. I am no tender upper-class bloom. I am a woman of the harsh and beautiful islands. Take me now. Love me. Beget children on me. I am strong and fierce. You won't hurt me."

He lowered himself onto her. Rubbed the head of his engorged shaft over her secret, sensitive sex. "Yes," she crooned. He pushed in a little way and groaned his pleasure. How he filled her, stretched her, completed her.

She raised her hips to take him in farther.

He thrust a little more each time, and then he buried himself to the root. She gasped. He ground out, "My beautiful wife," and then he began to thrust inside her, her inner self wrapping him and catching him, rubbing with that delicious friction.

His face screwed in an agony of pleasure. He thrust, harder and harder, and she met him, fiercely and gladly. Pleasure climbed within her, buzzing and sizzling. She writhed under him as her climax exploded and she fell into the wide sky. "My love," he choked out, pushed with three more urgent thrusts, and then his body wracked in his own release.

They lay in each other's arms, drowsy and replete. The fire flickered red and gold over the room.

"I love my life," Lochaber whispered. "The life you have given me. You have returned my heart to me. And it's not as black and damaged as I had believed."

"And you have given me a future. Full of Picts, professors, and with fortune, little Lucky Lochaber girls and boys with flaming bright hair."

"Would you truly want my children, my wife, my heart, my love?"

"So much so, my husband, that you had better prepare for much passionate lovemaking."

"Would right now suit my queen?"

"Perfect, my flinty warrior king!" They chuckled in unison. And then Lochaber rolled her on top of him.

They kissed.

Author's note on castles and artifacts in Pitching the Petticoat

I visited the Outer Hebrides in 2018, and those stunning, harsh landscapes have haunted me ever since.

After getting tangled in fact-checking my own outrageous, piratical McNeil and Ross family history and the compelling stories of other Scots clans, I decided the only way forward was to invent a castle, so Callanish Castle was born. Lochaber's Castle Clàrsach is also fictional.

An iron-age house really is located on a local island, but having my heroine continually row there changed the story pace, so I moved the ancient village to nearby Tolstachaolais. I have added fictional Picti stones, but the astonishing standing stone circles and neolithic broch are all there in location. I apologize to Hebridean locals for these misrepresentations of your beautiful islands and fascinating history.

Rhynie Man was not found until 1978, but how could I resist including a stone with a clearly etched warrior with long hair, beaked nose, sharp teeth, and a pointed beard, wielding an ax.

The Picti-stone star maps theory is entirely my invention—but who knows? Those ancient kayakers in sealskins somehow navigated huge distances across oceans.

Ruari is spelt Ruairidh in Scots Gaelic.

A word about the author…

Maryanne Ross is totally addicted to reading. She adores writing sparkling historical romances with wilful heroines, wounded heroes, and happy endings.

When not writing, she loves bushwalking and travelling. She works as a development consultant for an Aboriginal organisation.

Check out the first two books in the Victorians Unlaced series and connect with Maryanne at

https://www.maryanneross.com/

https://www.facebook.com/MaryanneRossAuthor

www.ingramcontent.com/pod-product-compliance
Lightning Source LLC
Chambersburg PA
CBHW051134030726
47504CB00004B/862